Ace Books by Joan Frances Turner

DUST
FRAIL

PRAISE FOR
DUST

"*Dust* is a thoughtful, poignant and frightening book about the undead. It is a truly original idea told from a viewpoint that will surprise and horrify, and may make you change sides in the next war between zombies and humans."

> —Laurell K. Hamilton, #1 *New York Times* bestselling author of *Kiss the Dead*

"*Dust* is spectacular. Not because it's about zombies and gross as hell, not because it leaves the genre in its 'dust,' but because it is such a great, unsettling portrait of raw hunger and hope. What George Romero started with *Night of the Living Dead*, Joan Frances Turner finishes with *Dust*, an undead romp among the American ruins."

> —Jeff Long, *New York Times* bestselling author of *The Descent*

"*Dust* is an amazing novel! Joan Frances Turner has done for zombies what Anne Rice did for vampires. With wit, fine writing and psychological nuance, she has created a compelling alternative reality, populated with sympathetic characters, in a gripping story that is guaranteed to interfere with your sleep."

> —Douglas Preston, #1 *New York Times* bestselling coauthor of *Two Graves*

"Turner's debut is a massively entertaining and seriously revisionist zombie novel . . . The author has taken the familiar zombie clichés and given them a good shake. Jessie, who's been dead for nine years, is as real and human a character as anyone you're likely to meet in the pages of a mainstream novel, and Turner has created a new zombie mythology that is smart, scary and viscerally real. Recommend this one highly to horror fans, even those who claim to have sated themselves on zombies."

> —*Booklist* (starred review)

"A fresh and exciting addition to zombie culture."

> —*The Fiction Enthusiast*

continued . . .

"*Dust* is grim and realistic but balanced with unimaginable beauty. Jessie's journey to save her world is engrossing. You forget about the nastiness which is inevitable when time meets dead flesh, and quickly find yourself caught up in the larger quest . . . a new paradigm where humanity has a much broader definition."
—*Fresh Fiction*

"A nail-bitingly good zombie romp that magically morphs into an intelligent treatise on life, death and the fallibility of being human. With its engaging protagonist, Jessica, and a host of well-imagined supporting characters—both alive and undead—*Dust* is a cut above the rest."
—Amber Benson, actress (*Buffy the Vampire Slayer*) and author of *The Golden Age of Death*

"A well-written urban fantasy, *Dust* is a new and unique take on zombies."
—Ilona Andrews, *New York Times* bestselling author of *Steel's Edge*

"*Dust* is both haunting and horrifying, blending the lines of the living, the dead and the living dead into a graphic narrative about friendship, family and what it truly means to be alive in a world where mankind is the main course."
—Anton Strout, author of *Alchemystic*

"*Dust* brings new life to being dead."
—Daniel Waters, author of the Generation Dead series

"With *Dust*, Joan Frances Turner does her part to revive zombie lit from the dead end of novelty-book silliness. Here the rotting, flesh-hungry ghouls are the heroes, and they roam the landscape bickering and horsing around like teenage hooligans out of S. E. Hinton's *Rumble Fish*. Lush gore abounds—this is a vivid trip to the dark side that could have been called *Twilight of the Dead*."
—Walter Greatshell, author of *Xombies: Apocalypso*

"An extraordinary achievement, and must not be missed."
—*RT Book Reviews* (top pick)

DUST

JOAN FRANCES TURNER

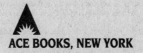
ACE BOOKS, NEW YORK

THE BERKLEY PUBLISHING GROUP
Published by the Penguin Group
Penguin Group (USA) Inc.
375 Hudson Street, New York, New York 10014, USA

🐧

USA | Canada | UK | Ireland | Australia | New Zealand | India | South Africa | China

Penguin Books Ltd., Registered Offices: 80 Strand, London WC2R 0RL, England
For more information about the Penguin Group, visit penguin.com.

DUST

An Ace Book / published by arrangement with the author

Ace Books are published by The Berkley Publishing Group.
ACE and the "A" design are trademarks of Penguin Group (USA) Inc.

For information, address: The Berkley Publishing Group,
a division of Penguin Group (USA) Inc.,
375 Hudson Street, New York, New York 10014.

ISBN: 978-0-425-26208-5

PUBLISHING HISTORY
Ace hardcover edition / September 2010
Ace trade paperback edition / October 2011
Ace mass-market edition / May 2013

PRINTED IN THE UNITED STATES OF AMERICA

10 9 8 7 6 5 4 3 2 1

Cover photographs: woman © Lea Bernstein / Arcangel Images; winter trees © Roy Bishop /
Arcangel Images; oil painting © iStockphoto/Thinkstock.
Cover design by Judith Lagerman.
Map by Claudia Carlson.

ALWAYS LEARNING   **PEARSON**

ACKNOWLEDGMENTS

To my agent, Michelle Brower, and my editor, Michelle Vega, whose advice, advocacy and inspiration helped make this a far better book. To everyone at The Berkley Publishing Group, Wendy Sherman Associates and Folio Literary Management for all their hard work on my behalf. To Nick Mamatas, who read parts of an early draft and offered very insightful suggestions.

To the owners and management of the Town Theatre in Highland, Indiana, where I scribbled the first page of notes that eventually became this book. To the staff and volunteers at Deep River County Park in Hobart, Indiana, the Taltree Arboretum & Gardens in Valparaiso and Marquette Park Beach in Gary, where all the knottiest plot points got wrestled into submission. To Roxann McGlumphy, Ann Larimer and Betsy Hanes Perry for encouragement, support and friendship above and beyond the call of duty. To Mary S. for love, fidelity, first draft read-throughs and every good thing. And to my mother, for everything and then some.

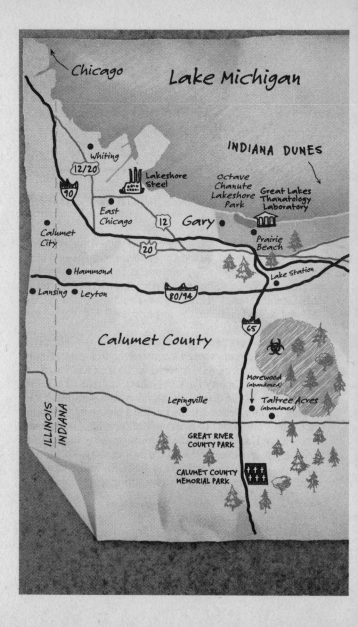

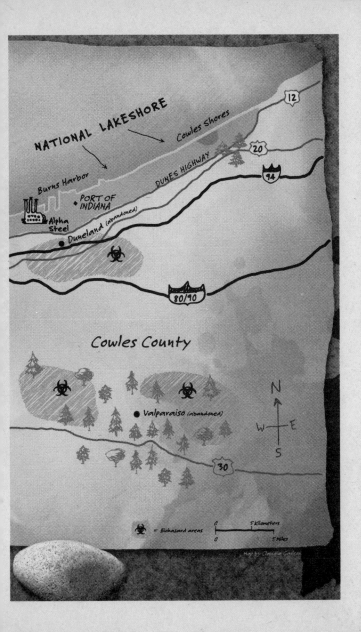

BOOK ONE

DRY BONES

My right arm fell off today. Lucky for me, I'm left-handed.

In the accident that killed me I rocketed from the back-seat straight through the windshield—no seat belt, yeah, I know—and the pavement sheared my arm to nothing below the shoulder. Not torn off, but dangling by thin, precious little bits of skin and bone and ligament. I had a closed casket, I'm sure of it, because they never wired the arm or glued it or any other pretty undertaker trick. I managed to crawl back out of the ground without its help anyway, and of course after nine perfectly uneventful years of fighting and dancing and hunting and getting by *fine* with the left arm, the right finally shuffles its coil right on the banks of the Great River County Park's not-so-Great River, smack in the middle of a meat run. Joe, my boy, my backup, was not sympathetic in the least.

"You're shaking," he muttered, as he led the gang along the riverbank, through the clearing that used to be the park playground. "Your arm's shaking, look. Is the big mean pointy-headed deer that scary?"

Mags snickered, waddling past the rusty remains of the jungle gym. Ben and Sam were right behind her, sniffing and sniffing for living meat; fat gas-bloated Billy pirouetted in their footsteps, and Linc brought up the rear with Florian, our oldest and dustiest. I gave Joe a shove.

"Shut it," I warned him, "or I'll set Teresa on you." I'd have to find her first, to do that: Our big chief and cheese never seems to show up for hunts anymore. Maybe she's sleeping in. Never mind that Florian, who's got a couple of centuries on her, still hauls his ass without complaining. "Now she's one mean pointy-headed thing I know you're too hoo-yellow to fight—"

Then a phantom dog got its teeth deep into my right shoulder, shaking and shaking, and a tremor shot down to my knees and back up again. The tremor became a whip crack and something snapped painlessly in my shoulder, and my poor useless deadweight arm broke off for good, wet purplish skin sliding off in sheets as it hit the underbrush with a squish and a thud.

The deer we'd had in our sights, foolish thing too stupid to pick up the stench of death (ours and his), rocketed up and bounded away faster than any undead could chase it. Ben broke into the same slow, sarcastic applause I remembered from when I was alive, when someone dropped a full lunch tray in the middle of the cafeteria. An oak tree bowed under Billy's back as he leaned against it grunting and growling with laughter; Florian's dry, ancient mouth twitched, Sam and Ben snickered, Mags giggled from deep in what was left of her throat and Joe threw an arm around me, sprays of maggots shooting from the rips in his leather jacket like little grubworm confetti.

"Congratulations!" he grunted around the smashed half of his jaw, eyes glinting with a mocking pride. "Nine years of hauling around that useless turd of an arm, and you finally drop it in the dirt where it belongs—she's a genuine rotter now, how about it? Three cheers for little baby Jessica!"

The hip-hip-hoorays rained down and I booted his ass, or tried to, while he laughed and stumbled in a mocking little circle. My right shoulder still jerked and twitched. "I've been a *genuine* rotter since I climbed out of the ground— I've heard the stories Billy used to tell about you, ant farm!"

He just laughed harder, looping arms around my waist from behind and whirling me until those poor maggots were light-headed. "Ant farm?" He grinned. "That the best you can do? And you know Billy's a gassed-up liar—"

"I told her you cried yourself to sleep every morning after you tunneled up, wailing for your mommmmmm-meeee." Billy smirked, rubbing his swollen blackened hands together eagerly anticipating a fight. "Weeping and wailing like a worthless little 'maldie full of embalmer's juice—"

"Yeah?" Joe just grinned wider. His brain radio, the waves of telepathic sound that help us talk around rotted throats and tongues, veered into a hard fast electric-guitar screech that could have been real anger, could have just been the need to fight. "We'll see who's spitting up formaldehyde by the time I—"

He grabbed me hard enough to snap bones, hauling me straight off my feet. I shrieked, groped behind me for his neck and throttled until I heard rattling teeth, felt blowflies and carrion beetles turn to mush and juice beneath my fingers. He wrenched my hand away and threw me in the damp riverbank dirt, trying to straddle me, but my legs are stronger and a few kicks sent him sprawling on a layer cake of dead leaves. The gang surrounded us to watch, the eagerness for good bone-breaking fun stronger than any flesh-hunger—all except Linc, who hung back drawn and worried. Linc's a sweetheart, he is, but however book smart he was alive he's got no clue about anything that matters. I turned to give him a little don't-worry glance, and that distracted second was all Joe needed to flip me over and force-feed me a heaping mouthful of dirt.

"Y'fuggr!" I coughed and spat, horse-kicking as Joe tugged at my elbow like a sailor hauling anchor. "N'my *urrm!*"

"What's that?" Joe laughed, a groaning guttural sound that would make a human crap bricks, and yanked harder. That dog-bite tremor was happening again, up and down my left side this time, and he was too excited to care. "Didn't catch that—"

He tugged more and I kicked more, and he pulled so hard that I felt vibrations through my arm socket and something close to panic. "Nuh! *Stuppit!*"

I finally found my legs again, rolling onto my back and getting a foot so hard in his chest I heard something snap and deflate. He gasped in pain, growled and pulled back, ready to kick something loose inside me. The whole gang roared with glee.

"All right." Linc stumbled over, gave Joe a shove. "That's enough."

Not the whole gang, then. Joe was on his feet again, looming over small skinny Linc like the biker bully he'd been while he was alive. "Says who, baby boy? You? Let's hear it." Silence. "Well? Let's hear it!"

"Easy there," murmured Florian, holding up a flesh-stripped hand, but with Teresa away or asleep we had no Fearless Leader, no rules to stop us. Not that she cared much either. Linc stood his ground, glaring. Joe let out a wet, congested hiss from deep in his throat, the warning of a worse beating than he'd ever given me or anyone else, and as he crouched ready to spring on Linc, I touched his shoulder.

"Joe." I used my low growling voice, the one he liked. "Stop."

We could all hear it in our heads, Joe's brain radio cycling down from hard screeching electric guitar to a soothing acoustic strum; right off, when I touched him, his fists started uncurling. That's what Linc just doesn't get, never will, about Joe and me. Linc glanced at my remaining arm, making sure it was still attached, then buckled to Joe's and my seniority and turned away. His own brain radio never changes: a lonely one-handed piano, each *plink, plink* a teardrop of notes splashing down. Awkward and silent now, a group blind date turned bad, we left my arm lying at the riverbank and wandered deeper into the trees.

We hadn't gone two hundred yards when Linc let out a sudden excited arpeggio, still hollow and lonely, and we all caught the scent: *Deer.* Again.

Linc stood waiting, silently challenging Joe not to let him

go chase it. An indifferent little *skrrrrrit!* on Joe's guitar strings, hunger beating back rage, and the tension broke; Linc turned and vanished after that good meat smell. We stood there, shaking, waiting.

The hoos like to make fun of how we walk and it's true, we can't really run, can't manage much past a stagger. But Linc is just that little bit faster, fleeter, than the rest of us, and he knows his business. We gathered in a tight semicircle, freeze-tagging shoulder to shoulder, still as winter trees. Waiting.

A big beautiful stag rushed terrified into the clearing, Linc right behind it as it bounded the wrong way in its panic. One great roar in all our ears, eight earsplitting dissonant brain-radio symphonies of triumph and we closed the circle tight around that deer, broke legs as it tried jumping over us, tore away antlers when it tried barreling through us, groaned triumph over its rising screams of pain before Joe wrapped a hand around the stag's neck and stopped all sound with a single, effortless *crack*.

So hot they almost steamed, those good fresh deer guts, and warm dripping blood and the solid meaty muscle of a heart still beating as we tore the carcass open, venison like you never tasted it on your little hoo-barbecue with the charcoal smoke making it filthy. Linc snatched the first mouthful of the liver, the best and sweetest meat of all, and Joe kicked him away from the rest and Billy kicked Joe and why's everyone fighting when it's so good to feed, it's so good, you can't stop and you can't think and you can't do anything but chew and swallow and want to bust out sobbing you feel so wonderful? Sam grabbed at the bones, fought Ben over the marrow. Should we save some for Teresa? But by the time we got it out of the woods and across the field and past the old mill and out to the gazebo how fresh would it be, anyway? Snooze, lose.

I was a vegetarian when I was alive, not the fish-and-chicken kind either. No leather shoes, no honey. I drove my mom crazy. All those years of good rich meat going to fly-blown carcass waste, just remembering it now made me want to weep. How was I ever such a fool? There's nothing in this world, nothing, that's as honest or as beautiful as meat and blood, beautiful as this bone gnawed white and stripped clean, this shredded hide, those hanks of flesh and tooth scrapings of veined yellow fat still stuck to the fur—

Ben shoved me away and I sat down hard on the ground, panting, letting him have the remnants of the rib cage. Billy and Mags were still working on the guts, tearing off greasy handfuls and shoveling them in like potato chips; Florian nibbled at bits here and there, too old to have much appetite anymore. Sad-sack Sam gave me a big happy grin as he licked the fat from his fingers. Linc looked half asleep as he shoveled in leftover shreds of meat. There was a red haze over everything and a stench permeating the air, the heavy fast-moving odor of life bursting out and spilling away.

Joe, good humor restored, sidled up looking embarrassed. Like always. "Your arm okay?"

"Fine." I wiggled my fingers. "No thanks to you."

He touched the empty shoulder socket like it might shatter. The maggots and blowflies and watch beetles feeding off him head to toe pulsed with the hungry sucking and clicking of thousands of little mouths: *shuck-shuck,* in rhythm, and then *crrnc-crrnc,* biting down. They've been feeding off him for decades now, feeding on bits of nothing, between bouts of silent stasis. Do we attract a special kind of bug? It never takes dead hoos who stay dead this long to get flesh-stripped, and I never heard of hibernating maggots. He shrugged, his notion of apology. I glared at him.

"The next time you decide to rip me into kindling," I said, "give me fair warning first so I can take out your eyes."

He let off an angry guitar chord. Blinding isn't funny— when Lillian, one of our seniors, lost her remaining eye in a gang fight, Teresa made me and Joe be the ones to take her into the woods and kick in her skull. Can't hunt if you're blinded, can't do anything. Even Florian couldn't argue with it, though he tried to. "You even try it," Joe said, "you'll end up with your teeth all over the ground. But you wouldn't try it."

"Because you're so big and strong?"

"You said it, I didn't." He grinned and started rubbing my back, a soothing apology. "And you said yourself, your arm's fine."

"Try that again, Joe, I will gouge your eyes."

"I'll knock out your teeth."

"I'll smash what's left of your skull."

"I'll pop these gasbags like balloons—" We wrestled again, shrieking, and this time Good Samaritan Linc just gave us a lazy smile. When I shoved Joe away he just lay there, eyes closed. I wanted to drop off too, but it was close to dawn and if we stayed away during the big sleep we'd never hear the end of it: Teresa likes us where she can eyeball us. Too near her to hatch secret plots and plans, which is how she overthrew old Lillian and got to be gang head in the first place. I was trying to shove Joe to his feet when Sam stepped in, pulling himself upright with a grunt.

"C'mon, kids." He was just a little older than Teresa but already as stripped-down as Florian, all exposed bones and dried-out leathery skin shreds that the bugs didn't want anymore. "Time."

Groans, jeers and mouthfuls of bloody spume didn't dissuade him, and we retraced our steps in a ragged, complaining line back toward the riverbank. My arm lay in state on the boggy grass, jarringly clean white bone and soft, blackened distended flesh. If you looked closely, you could still see tiny chips of polish on the nails. Fuchsia pink.

"Wait'll the hoos get a load of that." Mags snickered, doing a lurching little dance around it. "They'll faint."

Even Linc laughed. "They're not stupid enough to come here. Whose woods these are, I think they know."

Ben muttered something under his breath. He hates it here or keeps saying he does, out in Hicksville with Fearless Leader dogging our steps, but he's had a thousand chances to run off with a city gang and hunt humans every day of the week and he never does. Still too hoo for his own good, Billy says. That feeling, I think I know. I'd rather stay where things are wide open and quiet.

We marched beyond the sharp bend in the Great River, through the erstwhile playground, past a faded sign pointing to ye olde historic gristmill and sawmill and sugaring shack (maple syrup in Indiana, who knew?) and spilled into the parking lot, the late winter asphalt morgue-cold and soothing against swollen and bony feet. I was half asleep, wishing vaguely for a little marrow bone to suck on while I drifted off, and then suddenly wide awake as a pair of blaring headlights swung off the county road, knocked over the orange cones blocking their path, shot through the barricaded park entrance, peeled toward us in a wide screeching curve and came to a bucking-horse stop yards away, right there in the middle of the lot.

Unbelievable. The park is abandoned, the farms and subdivisions deserted, the roads strictly Drive At Your Own Risk, there's no guards and no safe houses and no barrier gates and not a sane hoo for miles around and the assholes still come barreling through thinking they can be Big Mighty Zombie Hunters? Hasn't happened in years, hasn't happened since the unincorporated-county hicks finally lost enough Billy Bobs to realize we can do anything we want out here— as long as we stay out here—and there's no National Guard to come raging in with machine guns like in the movies. This wasn't a pickup truck though, just a crappy little white Honda, and before we could react the driver's door flew open and a skinny blond hoocow crumpled onto the pavement and splattered herself with puke.

Correction: Mighty Zombie Hunters, and the occasional wrong-turn drunk. I fucking hate drunk drivers. I have my reasons.

If we weren't already stuffed sausage-tight with meat and blood we would have tried rushing her, hope she'd run toward the woods in panic, but we just wanted a little fun. She was too busy groaning and pulling at vomit-caked hair strands to register our presence so we moved in a little closer, and a little closer, and when she finally realized that wasn't more puke she smelled we were within easy stumble of dessert. She stared at us, bleary-eyed, face ashen. We stared back.

She dove head-first back into the car, slammed the locks shut and propelled the thing straight toward us. Sam just stood there, glowing and skeletal in the oncoming head-lights, and put his hands out to the front grille; the tires squealed, turning over and over on themselves, and when his arms shook with the effort Billy and I stepped up too, our palms splayed side by side like a chart of fleshly decay. She gunned the accelerator, giving me a good bodily jolt but not moving the car an inch, and as Mags and Ben and Joe swarmed around the doors her whole body went slack with fear. Joe rapped on the windshield, a light little tap that made the glass blossom in a cobweb of cracks.

"You *lost*?" he shouted, looming in close so she could see his gnawed-up face. *"Is somebody lost?"*

Mags staggered around the car groaning, her drooling-retard undead act, fingers buried in the mush of her own flesh up to the knuckles. The smell of terror poured through the door seals like gas from a vent; Billy and Sam on one side, Joe and me on the other, we rocked the car gently back and forth, up and back down again, and the hoocow tore at her own hair and screamed and screamed. Linc and Florian held back, like they always hold back, but they were both wheezing with laughter.

"Come on," Linc managed, "knock that off. Or I'll tell Teresa."

We ignored him, the car way off to the side, balanced on one set of furiously rotating tires, then back. The hoocow was puking again, from vertigo or fear anybody's guess.

Florian spat, a thin depleted stream of coffin juice, and stamped his bony feet. "You all a lot of pussycats?" he asked, drawing out the first two syllables. "How long you gonna stand here playing? Either kill it and eat it or leave it alone."

Killjoy. We rested the car gently on the asphalt, stepping backward with bows and curtsies. The hoocow just sat there, covered in sick, probably stunned. She had big bewildered brown eyes, actual cow eyes, that skin so pale it always looks bluish. Actually she looked plain old blue, a dark sickly tinge rising up and suffusing her skin like a blush. Billy made elaborate motions toward the park gate and she just sat there. Little chips of windshield had fallen out, bits of glitter sprinkling the ground.

"You better leave," Linc called out, pointing at the gate. He can't talk any better than the rest of us, lips and tongues and palates all moldered away, but his mishmash of syllables at least sounded friendly. "This place isn't for humans. You better go."

The hoocow drew her brows together, startled, then gazed in wonderment at the puke on her T-shirt, at her left hand grasping the wheel and the right pulling the brake. At me. Big, dark stupid eyes staring into mine, sidling on down to take in my face and the rags of my clothes and lingering on my one remaining hand and Jesus Christ, how drunk was she? I screamed at her through the windshield and she started awake, throwing herself into reverse and heading exitward at a downright leisurely pace. The car meandered from side to side, nearly wandering into a clump of trees, then righted itself and vanished slow and unsteady out the park gate.

"What the hell was that all about?" Joe demanded, like I would know.

Ben yanked the ragged remnants of his fedora further over his eyes. "So stoned she couldn't tell which hand was which. Big deal." He gazed across the parking lot, frowning. "I coulda used a little tasty treat, myself—if she wanted to stay that bad, you shoulda let her."

It was halfhearted protest; his voice had the same lazy edge of satiety as Joe's, and by the time we crossed into the wide, empty park field bordered by gristmill and sugaring shack and thick bands of cottonwoods Lady Hoocow was nearly forgotten. Uncut for years, the tall grass was choked by taller weeds, their stems sharp and crackling as we pushed through them to get home. Teresa's gazebo, its white paint peeling and carved patches of roof rotting away, sat across a little footbridge in an enclave surrounded by rusting park benches and clusters of oaks; the "Great" River, narrow and slow-moving and perpetually clogged with mud, circled around the rear and disappeared back into the forest.

The queen's throne, but of course Her Majesty was nowhere to be seen. Teresa loves to disappear for hours and days at a time, no saying where or why, no saying how she fed. Ben and Billy and some of the others wander off too, go human-hunting whenever deer and ducks and possum and coyotes stop tasting exciting, but they always bring back bones and stories for the rest of us, make it worth everyone's while. Teresa, she's just too good to share and of course *we* can't have a walkabout if she's having one; we all have to be right there, sitting tight, waiting for whenever she decides to stroll back home.

That act's getting old, dusty and ancient in fact. But right then I was too tired to care.

Ben groaned, crawling under one of the benches; the ground was softening with the approach of spring, but still cold and firm enough for good sleeping. "All that fuss to get back and she ain't here. Told you we should've stopped for a snack—"

Florian, curled up against the gazebo wood, was already sound asleep. Sam hauled himself up again, groaning. "Our turn for watch, Billy, c'mon."

He and Billy left for watch duty, to tramp around the near perimeter of the park looking for any more interlopers until all the sun and daylight exhausted them and a new shift took over. Not my turn yet, thank God. I get sleepy now the way little kids do, big wild bursts of energy evaporating in a flash, and falling into the tall grass was a relief. Joe settled next to me, front to front, Linc on the other side back to back. Mags was flopped out snoring at my feet.

"Wait'll she gets back home," Joe muttered, already half-asleep. "Th'hoocow. Stories she'll tell. Zombie this, zombie that—"

"Good." I shifted away from a sharp rock. "Keep her kind away."

The sunrise was full orange, striated with wide soft streaks of pink. Stomach full. It was time to go to sleep.

I remember, when I was alive, reading somewhere that Eskimos don't call themselves that—white men did, a corruption of some word that meant "raw flesh eater." They called each other "The People." Raw flesh eater. There actually is a gang up in the Dakotas that calls itself The Eskimos, but a lot of folks don't get the joke. My gang, Teresa and Joe and Sam and all the rest, is called the Fly-by-Nights. Our turf is what used to be the Great River County Park in Calumet County, right over the Illinois-Indiana border and just south of where the Lake Michigan beach dunes begin, and it's been their place, our place, long before I tunneled up and they took me in as family.

We're not the only gang around here, not by a long shot—there's the Carnies over in Michigan City, the Bottom Feeders in South Bend, the Way of All Flesh that practically runs Cicero and the Rat Patrol that goes wherever the hell it wants whenever it wants—but this is my gang, the best gang, and so that's what I call myself if you ask me, a Fly-by-Night. Undead, if you want something more basic. Jessie, if you're not such an asshole you never ask my name.

What I never call myself, ever, is "zombie." It's racist, for one thing, just like "Eskimo." I cared a lot about racism and animals and justice and all of that, when I was human. But I haven't been human for a long time.

2

Nine years ago, I was alive. Nine years ago, Jessica Anne Porter was fifteen and lived in a nice house in the very well-guarded town of Lepingville, an hour out of Chicago, and got okay grades and wanted to do something someday with animal rights. Her hair was auburn dyed something brighter, I forget what. I don't see bright colors well anymore. She had a mother, father, a sister in her first year of college, a brother in his last—neither of them could wait to get out of the house, they barely spoke to her parents. And her parents barely spoke to each other. Then one day they were in a rare good mood and took her out to dinner, and then there was the Toyota ride home.

Dad took the back roads home, the scenic tour. You weren't supposed to do that, you were supposed to stay on the main highway with the blindingly sulfurous roadside lights (the "environmental hazards," as we called them, you never put it more directly than that, supposedly hated bright light) and the toll booths. Each booth had a FUNDING COMMUNITY SAFETY sign so you wouldn't throw a tantrum as you forked over your money, a sentry bearing an emergency flamethrower. See? Safety. Suck on that, you suburban cheapskates. The small, cramped booths could serve as safe houses in a pinch, if a "hazard" somehow surprised you on the road. They had to let you in, that was the law. But my dad had paid four tolls in eighteen miles just to get to the restaurant and my mom complained the road lights gave her headaches and it was a pretty night and for once nobody was screaming at each other so why not take the old road, the long way home? Rest your eyes. Have a bit of peace and quiet.

It was two miles from the county line, where the former industrial park gave way to beachy dune grass and rows of half-built condos sat empty along the roadside, silhouetted in weirdly dim, soft white road lights. The old-fashioned kind. This was after they finally passed the moratorium on residential building in rural areas, the one the developers held up as long as they could, until the "hazards" somehow got into that gated community near the Taltree Preserve; whose woods, fields and ex-farmlands these are, even they then managed to figure out. Nothing hazardous that night, though, just the dark sky and the low fuzzy whiteness and everything peaceful and sleepy until suddenly there were two blinding headlights bearing down on us from the wrong side of the road, howling brakes and screaming and then, like the lost breath from a hard stomach punch, everything gathered into a fist and struck, and then stopped.

I remember a pickup truck, yellow, gone faded saffron under the road lights. And a woman's voice, not my mother's, moaning over and over like some nauseated prayer while I lay on the pavement dying, *Oh Christ, oh God, oh Christ oh Christ oh Christ oh my God* and I thought, Lady, it's a little late for that now isn't it? Her voice was washed out, staticky with the buzz of a million angry flies eating her up, and the buzzing became louder and louder and there were new flashing lights, red ones, but it was too late, I was all eaten up, and I closed my eyes and fell asleep for a long time.

Then, days or weeks or months after the funeral, I woke up.

In old horror movies where someone gets buried alive,

there's always that moment where they blink into the darkness, pat and grope around the coffin walls and let out that big oxygen-wasting scream as the screen goes black. Me, though, I knew I was dead, really dead and not put away by mistake, and another giant fist was gripping my brain and nerves and shoving away shock, surprise, bewilderment, only letting me think one thing: *Out*. And I knew, with absolute certainty, that I would break free. I didn't seem to need air anymore, so I could take my time.

I tried putting my hands out just like in the movies, to feel the force and weight I was fighting—six feet under, that's a lot of piled-up dirt—and that's how I found out my right arm was shot to pieces. The left could rattle the box a bit, but not enough. I raised my legs, each movement a good long achy stretch after the best nap in the world, and pressed my palm, knees, feet against the white satiny padding overhead. Felt a rattle. Pressed harder. Heard a creak.

Then I kicked.

The first blow tore through the satin lining and slammed into the wood without a moment's pain; the second splintered it, cracked it, and I kicked and kneed and punched until I hit shards of timber and musty air and then, so hard my whole body rattled, a solid concrete ceiling overhead. A grave liner, Teresa explained to me later, another box for my box, but I felt real panic at the sight and had to make myself keep kicking, harder, harder, and that awful concrete became fine white dust that gave way to an avalanche of dirt. I was gulping down mouthfuls of mud and I was sad for my shirt, they'd buried me in my favorite T-shirt that read ANIMALS ARE NOT OURS TO EAT, WEAR, OR EXPERIMENT ON and now it was plastered mute with damp black dirt, but I kept swimming one-handed, kicking, tunneling upward through a crumbling sea. The moist tides of soil were endless, then I felt something finer and powdery-dry and my good hand found thin cords of grassroots, poked through the green carpet-weave and ripped a long jagged slit open to the air. The *air*—I didn't need it, maybe, but as

I lay there drained and exhausted and felt it cool on my dirt-caked back I almost cried.

The sunset was a needle-thrust in my eyes. I crouched in my own grave hole, retching up pebbles and earth, and gasped at the smells of the world: the turned soil, the broken grass stems I clutched in my fist, graveside flowers old and new, the trees and plants and the thousands of people and animals that'd left scents behind traversing the cemetery grounds. My own dead, dirty stink, and it still didn't shock me, I was too distracted by the other million fits and starts of odor flooding my nostrils—this was how to experience the world, this note of mushrooms sprouting in damp grass, this trace of old rubber from a sneaker sole, compared to this banquet eyes and ears told you nothing! My head pounded, painlessly, like a great throbbing vein: the hard pulsations of my new brain, my undead brain, but I didn't know that yet. I reached up, like someone would be there to lift me, and touched something rough and cold. A tombstone, my tombstone: AUGUST 14, 2001. I died on August 14, 2001, but what day was it now? Where was I now? Where would I go, where will I sleep, do I *have* to sleep—

I smelled it before I saw it, darting quick and confused across the grass. Rabbit. Fresh, living rabbit.

Every other scent and smell in the world instantly vanished. Hunger rattled my skull and shook my bones—pork chops, hamburgers, steaks rare and bloody, everything that would have made me vomit when I was alive but I had to have them now, I had to have them raw and oozing juice and if I didn't get that rabbit, if I didn't kill it and devour it *now*, I had nothing to live for at all. I staggered to my feet and stood there trembling, legs stiff and exhausted, but before I could even try to run for my food something bloated and rotten in the shape of a man, his dark suit jacket torn and spilling fat little white grubs, crawled on all fours from the pile of dirt that had been his grave. The grave next to mine. The rabbit had halted too soon, crouching frozen with fear by our collective tombstone, and as I watched it spasm and kick against death, as I watched my father sink long teeth into its skull and spit out soft tufts of brown fur, I was small again and only wanted to scream and cry, Daddy, why did you take my toy?

Something crawled from behind a yew tree, feverish and fast. A woman in the rags of my mother's favorite blue sweater fell on him, grabbing the rabbit's meaty hindquarters for herself, and held on tight and chewed no matter how hard he punched and kicked, so hard she sobbed between bites: Whap, cry, swallow, whap, cry, swallow.

But, Daddy, that's *my* toy.

They rolled on the ground, snarling with rage.

And you. What are *you* doing in my mom's favorite sweater?

But they'd dropped the rabbit carcass, fighting that hard, and I was so hungry and it was so good and I knew the answers to my questions, I already knew.

A garter snake slithered over my mother's foot and they both went crazy, grabbing fistfuls of grass where it had shot out of reach. Arguing again, fighting forever, only with sounds now and no words—screeching violins, deafening pounding drums. I was gone already, walking away. I never saw them again.

I scraped a deep, gouging ridge in my back, crawling through a gap I'd torn in the cemetery fence, and felt only a paper cut. A pinprick. I ran my tongue along my teeth and almost screamed; the fence's barbed wire was nothing, but my teeth had all grown long and blade-edged and when I pulled my hand from my mouth, there was something thick and syrupy from the new cut on my tongue and fingers, almost like blood but black. Coffin liquor, Florian told me later, my own putrefaction flowing through my veins. My hand was swollen and livid, the veins and arteries gone dark.

I could barely walk. I staggered, tried crawling like my mom had but with the bad arm that wasn't any better. CAL-UMET COUNTY MEMORIAL PARK, read the sign; that told me I was in the middle of nowhere, if you insist on burying instead of burning they make you do it far away from everything and don't come crying to us if the funeral procession gets attacked, but where this particular nowhere was I had no idea. Other than me and that garter snake, no sign of life. I crawled and stumbled and crawled again, pushing through grass, gravel, leaves and underbrush. Snapping branches scared me, a single car speeding by terrified me; it'd find me and run me down if it got a chance. I didn't feel like a monster but I knew I looked like one. I cried from fear, wept from hunger, black syrupy tears splattering my muddy shirt.

I kept walking, deep into the countryside, no company but the animals I was too scared to stop and hunt. What the hell was I looking for? My throbbing skull started pounding in earnest, yielding to real pain, and my ears were flooded with a sudden off-kilter symphony of screeches, buzzes, trumpet squawks, strings sliced shrilly in half. The buzzing like flies, that sound I remembered from dying. I shook my head to get rid of it, like real flies stuck in my head, and it grew louder and sharper and became muffled disjointed words:

—*another one—grave—Joe—see—*

I started shaking. Never mind what had happened to me and my parents, never mind the guard posts along the highways and every Lepingville entrance and exit, never mind all the school safety drills and town committee handouts about the others, the "hazards," the reasons you either burn like a Good Responsible Person or you get buried behind barbed wire in No Humans' Land—never mind all that because it couldn't be true, *I* couldn't be true—

—*circles—follow—*

Circles, dizzy and hunger-sick around the same clump of trees, and I couldn't find those voices or escape them but I tried to follow them not knowing why: hot-hotter-COLD— turn left—warmer-warmer-COLD—not so far left—so hungry-hotter-COLD—straight ahead—too quiet—turn around. My guts twisted hot-hotter—ON FIRE with emptiness, no more meat, no nothing. Voices faded, returned in tinny crashes of music, then vanished. I was on the worst ice-cream truck chase in the history of the world, but if I kept going the voices would find me, they'd tell me where to go and feed me and take me in—but then I took a wrong turn and it was cold-colder-absolute zero, every sound gone. The clouds overhead seemed to burst and collapse like bubbles, inky night pouring in as I stood there covered in mud and black blood. All alone.

I doubled over, threw my head back and screamed. Frankenstein's monster, roaring, and it felt so good that I crouched in the leaves and shouted louder, ripping myself inside out with hunger and fear. Something small and furry shot past me, terrified of the sounds I was making, and I could have chased it but my head pounded and throbbed and everything before my eyes melted, sliding off my plane of vision as I succumbed to the vertigo. A spoon heated seething red scraped my gut away piece by piece, slow starvation cauterizing my insides, and I pounded my forehead, my good fist, against the ground and wailed.

I don't know how long I lay there. Silence, my horrible crying met with utter silence, and then I felt what I thought was an insect brushing my face. No, not an insect—soft swollen fingers. A stench pressed in on all sides, I was fresh and sweet in comparison, but I was too tired to move and it couldn't mean anything. I was all alone.

The fingers touched my ruined right arm, lifted it. It fell back with a soft thud. *Chit-chit*, I heard, a strange wet-dry click like someone chewing a mouthful of popcorn kernels. I pulled myself upright, and looked.

The whole right side of his face was smashed in, concave forehead and crushed cheekbone and one eye bugging precariously from a broken socket. He was purplish-black, and dirty white: Maggots seethed from every pore and crawled across him in excited wriggly piles, blowflies waving and blooming and wilting, the bits of bone they'd scraped clean glinting like tiny mosaic tiles. Scraps of jeans and a leather jacket clung to the sticky seething mess of his flesh. He was big, big-shouldered, a good foot taller; *chit-chitter*, he went, even standing still.

Behind him were more stinking, seething masses shaped like people, their skin in the thin moonlight every color bruises go: some barely rotten at all, one shriveled and bony as an unwrapped mummy, one so bloated and gas-blackened it scared me. Standing right behind Bug Man was a half-skeleton with wild dark hair and silver rings clinking on her finger bones, eyes bulging nearly out of her head as she sized me up, grinned and let out a loud, belching guffaw. They all groaned with laughter. Their teeth looked the way mine felt, long and jagged and dull gray like tarnished blades.

I can't explain it. You can be a monster yourself and still scream, puke, faint seeing what you are staring back at you, but none of it seemed monstrous. It was pretty, almost, the weirdest kind of pretty, seeing how they were all young or old in their own inhuman way, how slowly and methodically the bugs took care of everything, how clean bones and pulsating brains were underneath the skin. How natural it all was. But then those teeth, so dull and dirty but a glint at the tips, if you looked closely, the flash of a needle that could crunch through bones and penetrate to the marrow. Under their laughter a thrumming sound, not quite musical but not quite mere noise, and the longer I stared the more the shapeless sounds took on outlines, defined themselves, by whom I was looking at: That one there, with the bleary laugh, a trumpet; the one with the thin sad face, banjo; the black-haired scarecrow with the rings, shrill strings. Bug Man's noise was louder and stronger than the rest, so I mistook him for the leader. Electric guitar, that would blast you flat to the ground if you got too close.

I reached out and touched his face. *Chit-chit*, said the bugs. He grunted, almost belched the crude shape of words, a caveman with a rotted tongue—but soon as all that *hrruh-hrruh-mmmuhhhhh* shot through my head it became waves of sound, transformed radio waves, and then words precise and clear as pieces of glass glittering on the beach.

"I'm Joe," he said. "Happy birthday."

The others mumbled something in turn but I couldn't hear them properly just yet, only their noises that were almost but not quite trumpets and banjos and strings. The smell of fresh flesh wafted over me, and Joe the Bug Man stepped aside as someone in a ragged black fedora emerged from the trees, something swinging from his hand, and dropped a warm furry just-dead thing right at my feet. A possum, its neck neatly snapped.

My stomach gurgled and Fedora Man snorted, walking away. Dark drops fell on the carcass, *plink-plonk*, and Joe laughed, reached out to wipe the black drool from my mouth. "Go on. Eat."

I ate and ate and couldn't stop. Rich raw meat. Warm blood. Leftovers from God's refrigerator. When I looked up again, putting down the bones I'd been chewing to twigs to get at the marrow, they were all standing over me. The dark-haired one with the rings smiled.

"I'm Teresa," she said. Jerked her head toward a soft, bloated gaseous mass with a lone lamplike eye and ragged remnants of red hair. "That's Lillian. Remember her name, even if you don't remember mine."

Lillian, the chieftainess, though of course I didn't know that yet. Teresa was her second in command back then, already planning, scheming. They both watched me crunch another bone down to splinters, then Teresa smiled.

"Good girl," she said. "Now, time to earn your food."

Her fists caught me in the jaw, chest, gut, and when they all piled on me at once, my gang induction, all that meat came rocketing straight up again. Dry bony feet kicked me, squelching rotting ones, and Joe sat there watching it all happen. I crawled through a gap in the fists and feet, even one-armed it was better than tottering on legs that would never work properly again, and I rose up and punched Joe hard in the gut and he gasped, laughed harder, and hit me back more viciously than all the others. I hung on. Bones cracked, his and mine. They only pulled me off when we were both dizzy and spitting out mouthfuls of bilious dark blood, and even one-armed I'd passed my test so well that Teresa, then Lillian, beat me up again so I'd remember who was in charge. I couldn't move for three days. They brought me rabbit, squirrel, the dog-ends of deer. They'd been needing someone new who could really fight, they said, and didn't hide their surprise that the someone was me.

But there wasn't anyone to fight, not in the middle of nowhere in a former county park with only squirrels and deer and each other for company. They were the first gang for me, the only gang, and so I didn't question why we all stayed out here when other gangs routinely marauded in the poorer, unguarded human areas, the ones whose property taxes just couldn't float guard teams and electrified fences and infrared video security, it's like they all *want* to be attacked, too bad, so sad, why don't they all just quit their goddamned whining and move somewhere else?

"You broke six of my ribs," Joe told me, when I could stand and walk again; he said it nose-to-nose clenching my good arm hard enough to snap but there was admiration in his eyes, that little hiss in his voice that someone gets when you're not at all what they expected, when they realize they're not gonna get what they want without a fight and they like it. That singular sound of: *Damn, woman.* "Six. You stomped me like a fucking cardboard box."

"I'm hungry," I told him, and there wasn't any whining in my voice, no please-feed-me, just a hard flat-out demand for what I required. He liked demands, I could tell already. Hearing them, issuing them. "I'm always hungry."

"You're supposed to be."

He pulled me aside from the group, from everyone smirking at us both. Florian, the walking skeleton with the watery blue eyes, he was the only other one of them I liked. "It's time you learn to hunt," Joe said. "I'll show you how. Lillian's a shit hunter, don't let her tell you anything. You'll be good at it. Put some of that crazy to use."

Plenty to hunt. Plenty to hunt far outside our attenuated neck of the woods. Plenty of low-hanging two-legged fruit rotting on the vine in Gary and East Chicago and South Chicago and parts of Hammond and Whiting, plenty of what I kept being told, over and over again, secondhand, have heard, they say, everybody knows, is the only real meat. But turns out, I didn't want brains, I didn't need hoos; meat was meat, any fresh kill would do, and it did for all of us, for all their talk.

"So just what the hell are we looking for?" I asked Joe on our first watch patrol together at the wood's very edge, sitting side by side against a tree trunk, not watching anything but the wind kicking up the dry dead stalks of a neighboring cornfield gone to weeds. "There's nobody here. There's never anybody, Ben said, nothing but feral cats and every now and then a crazy-ass bum—"

"Do they still go around saying you can shoot us?" Joe interrupted, squinting into the painfully blue sky. High noon, the whole rest of the gang deep asleep. "Guns don't work. Not pistols, not machine guns, not automatic rifles, never be afraid of any little hoo who comes at you waving a gun—"

"So Sam said." I'd started liking Sam too, not half so worn out and dusty as Florian but with so much wearier, sadder eyes. "But they don't say that anymore. Didn't."

"Fire. That's it. Or a good stomp to the head, till your skull's kicked in." He folded his arms, a little humorous glint in his eye. "Like a flattened cardboard box. Otherwise you'll just crumble to dust, whenever it's your time. Stomping, or fire. Ever seen a crazy hoo-vigilante wandering around the woods with a flamethrower, thinking he's gonna toast our collective asses once and for all?"

"So what would we do then?" They don't go for controlled rural burns anymore, once they realized all that does is send the surviving "hazards" crowding closer and closer to hoo-territory. Gotta eat. Of course, hell with what the government does or doesn't do, all it takes is one crazy redneck with a book of matches. It's just been sheer luck. "By the time we see him, already too late."

"What do we do then?" Joe chuckled, still gazing up at the sky. "Mostly we die. But at least we die knowing who got us, and we don't die alone." He raked one leather-jacketed shoulder against the tree bark, working away at the ceaseless bug-itch of his own rotten skin. "Died alone once. I'm not doing it again." He turned to look at me, narrow dark eyes staring from a seething feeding sea. "Never. Ever."

I stared back, watching the perpetual movement of his skin as the maggots and flies crawled around and into every niche of flesh, made the worn creased jacket sleeves wriggle all of their own accord. Dead? Bursting with life, literally, all the life you could possibly want, that d-word applied to any of us was so ludicrous and willfully oblivious and just plain bigoted and how old and aged was Joe, anyway? Not by hoo-measure, but by our own lights? He'd said he died sometime in the fifties but couldn't remember just when. I'd forget too, he said, in time.

"I don't want to die alone either," I said. "Again."

Joe just laughed and shook his head. "Not a larva on her yet, and she's already hand-wringing—you have any idea how many decades Florian's got on you? Sam? You're a goddamned baby. You're so young."

"And you're not so damned old either," I said. Asked. Worried. "However much you brag." Silence. "Right?"

His eyes were adrift and lost in his own face, that whole ocean of insect life; I had to look that much harder at him to read his expressions, gauge his mood. Keep my attention on him constantly. If it had been me I'd have been creeped out, someone staring at me all the time like that, watching every last thing I do. Joe, he didn't mind.

"I'm not so old," he said, softly. Then he grinned. "And I can't drop even if I wanted to, now I've got a goddamned diaper-shitting baby to feed—"

I hit him, and he laughed again and louder and we wrestled until I shrieked for my arm, not my good arm, goddammit. The sky was pure cloudless blue that whole afternoon and the sun pressed in hard on dark-loving undead eyes but it was still beautiful, the sky, the woods, even that ratty old cornfield, all ours.

What the hell were we looking for? He never did answer that question. Him or anyone else.

They were the first gang, the only gang for me. Lingering out here in the middle of nowhere, years and years, shy kids at the perimeter of the playground, hiding and skulking when there was not a thing to hide from, there had to be a reason for that, it had to be some sort of deliberate strategy, I thought. It couldn't be that some of them stayed out here because it was easy. Because they really had been big noises in faster, stronger, more aggressive gangs, but they'd washed out or been thrown out or left thinking they'd be king hoo-killers all on their own, crowned and canonized, and it never happened.

Because they were old, some of them, older and dustier than they liked to say. Because they were young, and hiding was easier. Because they just didn't care for killing, not really, not once the hunger that never really left you got put in its place up on the shelf for another few hours, and that was a shameful thing even fleetingly to think so they just kept very quiet.

And then there was me. And now that I knew I could fight and that it wasn't hard to hunt I could have left any time, kept to myself for years or decades and avoided all the trouble that came after. I stayed because of Joe—his smile, the loud pounding music in his head, the way he hit right back and looked at me afterward with shrewdness, new respect, and then something more. Every time. What would repulse any sane human, the bugs, the smell, the casual brutality, the gleeful killing, meant less than nothing to me now. Even knowing then and later that I should have collected my strength and wits, turned around and left for good, no looking back. I stayed because of him.

Like I said, I was fifteen.

3

Losing my arm and catching such a huge deer and terrorizing a hoocow on a drunk was a lot of excitement for one night, and I could've slept right up until sunset. Could have, if not for Billy the Bloater returning from watch and splitting our skulls open with a rusty brain-radio reveille of *DA-DA-DA da-da-da da-DA-DA-DAAAAAAAAA*, so loud that Florian jumped and cried out and Sam, trailing Billy, let out an embarrassed growl and turned his back.

Billy, an Old Master's death's-head with a bloated, waterlogged tongue lolling perpetually from his mouth, ignored the shouts and showers of crab apples and made an elaborate show of stepping aside, clearing a path. Suddenly it grew quiet and I heard the little rattle of silver rings against finger bones, the barest hiss of breath: Fearless Leader was back. She stood over me, black broom-straw hair airborne in the breeze, and curled what was left of her lip.

"Up," she said.

Joe helped pull me to my feet and I quirked my head at the sound of a meandering little flute, a timid brain wave belonging to none of us, and then the smell of dead flesh plunged in a nasty, astringent chemical bath. It came from the gazebo steps, where something in a mud-caked dress and torn nylons sat with its arms wrapped around its knees, trembling and smiling at nothing. Perfectly rouged cheeks, perfectly red lips, a smooth pink-and-white face and eyes that wouldn't open and a mouth hovering in delicate, parted-lip repose: a 'maldie, a formaldehyde-pickled hoo, one of the undertaker's vain, whiny, tenderfooted useless finest. Displeased murmurs all around. Joe, already in a mood from being yanked awake, slammed his hand in frustration against a tree.

Teresa shuffled up to him, stroking the cottonwood he'd hit like that could bring back the bark. "The deer were out yesterday, I understand. So where's my share?"

I knew this would happen. It's hardly rocket science: You eat what you hunt, period, and if you miss a group hunt like last night's full of tasty treats, too bad. That's how it was, anyway, until Teresa suddenly decided that being gang leader meant she doesn't have to waste time hunting at all, that it's our job to drag back half what we catch to the gazebo for her to gobble on her own time—to leave her *snacks*, when even the weakest and oldest of us could kill their own, when anyone who couldn't met only one end. We'd been devouring all the deer kills and bringing her half-nibbled possum tailbones, muskrats, dainty little bites of field mouse, and now she'd finally decided she was pissed off. Fine with me.

Joe, unflinching, folded his arms. "So where have you been the last few nights?" he said. He glanced at New Thing. "Besides digging up worthless 'maldies for the fold—"

Teresa bristled. "We need new members, at least you're always whining that we do—and now that they're cremating nine-tenths of them the second they kick I can't be fussy about who I take. If she can't hunt, we'll just kill her." New Thing trembled. "And I had business elsewhere, that's all you need to know. So where's my meat?"

Joe shrugged. "Tell us the business, and we'll give you a meal."

She wrapped her bony fingers around his neck and lifted him straight off his feet, her tarnished silver rings sinking into his throat. "Your precious was first hunter last night," she said, not raising her voice. She never needs to. "Her job is to make sure my share got put aside. So why didn't she?"

Joe just hung there, oozing smothered fury. Teresa turned to me and smiled. "Get over here."

I got. The studs of Teresa's leather jacket glinted as she raised Joe higher; a nicer jacket than Joe's, the black leather less cracked and worn, but it wasn't *hers*. She and Mags got it off a hoo years before my time. Joe was buried in his. His second skin.

"It's nice and simple," she said, staring daggers. Her arm didn't even tremble. "Any hunt, first rights on half the meat is mine. And you were first hunter, and responsible for my share, so why'd you go and eat my share? And don't tell me"—a singsong falsetto—"'Oh, Teweesah, I was so *hungwy*.' If you're smart."

First hunter. Jesus, did she really think we had nothing better to do than play carcass cop with each other, wagging fingers over meat she had no right to touch? I just shrugged. "I got nothing, Teresa."

"You got nothing."

"I'm just saying, maybe you don't wanna hear it, but we wanted it, we ate it, we didn't feel like leaving you any." The truth is never a good idea around Teresa, but I was tired and my bullshit tank was down to fumes. "And there was no point anyway, because that was last night and here you are, half a day later? And you weren't anywhere in sight when we left or came back? Even if we'd left you the whole damned deer you couldn't have eaten it, the meat's too old. Ruined."

And what the hell's wrong with the bitch that I even have to say this? We can't eat stale kills, nothing over an hour dead's even digestible, so what kind of crazy power trip is she on to want tributes of rotten carcass that hasn't had a heartbeat in hours, days? Eat your damned fist if you need dead flesh that badly. Hell, make a hoo-barbecue and cook it, if you really want to make us all puke. That's the one thing about my appetites that hasn't changed since I died: There's just nothing out there nastier than cooked meat.

Joe shook violently, toes dangling, insects flying off his skin into the grass. Teresa hoisted him higher. "You didn't feel like it—well, I guess you think it's some kind of noble gesture, admitting it. So what do I do now?" She'd trotted out her weary voice, an all-giving mother faced with a rotten kiddie brat; the grunts and moans of it were like the spasms of a dying engine. "Tear off your other arm? But you'd probably like that, no more hunting duties at all. Give you a nice skin slip? Put you on permanent day-watch duty, so I never have to see your sorry face? But then what do I do about the rest of you—"

"Just where the hell *have* you been, Teresa?" Ben spat the words, scraps of his old black fedora flapping like wagging fingers. "You find some little nest of hoos too stupid to move to town and decide to keep it to yourself, 'cause God forbid the rest of us ever get a crack at some good meat—"

"You nearly broke my goddamned neck getting to the shitty meat last night, Mighty Hunter," Mags shot back, scratching doglike at her shoulder until a cluster of wasps and hide beetles flew up around her ear. She and Ben have always had it in for each other. "Only the nine of us on fifteen hundred acres and Monsieur still can't find any food that suits him? No wonder you can't figure out how to just follow the damned highway until you find an unguarded hoo-city, if you're that stupid right from the get-go—"

Ben growled, raising his good fist; Sam put a hand on his arm, coaxing, and Ben fell silent. Mags was right, of course, we weren't exactly tussling for scraps out here and even in the populated areas, where you'd be fighting the likes of the Rat Patrol and the Way of All Flesh for the hoo-goodies, there's always more than enough to go round—the old north-county steel towns, the unincorporated unguarded bits of what used to be a dozen different suburbs, that's a full larder by any measure. Ben, Billy, Mags, Joe, they all go hoo-hunting up there now and again. Never have myself, never tasted human flesh—yeah, it happens, and more than you'd think! Joe keeps trying to drag me along, keeps threatening never to come back from one of his meat runs, but he always does. They all do. It's quieter here. Mostly. There's nothing wrong with liking things quiet.

"So what do I do now?" Teresa repeated, eyes back on me. Her fingers clenched suddenly, crushing the beetles on Joe's throat with a thousand small crunches. "I still don't know. But since you all just throw away what's mine, not a second thought, maybe I should do the same for you."

She pulled her arm back, grunting, and Joe flew from her grasp, hurtled sideways and crashed into a cluster of wrought-iron benches. Under shouts and the clatter of falling metal came a gunshot crack and I stumbled toward him, my stomach a stone—she'd broken his back, she'd broken his neck, he was crippled and he'd be stomped in the skull for everyone's good and I wouldn't allow it, I'd bring him food and kill her to get it—while Teresa just stood there and laughed. New Thing, long since forgotten, moaned quietly on the gazebo steps. Her chemical stink was everywhere, perfuming the trees.

Joe lay curled on the upended benches, stunned but unhurt; the cracking sound was a tree branch he took down as he fell. Linc came stumbling up, offering him an unwanted helping hand; Joe shoved us both aside, wrenched himself to his feet and stalked into the woods without looking back. Teresa jerked her head toward me, then the 'maldie.

"Cal Memorial's vomited up another one," she said. "Take care of your little neighbor for me, I don't have the patience."

Lucky me. Mags, Ben and I went and yanked New Thing off the steps. I couldn't do this one-handed.

Ever read how they used to put pennies on dead people's eyes, to weight them shut? Florian had those. Nowadays, though, they use eyecaps: big plastic lenses with tiny tent-pole spikes on the outside, covering the whole eyeball and keeping the lids anchored like awnings. There's no way to get them out except to hold the 'maldie down, peel the eyelids back and pry them out, hoping you don't accidentally gouge out an eye. And we haven't gotten to the really fun part yet—the mouthpiece. It's always so tempting just to leave their whiny lips sealed shut. With every touch, New Thing flinched like I'd punched her.

"I'm gonna open your eyes," I said. "They're sealed shut, that's why you can't open them. Okay? You understand?"

No answer. As Mags and Ben gripped her arms, I pried gently at one eyelid; not sewed shut, good. Much easier. I gave the eyecap a little tap, got a grip on it—

—and tore her eyelid in two when she wrenched away and let out a muffled banshee-shriek of panic. I grabbed her hair, and her scalp slid sideways; a wig, I should have guessed. Mags slapped her hard, bellowing, "Stay still!"

She thrashed harder, back arching, and Ben kicked her. "For God's sake, Jessie, are you gonna help us hold her down?"

"I've got *one* hand, moron, how can I do this and help you? Billy, get over here."

Billy sauntered over, grinning; if New Thing was gonna be such a bitch, he was exactly what she deserved. I eased out the eyecaps with my fingertips, Billy pretending to help hold her head but mostly just enjoying the show. New Thing shook and whimpered and blinked, big blue-gray eyes screwed up in terror and agony in the failing light. She was tensed to run, not realizing she'd never run again, but that immobilized mouth kept its placid candy smile.

Mags grabbed New Thing's chin and poked at her lips. "Looks like a wire job—you sure you can get in there, Jess?"

"Sure. Have to break a few teeth to do it, but—"

That did it. New Thing screeched from behind her mouthpiece, donkey-kicking until I wrapped my arm around her knees and lifted her straight off her feet. "Listen up." I gripped tighter, silent warning I'd break her legs if she pushed it. "That thing in your mouth's held in by wire. It's sealing your jaw shut. That means I have to crack teeth to get it out—and if I don't, you'll starve to death. You wanna starve? Huh? You wanna starve?"

She shook her head, moaning between sealed teeth and trying to squeeze her eyes shut; the torn-away lid gave her a permanent wink. Ben laughed quietly, then reached up and plucked the dangling wig of soft blond hair right off her head, twirling it on one finger. She groped one-handed at her skull, feeling the huge spots of nothing where pretty silky curls had been, and started crying in earnest. 'Maldies. Jesus Christ. I just can't believe hoos still pony up for embalming; if you know your best beloveds might be tunneling up again, it's okay they die of flesh-hunger as long as they look pretty? But of course, I forget that nobody's own best beloved will ever, ever become one of them, one of *those*. I know how that sort of thinking works. I know it right from the source.

I parted her lips, running a finger over posthumously lengthened teeth, and finally spotted the little glint of silvery wire snaking through her gums. Targeted the spot next to it, one, two—

The three teeth bordering the wire broke off so hard and quick they flew into the grass. The 'maldie screamed out loud, plain old pain this time and not panic, and I groped around calmly in that tiny little space until I got my fingers on the wire and snapped it in two. I dropped it in the grass, next to the broken teeth, and she let out a hard, ragged sound, figuring out the worst was over. As she tried to open her lips wider I saw the hard plastic former shoved in behind her teeth, shaping her mouth and jaw into eternal pursed-up bliss; a few hard tugs, and it was out. She doubled over coughing and heaving, then retched up chunks of gauze, wads of cotton that stuck like wet toilet paper to her lips.

When we let her go she staggered and looked around in amazement, her flute notes coming high and fast and nervous. I remember that feeling. "So, what's your name?" I asked.

"Renee," she croaked, rubbing her head. "Renee Anderson."

Whatever. Last names don't matter. Ben folded his arms. "So? Let's hear it."

When she frowned in confusion he leaned into her face,

shouting low and slow like she was brain damaged: "How—did—you—die?"

She didn't flinch like most 'maldies do, seeing honest unembalmed rot like that up close. "Oh. I think . . . I was in a hospital." She nodded. "Yeah, I was. I remember the lights. And my head, it just . . . exploded, from the inside."

Aneurysm? Maybe. Florian died of that too, or maybe a stroke, but New Thing looked young, sixteen or seventeen at most. Like me when I tunneled up. She felt her skull again, the crisscross of surgical staples glinting between unshaven tufts of blond hair, and seemed surprised her whole head was there. If you looked closely you could see her clean new brain pulsating slow and steady beneath her scalp, a giant fontanelle.

Ben laughed. "Well, no kidding. My head exploded too—with a little help from a cracker-ass sheriff and some of his friends. See this?" He brandished his right arm, a blackened stump with the stubby memory of fingers flaking off at the ends. "They shot me, then tried cooking me extra-crispy. Lucky I woke up before my head melted. That's the last thing I heard 'em say: 'There's another one for the fire.' Nice, huh? So you gonna be like all the other 'maldies? The little pickled hoo-lovers who think they're God's special babies because they start going rotten in six months instead of three? You wanna tell me if that's fair, princess? Huh? Is that fair?"

Her eyes widened. "Sorry," she whispered.

"Sorry?" Ben snorted. "Here's sorry."

He hit her hard, and she went flying. Her gang baptism, no different than mine, but unlike Peachy Perfect I didn't sprawl on the ground and wail. Mags sauntered up, shoving me aside. "Oh, poor baby—he's awful mean, isn't he? Let me help you."

Slam, crash, facedown in the dry powdery dirt. Ben yanked her to her feet, giving Mags another crack, and even Florian and Linc didn't step in to help. Tradition is tradition. The new girl gave me a desperate glance, and I just shrugged. Kids today. "So, you gonna run off and cry, or are you staying?"

She panted, sagging in Ben's grip. "You mean with you guys?"

Unreal. "Yes, with us. Would you like—to stay—with us?"

She nodded, unhappy but also resigned. Where the hell else did she have to go? Teresa walked over and leaned in close.

"Thing is, you'll have to learn, if you want to stick around." She jabbed a finger in Renee's face, silver rings rattling. "First is hunting. You hungry?"

"Oh, yeah," she whispered, miserable and pathetically eager. I remember that too.

Teresa snickered. "Oh, yeah? Well, you get last rations until you can make a good kill yourself. If there's no meat left when it's your turn, tough. Second, I run this gang." Nice long pause, and a sudden throat grab that made Renee squeal and choke. "*I run this gang.* Understand? You eat when I say so. You sleep, talk, *think* when and how I say so, you kiss my bony flyblown ass twenty-nine times a day if I tell you to, and if you're too good for that you can piss off right now. And everyone else here is better than you, including that asshole I threw into the bushes. You're a piece of hoo shit." Her grip loosened. "Well? Say it."

Renee choked, coughed. "Piece'f hoosht," she mumbled.

"What was that?" Teresa shook her until her teeth snapped and rattled. "What was that? What did you say, 'maldie?"

"Hoo shit! I'm a piece of hoo shit!"

"What are you? Huh?"

"Hoo shit!"

Amid the chorus of jeers, Teresa nodded. "That's the second rule." Her finger traced Renee's ripped eyelid, delicate as a spider walking its web. "You already know the third."

Renee went down like a cement sack, gasping as Teresa's foot sank into her gut, and when she rolled on her side Billy grabbed her legs and tossed her flat on her back. I was feeling charitable, so I just pulled a few fistfuls of patchy blond hair and left her to Ben and Mags. They tore strips of flesh off her arms, her face.

"Easy now," Florian said, still sitting and watching, but he didn't try to rescue her. Gotta happen. Toughen them up. Linc frowned, took a step forward, but when Florian shook his head Linc didn't push it. Renee, now crawling trying to get away, flung herself recklessly at Sam's feet and nearly got her cheekbones kicked in for the trouble. Someone could've fed her first, at least, but it wasn't gonna be me.

Mags poked her fingers at Renee's eyes, getting within millimeters so Renee kept whipping her head back and forth to escape them; that let Billy get in punches on her left side, Ben on her right. Jab, whap. Jab, smack. Florian and Sam and Linc sat in a cross-legged choral row, just watching. Teresa turned to me, all hostility vanished. "Why don't you go have some fun?" she said, motioning toward them. "The little squirt'll thank you in the long run, for giving her a spine."

Run along and play, kiddie. No thanks. I shrugged, watching Renee get beaten, watching the watchers, remembering the meaty smack of fists and crack of bone when Joe and I first met. This little bitch wasn't even trying to defend herself, what the hell did Fearless Leader want with something so useless? Maybe just some fun. I closed my eyes, taking in the odors of dry musty tree bark and old possum tracks and peeling rain-softened paint, and that's when I caught it.

The smell, that strange chemical smell that I'd sniffed in the air earlier and thought was Renee. I could smell Renee too, the stench of formaldehyde and dyes and fixatives and cosmetics smeared over and shot through dead skin, but this was something different: just as sterile and alien but without a pedigree of its own, an orphan smell I couldn't place but knew was from nowhere in nature. It was coming from Teresa, emanating from her skin as she lolled under the rotting gazebo roof, and over the dull patina of her decay was a layer of soft, shiny dampness, marinating her in a pungent little sweat bath. Not rain, it'd been dry for days. Sap, it looked like, beads of it oozing up from freshly cut wood. I listened, not knowing what I thought I'd hear from her, but got only the same everyday brain music and wordless hum of thought I heard from everyone else. She was perfectly normal, except she wasn't. The more I stared the more she stank, of vinegar and varnish. Nothing dying, and nothing ever alive.

Teresa caught me looking. She just smiled.

Dizzy and punch-drunk, Billy reared back and let fly, intestines playing a symphony of farts, gurgles and sickening wet explosions like air ripping out of a balloon. Clouds of pure stink welled up from his gas-bloated guts, making us groan with laughter and shout, "How'd you like it, little Renee, how'd you like that," but our new baby sister had long since passed out.

4

The small, stifled sobs grew louder and harsher until they crested into a single sorrowing wail. The thud of a fist followed, and Joe's voice snarling, "Goddammit, bitch, go to sleep!"

So much for his sulk in the woods doing him any good. I winced as Florian and I crossed the footbridge and headed across the open park field. I wasn't feeling so good today, off-kilter and fuzzy-headed like a hoo catching a cold—Billy threw all my sleep right off, tooting Teresa's triumphant homecoming—but still more than glad to be on watch and getting out of earshot. They should've fed Renee first: It was the hunger pangs killing her, not any memories of Mommy and Daddy, but everyone had decided they were too tired to throw her a bone. I'd bring her back something, a rabbit or two. Florian was off in his own world as usual, humming some century-old song to himself as we went past the sugaring shack, crossed the second footbridge and another, handkerchief-sized parking lot and reached the welcome shadiness of the overgrown nature trails.

It was hot this morning, too hot for barely spring. We headed east toward the riverbank, passing the weed-smeared signpost for the Sullen Trail (a settler's name, John or Jim

Sullen of years past, or someone's stupid idea of funny?), and began our ambling walkabout of watching, listening, sniffing for hoos. There was no way two slow-moving undeads could cover the whole park in a day, there could be a platoon of Marines camped on the other side of the forest for all we knew, but Teresa insisted.

"She does this just to keep us busy," I muttered.

"That's no news, pet." Florian called everyone pet, even Teresa. "But also for some make-believe excitement—what if there are *hoos* in the woods, with *guns*? Or worse, matches? What if we're all in their sights?" He spat: not from a swampy mouth, he's barely got any coffin liquor left, but from long force of habit. "Hoos, hah. They started packing up and running away from here long before you were born—before Teresa was born, but she still sees 'em everywhere. Behind every tree." He pulled a jay from its hiding place in a bush, snapped it dead in his fingers and crunched it down feathers and all, not faltering a step. "Gives Billy and them something to think about, though, other than dethroning her."

This was true. Billy and Ben never said no to watch duty, always shouting about how if they did find a goddamned hoo then by God they'd make it sorry (unless, like always, they're so lazy or stuffed full of deer they can't be bothered). I didn't mind either; really, it got me away from her. And I liked trees and riverbanks now, in a way I never had when I was alive; I'd wanted to save all the animals, but nature bored the piss out of me. This way was better.

"You still gotta wonder where she goes, when she takes off." I rubbed my shoulder socket against some tree bark, getting in a good scratch. "I don't see what's so special and secret about—"

"You ever miss your folks?"

Florian loved to do this, pretend he was listening and then interrupt with some dispatch from Pluto—like I said, he was old—but the question made me tense up. "Why're you asking now?"

"'Cause I wondered, that's why. Do you miss your folks?"

I thought about the first few weeks after joining the Flies, how I would lie awake mornings waiting to hear their brain-sounds getting closer—those nervous strings, furious drums. Waiting for them to find the gang and get joined up too. But they never did. No other gang I knew of either. They just disappeared. It happens. Would definitely have happened to that Renee, if Teresa hadn't dragged her back. But it didn't matter; we always pretended we'd never had any other family. "No point," I said. "Gone's gone."

Florian watched me, one sunken eye moving independently of the other. "Gone may be gone, but that don't make gone fun. Just asking."

"And I just answered, so can you find a new useless question?"

He shrugged and pushed his walking stick—the branch Joe had torn away in his fall—against the softening ground as we headed forward. The birds twittered and screeched overhead in two-note complaints, rising to a roar of mass discontent as the river snaked through a clearing and past a wall of oaks; this was a migration stop-off, and twice every year that sea of bird sound up high signaled autumn turning to winter, then winter to spring. We paused to listen.

Fighting, they were always fighting. Fighting to the death, the last I ever saw them. That's all I really keep with me about my parents. They must've loved me, I suppose. I don't know. When I needed help with a science project, or a ride somewhere, or someone to yell back on my behalf, I went to my brother, Jim. Lisa, my sister, for everything else. I don't blame them for clearing out like they did—I was counting the hours myself—and I could call them whenever I wanted. And Lisa, whose college was closer, would come visit sometimes just to get me out of the house, but it just got worse and worse after they were gone.

"I still miss my children," Florian murmured, as the birds squawked and cried. "Sometimes. Two daughters and a son. Grandkiddies. Don't know what became of them. If they ever tunneled up too."

And even if they did they might just turn their backs on you for half a rabbit, old man, so what the hell do you want from me? They were always like that, since I could remember, my mom and dad. "Ma" and "pa," I guess Florian would say. I wonder why people say "mom" and "dad" now, instead. Language evolves, my English teacher said. He'd intone it all solemn like a Bible verse, lann-guaaage evolllves, but never explain how or why it did. Always shouting. Always fighting. Absolutely anything could set them off. When I got scared I'd go sleep in Lisa's room with her.

"I hate it here," she would whisper, not to me but herself, when the crash of something thrown downstairs made us both jump. She'd have her arms wrapped around me and I'd feel the sudden tensing twitch in the muscles, almost more startling than the noise that caused it. "I hate it here so fucking much."

I'd hear Jim sometimes too, shouting at them to shut up, control themselves. *You wanna know why you can't pay Jessie to talk to you and Lisa's scared of her own shadow why don't you both look in a mirror, get a goddamned divorce if you're that miserable, we'll all throw a fucking party.* He's right, we would have. The little martyrs, he'd call Lisa and me sometimes, he hated that we'd both hide in her room. What'd he expect us to do, take a hurled paperweight in the face for the team?

But he didn't take their shit and I liked that. One really terrible Thanksgiving he just said, "Screw this," right there at the table, and loaded me and Lisa and Grammy Sullivan into his car and we all went to the turkey buffet three toll stops down the road. They're entitled to ruin their own holiday, he said, but not ours. I liked that. We each had our own holiday, it wasn't theirs to keep inflicting on us their way. Grammy Sullivan, who'd looked ready to walk all the way back to the nursing home, cheered up and handed out chocolates. I'd already given up meat and all the vegetables looked butter-soaked so there wasn't much else for me to eat except plain bread and cranberry sauce, but it was still the best Thanksgiving in forever.

No, Florian, I do not miss my folks. It's just that sometimes I'm still listening for them, even now, and I don't know why. That's force of habit for you.

"Why's it so hot today?" I said, stomping my feet on the soil like I could force the coolness up through my legs. "It can't be later than March. I'll rot like a Florida feeder."

"It ain't hot at all." Florian sounded puzzled. "That wind coming in is—"

"—way too warm. It can't be later than March, there's barely any violets yet—"

"Ain't trying to be difficult, you know," Florian said, face still tilted upward. "I never thought much about old times when I was your age either, but it's different lately. Can't think about much else." He turned to me. "Thinking about the human days, of all the useless things. I knew my last times were on me anyway, and this about settles it—"

"You're not going to die," I said. It happened to be a fact: The sun would never come up in the west, Florian would never die. He was already a dried-up shrunk-down remnant when I first met him, had died in his sleep as an older-than-hell hoo back when this was the Northwest Territories, all Indian tribes and a few trading outposts. He remembered the Revolutionary War. (He was a Tory.) And the Civil War. (He was dead, no need to take hoo-sides anymore.) He remembered when Lepingville, where I grew up, was just a giant farm field (which it might as well be now anyway, if you ask me). He'd survived the Pittsburgh Uprising of '68, all the young undeads turning on the dusties when they got sick of killing and eating hoos; he'd survived fights, forest fires, starvation, hunting teams, the hoos deciding again and again that we didn't really exist and crowding into our living space like nasty little gerbils grabbing a new cage. You didn't see all that, live through all that and then just . . . vanish, like all those reserves and survival skills meant nothing in the end. I wouldn't accept it.

Florian smiled. His skin in the strengthening sunlight was jaundiced and tissue thin, sagging at every joint like a collapsing awning. "Don't be silly, pet."

I got sillier. I threw my arm around him, letting him laugh and pat my shoulder. We didn't hold with mushiness, but I didn't care. Things were easy between him and me like they weren't with anyone else but Joe. "You're not going to die."

"Course I will, I'm—" He frowned. "Well, hell, I got no idea how old I am now, but damned old, I know that. It's long past time. Sick of being sent on watch rounds, just so she can get rid of me. Sick of everything." He sighed, studying himself, the crumbling silhouette of his bones. "You'd never believe it now, pet, but this arm"—he made a joking flex of the biceps he didn't have—"this arm could bend an iron streetlamp post barely trying. These legs could kick through concrete, just like yours. That's why they wanted me. Now they're just waiting to be rid of me. So I'll go." His voice was light and pitiless, almost reveling in the pronouncement of death, but his face grew wistful. "All I wish is I could see my beach again."

"It wouldn't be the same." Florian had lived for a while, a long while, in the woods around the Indiana Dunes, way back when they were just unprotected piles of sand and not a park. "I know nobody's *supposed* to live out near there, but you hear stories sometimes about—"

"There was always hoos out there making one kinda trouble or another, that ain't nothing new. I remember when some damned fool company just took one of the biggest sand dunes away, two hundred feet high and they hauled it all off in boxcars to melt it down, make glass jars out of it—I said I miss my beach, not their beach. Hasn't been my beach in forever."

He stopped to rest near the shell of a dead tree, a blackened stub that made me imagine a long-ago lightning bolt. "That sand could hurt a rotten foot, all gritty, but there was still something about it, you lay down in it to sleep and woke up every night feeling good. All those woods, barely a soul in 'em, and that big long slope down to the shore and the shore was nothing but waves that kept rolling in, real soft. Like a lot of drowning people's hands laid all in a row, touching the sand and then getting pulled under all at once. All kinda flowers to look at, stuff you never seen anywhere else, and too many birds to count."

He watched the Great River meander past us, all slow-moving liquid mud. "The Indians left us alone. Well, they'd get mad when we raided their muskrat traps, but a body's gotta eat. Then they made 'em all leave. Built railroads and steel mills right there on the sand. Beach houses. Couldn't make us leave, though. They only thought they got rid of the Indians, the ones that tunneled up all came back too. Dozens of us, and we never had much of any fighting, 'cept when we got bored. Time just kinda stopped there. Every day the same as the next—"

"Yeah, not at all like being out here."

"Every day just like the next." Florian was long gone now, that look on his face old people get when they're all excited about something that happened before you were born. At least he didn't expect me to act excited too, like Grammy Sullivan would. "All flowing together, just one big day and one big night. All peaceful. And I don't know what it was, but you broke down so slow there, your body did. Took a good thirty, forty years before I found even the first bug on me. Hoos would see us and think we were still them, before they saw how we walked. Seemed like we all barely rotted at all."

He sighed. "If you ever get there, pet. I won't say heaven, but it was more beautiful than anything else."

I'd never seen the Dunes except in photographs, growing up. Too dangerous, though sometimes kids would go to the unincorporated areas on a dare. A few from the class a year ahead of mine did that and never came back. I knew I was meant to feel sorry for them, but it was kind of hard when all it meant for the rest of us was more goddamned safety drills and this was after we'd already suffered through it all in Safety Ed: endless variations on Don't Go Out There, You Idiots. Nothing stopping me now, of course, though no swimming unless I wanted to be reduced to a skeleton within minutes. Decaying flesh plus a steady water bath, it's like parboiling.

There were rumors of government facilities out on the beaches, research labs, in the Prairie Beach part of Gary and Burns Harbor and the other lake coast towns. Some out in the prairie preserves too. Thanatology labs, studying us in the belly of the beast. I knew a girl whose dad supposedly was a guard out there, though you weren't meant to know about it. Or that they were out there at all. He made way too much money, everyone said, for any ordinary security guard. There were rumors that my kind never killed the kids that disappeared, that they stumbled into a restricted lab area, got shot, left out for us or the birds and coyotes. Who knew. I've never heard much tell of it, but then it's not like I go out looking.

"So why'd you ever leave?" I asked. "If it was all so great."

Florian just shrugged. He reached into the little leather pouch he kept looped around his waist, as creased and worn down as Joe's jacket, and shook out a couple of old stones: Lake Michigan beach stones, flat and smooth and soft greenish-gray, pale pearl. He had more of them he'd dragged with him everywhere he went, hidden somewhere in the woods. Another old person's eccentricity.

"Can't stay in any one place forever," he said, running the bones that had once been fleshy fingers over the stones' surfaces. "No matter how much you like it. Gotta keep moving. I been everywhere. Everywhere I could walk." His fingers curled around the pearly gray stone. "And no matter where I been, no matter how bad things was there, if I had these with me I always felt like I was safe, that I'd come out of it alive and fighting. Even in Pittsburgh, back in the uprising. I got bit hard by a young feeder, I shoulda lost my arm. Didn't. So much damn luck. And these, right here, they're my lucky tokens. Ain't never been without them."

He put the stones back in their pouch with a happy little look in his eyes, like he'd just had a private conversation with them I didn't know anything about. I guess when you're verging on your three-hundredth birthday or so you've earned the right to be loopy. I nudged a clump of snowdrops with my foot, fresh salady green against twenty shades of dirty brown. The tree leaves were just coming in, lighter greens tinged with yellow.

"This is pretty beautiful too," I said. "Just like your beach."

No answer. I poked around an old duck's nest, found nothing and was set to head another mile down the river when the smell hit me. Florian caught it too, raising a hand for silence though there was no sound but birdsong. Human flesh, definitely, but also a note of something chemical that I couldn't place: like deodorant gone stale, cheap lotion turned metallic with sweat, but stronger and stranger than that. We kept staring and sniffing and finally saw a shadow zigzagging through the spindly trees, too fleet-footed to be an undead. Every now and then you see a few vagrant guys out on the forest edge, though if Ben or Billy or Joe's feeling hungry you never see them for very long. This one, though, was female, lolloping fast toward us, all hunched-over nervous speed like a little ape; she paused, raising her blond head to sniff, came stumbling barefoot along the riverbank and, just yards away from us, smacked straight into a linden tree and clung to it stunned. Her breath rattled, lungs fighting each other for the last gulp of air, and drool snaked from her open mouth.

It was the hoocow from last night, the one who'd come on a drunken tear through the parking lot. Her skin had gone from blue-tinged to outright blue, one huge fast-spreading bruise: *Cyanotic,* I thought, a word I remembered from health classes. There was a weird sheen on it too, like sweat if sweat was beads of tree sap, and she stared at us without fear or any other human look in her eyes. Nothing human about her smell, the chemical stink pouring from her skin, and nothing undead either, nothing I could call hoo or not-hoo and I shivered, smelling it.

"Hey!" Florian shouted, waving his skeleton arms, baring his yellowed teeth to try to scare her off. "We know you. This ain't no camping ground, you better get out of here. There's lots more of us and the rest won't help you. You understand?" She just stood there. "You understand me? Those old park bums ain't your friends either. Get out!"

Of course everything we said was so much *hrruhhh uggggh muhhhhh* to anyone but us, but if she hadn't got the gist she really was too stoned to live. I snarled at her, spitting a mouthful of black blood, and when it spattered her bare feet she gazed up at me in something like wonder. Her eyes were glassy and smudged and shadowy like she had cataracts, marbles smeared with greasy fingerprints, and as I stared back something about the angles of her face, the tilt of her chin flowed into a falsely familiar shape, some strange foreign substance poured into a well-worn mold; then the shape melted away and left only her, nobody and nothing, standing there gripping the bark for dear life. Why are you looking at me like that? I don't know you. I'm not your friend.

"No . . . camping ground," she repeated, in a croak, holding the words in her lips like little bits of sugar. Not the way humans said them, but the way we did. "The old bums . . ."

Imitating, I thought, as the chords pounded fast and feverish through my brain, she didn't understand us, hoos couldn't understand anything we said. Like a babbling baby. The old bums. Maybe she'd just learned the hard way they weren't her friends.

"What about 'em?" I gave her a shove, making myself go gentle because a hard push would snap her shoulder. If she really were the hoo she looked like. "What do I care for some old bums, some dead-meat eaters? You like 'em so much, go—"

She moaned, a high, scared horse's whinnying, and her little sob sounded so much like Renee's hunger pangs that I grabbed for Florian's hand. Her chin lolled back and she swayed, seizing the linden bark harder, and reached one shaking arm up to where a squirrel was splayed frozen and praying to be invisible. He went crazy, thrashing and biting in her grip, and she bit down. Her head jerked left, right, trying to pull off a piece, and he let out a horrible shrill scream of terrified pain and held it and held it until her teeth found his neck and wrenched it apart.

Mesmerized, we watched her. Her teeth seemed long for

a hoo's but they were white and squarish like any human's, and just as bad at tearing through hide and thick bones. She gnawed at the little bit of meat she could get, licked fresh blood from her hands, and then I heard a gurgling sound and she was looking up at me trembling in fright, dark bubbles of spume oozing from her ash-colored lips. She stared down at the torn-apart thing in her hands, warm and dripping blood and viscera and tufts of gray fur, and let out another moan, not of starvation but shame and horror; meat and bile rocketed back up, splattering the linden tree and the soil below, and she sank to her knees and doubled over, shaking and shriveling into a wracked little ball. Florian, forever too softhearted, must have decided she was one of us after all because he reached down and touched her hair.

"Squirrel ain't no good," he said, conciliatory. "Always hated it. If you come with us, we'll find a duck or two, some deer—"

She howled, fists drumming on the linden bark until her knuckles split and bled. Her body arched, jerked backward, and she made horrible gasping sounds pulling in air she could no longer breathe; her fingers loosened and she almost fluttered back to the ground, curling gentle and womblike around herself as her breath softened, slowed and stopped. There was a shudder that seemed to come from somewhere else, an invisible boot kicking her in the chest, and she lay still.

I touched her skin. It was sap-sticky, covered in congealed ooze, and cold.

Florian bared his teeth, snapping them shut on invisible flesh. "Blessed hell," he muttered, and turned her over and shook her and shouted at her trying to figure out if she were alive, dead, unconscious, what the hell had happened. I rubbed my fingers against the linden bark, scrubbing away that awful sweat; I didn't want her stench on me. She didn't move.

"No heartbeat," Florian said, pulling himself upright. "But she was trying to take in air. You think she's one of us? You think there's some . . . sickness out there, and she got it? That smell."

There isn't a disease that gets us other than rot, even with those hoo-scientists out on the beach, supposedly, trying their best, allegedly, to create one. "One of us? She was trying to breathe, you just said so. And you saw her yesterday, nobody dies, wakes up and goes under again in less than a day—"

"No hoo's out eating squirrels with their bare hands and teeth. This isn't nothing human."

"It's nothing *us* either!"

Florian stared down at her, confusion turning to anger, and let off a muttered epithet of good riddance as he kicked her. I held back. Whatever she was, whatever had killed her I didn't want to touch her or know her, I just wanted her gone.

The way she looked at me, just for that split second, staring like she knew me. Like I should know her. Nobody and nothing. That's all hoos are to me. Not even meat.

"So are we tellin' Teresa?" Florian asked.

For an answer I reached down and hoisted up the body, an awkward job working one-handed. Florian helped me get her slung over my shoulder, and we walked until the woods got thick and the ground hilly and we'd reached the concrete tunnel beneath the old highway underpass; we left her there, skull intact, a good warning for any of those old bums sheltering from rain. If Billy or Ben or whoever came this way, let them figure it out.

By the time we retraced our steps Florian was pinched with exhaustion; he curled up and dozed all day in the grass while I hunted. I still wasn't feeling so great either, hot and all tired, but I needed a good meal to distract myself from the nastiness I'd just seen and smelled. I didn't spot any rabbits but I surprised some raccoons, a badger, a couple of ducks, there were still leavings fresh to eat when we got back, and Renee wept so much when I gave her some it was disgusting, she cried and ate and ate and cried and moaned about how wonderful I was, I was her best friend now, and when I punched her she still followed me around, mooning, like a groupie at a hotel room door. Joe couldn't stop laughing. Neither could Teresa, who accepted the rest of the meat with the graciousness of a tsarina who'd finally got her serfs back in line. Florian, like he'd been doing so much lately, turned away and slept some more without offering a word.

No, we weren't telling Teresa. Because she had that same smell on her skin too, that dead hoocow's awful sterile rot, and until I had some answers to throw in her face I was pretending everything was fine.

5

Renee's grave was already pristine, the birthing hole filled in and covered with grass too even and green to be real. There's no gate guards, the alarm systems are defunct, the barbed wire's busted full of holes, weeds everywhere, but by God they still get those gravesites looking swank and undisturbed as soon as they humanly can. Maybe it's all people really care about, the handful that still come to visit. I hope the pay's good, if you've got that job. I bet it is. Nearly as good as a thano lab guard's. We crouched in a patch of woods above Calumet Memorial, waiting.

I gave Renee a shove. "Why are you so sure they're coming? And why today?" Why the hell I'd agreed to sit with her, of course, was another question.

"I just have a feeling," she said, a stubborn twist to her mouth.

"Nobody's coming. You're just lucky you got buried instead of burned, and they never like it when people come out to visit, they don't want the publicity if someone gets—"

"I just have a feeling." Her voice was a high, breathy singsong, air whistling through the space where I'd knocked out her teeth. "I just know."

You just know. That's about the only thing you know,

other than how to cry for food someone else hunted for you. Infant. "So what are they, stupid, drunk or suicidal? Because that's the only kind of humans who come out here now, even in dayli—"

"Oh my God, that's them. That's them. I knew it. There they are."

A blond woman, a tall balding man, a blond girl maybe ten or twelve came down one of the weed-choked walkways, looked cautiously behind and around them and clustered around the gravestone. The man knelt, crossing himself, then got up and clutched his wife's hand, shoulders heaving. The girl wiped her eyes, put a pink spray of flowers in a little vase attached to the tombstone.

"Jennifer," Renee muttered, teeth worrying her lip.

"Sister?"

"Yeah."

The little girl sat down cross-legged, running one hand along the gravestone as she wept. Renee stared at her, hungry, mesmerized. What the hell good did this do, hankering after humans, acting sentimental like a human when that all had nothing to do with our lives, ever again? I turned away, half-hoping I'd find a stag or a mastodon or something lurking in the trees and have an excuse to go hunt it, and when I turned back Renee was watching me instead.

"There must be someone you miss too," she said, like a challenge. She could make more actual words than I could, tongue not nearly so swollen and rotted: *Mussth be sssthum ye missssth.*

Didn't they even notice that grass on her gravesite didn't look right? Of course they didn't. They didn't want to. No hoo ever thinks one of theirs could become one of us.

It doesn't matter who I miss.

I came back here once, about two or three years after I died, after Joe and I fought and I needed to think. And I got no peace because there lo and behold was my sister, there was Lisa, standing over the family plot with daffodils and a rosary. How old was she then, twenty-one, twenty-two?

She was crying, teary shuddering sobs, and seeing it I

felt happy, foolishly blessed. Never before had I had a single flower, no prayer cards or stuffed animals or little flags, no gravesite footprints, not a single disturbed pebble or grass blade to show that anyone remembered my mom and dad and I ever existed. No friends. No Grandma Porter or Grammy Sullivan, though for all I know the shock of this killed them both. No Jim, or at least if he came by he never left any traces. And Lisa, my sister, was always so timid and so scared of everything I just assumed she'd never dare come out here where there's so much *crime*, where the *environment* is so harmful, but she fooled me. Isn't it wonderful when people do that, when you put all your faith in their being selfish and self-centered and not giving a damn and it turns out, all that time, you were all wrong? She'd be shocked to see me, scared at first, but maybe we could talk. Learn to talk, since I couldn't talk the old way anymore.

I thought, That's just how stupid I used to be.

I crept closer, and it was the smell that got her, of course. She frowned, put a hand to her mouth and turned very slowly, shoulders stiffened, like she knew she'd see something she'd never forget but couldn't stop herself from looking. I stood there and stared straight into her eyes. "Lisa," I tried to say. "It's me."

If I could still talk like humans talk, it would have been different. I know it. But I was trying to remember how to sound out her name; I got out something like *"Ruzzz . . ."* and it happened: I saw recognition in her eyes, dawning disbelief and sick shock. She opened her mouth square and tight around a scream, a marionette's jaw jerked to the ends of its strings, and then she let out a belch of revulsion, vomiting on her shirtfront, crying while she ran and running like I was Satan there to pull her into Big Catholic Hell. I hadn't moved. I was still standing there, holding out my good hand.

But that was all a long time ago, and now it makes me laugh—man, Renee, you should have *seen* the look on her face. Fucking hoos.

"I saw my sister here once," I said. "It could have gone better."

Renee stared at her hoo-family, not listening, then let out a teary gasp and lunged forward. I grabbed her arm just in time. "Get back!" I hissed.

She fought me, with hard desperate fists.

"Get back, you're gonna—" I kicked her, pinning her down with my legs, and dragged her ass over head into the brush. As I put a wall of trees between them and us she went limp, sagging against my shoulder like I'd shot her.

"I just wanted to see them," she moaned. "Face-to-face. That's all."

I wanted to hit her for being so foolish, but she was crying too hard. "Show some sense! Do you know what you look like to them now? What you are? What the hell are you—"

"I want them back," she sobbed, stretching out her arms. "I miss them. I just want to see them again. I just want them to see me."

Her parents were hugging, gripping as if they could bore through each other's backs and grab hold from the inside. I clutched Renee harder.

"Trust me," I said. "No, you don't."

"They'll smell you coming," I told her. "From far off. There's nothing you can do about that. But the good thing is that what they're smelling is dead flesh. You're not a *living* threat. Y'see? So you can be right on top of them, sometimes, before they realize they're in trouble."

I'd decided to try to cheer Renee up by teaching her to hunt for herself, no more begging infant favors from me or anyone else. We were deep in the quieter, more isolated woods on the park's west side, far from the old highway we'd crossed to get to the cemetery: I needed to keep an eye on her. She stood there slumped against a tree trunk, arms crossed and half-blond, half-bald head bowed so I could see her scalp pulsating steadily with that big new undead brain underneath; no more pinky-gray matter, her new brain, a bleached-bone white instead. Our brains are larger than a human's, more neurons. I read that somewhere, while I was alive. I bet hoos don't like to contemplate what that might mean.

"Of course, the downside is that sometimes scavengers go after you instead." I sat down right there in the underbrush; I was still feeling a little tired and peculiar around the edges, hadn't caught up on my sleep yet what with all her crying. "I got attacked by hungry yellow jackets once, in the middle of a nap. That was fun. Then one time this goddamned raccoon actually came up to me and crunched right down on my foot, I swear, like it was some sort of tasty scavenged snack and I—"

"I feel like I hurt them so much." She kept her head down, mumbling at her feet. Bare now, useless shoes kicked off, those ridiculous nylon stockings torn away. "I didn't mean to. One minute I was there, and now I'm not." She let out a laugh that sounded like a bad cough. "All of a sudden I'm not . . . a person, anymore. And I don't feel human either. I mean, I feel so different. Already."

It was that dull, resigned sound in her voice that was making me nervous. They get this way sometimes, the 'maldies especially, depressed, eating only when they can't control the urge, trying to make themselves just fade away. Then they get worked up all over again that it's not that easy. Can't handle what's happened to them. There's really not much you can say, honestly, other than get over it. All the rest of us did.

"Yeah," I agreed. "You're different." I plucked at an early cluster of violets, running my fingers up the stems. "You also have to think about what to go after, along with how. Squirrel's not much good, nasty meat and you're hungry again an hour later. Possum's good. Possum sticks with you. Ducks, I really like duck, if you can get one with the eggs still inside it that's a nice—"

"So how long before I turn into a giant pile of rot like all the rest of you? Or a skeleton, so this can all just be over?"

Okay, don't be too fucking rude or anything. My fingers twitched wanting to rip violets up by the roots but I'd done that once before when I was angry, killed a tree by kicking it, and I felt so bad about it afterward my stomach hurt. I pressed my palm flat against the ground instead, to ward off temptation.

"You're a rotter already," I told her. "A few months, a few decades, it depends. You'll get some extra time out of being embalmed, but not much. So don't expect it. You're in the initial decay. You won't look all that different, for a while." I showed her my feet, swollen up and turning bruised black. "Then a bloater, I've just begun that, that's when the bacteria really start breaking your insides down—"

She made a disgusted sound. I hate 'maldies, Joe was right to be pissed Teresa dropped this walking wailing wall on our heads. "—and you go all gassy. Like Billy. But sometimes you just bloat up a little bit before your flesh collapses, that's what happened to Linc. Then you're a feeder. That's when the bugs start hatching, like with Joe. It doesn't hurt." Itches like a bitch, so I'd heard, though. "They feed for a long time. It's like they keep hibernating and waking up on you, or something. When they've got nothing left to eat you'll be in dry decay, like Sam and Florian. A dusty." I pulled myself to my feet. "A skeleton. Then you can be happy."

No answer. I started walking off by myself. I wasn't hungry just now, but her martyrdom had officially turned boring and I wanted to look for more violets. When I heard steps behind me I didn't turn around.

When Joe first showed me how to hunt I loved it, it was all this secret knowledge I hadn't had before and he was the only one of the gang, even Florian, who got excited as I did to see me picking it up. We practiced on ducks, grabbing them from the nests and snapping their necks. Crunching down the egg clutch, shell and all, somehow felt weirder than eating the duck itself, spitting out bits of splintered bone and mouthfuls of feathers; I looked like a walking down comforter, afterward. The first group deer hunt where

I brought down the stag, he looked so proud of me he almost did a little dance. Proud of me and himself, of course, as the one who taught me. We had fun. Glad I wasn't too good for it, like some. Renee was walking in pace with me now. I ignored her.

"So we don't *need* to eat people," she said.

I could feel how twitchy and riled up she was, not just because reality had slammed her in the face but because that's how we are: tenser than hoos, angrier, always standing poised on the precarious, crumbling ledges of our own tempers and any slight, any sideways glance, any fleeting sensation of pique or boredom or melancholy can shove us straight over. I shrugged. "I've never eaten one," I said. "Not worth the trouble. If you wanna, though, you can find them. Just follow the road north. Mags or Ben can tell you how to steer clear of the flamethrowers. It's not so hard. And you get idiot hoos volunteering themselves all the damn—"

"So we don't have to stay out here."

"We don't have to stay anywhere." I headed for the clearing, spotting a little flash of faded purple. "It's just . . . this is where we are. Don't like it, go somewhere else."

That was the first real fight we had, Joe and I, when he wanted to take me hoo-hunting up in Whiting with Billy and Mags and Lillian. *It's the most fun you'll ever have,* he kept telling me, *the best you'll ever eat.* I was sure he was right because he'd always been before that, but every time I thought about heading back to the human areas and lying in wait upwind and grabbing one of them to snap their neck and eat (but not right away—Mags and Lillian both claimed that the hormones they oozed when terrified made the meat taste that much better, a savory pants-shitting marinade), something in my chest and stomach clutched up.

It's like I was afraid, and if you value your eyes never accuse any of us of being afraid of the goddamned sniveling soft-spined little hoos firearmed or otherwise, but it wasn't really fear. It was like my body's version of that sound Renee made, looking at my gassed-up blackened feet, and something else, something bigger, having to do with knowing how scared Lisa got of strange noises in the house, how Jim sometimes liked to be reckless and go walking on his own, late at night. I kept coming up with excuses not to go and finally Joe and I just had it out for hours, he nearly kicked my chest in and I broke his arm, and he kept getting smack in my face weeks afterward with the same failed sales pitch, over and over, exploding into a *rrrrwah!* of frustrated screaming like a fist to the teeth. Over and over. I couldn't fight him when he did it because I knew he was right, he'd been right about absolutely everything before, but I also couldn't say yes; that nameless thing stomping its gaseous feet all up and down the length of my gut wouldn't let me. Eventually, he just stopped asking.

"Are you following me for a reason?" I snapped at Renee as I pushed into the clearing. The purple was some sort of weed, not violets, but it was still pretty. "It better not be for meat, since you're too fucking dainty for it I'm not gonna go out of my way to—"

"I'm sorry I said you looked rotten," Renee mumbled, all fast and under her breath like an embarrassed kiddie.

Panicked along with embarrassed, she must have realized she'd insulted her one and only chance at a steady meal. I just laughed. "Well, I do, don't I? And guess what? I've never had a problem with it." I gave her a shove, enjoying watching her stumble backward. "And if you think 'rotten' is that much of an insult, you really are a miserable little piece of hoo shit."

She scratched at her skull, nails scraping like fretful, hungry insects at the surgical sutures. "Maybe," she said quietly.

She looked like I'd felt when Lisa ran away from me, when Joe screamed about what a useless sniveling hoocow princess I was for not going up to Whiting with him. Billy and Mags laughed their asses off, not at me but at Joe: *Gotta watch yourself now, Mister Joseph.* Mags grinned, hurling Joe effortlessly to the ground when he tried jumping her. She used to be such a bitch fighter, in her day. *Somebody don't have stars in her eyes anymore.*

"You're gonna have to learn to hunt sometime," I said,

nearly barreling right into a hidden clump of daffodils. "It's that or starve."

"I know. And I want to, all right? Please? Just, not today."

"It'd better be soon," I said, "if it's not today, because I'm not your mommy and I'm already running myself ragged trying to feed our bitch-queen, I don't have to keep fetching you—"

"I know. I know." She scratched harder. "I just worried I would want to hunt *them*. When I saw them." She gulped and looked back down at the ground. "Eat them."

I gave her a steady stare, that look you give someone to let them know they really can tell you, that you're not gonna fly to pieces or leave them standing there in the dust holding out their hand, but also that if they try to lie you'll know it and you won't have a moment's pity.

"Did you?" I asked.

I waited. She didn't answer. Something went burrowing swiftly through the nearby underbrush, kicking up little leaf and soil clumps in its path, and was gone.

"Possum's good," I said. "It sticks with you. For half a night, sometimes."

She nodded. We poked silently around the clearing for a while, fingering purple and white and pink and yellow blooms like shoplifters going through the aisles. I heard footsteps and the soft, soothing sound of insects chewing and there was Joe, looking from me to Renee and back like he couldn't believe what I was farting around wasting my time with, who could blame him. I hadn't seen him in a few nights; he was avoiding Teresa, who still smirked at the sight of him, or off on another hoo-hunt. I guess. We hadn't been out hunting by ourselves, he and I, in a long time. Not ducks or anything else.

"I need to talk to you," he said. He jerked his chin toward Renee. "Piss off home, 'maldie."

She stood there, glaring at him, working nails at her scalp like she was looking to strike a vein of copper. Another thing she desperately needed to learn, how to fight, though here she was cruising for the kind of extended lesson that'd really make her cry. Joe, though, just shook his head and grabbed my arm. "I cannot fucking believe what Teresa drags back from the hoo junkpile these days. Let's go."

Gladly. We headed south, in the direction of the old gazebo—or I should say Joe headed us that way, he kept trudging a step or two ahead and wouldn't let go of me as we walked. He got that way sometimes.

"You look funny," he said, still clutching. "Shadow-eyed. Worn out."

"A body can't get any sleep anymore," I pointed out, "between Teresa and the deadweight and you beating on the deadweight in the middle of the daytime. Where've you been the last few nights, anyway?"

He looked funny too, Joe did. Even though he gripped my arm tight and hurtful in the old way it was like that was the only flicker of life in him: His shoulders sagged and his feet shuffled along at an old dusty's pace and his free hand ran slow and meditative up and down his side, half-crushed bugs peeking up indignantly from between the fingers. His brain-chords were monotonous and subdued.

"Out and around," he said. "It's not like you ever wanna go with me, so what do you care?"

"It's not like you ever bother telling me where or what you—"

"Why don't you try asking me about shit that actually matters?" he said, gripping a bit harder like he'd enjoyed hearing the hurt in my voice. "Why don't you ask me why Teresa's gone. Again."

I shrugged. "Out and around. Right?"

I hadn't told Joe any of what had happened: the woman in the woods, the strange stink of Teresa's flesh. He hadn't been around to tell. But the thing was, I'd been waiting for someone else in the gang, anyone—other than Renee, who didn't know shit anyway—to notice that Teresa looked strange, that she smelled strange, that even after I brought her the goddamned meat she'd been moaning for she ate about two bites and then threw the rest away. There were a half dozen of us there to witness that and it wasn't like we didn't spend a whole lot of waking hours scrabbling to find each other's weak spots—if Teresa suddenly had a dusty's bad appetite what other vulnerabilities was she hiding? You'd think Ben, or Billy, both convinced they were the gang's anointed One True Leader, would at least sit up and say something. Not a word.

"She's acting strange," I said. "And she looks strange. And she smells really strange—"

"You think?"

"What do you mean, I think? I know. Anyone with the remnants of a nose can—"

"You eating lately?" Joe asked me.

That was such an insane question it stopped me right in my tracks. Joe tried to keep on going and I yanked my arm free. "I'm eating," I said, anger starting to snake its way through me. "Unlike some folks, I'm eating just fine, in case you didn't fucking notice me all over the carcass on the last deer hunt, what the hell are you asking me that for? It's Teresa who's not eating, I keep trying to tell you, she's acting nuts and playing these senile little power games and her skin smells like she took a bath in—"

"Senile," Joe repeated, and chuckled. "Well, see, Jessie, that's about what I think too. And not just me. Trust me on that. It's just I thought I wouldn't have to tell you what that means, but I guess I do." He took a step toward me. "I think it's past time you challenge her."

That was the last thing I'd thought to hear. I'd never forgotten what Teresa did to Lillian, how she made Joe and me finish her off, but then it'd been Lillian who jumped her first and if you finished off the gang leader all by yourself like that, no help, you'd more than earned the right to boss all the rest of us. Annie, everyone who knew Annie better said she might've challenged Teresa in turn, but Annie died; Joe, Billy, Ben, they all talked a good game but come right down to it, they just didn't want the big fun of herding feral rot-kittens and always sleeping with an eye open. Damned if I did either. "So fine," I said, "she's losing it. Let Mags challenge her, she's a better—"

"Mags's gone soft," Joe said, yanking at a big, healthy tree branch heavy with clustered blooms. "Her and Ben. Too much sitting around the woods doing nothing. Billy's a shit fighter, you've seen I can't fight the bitch, Sam and Florian are too old, Linc's scared of his own fucking shadow, who the hell else is gonna do it? You'd have backup, Jessie, trust me, we're all sick and tired of—"

"I wish you wouldn't do that," I said, as he worried the branch until the living wood started shredding, bending like tendons under teeth. "It's not fighting you."

"And I wish you'd goddamned listen for once when I talk, how about that?" He let go of the branch, too late; it dangled limply like my dead arm had once done, strips of detached bark curling in thick wood shavings from the tree trunk. Yellow petals showered the ground. "It's why she's down your neck all the time lately, why she's grabbing up stupid 'maldies who can't find their own asses—she's at the tail end and she's scared and you're her only big competition. And we'd back you up."

"I don't want to lead a gang," I said, plucking blossoms off the twisted tree branch. Not like they'd live much longer anyway. "And bullshit you'd back me up—yeah, you would, but Ben hates everyone who isn't Sam, Mags and Billy would sell their grandmothers for a deer's heart—"

"You could fight her," Joe said stubbornly, grabbing my hand away from the flowers. "Even without the arm. You could do it."

"And this is all for my benefit, right?" I demanded. I yanked my hand back, snatching up another handful of soft yellow flowers; pollen smeared my fingers, the loose, ashen nails going a faint pale orange. "Nothing to do with you. Other than that I stick my neck on the chopping block so you can be the big power behind the throne, you think, and convince yourself you actually stomped her and whisper orders into my ear, if I survive, which without any backup at all isn't exactly—"

"You never listen to me, do you? You never, ever listen to a word I—"

"Jessie?" someone called out.

We both turned. Linc was standing there, blinking blearily, pollen dusting the dark snarl of his hair and yellow petals sticking to his feet; he looked as out of sorts as I felt, up at this ungodly hour of the afternoon. Doesn't anybody goddamned sleep anymore? "I was looking for you," he said, "I'm on watch right now and Florian's not—"

"Fuck off," Joe snarled, before I could.

He and Joe stood there, bullied boy and bully-boy glaring dagger-teeth at each other and I hoped to God there wouldn't be a fight. Linc might be quiet but he was not in fact scared of much of anything and I wasn't in the mood to try to pull them off each other. "Florian's not what?"

"He's meant to be on watch with me, but he had to go back. He's not feeling good." Linc shook his head. "He shouldn't be doing that anymore anyway, so if you could—"

"What do you mean, not feeling good?" I dropped my handful of flowers, scrubbing my pollen-caked hand against my leg. "What's wrong with him?"

"What d'you *think* is wrong with him?" Joe interrupted. He'd always thought I made too much fuss over Florian, said it was stupid hoo-kiddie sentiment to go beating the bounds for some random used-up dusty to call Grandpa. "He's too goddamned old to be tramping around like—"

"He's just tired," Linc told me, like nobody else was standing there. "So if you could come finish the watch with me, I wanted to talk to you anyway about—"

"We're busy," said Joe, voice dropping into that low, quiet register that meant you straightened up and flew right out of his sight before you got your wings torn off. "You want company so bad, take the 'maldie. And set her on fire, if you wanna do us all a real favor."

"Are *we* busy, *Jessie*?" Linc demanded. His mental piano chords were going discordant and abrupt and his nails were curled inward digging back and forth into his palm, his peculiar little gesture whenever he was angry. "Or do you have anything to say about it yourself?"

God almighty. Gimme this, gimme that, feed me, love

me, go to my gravesite, come on watch, go fly a kamikaze plane up Teresa's ass—can I please just crawl into a ditch somewhere and go to sleep? "I can barely put one foot in front of the other," I told Linc, baring my teeth, "speaking of tired. I've been babysitting the 'maldie for days on end and she's worn me out and now you two are seriously pissing me off so please just take Renee, okay? She's wandering around here somewhere, probably sniveling about Mommy and Daddy again. I'll kill you an entire deer herd if you get her off my hands because I really don't have time for any of this shit." I pushed him hard enough that he nearly tripped over a rock. "Especially not yours."

Joe let off a loud, sputtering little chord of triumph. Linc sawed at his palm again, like Renee clawing her own scalp, then his fingers subsided and he just shrugged.

"Sorry," he said, and gave Joe a jaundiced glance. "Should've known you're not allowed."

He turned and staggered off without looking back. As soon as he was into the trees again I felt like an asshole: We were friends (or I guess we were—we never talked much but when Joe and I got in our worst fights Linc always jumped in on my side, even when it got him kicked stupid), he wanted to tell me about Florian, he was one of our best hunters, and I sent him packing like he was the new foundling. Joe just laughed and spat a mouthful of coffin liquor on the ground, splattering the crushed flower petals with a sticky, tarry stream full of drowned insect carcasses; then his guitar chords started slowing down again and he stood there with his hands shoved in his jacket pockets, dejected, tired.

"Should we kill Renee?" I asked, both to distract him and because I was seriously starting to wonder. I liked her, sort of—don't ask me why, clearly I was losing it in my sort-of older age—but she was a useless burden and with all her moaning about being resurrected it wouldn't be like sending up Lillian. We'd be doing her a favor.

Joe grabbed the half-torn tree branch again, twisting, wrenching. I didn't say anything, it was too late to salvage it anyway. "You never know," he said. "She could end up okay. Annie was a 'maldie, she straightened herself out. She could fight." He looked melancholy for a moment. "Goddamn, but she could fight."

She could fight. Joe liked anyone who could fight, anyone who liked fighting. I liked Annie too. Everyone liked Annie. She could've torn Teresa to pieces *no*-handed, everyone said, she'd have been our leader after Lillian if she hadn't had to go and surprise a hoo bum at his little campfire during a hunt; she surprised him and he panicked and pushed her into the flames. She melted off the bone, bubbling all over like roasting duck fat, and Mags threw river water but that only stopped the fire itself, not Annie's flesh and then her bones sloughing away in increments while she could still feel it. The bum ran off, we never found him. Annie's screams stayed in my head for months.

"This one's no Annie," I said. "She's barely even a Billy."

"We'll see." Joe snapped the last twisty greenstick strands connecting the branch, throwing it down into the mud and liquid muck. "I guess we'll see."

He stared down at the fouled tree branch, smelling vaguely of annoyance and guilt like he'd just now realized he'd ruined something pretty, that he'd hurt something that never did anything to him but be in front of his eyes at the wrong time. He looked that way at me sometimes, after our most awful fights. We didn't fight, though, the time I got it in my head he liked Annie better than me and got angry about it, knuckle-splitting angry. He loved seeing me jealous. He spent so much time jealous of whoever I was with when I was out of his sight, I suppose he thought of it as something of a righteous payback. Even angry as I was, though, when I thought that, I couldn't hate or fight Annie, I still just liked her too much. I couldn't help it. She was one of those kinds.

Teresa, though. Yeah.

"Let's go hunting," I said. I was still exhausted, Renee and the very thought of running up against Teresa had drained everything I'd had left, but Joe looked weirdly sad and a meal never failed to cheer anyone up. "Just us. We haven't in ages."

Joe pushed his toes at the fallen branch and shook his head. "I'm tired," he said. "Gonna go back and sleep. You should too. You wanna hunt? You said you could barely stand up."

"I'll be all right. Come on, Joe, we never—"

"I'm tired."

He picked up one of the old shoe-worn forest paths and I followed him. The insects traversing his legs and shoulder blades and the back of his neck looked shriveled up, withered; some were dead, you could tell looking closely when they were hibernating and when they'd just given up their tiny ghosts. Fifty or so years out isn't at all an unusual time to start going dusty—Florian was an outlier, being so old before it happened—but the thought of Joe bugless and bone-stripped and so near the second death made something in my chest and stomach seize up and I took his arm from behind, quickened my pace to keep up as he walked. He stopped suddenly and I thought he'd shake me off, mutter about how it wasn't enough the goddamned beetles had their hooks in him and now I had to start up too, but he just looked down at me and my hand holding him like he'd never seen me before, like I was some sort of intriguing stranger.

"I just want you to be all right, Jessie," he said, still gazing at my fingers. "Whatever happens. You just gotta be all right. Okay?"

"Okay." I shrugged, not letting go of him. I knew this already, he'd spent the entire time I'd known him trying to make things all right for me. He didn't need to embarrass himself saying it. "I just don't necessarily think getting in Teresa's face right now is the best—"

"Maybe not," he said. He laughed again, a short little fuck-it laugh. I couldn't decide if it was directed at me, or himself, or Linc or Renee or the moon. "You might know better, Jessie. You might know a lot better."

He took off walking again and I stumbled for a second, trying to stay in step. The sky was clouding over and I could smell a heavy rain coming; not great for dead flesh but not as bad as a lake swim, you needed to be completely submerged before real trouble began. The air was odd, almost tingling. There'd be thunder. I liked a good thunderstorm. The leaves and branches around us shutting out the fading sunlight already seemed damp and dark with the drops that hadn't yet fallen. Joe kept walking, stone quiet.

So where *have* you been the last few nights, Joe? You and Teresa? You never did answer that question.

6

An entire sunrise to sunset of passed-out cold, undisturbed sleep and I felt halfway like myself again, even though Linc was still acting cool and distant and Joe silent and brooding and Florian peaked and weary and nothing, not fresh meat or new violets or the comforting dark of the nighttime, could coax Renee from her funk of misery. I was going to grab Joe for watch duty, tell him what Florian and I saw, and smelled; all else aside it'd distract him, he needed some kind of diversion from whatever'd just jumped into his grave. I was going to do that, but there was a dance that night. Nobody ever announces one; you just wake up, same as always, and feel in the marrow of your bones that it's the time and the night. And you can't skip out on one, you just can't.

It was a cool, fresh-smelling evening. When twilight faded Joe rolled over, half asleep with one arm still around me, and sniffed at the air; there was something quiet, expectant, about the sky and clouds, and seeing and feeling it we all turned as one toward Sam. "Almost," Sam said, an ear cocked to the wind, seamed face breaking into a rare smile of joy. "Almost."

Before he wandered our way Sam lived in Kansas, on the

outskirts of Lawrence, and he still gets sentimental over the dances he and his old gang used to have. There was an abandoned, run-down amusement park on the edge of town where gangs from miles around would meet every time the spirit moved, everyone's mental music running together in a slurry of sound that coalesced into ceaseless waltzes and minuets; all fights and rivalries set aside, they would dance until sunlight and exhaustion made them stop.

Sam never talked about his old gang, or what happened to them—*There was this new girl,* he said once, and that was all—but he remembers it so well and dances with such feeling that it's always him who says when the time is right, when it's time to rise to our feet and become one. We lay there waiting, prickles of electricity all down our shoulders and spines, while Sam stared up at the rising moon and Joe, beside me, put aside the brooding and held his breath.

Everything, everyone had gone unnaturally silent.

"Now," Sam said, still staring at the sky as he rose. "Now."

Of course now. Could it be any other time than now? We shuffled to our feet, hunting hunger forgotten; this was a far more urgent need. Joe nudged me and pointed to Renee. "Go take care of her," he muttered. "She's spoiling it."

Renee lay knees to chin, looking sullenly into the distance. All this fuss over a family who'd faint if they saw her now—I kicked her until she stood up, pulling her into the rapidly forming circle.

"I'm tired," she said, shaking off my hand. "I want to rest."

"Too bad. Just wait."

She was twitchy with need like we all were, I could see it, but she didn't know why. "Wait? For wha—"

She stopped talking when she heard it. Piano, banjo, cello, violin, harpsichord, trumpet, sax, electric guitar, all those clashing and chaotic brain radios melting together into something that flowed lightning-fast from Sam, to Mags, to Teresa, to her, to me, round and round the circle. It gathered strength and energy as it traveled, electricity singing flesh, and together just by standing there we fashioned a tune from our collective head never heard before by anything, living or reborn, one that never, no matter how much we wished it, would ever be heard again.

The music is different for every dance, wild and melodic and gorgeous and elusive; you try to remember it, hum parts of it a week or a month later, and it's all gone save the memory of its beauty. There are other times when we're all in some semblance of mental harmony, during a good hunt or a good feed or when a dream of the peaceful underground passes among us in our sleep, but never like this. We weren't just choosing to play together; something else was playing us.

Renee's eyes widened, feeling it, and she turned to me like a hoo-kiddie ready to ride the big roller coaster. She looked so small and thin and shadowy under the moon. I pushed her in Sam's direction and she lunged forward with arms outstretched, a Frankenstein stagger, and Sam caught her hands and spun her dizzy. Our mutual song, traveling shrill and high as a winter wind on this mild spring night, slowed and thickened into a waltz so simple and plaintive that every note was a separate, irreparable heartbreak. Florian snuffled, melancholy at the sound, and Mags and Joe wept. Renee stood mesmerized, letting herself be spun.

Sam slipped an arm around her waist: step-one-two, step-one-two, Ben reached for Mags, Joe for me; Florian was a serene satellite, humming and shuffling around the spinning planets of Linc, Billy, Teresa. Perfect rhythm, perfect harmony, perfect unison. Renee whirled away, grabbed my hands, swung me right back round to Joe. Somewhere out there a hoo turned restlessly in his sleep, her sleep, dreaming of the calliope playing endlessly in some faraway carnival.

The music grew higher, sharper, the waltz more frenetic; we turned again and again around one another, rotating from night to day to night around each other's perpetually shifting suns. The calliope notes only we could hear drowned out all distraction, stifled caution. I kept my eyes tightly closed and felt my feet lift free as I whirled from hand to hand without plan or thought, the better to take in the whistling winds, the birds' night cries, the chitter of insects in the brush and the crawlers feeding slower than slow on our own dead flesh, the whole turn and tide of dying and rotting and earth-nourishing life and that smell, that lovely flesh-rotten chemical smell like formaldehyde except stronger and sterile like bleach diluting blood—

The smell made me open my eyes, that and a hand firmer and fleshier than any of ours clutching mine. I had wandered away, been carried away to a circle all my own, and the stranger dancing with me had sickly bruise-blue skin, a dazed expression and beads of sticky, slow-moving sweat congealing on his bare forearms like pine sap. Three or four others like him surrounded me, performing a mechanized stumble left, right, left and back again; their music was a shambling lampoon of ours, each tuneless note snot-sticky as the sheen on their skins and tense as guitar strings tightened to snapping point. They'd lurked on the perimeter of our dance, they must have done, awaiting their opportunity, and I jumped right into their arms and nobody even saw me go.

I pulled away, shouting, and they pressed in with shoulders, elbows, stinking skin—intact, fleshy, springy human skin—and formed a tight, insistently moving circle to keep me close. I pushed back, gagging on the smell, and they pressed closer, ashen faces and unseeing eyes dull as grimy glass shards in a gutter. They didn't see me. My gang didn't hear me. I threw my weight forward, trying to break through their Red Rover grasp, and slipped on a patch of mud. I was falling, they were closing in tighter. I flailed unable to right myself with only one arm and they grabbed me, squeezing tight like toddlers clutching a kitten, tighter—

The circle wavered and broke as Joe barreled in, striking at random with fists, feet; they released me, crying with pain. Joe hit harder. They had human blood, bright red, congealing the second it hit air. We yanked them upright and shoved them in the direction of the parking lot; they inched like failing windup toys back over the lot and toward the empty road, voices rising and falling in unmistakable hurt and confusion, like dogs wanting to play. We spat at them, bared our teeth, until they vanished from sight.

Nobody else had heard a thing, or if they had still couldn't tear themselves from the dance; I could hear the real music again, but it was ruined. Joe led me into the trees, out of earshot. "You okay?"

I nodded, shaking. "It's nothing," he said, rubbing my back. "Just some gang rejects from somewhere who heard the music way off, wanted a party—they'll wander back to the city, get an even bigger ass-kicking soon enough." He grinned. "C'mon, Jessie, they were pathetic. You have to admit it's kind of funny."

I waited for laughter to bubble up and banish fear. Joe was waiting too.

"Those things," I said, "whatever they are, they were breathing. I felt it. And they bled red. And the smell, I know you caught it, like—"

"Jess? No offense, but you need to cycle down."

"—like antiseptic and bug spray, not even honest form-aldehyde, and don't tell me to cycle down. That hoocow who drove her car in here? Florian and I found her wandering in the woods, looking just like that bunch, exactly like—and she died right in front of us. I mean, she wasn't really alive, and she wasn't really dead, and then she wasn't anything at all." I growled at a raccoon, who fled back into the brush. "Her body's beneath that old underpass, you can see it your-self."

Joe's expression had turned wary, that look you give someone who's raving about how the Jews shot JFK or Clin-ton was secretly elected pope. "Jessie, remember I was on watch last night with Billy? We went through the underpass, out to where that old cornfield is, and there's no body any-where around there. No smell of one either."

"You can't have missed it. She had blond hair, her skin was all sticky like—"

"Jessie, I didn't see a damned thing—and if you don't believe *me*, does this sound like something Billy would keep to himself? You know what a mouth he has. Ask him." He gave me a shove. "Well? If you're so sure I'm lying, go yank him out of a sound waltz and ask him!"

Could Florian have moved the body, got nervous and decided to hide it better without telling me? That wasn't like him, though, even if he'd still had the strength. I was somehow sure no animal would touch it. Which left only two possibilities: Joe was lying, or someone took the body away. My money was on Teresa, and would Joe cover for someone who'd humiliated him like that? Never. Which made me feel no better, because it meant he was in fact ignoring his own senses and acting like a fool. I couldn't figure this out with the help of dying old dusties and stubborn fools.

I shoved Joe back, a lot harder. We tussled for a while, more feet than fists, and when he got me pinned his mood lifted and his face grew thoughtful. "Of course," he mused, "the real question is how Teresa ended up with that stink all over her too—"

"So you did notice?" I sat up, squirming away from his grip.

"She had her hand wrapped around my throat, how could I not? I thought maybe it was from dragging that 'maldie back, but it didn't seem like an embalming smell. I didn't know what it was." He shrugged. "Hell, maybe the Rat Patrol knows something about it—Billy does walkabout with them a lot, you know, goes hoo-hunting with them, he says she wants to try to join back up."

Joe and Teresa both used to be in the Rat Patrol, before my time, or so they said. The Rat was the largest gang in our neck of the woods, hundreds, sometimes thousands of members, all constantly trawling the unsecured neighborhoods of Gary, Hammond, East Chicago, South Chicago, Whiting, Marquette, Calumet City, Lansing, Harvey for all the hoo-meat they could stuff down their throats and fighting to kill each other just for fun; hardly mattered if they stomped a dozen of their own at a time into the dirt, there were always more hungry recruits. Every now and then a handful wandered out to the countryside, hung out with us and hunted deer for the sheer novelty, but mostly they had far better things to do. I don't know when or why Joe left the Rat. I'd always had this feeling I shouldn't ask.

"What the hell would they want with her?" I demanded. "They can do better on a bad day." They sure as hell never wanted me, not with my hoo-shyness and deadweight arm. Or any dusties. Or know-nothing 'maldies. Or a loudmouthed bitch who won't even hunt for herself anymore. "She can't think she could challenge Rommel as leader, even she's not that crazy—"

Joe shrugged. "You sure about that? All I can say is, good luck to the dumb bitch if she tries." He snorted at the thought. "But that's her lookout, no point in getting worked up about it. Or about some weak little 'maldie shitheads stumbling into our turf—that's probably what we're smelling anyway, all that wood alcohol and crap they shoot into their skin. Hell, maybe we should both go after them, huh? Ask 'em to take that Renee off our hands?"

He smiled at me, the issue settled. I twitched, feeling beetles creeping over my skin, but it was just nerves. Joe was such an ant farm you felt itchy just looking at him.

"You're wrong, Joe," I said. "I don't know what all this is about yet or what those things are or what the hell Teresa's really up to, but you're wrong."

Joe slammed his fist against a rock. It cracked down the middle like spring ice. "Okay, so what's your brilliant theory? Huh? You're so full of superior wisdom, except you crap yourself when a couple of arm-flapping retards come wanting to play—"

I spat at him, sticky black like a tobacco plug gone rotten. "You're talking brain damage? That's just rich. I know what I saw and you know I'm right, you just can't stand that I could figure anything out or even find my own ass without your help—"

"You can?" He struggled to his feet, yanking me upright with him and then letting my hand slide out of his like it was something diseased. "So if you can take such good care of yourself, what am I doing 'saving' you from something a kiddie could kick to dust?"

"What do you want from me? I didn't even see them until—"

"Yeah! Exactly!"

"Well, if you think I'm that worthless, just don't fucking bother!" I aimed a hard kick at his leg. "But if that's how it's gonna be, don't try to hide behind me or push me into challenging Teresa because your time's running shorter and you're scared and you think you can't fight like you used to, or maybe you're just too damned lazy to get off your ass and do it yoursel—"

He pushed me so hard I went flying backward, stumbled over an exposed tree root, fell on my side sliding against rough bark and a cluster of pebbles so the skin from shoulder to hip scraped clean away. I lay there, clench-toothed and dizzy, and when the ground stopped tilting long enough to let me sit up again I saw Joe looming over me, arm held out, the old look in his eyes of genuine remorse mingled with the stubborn certainty that he'd been right all along, that he really was sorry for what he'd done but mostly very sorry I'd ever provoked him into doing it. I hated that look. I hated that I could never even see the sorry part of it anymore, the part that really mattered, all I could see was how it was still always me that was wrong and him that was right. Always. No matter what.

I turned my back on his outstretched hand, getting up again without his help; I stood there clutching a piece of broken rock, my knuckles slowly pulverizing it to powder.

"Just go back to the dance," I said, and walked away.

I went slowly, giving him a chance to follow, say he really was sorry—for all of it—but when he didn't I turned and tracked a bend in the old nature trail, seeking out the little wooden observation deck built over a bit of riverbank. You could look without being easily seen out across the river toward the gristmill and the cottonwoods, as far as the footbridge leading to the gazebo. I could still pick up the strains of music, merry and supremely indifferent, feel my legs moving in unconscious time but I was damned if I'd go scuttling back. Maybe some of my new friends would, dozens of them

I hoped, so Joe could find out firsthand how frightening it was to have something neither living nor dead nor properly in-between pressing in on you, filling your nostrils and mouth with a stink of skin scrubbed like a floor, shocking strength in its sterile unrotted muscles but only dust and hollowness behind its eyes—

Something was crossing the footbridge from the gazebo side, so thin and tottering that even from this distance I recognized it as Florian. Dust and hollowness. He took a few steps and stopped, clutching the railing like a living old man gasping for breath, and as I stood up in alarm he seemed to gather himself, moving with renewed speed into the open field past benches lost in swaths of grass. He picked his way toward the rise of a little hill right near the old sugaring shack. It took him so long. The dance had drained him dry.

As he came closer, pushing himself to move just a few more feet and then a few more, I felt the ache in my own arms and legs, a little clay ball surrounding a hard painful stone. Finally he curled up on the hillside, wedging himself beneath another rusted bench, and almost instantly fell asleep, alone and unmissed. He trembled in his sleep. He got tremors a lot now, he said it was just old age, but from where I sat he looked like a twist of dried-out paper folded into human shape, hiding and shaking with fright at the prospect of sharp scissors, a lit match, a good gust of wind.

I watched him for a long time, ignoring the fading notes of the calliope, and when my chest grew tight from sadness I lay down on the deck, my back to him, and fell asleep.

BOOK TWO

DANSE MACABRE

7

Florian died three days later.

Once he found that little hillside spot, the night of the dance, he never left it; he just lay curled on the grass, sleeping, rocking back and forth, singing softly to himself. "Go along, pets, go ahead. I'm tired," he'd whisper, every time we went to hunt. We brought him back fresh deer meat that he nibbled like candy and never finished. His brain radio was soft and fading, you had to strain to hear it, but it was still there: banjo, a merry strum when he was in his prime but now slow plucks of weak, tired fingers on strings he'd forgotten how to play.

A slow banjo is the loneliest sound in the world.

The sun was just coming up and we were wandering back from a hunt, drunk on blood and heavy with meat. We went past the gristmill and sugaring shack and up to the little hill and as we got closer we saw no movement in the winter-browned grass, felt only silence. My stomach lurched.

Teresa stood there for a moment, then walked away. Considering everything that happened later I should be fair and say it was our way, we left each other alone and in peace when it was time to die again, and Billy and Ben and the rest all followed her but I couldn't do it, Florian I couldn't leave like a dead raccoon on the road shoulder. I pushed my way through the grass and found him huddled knees to chin in a nest of tree roots, his jaw clicking in slow mute taps. He stretched suddenly, rolling flat on his back, and clutched at the grass stems like he might float away.

This wasn't right. He had to wake up, eat, tell one of his convoluted stories about ghosts and talking animals and spaceships heavy with radiation and always, no matter what, us triumphant against the frighteningly or comically stupid hoos; he had hundreds of stories, some decades old, invented to while away the long tedious hours of watch duty or hunting or travel or insomnia. His prophecies, he called them. All true in some time or place. He wasn't allowed to be a dry, wordless thing curled up in the dirt. I knelt by him, murmuring, "Florian."

I heard footsteps behind me but stayed turned toward Florian, stroking his skull; poor little skull, the bone flaky and almost soft beneath my fingers. "Florian?"

"M'eech." He moaned, his failed strength gathering like a fist in a single painful sound. He spasmed, gasping, and Renee and Linc were suddenly beside me slipping arms around his shoulders, holding him steady, and I kept rubbing his head as he kept repeating *m'eech, m'eech*, nonsensical but full of an urgency that sapped him.

"Tell me," I said, touching his face. "Slower."

His hands, all bone, clutched my shoulders hard as he yanked himself up for a single, agonized second and then fell back into our arms. "My beach," he murmured, calmer now. Like he knew what was coming. Like he couldn't wait. "Get—my beach—my lake—stones—"

His lake stones. Those ridiculous mementos. He didn't have the pouch slung around his waist, the one he always kept them in. I hadn't even noticed. What had he done with it? Where had it gone?

"Where?" Linc said quietly. "I'll get them." He would never make it back with them in time. None of us would. "Florian? Where—"

"M'lake." He grabbed at my arm and then his fingers

seemed not to uncurl but collapse, reduced to random bits of bone held together at the knuckles by strings: a plastic hoo-skeleton, curled up back in its box after Halloween. "Lake—stones—m'beach—I'll live—"

Tremors rushed through his body, the dust of his flesh and bits of bone coming off in sooty patches like plaster from a ceiling. His skull opened, parting as easy as a split seed pod, and his brain pulsated, ready to burst open too; it shrank and withered with every new beat, the rhythm slower by the second. A wrinkled, grayish-white little cantaloupe. A dust-caked plum. A peach pit. His eyes rolled backward, and then just melted from their sockets. He'd always had kind eyes, Florian did, steady and gentle and when he looked at you, it was like he saw nothing else. Now they were just streams of thin jelly that trickled out over his cheekbones like tears, dropping one by one into the grass.

Gently, we laid him back against the roots.

Blinded, Florian trembled, his jaw opening and closing *click-bang-click* like he was trying to shout in pain; even knowing he wasn't feeling a thing, brain shriveled up like that, I gripped Linc's outstretched hand tight as I could. Florian's arms were bare rattling bones now, his teeth going to dust as his jaw clicked harder and faster. His arms went to powder at the finger joints, wrists, elbows; his legs disintegrated, his lower jaw broke off with a clatter, a chunk of his skull and the peach pit of his brain fell into musty bits of nothingness. Then there was just the top part of his skull, empty staring sockets, and the long length of his spine half-buried in soft tan ash. I kept listening for the last faded, failing banjo notes, one lingering echo of him in my head, but when I wasn't paying attention it had all just gone.

Renee turned to me and Linc, stricken. "What do we do now?" she whispered.

Nothing, Renee, nothing but wait for the rain to come wash away this ash. Wasn't that a line in some movie? A guy wishing the rain would come through the city and wash him away? Some movie my dad liked. I couldn't remember. What did Renee care? He was kind to her, the handful of days she'd known him, but she couldn't miss him like I did. I didn't know why she was even there.

"What are we going to do?" she repeated, querulous. She just wanted to show off how human she still was, sniffling over someone she'd barely known and hadn't loved. Fresh out of gold stars, sorry. Linc took my hand again and after one last look, we turned and walked away.

"Don't we at least bury him or something?" Renee shouted. "Don't we do anything?"

We kept on walking. She had to work to catch up.

8

Linc and I were on watch that next morning, a relief as he never expected me to talk. I told him I'd take the Sullen Trail to the underpass, not explaining I meant to check on our dead girl; he could beat bounds the opposite way. I moved slowly, letting my thoughts drift as the riverbank disappeared behind me, the trees became denser and the flat ground gave way to slow-rising hills matted with last fall's leaves. Everything was quiet, all the sounds and smells what they should have been, and then I saw something that made me pause: a single young, slender ash, standing in a handkerchief-sized clearing, its trunk encircled with flat, colorful stones laid out in neat spiraling rows. Sitting near it, weighted down with ordinary forest stones, the old leather pouch Florian had always worn round his waist, looking bulky and bumpy like there was still something inside.

I picked up one of the stones, a smooth slate gray, put it down, pulled the pouch free and took it in my hand. Heavy. I couldn't remember seeing him wear it, I realized, since that day in the woods; it must've been too burdensome on his old bones, those final days. His stone collection, the water-polished bits of Lake Michigan he had carried with him over miles and decades without, he once told me proudly, ever losing a single one. Precious bits of junk. He'd never say where he buried them but he'd take them out and count them sometimes in secret, like miser's gold. I'd never realized he had so many.

He must have stuck them here meaning to organize or bury them or just look at them one last time, but never got the chance. *Get my beach. My lake.* That's all he wanted, to look at his souvenirs one last time and think of the beach, the lake, the place he'd been really happy. But I didn't get them. I couldn't even be bothered to try.

I sat down on the ground and made the sounds that had to pass for crying now, not touching any more stones lest they turn to dust too. I heard footsteps behind me and Linc was next to me then, holding something in his hands, and when I saw what it was I couldn't get angry at him for following me. He sat next to me with the bit of skull cradled in his palms, that and a strip of dirt-stiff cloth torn from his own shirt, knotted into a makeshift bag around a handful of gray ash.

"I had to go back to get it," he said. "The rest disintegrated when I picked it up. The backbone. But this part looks pretty solid. Please don't cry."

"Renee did." I wiped my eyes. "She barely knew him, so why shouldn't I? I didn't want him to die. He wasn't so old—"

"Over three hundred? Not so old?" His voice was gentle, not yelling at me about hoo sentimentality like Joe would have. Like he already had. Yelling louder when I just walked away. "Almost a century as a hoo and two as one of us, that's a lot of life." Linc put the cloth bundle down near the stones. "A whole lot of life."

His shoulders sagged, chin dipping down toward his chest. A big black beetle emerged from the tangle of his black hair, crawling slowly down his shoulder; Linc was getting more of those lately, making the slow transition from bloater to feeder. I took the skull from him, its eye sockets softening and flaking away but most of the cranium still solid: our old man, all that was left of him. *I been everywhere.* Nothing left now but the pieces.

Did they take my mother's organs at the hospital? She

had the back of her driver's license signed, my father didn't. I never even thought about it before. Pieces, all cut up. The thought of meat cutting up pieces of meat to stick in another carcass of meat, it gave me a little shiver of disgust.

Linc touched my shoulder. "You okay?"

"I'm fine." I never liked mentioning parents around Linc, considering that his killed him. It seemed rude. "I don't want to put him here—this tree's too young."

We found a big mature oak with deep fissured bark—good scratching bark, Florian loved a nice back scratch—dug with our hands in the stiff dirt next to it and pressed the skull and the tiny bag of ashes into the ground. I picked up Florian's old leather pouch, weighted with lake stones, and with Linc's help tied it around my own waist; maybe he'd meant it never to be found, but he wasn't here to tell me so. I felt a bit better, feeling that little weight, Florian's weight, against my hip. Another stone in my pocket, pale brick with striations like mother of pearl. Linc took a couple, slate gray and deeper brick, and at the last minute I took a green one for Renee, consolation for missing the funeral. A pink one, in case she didn't like that color. I thought of Florian freed forever from old age, fighting, Teresa's incessant insane demands, and that also felt better but not really good. Good had snuck away while my head was turned.

"I'm not really up for watch tonight," I said, fingering the pouch, the stones in my pocket. "If it's all the same to you, let's just go back." I laughed. "Teresa won't be there to scream at us anyway, bet you anything."

Linc looked suddenly wary. "I know how you feel," he said, slowly like I might jump on him, "but I really think we need to anyway."

I stared at him. "Because why?" No answer. "Because what have you seen, Linc?"

No answer. I started to laugh. "Okay, so exactly how many of us know something weird's going on and are pretending we don't? Huh? Me, Joe, you—"

"You didn't say anything during the dance, Jessie, when those . . . things came along, so I thought—"

"You saw that happen?" I shoved him. "You saw it. So why the hell didn't you help me?"

Linc looked stricken. "I thought you were just fooling around with them, before Joe chased them away. They didn't seem dangerous, whatever they were, and Joe said it was nothing but later I thought, that's still awful strange, maybe I should look around the woods and see if they're—"

"Yeah, well trust me, they're stronger than they look." I was furious now, at Joe for spreading his fairy tales and at Linc for swallowing them so meekly. "You saw it and you just stood there with your mouth open, now you're Johnny on the spot a week after the fact? So what're you gonna do if they ever do send the National Guard or Marines or something after us, whine about how you weren't *sure* those were really flamethrowers until your own head's a big pile of ash?"

I shoved him again and he didn't fight back, just curled up on himself looking ashamed; I glared at him with his beaten-in face and slumped shoulders and shuffling feet, his eyes the only sparked-up thing about him, and saw the shadow of his living self, shoved around so much and blamed for so many things that he expected no better. I hate people who can make you feel guilty when they've pissed *you* off, but hell, who else did I have to talk to now? Renee was too new, Joe and I weren't speaking and I couldn't trust anyone else to keep their mouths shut. One big happy family.

"Come on," I said, pulling at his arm. "You want a watch? We're gonna look for a dead body that might never have been alive. It's a lot more interesting than whatever Joe's been telling you, so shut up and listen . . ."

When I got to the part about Teresa and our new friends using the same perfume, Linc nodded. "She says it's industrial solvents," he said. "Don't laugh—Sam and I went hunting once outside Whiting, stepped in a leaking barrel of something outside the refinery and our feet stank like that for a month. Lost a whole layer of skin too. But that doesn't explain her face." He lowered his voice, as if the squirrels might go tattling. "She looks like she's got . . . modeling clay or something on her face, I don't know, like the decayed bits are filling in but it's not real flesh. Just in the last day or two, you can really see it—and the bugs are crawling off her, like there's nothing for them to eat anymore. Some of them just falling off."

I slowed my steps, thinking. Bugs falling away en masse was nothing strange, not when they'd finally stripped off the last flesh and left you a skeletal dusty—but Teresa wasn't that much older than Linc, she still had flesh to burn. Unless that chemical smell, or taste, was driving them away. It couldn't be plain embalming fluid, the bugs ate you anyway (a nasty surprise for some of the vainer 'maldies). So maybe just something industrial, something she stepped in or fell in that made her reek? And those creatures from the dance, maybe they were real undeads who'd been buried near a waste site, a paint factory, something that leaked nastiness into the soil and mutated them—I'd never heard of such a thing before, but you never knew. There were mills and factories and refineries and landfills all over the county, farms soaked in pesticide runoff, stenches bubbling up from clean-seeming soil that no human had the nose to catch. I was jumping the gun, thinking this was anything sinister. Shit happens.

None of which explained her face. Or the blond girl, who I'd stake Joe's life was real, corrupted living flesh.

"So is this why you were so antsy to get me on watch with you, the other morning?" I asked. "To tell me about this?"

"I wanted to hear what she'd told you. Solvents, or . . . some other excuse."

"Fuck-all," I said. "That's what she's told me. But what else is new."

The concrete tunnel floor was soothingly dry and hard underfoot. Joe hadn't lied, the body was gone; there was a lingering disinfectant-like odor where I'd laid her out, no other smell but moss and old graffiti paint. Past the tunnel were more woods and steeper hillocks, only another half mile or so before the trees abruptly gave way to the old aban-doned cornfield—overgrown Living Pioneer park exhibit, or actual erstwhile farm?—thick with shoulder-high weeds and dead fallen stalks. Thick with rats too, we wouldn't go hungry today. It was where we marked the end of our world. We'd never pushed through to the other side, but today Linc and I crossed the wood's edge, shoved through the stalks and waded in, sniffing and listening and pausing like cautious cats. The papery husks sliced at us and I heard Linc wince and swear. Other than the robins and mourning doves, silence.

Something small and skinny rushed past our feet: an actual stray, part of a rat wedged in its mouth. Disgusting stuff, cat meat, outside of starvation none of us would touch it. I ripped at the stalks, trying to cut a path, and heard the rustle of something bigger, a moaning sound beneath it abruptly cut off. The stench rose slowly like steam from a stagnant puddle, fresh flesh smothered beneath a stew of solvent, rubbing alcohol, paint thinner, polish remover, oil. A thick smear of rancid margarine. Old eggshells with the taint of sulfur. A high, tuneless melody circled overhead like a thin little bird as we pushed toward the heart of the field. The stench made us gag. I thought of puddles, fetid standing water full of hatching insects and floating islands of oil.

There, in a chopped-out clearing, a dozen-some of our newfound friends. Some bluish-black, some outright rotten, some still tinged living pink or brown but sap-sweaty and stinking, all gathered round one crouched in the middle trying to scrape out a ditch with his hands. He kept digging, taking up the tiniest nail scrapings each time, while his friends swayed and rocked and tried to sing. It took me a minute to place the melody: "Amazing Grace." I remembered his green sweater from the dance night; he was unrecognizable otherwise, his ashen skin now a head-to-toe bruise and his hands puffy and soft with the fingernails pulling loose.

"Can you kill us?" he said, still with hoo-lips and hoo-tongue but the words so soft and slurred I could sense the rot forming in his mouth. His face was slack and drooping like he'd been autopsied, muscles cut through with a scalpel. "We want to die."

"You're not dead already?" Linc asked, voice slow and loud. "How long have you been here?"

The others ignored us, moaning and scratching at the dirt; Green Sweater seemed to be the spokesman. Maybe the only one who could still talk. Talking like a human, all delicate articulation, but he still seemed to understand our gestures and grunts. "Make us dead like you," he pleaded. "Or just dead. Help."

He staggered toward us, hands held out in supplication. One of the others picked up a rat, holding it struggling and squalling in her grip, and looked at it longingly and drooling and then dropped it again with a shudder. They were all shaking, from hunger for things like that squirrel that they couldn't keep down or kill properly. They sang without words, each note a penknife nick to the brain; the stench was searing. They trembled when I looked at them, they trembled when I stepped back. What was this ruined mockery pretending to be us? Pity was impossible. My fist clenched with the need to smash it.

"Why aren't you dead?" I said, slapping Green Sweater's outstretched arms aside. "What are you? Are you human?" No answer. "You're not one of us! Tell me what you are!"

"Why wouldn't you dance with me?" he demanded, the tones of a betrayed lover. "Why wouldn't you infect us? We want to be like you—or just die. You like killing things. Kill us."

I just stared. He shivered and snuffled, bewildered this meager bag of tricks hadn't worked, then let out a frustrated hiss and grabbed me hard around the throat. Linc came staggering to the rescue but Green Sweater had weakened, gone soft and putrescent since the night of the dance, and it was easy to throw him to the ground, kick him again and again until he huddled up screaming in fear. His friends didn't even turn around. His bones felt almost soft on impact, bendy as greensticks. I spat on him, a long black trail of coffin liquor.

"Kill yourself, coward. You're not worth the trouble it'd take me." I wiped my feet against the dirt, trying to scrub away all contact. "And you must be a hoo, everything you think you know comes from movies—we're not contagious. If we only were, we'd run this fucking planet."

He just lay there. Another one started scratching at the ground and they all kept moaning in imitation song. Linc was now awkwardly patting something in a mud-caked red skirt that clutched his arm and sobbed. "C'mon," I said, yanking him off. "We're leaving."

"But we've got to find out—"

"You know what I've found out? That they're psycho and their smell's going to make me pass out. Let's get out of here and go someplace we can talk."

The cornfield is wide, I cannot get o'er. The stench over-powered everything around it, our smells too, so that picking up our path again was a wearying chore. Florian and then all this, it was too much. I was vibrating with exhaustion, the hard sunlight beseeching me to lie down and sleep, and I had the trees and cool shady rest nearly in my sights when Linc and I started, and froze.

Someone was standing fifty yards away in the grass and bare dirt, strands of hair blowing over his face, frozen tense as a rabbit in sight of a cobra; he had a bulging red rucksack slung on one shoulder, a big damp spot on its side. Maybe a birdwatcher, camper, some hoo who came out here last night or at dawn and then got lost. At least he wasn't trying to sing. He stared at me and I stared back, and it was as if something unspooled between us, a thread, a wire filament too thin for the eye, and he had one end and I had the other and our fingers were caught and tangled together like fish flailing in the same net. I couldn't pull away. Behind us our friends grew fainter, wailing outright in lieu of making music.

"Just a hoo," Linc murmured. "Just what we need. Let's go scare him off."

The human didn't move as we approached him, as that thread between us wrapped tighter and tighter around my fingers and tugged me forward. Did I know him? How could I? Early thirties at most, neatly combed hair gone prematurely gray, wire-rimmed glasses, jeans, a rumpled blue shirt, a face so bland and ordinary you forgot what he looked like looking right at him. His smell was pure hoo. The rucksack gave off an odor of greasy plastic and, beneath that, something raw and meaty. He swallowed hard when we approached, eyes wide. He was getting our smell now too.

"Out," Linc said, and showed his teeth. Linc has very long, very sharp teeth, even for our kind; he almost never needed to do more, the few times we had to frighten away vagrants. This fellow, though, didn't even seem to see him. He was too busy looking at me.

"Jessie?" the stranger said.

Surprise turned me still. It couldn't be someone from school—what would I be now, twenty-four, twenty-five? Unless I really had lost all touch with time, he was too old. Someone I knew. How would I know him? It was a guess, a joke. Linc smelled my anxiety and growled, drooling coffin juice. The hoo took a step backward.

"Can you understand me?" he said, his voice shaking, a hand to his nose. He looked like he desperately wanted to bolt and run, like he couldn't, like whatever thread, filament had tangled me up had caught him fast as well. "Please just nod, or . . . something, if you can, I—"

"Jim," I said.

That's what came unbidden from my mouth but of course, he couldn't hear it: just the throaty grunt of a creature without a tongue, even less human-sounding than when I'd tried to say Lisa's name, years past. His voice. I didn't recognize this gray-headed weary-eyed shit-scared stranger but he'd somehow stolen Jim's voice for himself, my brother, my older brother, Jim. I could *feel* his feet twitching like they were my own, itching to run away, but he didn't. Could sense the nausea rising in his throat, at how Linc and I smelled, but he didn't get sick. He stood there. He let us both come closer, eyes full of shock and longing like I'd somehow turn back into the human he'd known if he just stared at me long enough. My stomach had become a vast hollowness, the full measure of the air you fall through jumping from a sky-scraper to the pavement.

"Your arm," he said, "what happened to your arm? Where'd it go?" All thick and congested-sounding, like he might cry. "It's me, Jessie, it's really me. You can understand me, can't you?" Now he was blinking back tears in earnest. I could smell the fear seething inside him, rising like steam from his skin. He stood his ground anyway. "Your eyes are just the same, Jessie, I—"

"Jessie," Linc said, a hand on my arm, "let's get out of here."

"I'm sorry, Jessie," Jim said, drawing shallow, ragged breaths. "I know I shouldn't be here, I'm so sorry—"

"Jessie?" Linc's fingers were gripping harder now, insistent. "This does no good. You know how little good this does. We're getting out of—"

"Tell me you understand me," Jim pleaded. "Nod your head, anything, please just—"

"No," I said, I shouted, to him, to Linc. It wasn't "no" to those human ears, though, but a guttural grunt of *unuhhh* that could have meant anything he wanted it to, and Jim kept wiping tears from his eyes and it was really him, Jim, my family, seeing me standing here in the full sunlight stinking and rotten and suddenly I was more scared than he could ever be, I wanted to turn and run fast and mindless as Lisa had when she saw me, but that luxury of swift movement was gone forever and I could only start backing away, shaking my head. The rucksack banged against Jim's shin, releasing a fresh burst of its greasy, meaty smell as he shoved aside his own fear, as he came right up to me like we'd been parted a day, an hour.

"Jessie," he said, a sound like crying and laughing at once. "Oh my God. You're still *here*. It's all right. It'll all be all right. You're still here."

He threw his arms around me, and I cried out in fear.

9

Linc growled and leapt, and if I'd let him break my brother's neck then and there maybe somehow it'd all have been different, we'd all be safe in the woods laughing our asses off right now, but some buried, accursed thing in me wanted to hold Jim next to me just as much as push him away, and I pulled Linc off before he could snap bones. Jim staggered backward, breathing hard, holding his greasy rucksack before him like protection or a bribe.

"I won't hurt you," he said, giving Linc a quick, fearful glance. "I can't anyway. There's nothing flammable in here." He put the rucksack down on the ground between us, backed away from it. "I'm alone. Can you understand me? Jessie? Just a little bit?"

He won't hurt us, can't hurt us. He actually thought that needed telling. All hoos are alike. Jim, my brother. He came back. He's not running away. The smell, when he touched me. Linc stood between us, ready to spring.

"Please," Jim kept saying, holding his hands up like a hostage. "You can understand me, I see it in your eyes. You're still in there. I know you can't talk to me, I know it's—just nod or shake your head again, or something? Please, Jessie. Please."

I didn't have a damned palate anymore, and he wanted to meet and greet. I drooled down my front, spitting onto his stained shoes, and he trembled a little bit as he scraped them clean against the dirt.

"I fixed up the house," he said. His voice skittered and hopscotched over the syllables, the desperate hollow chatter of someone who knew they had absolutely nothing to say but had to keep blithering, blathering, anything but the horror of silence. "It's pale blue now, sort of weathered blue, New Englandy? Remember those pictures you liked when you were little, the saltbox homes in Maine and Massachusetts? That blue. The old house. We're still there, Lisa and I. She was with this guy, it didn't work out, she moved back home again. I mean, the thing is, I mean, she was there, she moved back, but now—"

"Why are you here?" I said, and saying it shook something loose inside me, like fingers relaxing an arthritic grip, so I kept saying it even knowing he didn't get a word. Human words. He was showing off to taunt me, all his fancy tongue-palate-teeth family talk-talk-talk. "Why now? Nine years of nothing, and now you—"

"Your arm," Jim repeated, almost mournful like it'd been his own limb lost. "What happened to it?"

"Jessie." Linc kept pulling on my wrist. "This is a farce. Let's go back."

"—can't even understand a word I say, can you?" I gave Jim a shove, just a light punctuation of speech for us but it made him gasp and throw his arms out too late for balance, hitting the soft ground with a squishy thud. "Can you, human?"

"Jessie, I don't know what's going on here but if this is your brother, I'm President Carter. Let's go. *Now*."

"Caaaaaaa-huhhh." Jim suddenly moaned, a perfect echo of Linc: mouth fallen open, the C almost a G, the T entirely lost when voiced to a ruined tongue. "That was a name, right? Wasn't it? Somebody's name?" He hunched his shoulders forward, imitating the gesture we used to mean *proper name*. "As opposed to *car*. Caaaauhhh." A shorter sound, palm held flat and sweeping away from his body to indicate *moving vehicle*. "As opposed to *care*. Cayyuhhhhhh." Chin dipped groundward, arm curved like mother around infant. Then he looked up, shaking again. "I got that mostly right, didn't I?"

I was cold all over. Linc looked to me in utter astonishment, but I had nothing. How would you feel if your slice of pot roast started talking to you, fluently? Jim sat there in the dirt, not gloating or savoring our surprise, just waiting to see what we'd do to him now.

"We've worked out maybe a hundred, hundred and fifty of your words," he said, a new note, quiet, a bit authoritative, creeping into his voice. Seizing on something he'd proven he knew about to try to calm himself down. "Our psycho-linguistic researchers, I mean, not me personally—I'm a biologist myself. A dime-a-dozen biologist. We've *guessed* the words, saying we've actually worked them out is being kind. It's hard to do when half of your communication is telepathic. Your brains are still black boxes to us."

I remembered the first time Joe spoke to me, the nonsensical sound-strands that twisted themselves immediately into a tight, taut thread of actual words. It hurt, that feeling, but a good hurt like that sore tooth your tongue needs to worry. Humans didn't understand it, couldn't talk head-to-head, didn't have brains like ours. But apparently they were trying. I supposed I shouldn't be surprised. I thought all they ever wanted to learn about us was how to kill us. Or maybe this was somehow part of that. Why *are* you here, exactly, big brother?

I motioned for Jim to get up. He'd done the right thing, he'd gone and made me curious. "Get me a stick," I told Linc.

"I don't believe this." Linc actually bared his teeth at me, something he never did. "Jessie, this is about the most piss-poor idea since—"

"So go running to Teresa if you don't like it, if you can find her—but if you're staying, go get me a goddamned stick and then let me do the talking."

He gave me a look of the martyred and staggered off to the nearby trees, pulling away a suitable branch and practically slapping it into my palm. I pointed the branch at Jim, making him take a few more steps backward, then wrote in the rain-dampened dirt between us:

Lab?

My letters were clumsy, scrawling, it took me a few seconds to remember how to shape a B. Jim nodded, all excited we really could somewhat, somehow, speak to each other. Looked a little scared too. "Great Lakes Thanatology Lab," he said. "Near Octave Chanute Beach in Gary, there's been a large zombie infesta—presence out there forever. It's possibly interesting for other reasons too, but that's for the geologists to work on. Like I said, I'm biology." He smoothed his hair, his hand like a soft pink paddle. "I got an internship there my last year of college, right before you died. You wouldn't believe the fights Dad and I had about it. It wasn't 'safety' he was worried about, just, God forbid I go and study zombies because that means having to acknowledge out loud that zombies actually exist—"

Okay, enough of *that* word; Linc was starting to growl, hearing it, and I didn't blame him. I waved the branch until Jim quit babbling, then wrote it there in the dirt, *Zombie*. Big, flourishing Z. Then wiped it out with a sweep of my foot, shaking my head violently. Jim got the point.

"Oh," he said, and laughed nervously, the light dawning. He had the decency to look halfway embarrassed. "Undead? Living dead? Revived?"

I shrugged. He nodded. "I got an internship," he repeated. "There's a lab in New York that wanted to recruit me but this place is ground zero for the really interesting research, all the—anyway, after the accident I couldn't leave. Lisa wasn't doing well, she had to leave school, she needed someone to be with her. She was wandering around, going out to all the graveyards, saying she wanted to see where the accident happened . . . and then she came home one day, crying, sick, looking like she'd seen a ghost." He swallowed hard. "And, well, she had."

He waited, like this was my cue to burst into tears and give him a big hug. I kept my arm down.

"I looked for you again," Jim said. His voice was too steady, too calm, like he was balancing something fragile on it and if it broke he would break too, everything holding us both upright would shatter. "Lisa never forgave herself for running away. Never. She just wasn't . . . ready, for what she saw. She never went wandering again, after that. But that's the good thing about being affiliated with the lab, you get clearance to go places where otherwise—I looked for you, Jessie, I looked everywhere. For Mom and Dad too—"

I held my hand up swiftly, and Jim saw my silent question. Shook his head, a shadow of grief flitting over his face. Like I'd thought, then. Linc shuffled his feet, awkward and restless at all this family blather, but didn't try to jump in.

"I came out here," he said. "I looked but I thought you were around the cemetery instead, I didn't know exactly where—I mean, I wasn't even sure how much of you, I mean, the real you, was left—"

I *recognized* Lisa, you hoo-asshole, I tried to talk to her, she's the one who turned tail and ran and you stand there asking what's left of *me*, of my insides, my memories. Goddamned humans. Goddamn all of you—

"Please don't," he said, his voice skittering higher, as I started growling at him too, my body tensing to leap. "I'm sorry—"

"Coward." Linc laughed. Stepping back to see what I'd do to him next. Coward. Gawwwwwwhh. No hand signs. Add that one to your C-words, human.

Jim stood there, staring at me, curling his fingers into fists to stop them from trembling with fright. And he studies us for a living, or so he says. This is Jim, my Jim, my brother? What happened to you? Remember how you used to take me for rides down the abandoned back roads, so fast the car would rattle, you could shriek out loud with the fear and fun of it, and a couple of times we saw shambling, half-hidden figures at the side of the road and you just laughed, shot them the finger, sped up even faster? Never saw any cops, though, none of them would patrol hazard country for any amount of money. Remember when I pulled one of the town break-in alarms, everyone screaming and running to their basements like they'd be eaten alive and *you* dared me to do it, I could've been arrested, sued, expelled but you helped cover for me? How Mike Hinshawe from my class, always shouting about how he was gonna go out there and kick some fucking zombie ass the first chance he got he wasn't some goddamned fucking pussy no sir, heard that siren go off and literally wet himself? Pissed his pants in front of everyone. We laughed until we cried. Nobody ever found out it was me. Remember the time you got between me and Dad, and hit him back? Who are you now with those beaten-down eyes, bathing in a stench of defeat and fear? I can't recognize you. Why should I listen to a word you say? A reason. Just one good reason.

"I won't lie to you," Jim said. His eyes sad and regretful now like he could see just what I was thinking, like he knew and didn't blame me. "My job is about finding a safe, effective way to wipe all of you out. So 'all of you' were family? Loved ones? Doesn't matter, does it, when you're supposed to be dead anyway? Right?" He paced back and forth, agitated. "I told myself that for a long time, Jessie, that that was what you'd want, that I'd be releasing you from your torment. You and Mom and Dad. What are you all but a lot of moaning brain-dead cripples, staggering around rotting in slow motion? Right? No more than that?"

The pleading defiance in Jim's voice as he babbled at me, that was Dad after a fight, after another explosion of temper drained him dry, the *please please look you gotta,* a saliva bubble forming on his lip. He had Dad's hands too, broad meaty palms with long thin fingers stuck on like twigs in clay, that same sharp curve to his lower lip. I was a little copy of Mom, everyone said. Me and Lisa both.

"It's not genocide," Jim was saying. Talking to himself now. "It's euthanasia. Then you find out the brain-dead cripples actually think, and those moaning sounds are them talking to each other, God knows what they say but still their own language with its own rules, and then you see a body and a body walking in the trees, always the same two bodies together, like they mean something special to each other. And they laugh, and if something wakes and sleeps and thinks and reasons and laughs and communicates and pair-bonds that means it might even have emotions, it might feel grief and pain—"

Was I supposed to applaud all this? Seriously? My God, Jim, I know nobody credits even full-fledged hoos who can't talk properly with working brains but you're a *scientist* and this all shocks you? Sad, that's just damned sad. He stood there, rocking back and forth on his heels, vibrating with tension. I don't recognize you, brother, my flesh might be different but *you've* transmogrified straight down to your bones. But what you are, you are. Sad as that is, apparently.

"I changed my mind, Jessie," he said, quieter, hands thrust into his pockets. "Even before I knew I had family out here. But you can't say that, not where I work. You can't say it anywhere. There's more than a few of us, you know, that feel like this, we wanted to do something to—"

I poked the branch at him for silence, then bent over the dirt. It took me a few minutes, clumsy and hesitant, to scrawl it all out.

Why am I alive?

Jim let out a quiet laugh, and shook his head.

"Nobody knows," he told me, giving Linc a nervous little glance: *Don't worry, I'm not ignoring you, if I did that might give you an excuse to kill me.* "We're no closer to figuring that out than we ever were. Or why you're so much stronger. Or why you decay so slowly. It could be a virus. Doesn't seem to be genetic." He dug a heel harder into the ground. "Nobody knows why at certain times in history there's this great outburst of zomb—revivalism, bodies everywhere returning to life, and then other times, nothing, the cycle dies out. Boom and bust. And it used to be a lot more bust than boom. Centuries ago, you believe the thano-historians, you could go your whole life never seeing an undead, never knowing they existed."

He shoved his shoes against the soft dirt like he was trying to leave a fossil-deep footprint, a permanent artifact. "Now, though, since the Industrial Revolution, a big speedup, a lot less bust and a lot more boom, boom, boom. The 1918 flu epidemic, so-called. Detroit and Alameda in the forties. Pittsburgh in '68—so many outbreaks in the sixties. More and more and more."

Linc glanced at me, that look in his eyes of someone drawn in despite himself. They never told us any of this in school, only mentioned it in passing in books. Nothing but safety drills. Jim must have seen that look too because now he was staring up at the sky, the first time he'd dared take his eyes off me or Linc.

"Maybe it's industrial pollutants," he said. Talking, talking, like he'd been dying all this time to be someone's, anyone's little expert. He should've been a teacher, Mom always used to say that. "All the steel mills around here, refineries, factories, farm runoff, the whole region's bathing in it. And we've been lousy with revivals here, the last decade or two." He shook his head. "Hell, maybe it's the beaches. You want to see a loved one rise from the dead? Bury them in a good sandy soil, near the lake coast. You know how much longer your sort lives, around the beaches? Decades, centuries. The geologists have their theories. But I'm in biology."

I don't know what it was, but you broke down so slow there, your body did. I'd always figured Florian was just lucky that way, but then, we'd always stayed away from the beaches, we wouldn't know. Too much water. Those rumors about the labs. God knew what went on there. A lot more than I'd thought, it sounded like.

"Industrial pollutants," I repeated.

"I told you," Linc said. "Go on. Ask him."

Jim shook his head, uncomprehending. I pointed at the cornfield. Then at his rucksack, full of something meaty and greasy and dead. He actually trembled again, like I'd reminded him of something he'd been praying to forget.

"I have to go feed them now," he said. His eyes were grim.

He retrieved the leaking rucksack and we followed him unbidden back to the cornfield's heart, the wailing and moaning picking up at the sound of our footsteps like a needle jumping on a seismograph. The burial ditch was no bigger, but now three of them were scratching at it like they could burrow right through the cruel earth; the others gathered, ready to throw themselves in. At the sight of Jim I saw recognition on their faces, pleading fury, and Green Sweater came forward with the cringing servility of Igor before Frankenstein.

"Are you here to kill us?" he demanded. His sagging, ashen skin had deteriorated even further in mere minutes. "You have drugs that could do it, that's what they say, please kill us. Or make them."

"I'm back!" Jim held up the rucksack as if no one had spoken. "I've got food!"

The others cowered together, drooling, as Green Sweater clenched his fists and screamed. "We want to die! God, please just let us die!"

"I'm sorry," Jim said, and he really did sound sorry, had that look like it was killing him to watch this, like he was ashamed of himself for wanting to run away. "I've got food. You'll feel better if you eat." There was this sudden flicker in his eyes that told me that was a flat lie. "I've got it right here."

The moans and supplications rose as he reached into the rucksack and pulled out something skinned—a squirrel, a rabbit—and threw it into a volley of clutching hands. There were wrapped things too from some obliging butcher, raw cow hearts, plastic containers of blood he opened and lined up on the ground; they ran up to grab them, cried and retched with revulsion, crammed it all feverishly into their mouths. Green Sweater screamed louder and threw himself on the ground, not touching a bite. I had a horrible desire to laugh, the way he looked like a huge rotten baby throwing a fit in the grocery aisles, but smelling all that dead flesh made me feel sick too. The only thing worse would have been cooked.

"C'mon," Jim muttered. "We'd better go while they're distracted."

Once out of sight and stench, his hands started shaking. "I hate this," he said, rolling up the empty rucksack like a big befouled cigar, "but every time I come out here they beg me and they look so miserable, and in a way I feel like I owe—I'm just lucky they haven't tried to attack me. They're too weak now, but they'll eat living flesh just as soon as dead—"

Linc reached out and clasped Jim's shoulders, the soul of inquisitive friendliness. Jim stood there, wincing in pain as he clutched the crumpled rucksack, eyes watering from the smell.

"They're not you," he said. "They're living people. Very sick ones. Or were."

The sounds of retching started behind us, choking noises like someone spitting out something in chunks.

"Pest eradication," he said, fingertips worrying the stained cloth like he was trying to unravel and reweave it standing there. "That's what my job, our research was all about. I could have quit. But I didn't. The money." He laughed, a hollow, self-mocking sound. "That was my job, anyway. Now it's trying to figure out how to keep . . . that, you just saw, from killing us all."

He lowered his voice, as if those retching, stumbling things behind us had the cornfield bugged. "Before I was in the bio labs," he said, "I interned as a collector. We would go around the beaches and woods after zomb—undead fights, collect the bodies of any with smashed skulls and bring them back for research." He gave me this unblinking look like he knew exactly how repulsed I must be hearing this, all perversely proud of his own shame. (He was a shit mind-reader along with a coward. What did I care if they cut up some combat-stomp I'd never even met?) "Never got anywhere neurologically, but we got a pretty good handle on your digestive tracts. All sorts of amazing intestinal flora, not like a human's at all. But then, a year or two ago, we started finding something very strange: a strain of what looked like *H. pylori* in the gut. The bacterium that causes stomach ulcers. Just sitting there, doing nothing. Strictly a human bacterium, we'd thought. And its gene sequencing was . . . off. It had mutated."

The moaning from the cornfield grew louder, up and down, a call and response of impassioned agony. I walked away, clutching my branch and cursing my slowness, and Linc and Jim followed.

"But it just sat inside them, dormant." Jim reached up to a tree as we walked, snapped off a small branch of his own like a fencing duel was imminent. "No inflammation, like you'd find in a human stomach. Then a few months ago, more bodies, that same germ in the gut. It mutated again. And never mind inflammation, it ate holes inside them, great ulcerous holes. And there was something strange about their skin. It was sticky, like sap or Scotch tape, and it had this strange smell—not of decay, mind, but live, diseased flesh."

Linc and I stopped in our tracks. Linc clutched my hand, still holding the branch. Jim looked from him to me and back again, not the least happy at this revelation but just vaguely relieved.

"You know what I'm talking about, then," he said.

It was Linc who nodded back.

"The stomach contents were strange too," Jim told us. "You're obligate carnivores, you need fresh kills. This lot, though, we found the remains of berries, leaves, garbage scraps. Rotten food, leavings you'd find in large trash bins. Anything and everything but raw flesh."

Teresa. Teresa refusing to hunt with us, demanding leftover meat and then putting it aside barely touched, because if the kill were too fresh she might not keep it down. Disappearing for days at a time, knowing if we found out her secret illness, the thing gnawing holes inside her so she couldn't eat like us, had to rifle through garbage cans like a raccoon, that'd be the end of her gang leadership. And of her.

"Then, not long after that, the rumors." Jim stared over his shoulder, nobody there, those things not us and not him now mercifully out of earshot. "Then on the news. People, living human beings, whose skin went black, who couldn't keep down anything but raw meat, who smelled like they'd bathed in paint thinner. We found some of them, wandering the beaches, the fields. Just like those back there. They'd been thrown out of their homes, their towns, because people thought they were infected. Made undead, I mean. Never mind everyone knows you can't spread undeath by biting— the old superstition. They were rotting from the inside. Finally they couldn't even try to eat. They died. When we autopsied them, we found the same bacterium, that mutated *H. pylori*. The same holes in their guts."

Those things in the cornfield. I was right, Joe, I told you, I *told* you. I handed Linc the branch, pointed toward the cornfield, to myself, drew a finger across my throat. Looked questioningly at Jim. Keep it from killing us all. Which us?

"Our 'information' is all hysteria," Jim said. "Super-staph. MRSA. Flesh-eating bacteria. All wrong. Remember when we were younger, they never talked about any of this, they'd scream at anyone who did? All happy-chat all the time? Remember what hypocrites we thought they—"

I glanced over at Linc. He nodded at my cue and gripped Jim's shoulders again, tighter this time; it must've hurt like hell because Jim shouted, squirmed, couldn't shake free. Too bad, brother. Talk.

"The bodies of the undead we collected," Jim said, sounding pained and sick himself. "Other things were different about them. *Less* decay. More muscle mass. A higher core body temperature. That same smell, like something living that bathed in gasoline or—all over the beaches and woods, around the observatories, that stink is everywhere they go. And they're not dying. You're not dying." He shook his head now, kept shaking it, the panic he'd barely been hiding oozing like a vein of oil into his eyes, his voice, his tense clenched-up hands. "You're getting stronger. Omnivorous. You're de-decaying. While us humans . . . our labs are working on it, Jessie, but if this spreads any further we're in real serious trouble."

The sun had risen higher, and a dry wind sent a whiff of solvent like a ribbon trailing under our noses. We would have stopped for a nap already, Linc and I; you get careless on watch, this many years without anything to watch for. Linc let go of Jim, pointing to the cornfield and himself and me in quick succession, and when Jim shook his head Linc grunted in exasperation and branch-scratched at our feet:

Contagious?

"We don't know. The answer could change tomorrow, it's still mutating like crazy. But I've been swimming in it, and I'm not sick." He ran a hand through his hair, stared at the ground like this was a shameful confession. "I'm not. Lisa is, Jessie. Lisa's sick. I hid her, you don't know what it's like if anyone suspects you have this, there's been violence, I had to lock her in the—Lisa's sick. Don't know if I brought it home, or . . ." His fingers grabbed at the cloth of his cuff, buttoning, unbuttoning, rolling it up and down, worrying it compulsively. "I need your help, Jessie, or she's going to die."

Something hard and sharp twisted inside my stomach. "You're lying," I said quietly, and grabbed his neck and rattled until I heard teeth scrape and snap. He was blue and gasping, curled up retching when I let him go. Jim's stick had gone flying, the rucksack lay yards away, split in two.

"I'm not—" Gasp. "—making it up, I—" Swallow, choke. "Jessie—" He retched again, scrubbing a sleeve against his mouth as he sucked in air, crouching against the ground like it might shield him from me and Linc. "Jessie, the last thing I ever told Mom and Dad was to fuck off and die, and then they went—" Cough, choke. "—went ahead and did it. And you too, and it was too late, and now Lisa, I used to hate everyone else for being so scared and now it's like I'm being punished for it over and over again, Jessie, I love you, I can't help how we are now, please don't kill me. Don't kill me."

His voice had unraveled from desperate pleading into gasping sobs, his eyes dry but grief and horror weighting down his voice so it stumbled, lollopped out of his throat: genuine sadness, unfeigned shame, the smell of it seeped out of him like that solvent-stink off the dead girl. Off Teresa. *I, me, mine, I've got, I had, I don't, I've got, me me me*. But Jim was always like that, he never apologized for it, he wanted me and Lisa to be more like that too. Stand up for yourselves. Look out for yourselves. If people call you selfish, it means they know they can't push you around. Some things really do never change.

Jim scrubbed his mouth some more, looked desperately up at me. "I've been trying to treat her," he told me, nails sinking into the dirt. "I'm running tests, see if there's a genetic weakness, something, behind this. You can help me. Just, tissue sample, a mouth swab, I have them from Lisa, myself—"

"He doesn't deserve anything from you, Jessie," Linc muttered, watching Jim flatten himself against the grass like a cat sighting a coyote. "No use for you at all until he needed something. Typical hoo. Let's go."

"Jessie. I know you must hate her, hate me, but she doesn't deserve this. Please."

Desperate, smelling not of the fear we'd kill him but that I'd turn my back on him and leave him in the dust. "I don't want to kill you, I want to make things better, for everyone—I don't know if this disease hurts your kind or not. If I help Lisa, maybe I can help—"

"Stop," I said, holding out my palm because I couldn't listen to it anymore, all that begging and pleading and cringing pouring from the tap embarrassed me so much I wanted to hurt him to make him stop, make him back into the Jim who never begged anyone anywhere for anything. *Make* him be what he was supposed to be. Just look at him, right now, thinking the exact same thing about me.

Florian couldn't eat, right before he died. I'd thought it was just old age, but a new possibility crawled beetlelike into my head and latched on with deep, sharp pincers. That girl in the woods. That girl he got so close to, right before. The sick one. Contagious? We don't know. We don't know a damned thing.

"Jessie," Linc murmured, gently rubbing my back. "There's nothing we can do here. There's nothing we can do for any human. I'm sorry. We need to go."

Sometimes I missed being human so horribly, shamefully much. I could talk about that with Florian, stupid things like missing what human food tasted like: strawberries, potato chips, ice cream. He would get upset about his children sometimes, all dead and never revived, and distract himself humming soothing bits of nonsense as we walked the woods, over and over until it had the cadence of a real song. Lisa sang to me too, a lifetime ago. Nonsensical made-up songs as she braided my hair, snuck me Corn Pops from the forbidden giant box. I could have lived on dry Corn Pops when I was three or four. Couldn't imagine the taste of Corn Pops or strawberries or any of it anymore. Or having enough hair to braid. Or a home.

I took the branch back from Linc. *Yes*, I wrote, there at Jim's feet. Laid the branch aside.

Linc sighed aloud, but his hand soothed my shoulder blades just the same. Jim pulled himself to his feet, shaking again with fear or gratitude or both, and rooted around in his jacket pockets.

"A mouth swab," he repeated, unscrewing a slender cylindrical tube and taking out what looked like a long Q-tip. "I have them from Lisa and myself too. I can compare them side by side. It might help."

I opened my mouth and he swiped quickly, daintily at the inside, dropped the sticky inky-tipped swab back in the plastic tube. I saw him shudder as he got a close glimpse of my teeth. I didn't mind. I was relying on his cowardice to keep further trouble away.

"Thank you," he said softly, as he returned the tube to his pocket. He turned to Linc. "And thank you, for . . . hearing me out."

Linc just stared back at him. There was a flash of defiance in Jim as he locked eyes with Linc and for that split second I saw the real Jim, my Jim, shooting the finger at all of us from a car going eighty-five down an abandoned road, doubling over laughing at everyone else's silent, complicit fright. Hitting back, all kinds of ways. *You don't have to listen to them, Jessie,* he told me when I was ten, after I broke town curfew for the first time just riding my bike around and Mom and Dad screamed at me for hours. *All they do is believe what they're told. In their heads you're dead right now, because someone told them if you break curfew that's it, you die. But here you are. Alive. So who're the idiots here?*

I could have been a scientist. An animal rights scientist. Find new ways to do tests without lab animals. I liked chemistry, when I was alive. Jim would've been thrilled. Did he work with rats and monkeys and all of that, not just old dead fight-stomps? I bet he wouldn't tell me if I asked. He used to lecture me about how getting insulin for diabetics was more than worth a few dead dogs. We'd argue. But he actually listened to me, heard me out before telling me I was wrong, he didn't just stand there and scream. Or pretend to agree with everything I said, like Lisa did, just to avoid even the chance of a fight.

I reached out, saw him brace himself for a blow. Touched his hand and drew back. He reached out, clasped my swollen, darkened fingers in his so delicately I knew he was imagining they'd come right off in his palm, that he'd end up holding a handful of rot and there'd be me left with only finger bones. He works enough with us to know we're not that fragile, or he should, but still there's that fear right there in his eyes. Just like everyone thinking those cornfield people are us, that they can bite you and gotcha, you're nicked, even when they know perfectly well undeath isn't catching. Just like the sad sacks, the crazies, the tireds of life, who know guns won't work and still try shooting us anyway.

"So, are you okay?" Thoroughly embarrassed, like he could hear just how absurd he sounded but couldn't help himself. "Is . . . do you need anything?"

You tell me, Jim—some real answers? A plan? A clue? Some genetically engineered cow-sized deer? How about you work on wiping out your cornfield buddies, if your bosses really want to do some pest control? I wanted to laugh but I just shook my head. Linc was gazing fixedly at a clump of catmint, waiting for this to be over.

"Will I see you again?" Jim asked.

I shrugged, pulled my hand away and pointed at him. *Up to you.* He looked sad for a minute, then just nodded. "Well . . . good-bye then, Jessie." He managed an awkward smile. "Not for good."

We watched until he was a speck against the trees and then a pinpoint. Linc took my arm and we headed for the woods.

"He'd better watch himself," he said. "Getting back wherever he's going. Billy's been sounding hungry lately."

I kept walking. Linc seemed unfazed by my silence. "Well, that doesn't happen every day, does it? Fortunately enough." He looked thoughtful. "We should've asked him just how far this has supposedly spread, shouldn't we? I know hoos get hysterical and exaggerate everything but still, he sounded like—"

"I know he could be lying, Linc, okay? You don't need to say it, I'm not stupid."

"I didn't say that, Jessie." He glanced at me. "He's hardly making up what we saw back there, is he? And if this is all an elaborate scheme to wipe us out, which we already could've guessed they wanted to do, it's a pretty weird way to go about—"

"You know I'm not stupid, Linc." I curled my arm tighter in his. "I know he could be lying about Lisa, it's not like she's gonna come barreling out here to tell me he's full of shit, I'm not completely—"

"Jessie, don't look for me to say you did the right thing, okay? I wouldn't have done it, but it wasn't my brother. Or my sister. Little late now, anyway." We were back in the concrete tunnel, stopping every few steps to rub our feet clean of cornfield stink; he scraped his toes hard against the rough gray cement, enjoying a sound scratch. "Those things in the cornfield knew him, and it explains Teresa and all the rest of it, so maybe he isn't lying . . ." Linc flung out a hand, helpless confusion creasing his face. "Hell, I don't know. Maybe it explains it too well."

I glanced down at the tunnel floor, the fleshy footprint streaks like smears of blistery butter. What was I supposed to do, break Jim's neck because he said stuff I didn't want to hear? They lie, the hoos, when they say we don't care if we turn on our own flesh and blood (unlike *them*, all their revulsion, their screaming, their hate)—it's our nightmare, just like theirs, only sometimes the hunger is just too strong to resist. And then, it's too late.

Linc pushed through the trees with an odd urgency, and it wasn't until we were on top of it that I realized what he'd been looking for. My arm, eaten and rotted down to chipped-polish nails and too-white bone, lay at the river's bend where it always had. I doffed an imaginary hat in tribute. He didn't crack a smile.

"Okay," he said, "at least he doesn't know about this. He being so specimen happy and all—"

"Linc, you saw him back there, the forest might as well be radioactive. He's not coming in here. He knows what's waiting for him."

"What did he say about the sick-stomps? That they had more muscle mass? Teresa tossed Joe halfway across the damned park. You saw her."

I saw her. We all did. Did Joe know any of this, after all that yelling and carrying on? Didn't know squat, I'd bet, because there was no way he'd keep any of this to himself after what Teresa did to him, after everything else between them—unless he'd meant to tell me, before we'd fought, and then said fuck it. But I hated Teresa too, he knew that, neither of us had ever forgiven her for Lillian; was he really pissed enough to shove something this big under his hat? Joe's anger was a flash fire, flaring up huge and bright and scorching everything in his path but when it was over, it was over: He'd give you his hand, a good word, the last of the deer liver seconds later and mean it, what Linc and everyone else didn't understand was that it really, truly wasn't personal.

That hoo-hunting fight was the only time, ever, I'd seen him carry a grudge.

"Does anyone else know about this?" Linc asked me, gazing down at my arm like it might arc up on its fingers and scuttle away. "In the gang?"

"I'm not sure." I imagined the arm as some sort of deep-water creature, the remnants of decay on the bones the barnacles. The dry waving grass stems around it as seaweed. "I don't think so."

Linc nodded. "It might be better that way. Maybe."

Maybe I shouldn't have just walked away from Joe, during the dance. He'd been sorry. I could tell. But what the hell was I supposed to do, lie about what I'd seen because he felt stupid he hadn't seen it first? I'd seen Lisa do that placating crap with Dad while we were alive, all the time, and it never helped. Screw all his stewing in it, when he was ready to listen he knew where I was; he wasn't getting any begging and pleading from me. And Linc wasn't getting any vows of silence either.

I reached into the pouch at my waist, stroked the surface of one of the lake stones; its solid smoothness felt restlessly alive somehow, all pins-and-needles, like the prickly sensation of touching a magnet covered in clusters of iron filings. I felt strangely better, a bit restored, cradling it in my palm. I was still so tired so much lately, no matter how I slept. Linc took a stone from his own pocket, tossed it idly from hand to hand, dove for it quickly when it dropped.

"Do you think we'll get sick?" I asked Linc. "I mean, sick like those things? Jim said he didn't know how the disease works in us, what if we just get a few good weeks or months and then—"

"If I do, if I get sick like that, I want you to kill me. Just knock me down and stomp until the job's done. I mean it, Jessie, no joke." He shuddered. "I'm not hanging around to turn into that."

"Only if you do the same for me."

Instead of answering Linc flung his arms around me, an

insanely beatific look on his face, and when I realized he was only lampooning Jim we were already punching and kicking in the dirt, laughing but still fighting, raggedy hostile waves of shock and exhaustion oozing out like asphalt tar in the summer heat. My lost arm went to powder under our weight, whitish-gray ash smeared all over our legs and backs. We backtracked and found a little hollow of mossy dirt among the oaks, fell asleep in it clutching lake stones in our fists. At some point I was half-awake thinking how Florian would never believe any of this, and then I thought, *Oh, yes, that's right, never mind,* and I squeezed my eyes shut around thick inky tears and went to sleep.

The next night, I went back by myself to see. Jim was nowhere to be found and no more singing, no more moaning and begging, all the cornfield hoos were dead. A couple looked like they'd dropped where they stood, but most had broken necks, stomped skulls, guts neatly torn open but none of it eaten. A pile of smaller skinned dead things lay near them, untouched. The stench rose from their bodies without stopping, not rot but a smothering, sweaty miasma like a damp toxin-steeped fog, and I had to stop to be sick before I could get away.

Who'd done this? Teresa? She was too strong to be sick, much too strong. I didn't know what to believe. Like Linc had said, now it was too late.

10

Renee didn't even thank me for the lake stones. Why had I bothered? She kept them, though, ignoring Billy's taunts about hoo-wannabes and their two-bit tombstones, and started following me everywhere, asking to be hunt buddies, wanting to go with me on watch. So whatever happened to I don't waaaaaanna learn to hunt, I can't haaaaaaaandle it today, I'm traaaauuumatized? I had no time for all this, let her go be Teresa's new best friend—if Teresa ever showed up long enough to accept the honor. The others were getting restless too, missing even the onerous nightly fetching of flesh too long dead: At least it was a routine, like something normal, though it wasn't normal at all. This new feeling, it was just a void.

Me, I kept my mouth shut because there wasn't any chance to talk. Less than a dozen of us, over fifteen hundred acres of space, and still there was no place to go without someone tagging behind you, Ben shouting, Billy bellowing, Renee pleading, Mags picking fights, everyone in everyone's business every single night and when had we all grown so damned loud? Only Joe was quiet, sullen and turning his back whenever I approached, and with no way to get away without someone dogging our steps Linc and I kept mum, quiet as he'd ever said we should be. Then one night as we were stripping a deer to the bones along came Teresa, walking in from the north road with a tin bucket swinging from one hand and something clenched tightly in the other.

"So, the prodigal leader smells fatted calf and comes scurrying back." Billy deliberately took another large bite of the liver, Teresa's favorite. "Sorry, we really woulda saved the best bits but there's just not enough to . . ."

He trailed off, startled, when he saw the box of matches in her palm, then laughed. "Well, souvenirs now. Some hoo must've dropped them. They already wet, or should I toss 'em in the drink?"

Teresa headed right past him across the old baseball field, little tremors coming and going along her arms as if the bucket were weighted with bricks. We followed, all of us, as she stopped at a cluster of benches near the riverbank. There was an old fire pit built in the center, a bare dirt square bordered by bricks; she put the bucket down and with her free hand yanked branches from the nearest trees, tooth-stripped them straight and bare, threw them into the pit until she had a good-sized pile of kindling. We just kept watching, certain this was some kind of stunt or joke.

"What are you doing, Teresa?" Joe asked, without a trace of belligerence.

Teresa fumbled with the matchbox, lips pressed together in concentration—she had lips again, grown newly full and fleshy to cover her dead grinning teeth for the first time in years. Her cheeks were fleshy too, the rot retreating, and under saplike beads of refinery-stinking sweat her skin was smooth and firm, almost springy over solid cushions of flesh. Her hair was still lank and limp but it wasn't dead straw anymore, it had stopped falling out. Her hands, still inhumanly bony, trembled badly but she kept at it until she pulled out a match, her whole body taut and twitching with hunger. A newborn's hunger.

"Teresa?" Mags said. "Put those away."

Teresa pursed her full new lips, studying the thin strip of striking paper. "Just go back to your meat."

We didn't go back to our meat. We couldn't go back to it because Teresa was trying to light a match, set a fire, and even without Ben's half-charred face to remind us we knew what fire could do. Even Renee had heard Annie's story, poor dead Annie. All those gate guards, with their flame-throwers.

"Put those down," I said, the words springing from me by themselves. "Now, or we'll take them."

Teresa gave me a long, triumphant stare. She knew I knew, I could see in her eyes she knew, and it didn't matter because she was far beyond us now, her illness making her something *other*, no need to be careful around us because she wasn't us anymore. "Try," she said.

I didn't know Linc was beside me until he took my hand, and then of all folks Renee was there too, the three of us heading for a fight before Joe grabbed and tackled me, pinning me as I flailed and cursed and spat. Renee fell back, scared, and Ben and Linc threw themselves on Teresa, grabbing for the matchbox; Teresa tossed Linc aside like trash from a speeding car and then there was the sound of lightning cracking a tree trunk in half, the sound of Ben's arm wrenched sideways and back by Teresa's clenched teeth. His hands lost their grip on her neck and he screamed and screamed.

Mags gasped out loud. Teresa bit and pulled and crunched at Ben's shoulder until I heard another snap, and then he staggered away moaning in pain and tumbled heavily to the ground. Teresa, the soul of calm, picked her matchbook up from the dirt and stood there, grinning, happy, shaking so hard with hunger pangs her rings clinked on her fingers like wind chimes.

"Anyone else?" she said.

Renee grabbed my hand like Linc had, and I pressed back without thinking. Joe stood beside us, ready to jump again if we went anywhere near Teresa. Linc crawled to where Ben lay twitching on the ground. Ben, oozing from the mouth, didn't move.

After several clumsy tries Teresa lit a match, tossed it

into the pit and watched the pile of kindling slowly flicker to life. She yanked hunks of deer meat off our abandoned carcass, speared them on another branch and held them over the flames, pacing and skirting like someone waltzing with a live grenade; the smell of roasting flesh crawled through the air and Renee started to retch. Teresa chewed greedily at every burned scrap, sucking her fingers for the grease and letting out little sated sighs. I studied every face to see who else was properly sick at the sight and who looked like they wanted a taste, just a little bitty taste, and when I growled low and threatening at nothing, I saw Joe smile. Billy growled too, confused but not wanting to be left out. Ben still hadn't moved.

Her meal complete, Teresa picked up the tin bucket and tossed it at Sam's feet, waiting; finally he grabbed it, shuffled silently to the river and back and doused the fire. I felt a weak sort of gratitude, watching it steam up and die. Some water splashed from the pit and Billy, feet dampened, jumped and shouted as if flames were curled up in the fat droplets ready to burst forth. Teresa shook her head in disgust.

"Pathetic," she sneered. "Scared of a little fire. No wonder we're stuck out here, while the Rat Patrol's roaming all over the whole county, half of Chicago—I should've known better than to come back to this hellhole. None of you could handle what I've seen. None of you could make the change."

Her voice snapped with fury but it was happy too, a high-flying manic happy like her eyes when she stared into the fire she'd made. Nobody tried to stop her, nobody got in her way as she headed for the footbridge leading to the parking lot and the outside road. Billy kicked and stomped on the bits of branch in the fire pit, reducing them to splinters.

"Careful, sweetie," Mags pleaded. "They might still be hot—"

"What the hell was that all about?" he shouted, grinding his heel into the ash. "Huh? What's wrong with that bitch?"

Billy and Mags danced on the fire pit's stone border, crushing it to powder, while everyone else gathered around Ben. I pushed my way through and found him rocking back and forth on his side, trying to hide his arm beneath him like something shoplifted.

"You okay?" I asked, knowing he wasn't. "How bad is it?"

"My arm," Ben whispered, cradling it as it crooked nearly backward from the shoulder; his teeth chattered, he was fever-warm. "I can't move it, it hurts." Linc tried, gently, to straighten it out and Ben stiffened with agony. "Don't."

"You'll live," I said, because that was how we talked to each other when we were really hurt; pity was wasted, panic fatal. "Hell, look at me—even if you lose it, you'll hunt fine."

Linc glanced at me, both of us silently thinking the same thing: Should we just tear it off, right now? It'd hurt, Ben would pass out from the pain, but he'd live. Adjust. Hunt again. We might have to, if it didn't heal. Sam looked up at both of us.

"No," he said, baring his teeth.

"It hurts," Ben repeated, and closed his eyes. "Please go away now."

We left Sam sitting with him and headed for the gazebo, appetites gone, everyone staring sidelong at everyone else for a hint of the secrets they were concealing; I heard the word *change* in murmured snatches of talk like a coin glinting in a river, pretended it meant nothing to me. Why had she done it in front of us, why didn't she just keep scavenging in private? Maybe just to show she could. Maybe it was a test, we were supposed to have been intrigued and amazed and demand to be transformed too. If this is what it does to you? I'd rather be ground into compost.

Joe held back, taking my arm, and drew me aside into the trees. He looked me in the eye for the first time since the dance.

"So I guess you know," he said. "That Teresa's . . . changed."

"I told you," I said, hard and cold. "I told you it wasn't just 'maldies. Now let go of my goddamned arm."

"I didn't know what the hell they were," Joe hissed, sinking his fingers in harder. "Or if it had anything to do with Teresa. I've been following her, trying to figure out what she's up to, she's been buddying up to the Rat Patrol just like

I said—I told you that, didn't I, you can go check for yourself if you think I'm such a liar. Inside that abandoned church out on the highway, the big gray building. There's a bunch of them there right now."

"You're sure it was them? You got close enough to—"

"Jessie, I was in the Rat for a good decade or three, I think I know Rommel and Ron and their little psycho inner circle by sight. They were all out there, just cooling their heels, a little country vacation. I left before they saw me." He leaned in closer. "And tell you what, they all had that same smell to them. Like she does. That same look, like their faces were filling out again. You couldn't miss it, not from yards away."

He paused, letting that sink in. I stared right back, letting him make whatever he wanted of the silence, and when he smelled the animosity on me the guitar chords in his head started up sharp, angry, loud.

"You're getting fucking paranoid," he said.

"Hard not to, when you've been flat-out lying to me—"

"Jessie, I didn't *know* what they were, okay, and I just goddamned told you what I do know. Whatever this is, Teresa's got it, the Rat smell like they've got it." His grip loosened, eased, and he slid his hand away. "And you said you've been feeling sick."

I just kept staring at him. I couldn't think how the hell else to react to that.

"What are you talking about?" I demanded.

"You've been tired all the time, right? Feeling hot? Feverish? Under the weather?" He was looking down at me not in triumph, no gotcha glances, but genuine concern. "You're eating okay, you don't smell all that different but—"

"*All that* different?" I shoved him, I didn't want a fight, not another one like the last one, but he was revving up to deserving it. "So who's the crazy paranoid here? Yeah, I'm goddamned tired and worn out, I have a right to be: Teresa's acting nuts, Renee's up my ass, you're always pitching a fit, those sick hoos are all over our woods like beetles on a feeder—"

"I took care of them," Joe said. "Don't worry."

Those bodies in the cornfield. Another question answered. Maybe. "All that different? I wanna know what you mean, 'all that' different—"

"Jessie, it's like I keep telling you, I just want you to be okay." He folded his arms, stepping back when I tried to push him, not letting me set him off. "If you're just tired and that's all then fine, great, but Teresa's watching you, I told you she's got you singled out—"

"So the best way to make sure I'm okay is to make up some bullshit story about 'maldies and—"

"*I told you*, I didn't know what the fuck they were! You were right, they smelled human, they bleed red, I should've guessed it myself, I'm sorry!" He curled his fist to strike out at an oak in frustration; his arm hovered clenched and suspended in midair like a stop-motion frame, then he slowly let it drop. "You were right. And Teresa, the Rat, I know they know something, they know a lot. All Teresa ever let slip once was that it has something to do with a lab."

I nodded, calm and easy like this didn't signify anything in particular to me. Joe bared his teeth, irritated as he always was when he couldn't be my expert on everything. "The Rat's all over Gary and Burns Harbor and everywhere else the scientists are meant to be, they'd know all about this better than she ever would. Maybe that's another reason she wants in with them, they can all—so who the fuck asked you two in on the conversation? Get the hell out of here before I crack your little skulls in half!"

Linc and Renee turned and walked away; I saw Linc's sardonic expression, Renee's long sharp mother-of-pearl teeth scraping and grinding at her lip, and then they went back through the trees arm in arm.

Joe sneered at their retreating backs, spitting in their wake, and I rubbed at a temple starting to ache. Yeah, look here, Joe, this means I'm a plague-dog for sure, it can't just be you're all a goddamned pain in my head, my neck, my ass. I was holding a string of half-truths and unfinished stories fragile as Florian's dusty powdery bones, a paper chain dropped in a puddle, but I had to figure it all out because hoos were getting sick, when they got sick they always took it out on us, what if they decided to try to burn us out, if we all—enough. Enough decline, enough dropping into dust, enough of everyone falling ill. There had to be a way to stop it.

"I don't know much either," I said. That was nothing but the truth.

What if this really was just as bad for us as hoos, if we all died? Like Lisa might die, and Jim? Joe. Linc. Ben—I shoved that last thought out of my head, you couldn't kill anyone just with teeth, not for trying. Ridiculous. Joe was right, he'd heal up.

Joe actually smiled at me, the proud, almost proprietary smile of someone who thinks you have a problem only they can solve. "We'll figure it out, Jessie," he told me. "One way or another, we'll get the jump on Teresa. If she thinks this is gonna be good for her, all this, whatever it is, she's in for a surprise."

When Teresa made us take out Lillian, after Teresa jumped her for the gang leadership and blinded her and Happy Tsarina's first royal decree was making us two stomp her, we did as told; we let Florian and Annie and Sam kiss her good-bye and dragged her far out in the woods where nobody'd have to hear or watch, she was sobbing, she'd lost all her courage when she lost her remaining eye, *Don't do it, you fucking backstabbers, you're happy about this, I don't deserve to die again. Don't do it. Don't.* Joe kept talking to her all the way to the clearing, calm, quiet, no furious guitar chords and no sneering at her soft-headed hoocow pleading. *We're doing you a favor, Lillian. You can't hunt this way. Can't fight. You'd die slow. We're making it quick. You'd do it for us. You know you would.*

"We'll figure it out," I repeated. "What Teresa's up to. This sickness. All of it."

"Together," said Joe.

Lillian just stood there in the clearing, waiting, no matter all her hoocow pleading and sniveling she wouldn't lie down to die, we'd have to knock her down. We'd have to fight. Joe nodded slow in renewed respect and I started backing away, backing away and now he was grabbing me instead, I couldn't do it, I couldn't do this to her. *Yes you will,* he told me, still quiet, still calm, so much merciless pity in his eyes I couldn't stand looking at him, at Lillian. *Yes you will. Because you're not leaving me to do this all by myself, Jessie, not if you love me. I'm not shouldering this one all by myself.*

"I'm not sick," I told Joe. "I'm just tired. Sick and tired. Of everyone and everything."

Joe nodded. Sadness flittered fast and evasive across his face.

"I know the feeling," he said.

Joe, I can't do this, I can't stomp a blind—

Lillian's my friend. Not yours. And she won't last like this. That's why I'm doing it, not for Teresa. But I'm not living with doing it all alone.

So we both did it. Quick. She started crying again when we were on her but that didn't last long. Afterward we sat in the woods together, far from her body, not saying anything. So that's that, was all I kept thinking. That's that for that. And now there's no there there. One thing when it's an out-of-control pickup truck that does it, another when it's me. Us. Joe was right. Let it be both of us.

Where have you been, Joe? You and Teresa?

"We'll find out what all this really means," he said. "Okay?"

I nodded and smiled, the reluctant sort of smile you're supposed to give someone to show they've cheered you up, and we went back to the gazebo together in silence. The bugs still chittered and clung to the remains of his slowly disintegrating leather jacket, his face was still sunken and decayed; he looked the same, he smelled the same. But things were different. I could feel it. And I knew I wouldn't figure out why unless I did it without him.

11

Ben died that night. We found him huddled stiff and motion-less next to Sam, the arm Teresa bit gone black to the shoulder; it was charred-looking like his face but sticky and disintegrating, like tar bubbling up from asphalt. The bugs had deserted his body and a smell like human flesh, cooked flesh, seeped from his skin. We dragged him to Florian's spot on the hill and left him there: me, Linc, Joe, Billy and Sam, who'd been Ben's best friend. Sam took Ben's old fedora hat, the only remnant of him, and stood there turning it over and over in his hands, wringing it like a dishcloth.

"She's dead, Sam," Billy reassured him, with vigorous nodding from Mags. "The bitch might be flexing her muscles lately—and I'd like to know where she *got* muscles—but even she still needs to sleep. We'll track her down, if she doesn't come back, and then she's gone. Slowly."

We all murmured our agreement, Joe included—he really had thought Ben would get up again, he looked just as shocked as anyone. We all knew, inside, that we wouldn't see Teresa again. We should've let Sam take the watch shift, so he could go mourn in solitude, but Linc and I had bigger priorities lying at the wood's edge and we left him sitting on the side of the hill, still turning that rag of a hat around in his hands. I gave Linc Joe's version of events as soon as we were out of earshot.

"Jim won't be there," Linc warned me, as we followed the Sullen Trail as fast as we could. "He'll be holed up in that lab playing with his little samples, God knows what else he knows about all this that we didn't get to—"

"I'm not looking for him, for Christ's sake," I snapped, kicking aside ancient, petrified horse clods as I walked. *None of you could make the change.* Jim "didn't know" what this disease did to us? I could help him out there, save for those few hunger pangs Teresa was about as weak and delicate as an Olympic athlete. "Who we should be looking to talk to is the Rat but not if they're anything like Teresa now, we can't fight them off by ourselves—I just want to go back to the cornfield, see what's there now. See if anything's there."

"Yeah, well, you won't find anything, even Joe the great all-seeing prophet made that clear—if he told the truth about killing them himself. I wouldn't even believe they were dead except you saw it." Linc kicked at the clods in turn, expression sour. "Well, Joe or someone did your brother and all his scientist friends a huge favor, didn't he? No more disgusting sick hoos wandering around, needing feeding—"

"Because Jim would look just that panicked if those were the only ones." We'd reached the turnoff to the Sunlit Trail, a skinny hilly thread of a footpath that shortcut through the darkest parts of the woods; I had to struggle for balance climbing up it with just one arm, Linc reaching out at intervals to steady me. The trees bowed inward and a comfortingly damp, fungal stink surrounded us like a tunnel. "Right so far, isn't he, about this being a lot worse for humans than us—did Teresa look sick at all to you? Other than in the head?"

"You really think we'd get the full story on anything from a human? Family or no family? Don't go in too far, Jessie, you'll drown in the sea of bullshit." We reached the summit of the trail's steep first hill, collecting mud, mats of dead leaves and rain-dampened dog crap with every step. "And the sad part is, I'd even believe him before I do Joe—"

"Linc, this he wasn't expecting, trust me. He thought Ben would get better." I felt weird and guilty, dissecting Joe's talk with anyone else. "We all thought Ben would get better—"

Linc let out a brusque laugh. "I didn't," he said, nearly stumbling over a tree root. "I didn't. I could see it in his eyes. And that means this *is* bad for us, Jessie, at least for some of us, whether your brother knows it or not. And maybe it's better if he doesn't, because he said right out he's all about wiping us off the map and screw all his talk about 'changing his mind' and 'making things better,' if he really thinks something's out there killing hoos and making us stronger, more adaptable—"

"And he does." I pulled twigs off a dead gray branch, feeling both glum and foolish. I'd wanted to believe Jim when he said he didn't want to kill us, that he just wanted to try to help Lisa, figure out why this was happening, but if humanity's shit really was hitting the fan he'd hardly stand on untested principles, now would he? I wouldn't, in his shoes. "Whatever Teresa's got in her, that she could do that to Ben? Maybe that's something else he's trying to isolate—"

"Are you sure Jim never ran into Teresa?"

I shrugged. "He could have, if he's been out here looking for me so much. Or Joe, or anyone, though I don't know why they wouldn't just kill him where he stood. I don't know where Joe's been, I don't know if he's been with Teresa, I don't know what anyone else knows . . ." I scraped my fingers down the branch, its dry ash-colored bark peeling away in flakes. "I don't know a damned thing."

But I knew who might. Joe was right, the Rat were all over the place, all over the hoo-towns and lab-lands helping things fall apart, they weren't just sitting around the ass-end of nowhere waiting for the rest of the world to come to them—and why, especially now, would they give a damn for a half-crippled country cousin and her dumbass questions? You want your answers, bitch, go to the cities and beaches and look for yourself. Not that you'll be walking out of Rat turf to do that—we're all pumped up lately, high on the hoo-germs, wanna have ourselves a little fun with the weak sisters. A one-armer and a stringbean, trying to fight off any number of them by ourselves? Might as well just strike Teresa's matches on our heads and call it a day.

"I think we have to go to church," I said. "Rat or no Rat."

Linc laughed again, and clapped my shoulder. "Why do you think we're going down the Sunlit? It's a straight shot from here to the highway. At the cornfield, you have to loop all the way around."

The church was a big brooding two-story box, gleaming eggshell white peeled down to a dirty gray cinderblock yolk; there was a plain rusting cross on the flat roof, window holes framed in shards of pink stained glass, a letter-dropping marquee reading JUDG NG BY CHU ATTEND NCE, H VEN WON'T BE CROW. That used to be another hoo myth, that we were magically unable to set foot in churches. Nobody out front, and as we crept from the cluster of elms near the roadside into the church parking lot we didn't see anything inside. Steeling ourselves, we flung open the doors.

Empty, no Rat traces. Unless you counted the mess all over the floor, that is, the slick smear of dried fat and blood and human-smelling body parts scraped down to the bones. Human flesh, and the faintest lingering traces of human fear—instead of breaking necks right off the Rat might have dragged them here to die, unable to resist having their own sacrificial altar. They were boring that way, sometimes. Nose-twitching hints of dust and mice and, everywhere, that chemical stench, Teresa's stench, strong as a soaked cotton ball against the nose. Linc bared his teeth in disgust, then drooled; we hadn't eaten in a good three hours and the reminder of meat was taunting us. Nothing fresh here, though, and all the bones were sucked dry.

Another human body lay near the altar steps, most of its head missing and the rib cage scooped clean; it had shat itself. A lot. Guess I would have too. Other than our footsteps the place was tensely, heavily quiet, like a sky right before a thunderstorm. Linc poked around some of the pews, motioned to a side door leading to a chapel, choir dressing room, who knew.

"Horrible stink back there," he whispered. "It's oozing under the door. Maybe they're—"

"WHOOOOO'S THAT EATING FROM MY BOOO-OOWWWWL!"

Linc and I let out bellows of surprise. Screaming laughter echoed from the eaves to the pews, drowned out by a chorus of crashing stomping footsteps and a symphony of mental noise, horn and cymbal and the deranged screech of strings. With a volley of ululating war whoops Rommel hurled himself over the balcony, plummeted through the air and landed just shy of the altar with a thud that would have shattered a hoo's ankles, and back, and pelvis; another half dozen Rats followed like paratroopers in his wake as he rose to his feet, all six five of him swathed in tatters of black leather bristling with bent spikes and rusty nails. Carny, always an idiot, nearly impaled himself on a music stand as he came crashing down in the choir pit. Ron grabbed him, slammed his skull against the floor for being so stupid and rolled from the altar steps; after a wet smack on Linc's forehead he tossed him aside and shook me like a stuffed toy.

"Jess-ay! Baby! *Kiddo!*" Ron finally let me go, eyes lingering on the stump of my left shoulder. "What the hell are you doing here?"

I looked from one face to another, familiar from a dozensome of their little countryside deer-hunt vacations: Rommel, the big chieftain; Ron, his lieutenant, small and wiry and crazy like a rabid maggoty ferret; Adriana, massive and bristling with teeth; Stosh, still in his voltage-blackened electrician's overall, Union Local 942 cap jammed on his head; bullet-headed, thick-skulled Carny. The Rat Patrol's inner circle, such as it was, plus a rotter newbie Ron called Dembones, crouched drooling on the floor with a length of motorcycle chain wrapped leashlike around his neck. He just let himself be dragged along, grinning, teeth jagged and gleaming with febrile spit. His undead brain hadn't come in right, it looked like: It happens every now and then, you get some that revive but are too damaged to know how to hunt, how to fend for themselves. Usually they just starve or get stomped quick for their own good, but the Rat sometimes took them as pets. They could afford the feeding expense.

"I could ask the same question," I said. "What the hell's the brains of the outfit"—I gave Carny and Dembones a pointed glance—"such as they are, still doing holed up out here?"

The church's front door flew open. Renee stood there in the doorway, gaping, and when she saw, and smelled, the Rat and the messy remains of their dinner she whipped around so fast her bones clicked. Not fast enough, though; Stosh got her arm twisted behind her, dragging her inside, and threw her into a pew.

"I heard you and Joe talking," she said, glum and dejected. "And Linc." Then pressed her lips shut when Rommel and Ron loomed over her, leering.

"Beautiful," said Stosh, producing an agitated palmful of soot as he rubbed his charred face. "So what's that bug-faced cretin found out that he's blabbing to the whole goddamned—"

"Shut it," Rommel muttered, and clapped Renee on the back so hard she gasped and doubled over. "Of course he talks to the family, he's a good boy—you didn't have to sneak in, baby, there's always room for another pretty face. What's your name?"

Renee just sat there wide-eyed. Coward. "Renee," I said, "this is Rommel. Rommel, Renee. Say hello to the nice Rommel, Renee."

Renee mumbled something unintelligible. Ron took one last bite of his midnight snack, a fresh-torn human arm, and gallantly threw her the rest; she let it fall at her feet, cringing. Ron shrugged, scooped it up again and broke off bits like a candy bar. "Plenty for everyone, you know," he said around a mouthful. "Just bagged a couple refinery workers with car trouble—"

"What about the police escorts?" Linc said. Dembones chortled happily at nothing, slapping a palm into his drool as it spattered the linoleum. "The guard posts?"

"You haven't heard?" Rommel snorted with laughter. "They're cutting back. Budgetary priorities, don'tcha know, enough trouble keeping the rich folks' towns and roads locked up tight without wasting money on the dregs. They get escorts in and out of the refinery, but once they're on the road, they're on their own." He threw himself into a pew, stretching out his long tinder-stick legs. "Lotta new 'security breaches' lately, that's the word. Hard enough plugging those holes without diverting patrols to work every steel mill, brewery, housing project, factory, backstreet—besides, they can't totally reroute, can they? All them roads and highways, they gotta squeeze together to get around the bottom of Lake Michigan, feed into the city. And there we are."

The severed arm looked weirdly pathetic in Ron's grip, like any moment it would start waving and signaling its buddies for help. "Hours old," I noted, glancing down at it. "Maybe days. Nothing like the taste of good, aged meat, is there, Ron? But you sure you wouldn't rather have that cooked?"

The sudden silence was like a quick, painful pinch. Then Rommel grinned. "We're there. All the way down to Hammond, all the way up to South Wacker Drive. Just make sure your car doesn't break down and your front door's bolted and all your pets are inside and you have a basement to hide in, and you might be okay. If we're in a good mood." He leaned forward with a hand on my arm, his new solvent smell and the sticky sap-bead touch of his skin oozing into my senses. "That's hundreds of us, y'know, so many, I lose count—hell of a lot more than you find in those little pissant tribes, those country-cousin chickenshit clans with a few half-wits living off dog and deer and smart-assing like they know a thing about how life really works."

His fingers tightened, gripping and gripping so I couldn't wrench away. Renee rose from her pew and Stosh pushed her back down; Linc kept watching, judging his moment. There wouldn't be a good moment. "You're right," I said. "I don't know much about life outside. If I did, maybe I'd understand why such a big bunch of bad-ass undeads seem so proud of looking and smelling and eating like a lot of freaks of nature, eating the same as a lot of soft weak little hoos—"

Rommel hit me and I fell, Linc jumping to the rescue a second too late. "—weak little hoos," I repeated, wiping the black ooze from my mouth. "Lotta folks looking and acting all human lately, all of a sudden. Like Teresa. Doesn't make sense at all, you know?" Was any of this working? Not exactly a shock if they kept me in the dark, but I didn't need a busted jaw on top of it. "Or didn't you know about Teresa? Joe could tell you—"

"Aaaahhh, Joe." Stosh quit fondling Renee's hair long enough to spit in my direction. "Mr. Genius, Mr. Superspy, your old man. He came sniffing round here the other day, wouldn't even come inside he was so a-skeered—always did think he could piss in the big kids' sandbox without anyone else smellin' it. Your old man charity case. I remember him from the old days, all tongue no teeth, talk talk talk then turn tail and run—ain't even a damned hoo, he's what a hoo craps out!"

Stosh and Carny and Adriana hooted like he'd told an actual joke. I smiled at Stosh. "That's real nice," I said, "but it's not an answer. So you don't know anything? Then I guess for all the talk, you're as backassward ignorant as he is."

Stosh just sat there, letting the silence build up around us like steam in a shower. His face, once so charred Ben was a beauty next to him, was filling in again, cheeks and chin regrowing beneath the huge scab of blackened burns.

"Do you know what we can do to you now?" he said, softly.

"I saw someone die that way tonight," I said. "I know."

The steam heat kept building. Then Rommel whistled, and I saw the balcony above us slowly fill up as more Rat emerged from the shadows: rotten faces, half-eaten faces, faces once stripped to the bone by drowning or burning or decades aboveground and even from a floor down they all looked restored, skin taut and plumped up and all rosy and amber and brown. Almost human-looking, some of them; if not for that smell of death and motor oil, they could have passed. They leaned on the broken railings with newly fleshy arms, waiting for their signal to jump. Or just enjoying the show.

"Boo," said Rommel.

"So is it true?" I asked, taking one of the pews. "The plague, the sickness. Don't pretend you don't know what I mean. Did they inject you with something, those labs? Use you for research? Or did this all start spreading on its own?"

Rommel sat down beside me and smiled, the smile you give a toddler who just used a word the wrong way trying to sound grown up. "Y'know, Jessie, you wouldn't know it stuck out in Cloudcuckooland like you are, out of touch with everything, but this is way beyond what any damned lab can control."

"I'm not sure their scientists know that either," Linc said.

"No, they probably don't. Typical hoo antics." He leaned closer, the badges strung round his neck—police, fire, a state trooper or two—clinking like wind chimes. "Can't follow an eight ball into the corner pocket, the lot of them. Okay. So, if you really wanna know so bad—a month or two ago, see, we start seein' undeads walking around looking a little funny, kinda tired, kinda draggy, skin all hot and clammy like they're running a fucking hoo-fever. Dusty, young rotter, didn't seem to matter. So, whatever, suck it up and keep on going. Then they started looking kinda—Ron, for Chrissake hand that over, I'm starving." He grabbed part of the too-old arm from Ron, started munching away. "Looking kinda funny. Sorta clammy, and then like the flesh was growing on 'em, not decaying. New muscle. New fat. New skin. Then, little while after that, we start finding these hoos walking around looking messed up bad, rotted from the inside out. Can't figure out what the hell it is. The undeads are looking more alive. And the living are walking around looking dead. Hmmmm, we say, what signify this?"

He tapped a finger against the soft hollow of my nose.

"Interesting coincidence, both those things happening so close together, don'tcha think? 'Specially round these parts, all those damned scientists prowling around the beaches, the woods, those fortresses of labs they got set up? Maybe whatever it is was always out there, like, latent, and something made it start to spread. Maybe it's one of their experiments gone wrong—they spray it all over where they know we are, like pesticide, and then we end up bringing it back home to them."

He snapped his fingers at Stosh, who scowled, shuffled over to the pile of hoo-remnants near the altar, brought him back hunks of dead flesh Rommel nearly swallowed whole. Just like Teresa, wanting her little snacks. "*One* of their experiments?" I said. "Or many? How d'you even know it's the same disease that—"

"Don't." Rommel shrugged, mumbling around another mouthful. "No idea. Couldn't tell ya. More to the point, dear sweet Jessica, who the hell cares?" He gulped down the last of his meal, licked his fingers, smiled. "'Cause I mean, as you can clearly see, our own prognosis is a little bit better than any damn human's."

He flexed a bicep, letting me see the solidly forming muscle under pinky pale skin, the slow throb of a vein snaking underneath. The blood in them was darker than a hoo's but it was still real bluish blood, not the tarry black mess a true undead bled when cut, and up close under the chemical stink was the smell of human flesh, cooked to a turn. Ben's death smell. As if he saw my thoughts—and maybe he did—Rommel smiled wider.

"Getting cozy with the meat?" someone shouted from the balcony. "C'mon, Rommel, you promised us a show."

"Rommel's *all* show," drawled another, unfamiliar voice. "Strut here, strut there, promise all that good mayhem and leave us spitting out pieces of steel-town chicken crap—"

Rommel made a wet, crunching screech like a tiger splitting through thighbone, and the crowd retreated from the railing.

Linc sat down and slipped his fingers around my arm.

"Rotted from the inside out," he repeated. "We heard it's spreading pretty fast—"

Rommel threw his head back and roared with laughter, Dembones barking in excited response. "Pretty fast? Yeah, unless you think a forest fire moves slow—the hoos are shitting themselves, they don't know where the fuck this came from either, though I *hear tell* the trouble started at that lab over in Gary, by Chanute Beach. Me, I wouldn't know, I just go to the beach to hang out, keep the rot from setting in too fast. It's true what they say about the sands up there, y'know, they keep you young—but then it's our own Mother Earth, isn't it, the beaches. They say. Not that you hoobillies out here would know anything about that either."

The story's always been that something happened on the shores of Lake Michigan, thousands of years ago, something that altered the sands or the nearby soil or the atmosphere to make the dead start coming back to life. They say. Another reason the scientists swarm around the beaches like blowflies on feeders. Maybe it was a meteor, crapping out extraterrestrial bits and pieces that hitched a ride here on the Ice Age glaciers, then penetrated deep into the dunes themselves. Or meteoric debris or radiation, infecting the air, making things mutate. Hoos used to think everything about us was down to radiation. If they're right, who knows how it spread. Who knows why whatever was in that meteor, if it was that, yanked us all out of a sound sleep and up from underground—the scientists sure as shit don't and you were never allowed to ask. We never talked about it in earth science, never did a damned thing but sit there listening to meandering blither-blather about igneous, sedimentary, metamorphic rocks.

"I know all about it," I said. "Just like you. I just don't know what the half of it means. And you don't either."

Rommel kept on grinning, his teeth still just like ours even if the rest of him wasn't. "Yeah? Well, we're both still one up on Hooville either way. Can you imagine if they did this to themselves? Seriously? Trying to get rid of us? That's what I'll never understand about humans, how they waste everything. Themselves included. I mean, it's just pathetic, how they all walk around acting like they actually got world enough and time."

Renee slid down her pew away from Stosh. Adriana was waiting on the other side, all gleaming teeth and bladelike joints. Dembones licked Renee's hand, then tamped his teeth down just hard enough to make her jump back. The lab at Chanute Beach. Where Jim worked. *Us humans are in trouble, Jessie. It's mutating like crazy. Mutating like it just got blasted by a meteor.* So just how much help did you all give it, Jim?

"So how'd you get it?" I asked.

"Fuck knows," said Ron, lounging on the altar steps. "Rommel here, he got it first. Big leader, like always. Then Irina, and Phoebe"—he jerked his chin toward the ceiling, at a couple of Rat I'd never met—"then Adriana, then a couple more of us, and pretty soon we were all staggering around tired, hot, hoo-shitty, and then, just like that, it all got better. A lot better. Seriously, I tell you, kid, I feel . . ." He flung out his arms. "Magnificent."

Mag-nif-i-cent. Perfectly pronounced, every consonant needle-sharp, just to show me his tongue and larynx had made a triumphant return even if he still deigned to speak our dialect. "Teresa's got it," I said.

Ron shrugged. "Bully for her."

"She killed one of us," I said. "Just by biting him. She did that."

Rommel smiled again, slow and sharky. "Yeah," he said, looking happy, looking proud, his eyes boring straight through me. "We do that."

He twitched a little, looking strangely worn out all of a sudden, his smile fading. "Carny, get me more of that meat, I'm hungry."

"You're always hungry," Carny snarled, stomping over to the altar again and hefting an entire corpse over his shoulder. Walking too swift, too easy, no more stumbling and staggering on half-rotted legs; his calves were solid, thick, as wholly restored as Rommel's arms. "Don't know what the hell's wrong with you, ate two whole goddamned deer by yourself just three hours ago, fuck-all for the rest of us, and—"

"I'm hungry!" Rommel roared, teeth clenched and fists shaking like they ached to split Carny's face straight open. "Fucking bring it here *now!*"

Dembones snapped at Carny's hand as he threw Rommel the meat and Carny spat in disgust, at which of them I couldn't have said. Rommel dove straight in, tearing off ribbons of gut that smelled like they'd been sitting there for days; Renee watched him in transfixed queasiness and then turned away. I saw a split second of what looked almost like worry pass over Ron's face, a quick brow-furrow and dark little glance. Linc's hand tightened on my arm.

"Joe said Teresa wants to join up with you again," Linc said.

"Like I said, bully for her." Ron chortled. "We got no use for that bitch. Not anymore. Too damned stuck on herself—"

"Has *he* got this?" I asked.

Ron started laughing harder, almost rocking back and forth in mirth right where he sat. *"Him?* Your half a boy? That piece of shit washout that couldn't track a hoo a mile without losing him, couldn't get in fifty yards of a city gate without pissing himself about the flamethrowers—"

"Ron, for the love of Christ just kill them already." Adriana tugged on Dembones's chain, her voice all guttural grunts; her throat had been cut clean through, the windpipe bone-white and pristine against the mess of her neck. Her brain radio was a double bass slowly splintering under a hammer. "I don't wanna be stuck out here all night."

"—or getting all no, no, *I* can't kill a bitty kiddie, I'm too sweet and good to go after an old grandma, I can't do this I can't do that I'm no goddamned use to anyone except dumbass new-rotters who'll believe anything I tell them about myself, fuck no, Jessie, that loser ain't got it." Ron threw a few uneaten fingers at Adriana, who hissed in reply, then gave me a downright gentle smile. "He thinks you do, though. He said so."

"There's a lie." Linc was bristling, a terrier trying to intimidate a Doberman; less than no interest in defending Joe, but he'd seen the look on my face. "Like you'd ever even listen to him, give him the time of night outside his dreams—"

"Oh, we listen when we feel like it, bone-bag—don't matter who it is, where they're from, we'll listen to anyone who's got an interesting story to tell." Sated, for the moment at least, Rommel clasped his hands comfortably behind his head. "We ain't prejudiced. We like everybody's fairy tales. We really like this one. We like the ones we can test for ourselves, see if they're true or not."

They were grinning at me now, Dembones included, because we'd all known from the start how this little interview would end. Ron pulled himself from the altar. Rommel rose from his pew. I looked up to the balcony, for respite, and saw another row of eager faces and fixed smiles like masks on sticks.

"You been tired lately, Jessie?" Ron asked. "Kinda hot? Kinda feverish? Like Teresa was? That's the first phase of it. Then your appetite starts shifting—"

"Fuck you," I snarled back. "I can't eat that age-old shit." I jerked my head toward the altar, the pillaged hoo-remains. "I'm normal, I'm not sick, I'm not some half-hoo laboratory freak—"

"You sure?" Rommel said. "You too, 'maldie? Bone-bag? You really sure?"

"Then your appetite starts shifting," said Ron, like he'd never been interrupted. He was rolling up his sleeves, slowly, revealing the new flesh easing out old rot. "And you get strong, even before the muscle starts showing you get so damned strong. Pound anybody into the pavement, the dust, that you wanna. Anybody getting on your nerves. Standing in your way."

A slow foot-tapping rhythm started against the balcony floor, and they all took it up one by one until the gallery was dancing for our flesh. Whose bright idea had this been? Oh, right, mine. All that new hoo-muscle. A one-armer, a string-bean, a 'maldie know-nothing. Renee gulped and tried to crouch down in her pew. Carny, who'd been pacing back and forth seething for the talk to stop, strutted up to Linc and punched him square in the chest. Linc flew backward, clutching a pew arm to keep from falling.

"Hey!" Carny shouted. "*Hey!* This Horton here? Huh? You Horton?"

"You know my name," Linc said, with bland politeness. "My name's Linc."

"*Hey!* You Horton? This little Horton the Wannabe Hoo?" Carny shoved him harder, making him stagger. "This the Horton who prances around eating his squirrel sandwiches 'cause he doesn't have the balls for a real hunt?" He slammed one bloated, greenish fist into another with a hatred you could smell. "Listen to you. '*My* name's Linc.' Aren't you cute. So is it hoo you won't eat, or just hoocow?"

Linc shook his head. "Someone thinks *we're* wanting hoodom," he said, chatting all calm at me and Renee like Carny wasn't still there in his path, seething, boiling over for a fight. "Someone's getting on *us* about what we eat, with their dead meat. Cooked flesh. Old scraps. Garbage guts. Pathetic." Grinning now, Linc was, as he walked around Carny right up into Rommel's face. "Sick and pathetic."

Laughing coolly as you please, he started walking back up the aisle. He didn't even turn when he heard Carny screeching dementia behind him, just let himself get kicked square in the back and go sprawling to the floor. Ron and Rommel screamed laughing, clapping Carny on the back as he roared and pumped his fists like he'd just conquered Normandy. Linc shrugged and pulled himself to his feet.

"If you want it," Linc said, and threw himself at Carny. Carny and Ron got him pinned in the aisle, one hitting, one kicking. Renee stumbled to the rescue from behind and got a motorcycle chain snapped whip-hard in her face; she fell screaming, clutching her cheek in her palm, and Dembones knelt down laughing, stroking the chain links of his own leash slicked with smears of Renee's skin. The sudden glint of eager, sharp intelligence in his eyes, as he cooed over his handiwork, decided me: fair game.

I grabbed the chain and whipped the other way, hoping for a clean neck snap, and Dembones reeled me in like a cat toy on a string, jumping on my back and pounding until my ribs crunched broken into my useless lungs. Fighting the new strength in him was like trying to toss a lightning strike back out of my body, trying to waltz with a bank safe crushing my chest, and I wrenched myself back and forth, kicking, punching, snapping my teeth at anything in range—and then all that iron and steel suddenly melted into puff pastry, he was beneath me and I pounded and punched at the flabby dough of his face with no idea of how I'd flipped him. Dembones wailed in protest, and Rommel stumbled toward us, grabbing Dembones's chain and holding up a hand. Ron pulled back from Linc, instantly obedient, and Linc loosened the arm he'd wrapped around Carny's neck. Rommel grinned.

"Family pet's off limits," he told me, patting Dembones's sides possessively. "Want some more fight, though? Take it."

More fight. Yes, I wanted some more fight. There was something inside me like a pain, stronger than the stabbing of my ruined rib cage and I thought, *This* is the curiosity that killed the cat: that sudden need to know, have I really got it? Could I outrun that freight train a second time? Let's find out. I smiled at Adriana, who slid from her perch next to Stosh and strolled slowly up to me. Carny, panting with humiliated rage, bared his teeth at Rommel and got a shrug in return.

"Okay," Carny murmured, his voice the low slow growl of a dog about to spring. "Not funny."

He fell on Renee. Linc jumped Stosh, rolling toward us in a tumbleweed of arms, legs and open jaws. Rommel had pulled back completely, Dembones at his side, watching and testing his crew. Renee yanked Carny's arm backward until it snapped, and he dropped her with a furious howl; Ron dragged her like a wheelbarrow, her scalp in shreds. Stosh pounded on Linc, got his neck square in his teeth and crunched. There was a loud, snapping crack, and Linc fell limp to the floor and didn't move.

My vision was a sudden blur, seeing that, but I made a grab for Adriana's throat all the same. She bent back my arm, almost giggling, then pinned me flat on my back and started punching. I was a crazy thing underneath her, legs and arm flying like I was breaking out of that underground box all over again, and it did me no damned good. Renee, a fish convulsing in Ron's net, screamed encouragement between punches, and Carny bellowed obscenities even louder and the balcony Rat were in a stomping frenzy, I was going deaf, I would shoot straight out of my skin hard as Adriana's fist meeting my face if the noise all didn't stop, *stop!* Carny loomed over me, ready to stomp my head to teeth and tissue, then he was suddenly gone with a howl, and a crunch, and silence.

I spat bile, gasping, whipping my head from side to side as the thick steel bands of Adriana's legs tightened and squeezed. She punched my arm, my head, flipped me face-down on the linoleum with my spine twisted and my broken ribs a bed of nails. She couldn't break my back. If I got out of this alive I'd still be stomped, just like Lillian, because the Flies wouldn't shoulder a cripple. She was going to break my back.

I was half-blind from exhaustion and panic, getting only crazy formless snapshots as I tried to twist away: Renee crawling moaning to a pew, holding her tattered head, Ron circling us like a wrestling coach dying to join in, Stosh standing in a strange grim silence. Rommel scratching Dembones idly behind the ears, all the time in the world. Screaming, I sank teeth into Adriana's arm, and she grabbed my shoulders and slammed my face full force into the lino. I was gone for crucial seconds as she twisted my arm immobile and got her other hand around my neck, and the gallery was screaming and I awoke just long enough to wait for . . . welcome oblivion—

Rommel let out a shrill cry of victory, and the rafters echoed as the Rat all picked up the sound. And for a half-second, no more, Adriana turned and forgot herself in that flood of impending glory, loosening her grip just enough so

I could use a sudden, enraged new surge of strength to push back around and bite her arm, sinking in until I heard a lovely, splintering crunch. She bucked backward, falling hard on her ass trying to shake me off, and I rose up, threw her face forward, planted my soles on her back and jumped. As her spine broke there was no gunshot crack, just a soft thick sound like an egg carton crumpling underfoot, like peanut brittle crumbling in a hoo's teeth. The balcony gasped. Then they laughed.

She was done, there was no need for more, but I bit and sliced into her cheeks, her nose, her nasty stinking regrown face, pulled out handfuls of seaweedy hair. Rommel stood over me, grinning with a mocking joy. Blood was blood, and he didn't care. I could hear him like he'd spoken: *Just do her. You know you wanna. She'd do the same to you. And what good is she to us anymore?*

I took her eyes. She was so dazed she never saw it coming but I did it, I knelt there and shoved in my thumb, left, right, out, vile jelly. I tore them out. Adriana screamed and screamed, eye sockets streaming human red, and Renee laughed. I'd never heard her laugh like that before. I smashed Adriana's skull, fast, furious, the nauseating liquid softness of her brains scrambled eggs under my pounding fist. She twitched violently, and fell still, and her diminishing brain radio went forever silent.

I staggered backward, dazed, surveying the damage. Carny lay sprawled across a pew, skull flattened. Renee crouched near him; she was bald in wide strips now, scalped, her one torn dangling eyelid now ripped away and gone, and the metal chain had cracked one temple open so I could see the clean white pulse of her brain inside. Mind the gap, I thought, and started to giggle. Dembones rooted in Carny's remains until Ron shoved him away, all of them staring at me with shock, confusion, something like genuine respect. I spat like Billy would and turned away.

Linc was standing now; that cracking sound hadn't been his neck after all but his collarbone, now sunken and collapsed on one side. It must have stunned him. And then he must've played possum, that little country squirrel-eater's trick, until he had Carny back in his sights. I helped him keep upright while Renee retrieved the lake stones fallen from her and Linc's pockets, all three of us jangling with the nervous energy of a dozen successful hunts. This must have been what sex felt like, or what hoos kept wanting sex to feel like: this great wrenching push of sound and light and flesh-lust that knocked me over and hauled me back up again and kept me dizzy where I stood. Rommel circled us and glanced at Carny, at Adriana, nudging her with his boot.

"That bitch," he said. "She never could resist playing to a crowd."

"We're leaving now," Linc said. "All of us."

"Yeah? Well, you can have the 'maldie back, she ain't pretty anymore. That might change, though. In time." Rommel laughed like he'd planned this, like he wasn't as flummoxed as that balcony full of murmurs and buzz. "Get what you came for? Come to surprise us with how the country cousins got some doctor's medicine too—"

"We haven't," Renee snarled. "We're not changed. We're not freaks. We're just better fighters than you."

Rommel chuckled like an indulgent grandpa, chucking Renee under the chin. "Long as you're sure, sweetie. All I know is, some of us are changing, adapting one way or another, and some are stuck on the outside looking in. Like your old man, Jessie. So any time you get sick of him and the country life and living off baby food, you know how to find us again. Not Teresa, though, you can keep that sorry bitch. Don't much care for folks who walk around bellowing about kicking ass and taking names and have to find out the hard way they ain't nothing. I like the ones who crawl in all weaselly-like and then . . . surprise me."

He winked at me, a small flicker of exquisite muscle control he would never have had before. Linc got his feet steady and I let him go.

"Later days," Ron called out. By the time we were out the door he and Rommel were already laughing free and easy, no more regard for Adriana and Carny lying there amongst the human corpses than for a pair of rabbits. Stosh, and the balcony, stared after us in silence.

Once we were safe on the Sunlit Trail Linc brushed off the church dust with slow, precise gestures, fingering the new punched-out hollow in his collarbone. "How did we do that?" he asked, a little tremor of shock in his voice. Shock, and eagerness. Silent Renee stared at me with shiny wet rabbit eyes, twitching with energy, waiting for the answer.

"I'm starving," I said. "I'm gonna get sick if we don't eat."

"Possum just ran by," Linc said, pointing into the trees. "Nasty stuff, but—"

"So that was all for nothing?" Renee cried, rubbing fretfully at her wounded head. "We still don't know much of anything—"

"We?" I demanded, pressing at a broken rib to try to shove it back into place; the pain was like a hard little jolt of nausea, then it snapped to like a jagged Tinkertoy. "Just how the hell much nosing around and listening in have you been—"

"I wouldn't say it's for nothing," Linc said, craning his neck for the possum. "We know this thing is everywhere, that it's spreading. That it spreads fast. And that even the Rat don't know how this happened, or aren't telling. And that Teresa's definitely got it, though it sounds like they didn't know that until we told them—"

"Joe knew," I said. "He knew all along. He just didn't want to believe it."

"Joe." Linc let his name hang in the air, a joke fallen flat. "That's bullshit that he told them you were sick or anything else, they just wanted to rile you up for some fun. Careful what you ask for." Grim satisfaction flashed across his face. "And it sounds like it's contagious, but spread how? Biting? Spitting? I bet Jim could tell us. I bet he could tell us a lot more than he did."

The lab at Chanute Beach, where all the trouble started. Maybe. Supposedly. The Rat had no idea who Jim was to me, they had no reason to make that up. Fucking Rat. Fucking Rommel, those nasty fleshy springform lips of his twisted up sneering over Joe, *can't kill a bitty kiddie*, pissing himself about flamethrowers—after all Joe's talk, his *screaming*, about how I wasn't any sort of hunter if I never learned to hunt that. Unless he'd always been just that scared. Unless, even worse, no matter how he tried he had no true gut-burn to kill something he'd once been himself, and that was why the Rat booted him out on his ass in the first place. What if he'd always wanted me with him not to show me what's what, but in case he needed help, needed rescuing? Because he was so scared he'd die, if he did go gate-crashing and ended up snared in a circle of swift-stepping flamethrowing hoos, and he just didn't want to take another chance on dying without me, on dying alone?

Because, for all his talk, in the end he was just like me. Both of us so scared of the fucking hoos, in our own worthless ways, and so damned we'd never admit it, and so slow on the uptake when we saw it in each other. Pathetic. Completely goddamned pathetic.

I slipped my fingers into Florian's bag of stones, grabbing one tight; I was doing that a lot lately, needing to feel that cool smoothness, that strange tingling in the palm of my hand, like a little last reminder of something good I'd once had in abundance. Renee took one from her pocket as well, rubbing it between her fingers, and the agitation on her face started to subside. I gripped tighter. The lab at Chanute Beach, where Jim works. *Joe told us you've got this.*

"Maybe Jim doesn't know anything else," I said.

"Or maybe he's lying," said Linc. "Or maybe he's not lying, he's just got these suspicions, but he won't say them out loud without proof, he's gotta study his samples first. Be a scientist. Looks to me like everyone just knows bits and pieces of the story, and they're all keeping their bit quiet so they can have the advantage. Not that they even know what the advantage is."

"So like I said," Renee retorted, "we didn't learn a damned thing."

Except that we can fight, I thought. That we can fight *that*.

Linc scratched vigorously at his shoulder, dislodging a new cluster of watch beetles. I raised my arm, sniffing at my skin: dirt, forest, cornfield, Adriana's too-reddened blood and the rot that was uniquely me, no hoo-smell, no solvent or sap-bead sweat. But Teresa had looked normal—for a while—and Joe, and Linc and Renee for that matter, and Rommel said the first thing that happens is you feel tired, and hot, and worn out, and how the hell was I walking side by side with Renee the little superspy like she'd been part of this all along, not just the stupid new girl sniveling about her embalming going soft? I reached around and gave her a shove just to set things right and she stumbled, shrugged, clung to my armless shoulder as the hill got steeper and we turned back onto the Sullen Trail. The snow-drops lining the path were withered now, the violets thickening in earnest.

"What do we tell the others?" I asked. "They must realize something's up by now."

"Maybe," Linc said, "they realized it weeks ago. Months. Right?"

Renee, smelling of confusion and worry, kept her eyes on her feet. Billy liked to wander around hoo-country too, what did he know, what had Ben? Not a damned thing, that I could tell, nor did they really want to. Poor Ben. Poor crippled blinded stupid Adriana. Poor Florian, coming apart in a spill of dust like sand shaken from a shoe. Poor things in the cornfield, poor Lisa, sick to death, begging for death. What had Jim really done, what did he really know, what did he really want with me and my remnants? Why was Joe so sure I could fight Teresa, knowing her plague-strength, knowing it all along—or had he changed his mind, actually looked where he was asking me to leap, when he saw what happened to Ben? He hadn't seen that coming. I knew he hadn't. Distracted, I stumbled over a tree root and Linc cut in on my thoughts with a laugh.

"Remember that movie?" he asked.

"What movie?"

His voice oozed false hoo joviality, a cut-rate Bela

Lugosi: "'They're coming to *get* you, Bar-buh-rah.'" Then he faltered, his eyes fearful, a palm resting on his newly broken collarbone. "Jessie, what's happening?"

A graveyard, a car that wouldn't start, an old farmhouse, a gas pump bursting into flames. A local station showed it every Halloween, overexposed black-and-white with bad makeup and worse acting, and I remembered all the rumors that some of it wasn't acting or makeup at all—some of it was real footage, the start of the real '68 Pittsburgh massacre caught on film by a few foolhardy hoos, and when nobody wanted to watch or admit the actual truth they threw in some junk about Venus probes and radiation and made a monster movie. But those were only rumors, like Joe's stories that Teresa had an eye on me, and Jim's of a strange new sickness burning up out of nowhere, and Rommel's of new speed and flesh and strength all down to one particular beach, one particular lab. *What's happening*, the female lead pissed and moaned when she finally made it to safety in the farmhouse, *what's happening?*

And do we try and find out, really try—or do we do like we all learned when we were alive, when we'd be driving down the sulfurously lit roads and see human-shaped shadows huddled by the roadside, ravaged faces of those we'd buried years ago illuminated in the headlights, and just look away and pretend they're nothing? Retch and run away when they hold out a hand?

"I don't think anyone but us really cares to know," I said. "Including the Rat."

Renee gripped my shoulder tighter and Linc slipped an arm through mine. I felt foolish slowing my steps for them, marching abreast and intertwined like we were dancing our way to Emerald City (speaking of stupid movies I'd hated), but glad at the same time, protected from some shapeless, sulfurous shadow behind us, inside us, that I couldn't and wouldn't name.

12

Back at the park I could smell agitation and anger in the air, thick and heavy as grease. Since when did we need Billy's permission to scupper? I bared my teeth for another fight as he staggered up to us, Sam and Mags tight-lipped and tense behind him. Joe was nowhere in sight.

"So where the hell have you three been?" Billy demanded. "Did *you* do it? No, what the hell am I saying, Saint Linc would never prank like that. Ben's gone," he said, waving his gas-puffed hands. "Gone."

"He disintegrated? Already?"

"No, Madam Curie, I said he's gone. He was just lying there, stone dead, and now he's not and there's no trace of him anywhere, ash or otherwise, and if someone— something—carried him off, we've got no clue where." He grinned, a wet tarry smear of fury. "Goddamned Sam, fall-ing asleep at the—"

"Don't you start on me," Sam snarled, hands curled into bony fists. "If you're too busy stuffing your face to pay atten-tion to what's in front of you—"

"What's in front of *me*? You fell asleep right next to him, you senile bag of maggots, and you just let them take him!"

Billy let out a rumbling, swampy belch and cobra-spat at Sam. "Hears nothing, sees nothing, as much good on watch as a deer skeleton—"

"Boys, boys," Mags cut in, mechanically weary; this must have been going on for hours. "Jessie, we've been looking and looking, and not even a smear of ash. Sam didn't hear anything, and Billy and I were off hunting."

"Where's Joe?"

"Off searching the woods—he thinks maybe Ben was just stunned, woke up and wandered off. Now, I know doornail-dead when I smell it, but your boy's an optimist."

Off searching the woods, I thought, remembering the tarry disintegrating mess of Ben's arm, or tracking Ben to kill him, like those cornfield hoos, kill what was left of him for his own good? The mere thought of trekking all over the park or back to the cornfield to try to find out made me sway with exhaustion, but as my father used to say about med school, fortune favors the sleepless. "I'll go help him look," I said.

Mags shook her head. "No, you're tired, dear heart—you can stay. Stay and explain why you've been acting so innocent face-to-face and then sneaking around talking to hoo-scientists, kissing up to the Rat, behind our backs like a little pissant 'maldie bitch." Her hand clutched the back of a wrought-iron bench, twisting it into new designs. "Or like Teresa."

I smiled, the bright sunny smile we always flashed before fights. I couldn't take another fight, I'd collapse and Mags knew it. "Guess Joe's been telling you some stories."

"Joe's got nothing for anyone but a shitload of stories," said Linc, trying to angle himself between me and Mags like he could shield me. "He never did. You're a fool if you listen to—"

"Joe said you knew something about what Teresa and them were up to, and were keeping it to yourself." Sam's voice was dry and punctilious, his expression sympathetic. He'd never liked Mags. "He keeps saying you know stuff and you're keeping all the rest of us out of it—"

"Out of what?" I snarled. "Out of what? If I'm such a sneak, I'd like to know what I'm hiding."

"Don't play cute," Billy hissed, circling. "If you think we're that stupid—"

"Why don't you leave her alone?" Renee shouted, yanking at the remains of her hair. "You think you're so tough? Well, we just killed two Rat Patrollers without any of your help, ones just like Teresa. We did. You can ask them. And we can do it again!"

We killed them, kemosabe? We? That was just downright cute—but it did stop Mags and Billy in their tracks. Mags shot a glance at Linc, who nodded confirmation. "So spill it," she said. "And explain how you could go up against . . . that, when you don't stink like Teresa stinks or have new flesh like she does."

"Why the hell should I?" I threw myself onto the grass next to the bench. "You've got Joe to set you straight, don't you? What do you need me for?"

"Are you going over to the Rat?" Mags demanded. Her eyes were tired and scared, sunk deep in the moldy folds of her face like dried-up currants in old dough. "He said you were, you and Teresa. And that the Rat Patrol's already changed over, like Teresa has—"

"And that some hoo-scientist somehow helped cause it all," Sam added. "And that you snuck out to be with him. To help him. Like his little lab rat."

My stomach twisted like Rommel was punching me all over again. So, Renee wasn't the only spy around here. Shouldn't surprise me. Shouldn't throw me off. Just what did Joe see and hear, the night I found my brother again—and why feed me those stories about the Rat, why tell me how they'd changed over? Because he knew me, better than anyone did. Because he knew I'd want to investigate, knew I'd end up smack against a rejuvenated Rommel and Ron and all-else without their numbers, muscle, energy. Just like he'd been pushing me so hard to challenge Teresa, knowing all along how much stronger she was now. Which made something in my chest wind itself tight and snap, snap as it went around and around, each revolution a new little jolt of fury. Mags just stared at me, almost timid beneath the smear of bravado. I got up again and started doing a tiger pace in front of the gazebo, too angry to lounge around.

"The answer's yes and no," I said. I had to force the words out, with the rat-a-tat snapping, snapping all inside me so it was hard to talk. "So just keep your mouths shut until I've finished." And then with Linc and Renee as backup chorus I told them everything, starting with the woman Florian and I saw drop dead—and then vanish without a trace, just like Ben—and ending with Adriana flat on the church floor. Halfway through Sam shuffled off into the trees, returning with some squirrels; he was testing me, I knew, making sure I could still eat real flesh without getting sick, but I was too hungry to care. Linc and Renee devoured my leavings and drifted off in mid-narrative, huddled together half asleep.

"Well, damn," Billy finally said, laughing like his old self, "hell of a family affair you got tangled in, isn't it, Jessie?" He sighed. "Florian would've known what to do. Prob'ly seen all kinda crap like this. I miss that old heap of bones."

I felt pathetically grateful that even brutal, unsentimental Billy had been thinking that. "He didn't know what to do about that woman. Neither of us did."

"And so Joe's a damn liar," Mags said, close to an apology as I'd ever get, and spat at the gazebo steps. "Half-liar, quarter-liar. There's a shock. He know all about this?"

"Maybe," I said, "but not from me. I don't think he's changed—"

"Hell, I could've told you that—he ain't anything like them new freaks, they got flesh to burn. He's withering up like Sam here. Like Florian." Billy let out a single disconsolate toot of gas, pulling himself to his feet. "You, though, you and Linc and the 'maldie—"

"Yeah, you know what, don't you start with that." I flourished my arm for him, for anyone to sniff for confirmation. "Don't you start. I'm still rotten. *I* don't stink of disease. I don't have it."

"You wouldn't stink," he said, Mags grunting in agreement. "Not at first. Not right away. Later on, though—"

"Later what?" I took a step toward him, watching his eyes narrow with a strange new wariness, Mags brace her soft, swollen feet against the grass. "What later? You see me. I don't smell. I still eat like us."

"They can eat like us," Mags said. "If they have to. And anything else too. Plants, scraps, garbage, dead meat. They can eat anything."

"And hip-hooray for them. I still eat like us, still talk like us, walk like us, smell like us, look like us—"

"You don't fight like us." Billy was growling now, the angry, confused sound of an undead not knowing if that little flicker of light was a firefly or a lit match. "You don't fight a goddamned thing like us, you couldn't have killed that, you'd be lying in a brain-stomped heap if you were still—"

"Sorry to fucking disappoint you!" My voice was high and almost shrill, like I'd been caught sabotaging a hunt, throwing a fight, and needed to lash out to save myself. "Maybe I'm just a good goddamned fighter, okay? Maybe we got lucky. Maybe Carny and Adriana just weren't working it tonight, they were off their game, maybe they were hurt and Rommel threw them to us on purpose to finish them off, I don't know, all right? I'm not sick! I'm not changed, I'm me! They're them! And Linc is right, you know he's right, Joe's nothing but a lying backstabbing—"

My hand slid of its own accord into my pocket and grabbed at the pearl-gray lake stone, clutching it, clenching it in my fingers as I tried to settle myself down. My teeth were grinding, sharp points sliding up against blade-edges as I clenched my jaw. Billy didn't answer. Mags gazed at her feet, the ground, like I'd just embarrassed her. Sam just stood there. Linc and Renee had barely stirred, hearing us; he had his head buried in her shoulder, she was already snoring. Angry as I was, the sight made my last vestige of energy drop away.

"I need to sleep," I said, turning my back on them all on

purpose; I lay down next to Renee and closed my eyes. Someone else, Sam from the dry bones of him, lay down beside me back to back. As we drifted away I heard Billy and Mags mumbling, their voices muted and far off like I was a kiddie back in my hoo-bed, parents in the next room.

"—did eat the whole thing," Mags muttered. "They all did. Maybe she's right, you know Adriana was all talk and that other one, what's-his-name, could've—"

"Could you fight that and live? I know they don't look it, but something must've changed. At least in her. Joe said so, he said—"

"Joe, the liar."

Billy snorted. "But he ain't all lies, is he? She said it herself, he ain't all wrong. Yes, and no."

"I don't care yes or no, Joe's always lied. Always. Whenever he thought he'd get something out of it. Jessie ain't like that."

"It don't matter what she's like, it matters what she *is*."

Mags made a little whistling sound between her teeth, the sound she always let out when Billy was running her nuts. "Sweet William, sir, Joe's a liar, that hoo-scientist sounds a liar, the Rat are all scum-stinking liars. She don't know what's really happening. They don't know. We don't know. Nobody does. Nowhere."

"Yeah, well, whatever's happening, I ain't hanging around to turn into a half-hoo freak. From now on, we keep our bags packed." He laughed. "Don't care how strong Teresa's now, though, when I find her we're knocking out her teeth and then we're working her over. Slow."

"Slow, and painful." Mags laughed her old, rollicking chuckle. "Bad as we can make it."

"Tell ya, Mags, I've been out around that cornfield plenty of times and I never saw—"

"I ain't going anywhere near it." Mags's voice was sharp and fearful, pushing a suicide away from his gun and pills. "Not ever again. You watch yourself."

"I am watching. Never said I was going back, did I?"

"Lookit Sam, sleeping like he didn't already spend the whole night snoring. Useless sod."

"Wish he'd gone up, 'stead of Florian."

So afraid, I thought as I drifted away. It occurred to me that if they were that afraid they might just decide to send me up while I was out, and how easy that would make it for Joe, but vigilance and heartache were both undercut by sleep.

When we woke up, Mags and Billy were gone. I wasn't surprised they'd lit out for the territories, not after what I'd overheard, but it was weirdly hurtful all the same. Poor Sam sat there all by himself on the gazebo steps, picking indifferently at the carcass of a duck.

"The mister and missus got nervous, decided to head out Valparaiso way," he said, with the permanent inviting grin of death but tired, tired eyes. "Ain't heard no stories of sickness there. But I guess they'll find out. I guess it's just you and me, kiddies. So, who's got the energy for a manhunt?"

Hardy-har. We grabbed the slowest-moving possum we could find and gorged ourselves, talked about nothing, told stories until the sky became streaky and pale. I went on a flower search with Sam, who'd been a gardener when he was alive and still got a kick out of spotting the first crocus. The bulbs must have been late this year. We fell asleep all in a pile, firm still-elastic 'maldie skin up against rot-softened bloater and bone-stripped dusty, and for the first time in forever it was like being a real gang again, a real us, however foreshortened. I pressed my forehead into Sam's exposed shoulder blade, my feet into Linc's shin where it softened like a blister, and dreamed of running around the park playground like a kiddie. Running. Had I really once been able to run? My feet twitched as I chased sleep.

Running. I wasn't just running but breathing in this dream, breathing with my lungs like a hoo instead of through my skin and bones, and I heard my own short, tired pants of breath in my ears as I slowed down, walked, tottered like a proper undead into the playground's sandpit. The pit got bigger and wider and stretched out like a beachfront, the water a vague greenish-gray streak in the distance, and Florian was lying in the sand in front of me half-buried, curled on his side. Sand up over his arms and streaking his shoulders like folds of a rumpled blanket. I winced at how much all those infernal glassy grains must have hurt.

"I gotta congratulate you," he said to me, and smiled up at me calm and sweet. His eyes were the same quiet, peaceful blue. "You're gonna have a baby."

The hoos used to think we really could get pregnant, have "zombie" babies, or maybe that was just their worst made-up nightmare. A whole new *breed* of undead. The uterus is one of the last things to decay, I remember I read that somewhere. All that thick muscle. Maybe that's where they got the idea, that and seeing our bellies swollen up with rot-gas. Sometimes I do wish I'd had sex while I was living and actually had a sex drive. Not that it matters now.

"Quit talking like a crazy hoo," I told Florian, even though I was smiling back that he wasn't dead after all. "I'm about as knocked up as you are."

"Not that kinda baby." Something glinted in the sand beneath us and I saw the corner of a pale green lake stone, half-interred. He reached a hand out, brushed its surface clean and I suddenly saw stones laid out everywhere around him: pink, brick red, gray, pearly white, dusted with sand, organized in close spiraling rows, like a mosaic being uncovered in an archaeological dig. "You. It's you who's the kiddie-to-be. You're gonna birth yourself."

Another one of his dusty flake-outs. Some things never change. "I'm not a baby," I pointed out, then immediately felt like a foolish toddler saying it: *I'm no baby, I'm nearly three!* "You're out of it, old man."

"Born once," he said, a fistful of stones cradled in his hands. "Born twice. Born times three. Third time's the last." He gazed down at the stones, grinding them slowly with his fingertips into a fine, variegated powder. "The last for everyone. Everything. Everywhere. Unless they learn how to lie down and rest."

He blew on his palms and the ground-up bits of stone scattered in that little breeze, sprayed all over my sand-caked feet. The bruise-dark, gassed-up flesh there seemed to collapse, disintegrate like I'd passed through my full feeder time in seconds, and I was suddenly buried in pink and pale green and pearly white sands up to my shins, my knees, it was eating like a painless quicklime through all my rotten skin and as I became bare bleached bone I col-lapsed right next to Florian in the sands, tunneling my stripped-down skeletal self through the sand-sea's dry tides downward, and downward—

He's dead, I remembered then, even as I slept. Florian's dead. Never again, not on the beach, not in the woods, not anywhere but in your own idiot head. No more. I sank fur-ther into sleep, beyond that knowledge, beyond any sort of dreams.

When I woke up, Joe was still gone and Sam was missing.

We tramped around and around the woods and found nothing but a strange heavy smell of living hoo-flesh mixed with our own rot, a smell that led nowhere and seemed to come from nothing. That's what we'd come to, wandering the woods like idiots tracking our own stink. A too-warm sun rose steadily higher in the sky and none of us could sleep that day. The air felt funny, heavy and almost spongy as it soaked up the weight of quiet and emptiness.

"He must've gone to Valpo too," I said. I knew he hadn't.

"Didn't your brother ask when he'd see you again?" Renee demanded. "So let's . . . find him, somehow, and make him explain all this."

"How?" asked Linc, his voice harsh with anxiety. "How the hell are we supposed to do that? He got what he wanted, we won't see him. Never again."

All that day and the next night he and Renee and I tramped through the woods, fields, trails, underpass, corn-field, and no trace of Sam. On a hunch—a hollow hunch—we headed for Renee's cemetery on the opposite side of the highway, and found it empty as we'd expected: gates swinging wide open, grass unmowed, old floral arrangements scattered thick on the ground. The old church building was empty, nothing but human leavings and Carny's and Adriana's bodies eaten down to mere splinters of bone, sucked marrow-dry. No Sam. No Ben. No Joe.

That next morning, we slept in shifts. When Renee took the watch she gripped our hands in hers, glaring fiercely toward the woods waiting for the strange entity that would swoop down and tear our entwined fingers apart. I wanted to laugh at her and couldn't. Florian came alive again in my dreams, this time big and gassed up and mocking like Billy, and wrapped his finger bones around my neck and throttled until I woke with a jolt. Renee had fallen asleep on watch, her hand slipping from mine; she and Linc were there and snoring, no boogeyman in evidence. I lay there twitching in the fading afternoon sunlight, finally gave up on sleep and headed for the riverbank in search of some luckless otter or squirrel.

The sunset was building, streaks of raspberry and orange jam filling up a big shallow jar, as I headed down the Potawatomi Trail and farther into the trees. The deer loved to hide there. A mile in by the river's bend I heard footsteps behind me, and then the unmistakable *chitter-chitter* of bugs in their most active, greedy phase, methodically devouring whole square feet of flesh. Joe stood there in a little thread of pink light. He might've been not half a mile away, all this time.

"You," I said.

He looked me up and down. "So, you having a fine old time running around with Linc? And the 'maldie?"

"You having a fine old time hiding from us?"

He put a hand to my new fight spots: the small smashed-rib crater in my side, the long strip on my thigh torn open to the bone, the black-bleeding bruises surfacing on my arm and neck. His fingers lingered on my throat, where I'd always liked being touched. I shook them away.

"The apple trees haven't bloomed yet," he said. Like nothing had happened. Like there was nothing bigger to say.

"The ones by the old baseball field? It must still be March. I could never get over that—one day bare branches and the next, boom, fluffy pink everywhere." He tossed a dead branch into the flowing water. "But I don't know anything about trees or plants, not like Sam—"

"You lied to me," I said.

He just shrugged. "You don't understand. You don't understand what I've been—"

"Yeah, it's incredibly easy not to understand when someone won't tell you a damn thing, Joe." My voice shook and I hated it. "Really easy, when they go on and on about how much you mean to them and then stab you in the back without—"

"Are you gonna stand here bitching and moaning all night, or are you gonna come with me and let me explain?"

I sized him up in the weak watery moonlight. Whole patches on him now where the bugs had done their final work and departed: scraped-thin skin flapping like an empty tent, no fat or muscle left beneath, shriveling into the parchment-paper bone covering of the dusty, the *zombi ancien*. His eyes were sunken and mournful and giving-up tired. When, how, had he suddenly grown so damned old? Rommel died decades before Joe—he remembered World War One if he wasn't lying—and he'd never looked like this. I felt Joe take in my shock and pity, loathe me for it, realize it was all he had left to keep us on speaking terms. He led me along the path toward the old playground, over a footbridge whose wet, rickety wood made him grab for my hand, to steady me. I reached over and gripped the railing instead, crab-walking across.

"I've had to talk Mags and Billy out of stomping my skull in, thinking I was like Teresa," I said. We picked our way through the underbrush at the bridge's end, thick and knotty with no more work crew to cut it back. "Thinking I might kill them like she killed Ben. Scared of me. Can you explain that one?"

"You're a lot safer with Billy scared of you. That's common sense, woman—"

"Don't you pretend that was to protect me!" I shoved him, hard enough that he stumbled into the bushes. "You told them I was changed, a freak, you said I was going behind their backs, collaborating with hoos—"

"Weren't you?" Joe said.

"I was trying to find out what's happening! I wanted to find out for *us,* like you kept saying, and you—"

And *you.* After everything between us. I wanted to hit him again, knock him down and punch until my knuckles were thick with syrupy black but he looked too old to hit now, too bone-stripped to bleed, he couldn't have gone dusty so soon. Time doesn't give a shit what you want. Slams right into you and leaves you bleeding, broken, dying on the pavement while you weren't even looking. Fine, Joe. Go ahead and laugh. Laugh at how fucking stupid I've been, all along. Well? Go on.

"Go on, then," Joe said, backed up now against an oak's peeling, desiccated bark. "Hit me. It's all in your eyes, I can see it. Kick the shit out of me for lying to you. It's what I deserve, right? Look at me, look how fucking old I am now, fuck knows you could grind me to powder without breaking a sweat—right? That's what you want, *right*?" Glaring. Waiting. "Well? Go on!"

He was vibrating with anger but his limbs were slack, relaxed, like he wouldn't strike back or even duck if fists and feet came at him. Waiting, resigned and open, for oblivion. There was a little tremor in his fingers, as he clutched at a branch.

"You're not old," I said.

His eyes were giving-up tired, hollowed-out sad. Like Sam's, before he disappeared. He turned and kept walking and I followed him.

That smell was back again: that same strange, heavy mixture of living and undead flesh saturating the air, like whole milling mingled crowds of human and undead. The park playground was empty, though, nothing but rusted-out swings and a jungle gym of thick softening wood planks; its metal was a ghastly, peeling shade of sulfur yellow that must have been blinding when it was new. And that huge sandpit in the middle, roiled and lumpy as old oatmeal, ground glass to rotting skin. No pretty faded lake stone colors in it, just a dull listless swath of beige. I gave it a wide berth, sitting on the swings. There was something else in the air around us, something urgent and expectant making a slow burn of my skin and nerves; it wasn't anger or sorrow or anything like, it was the tremors that echo through the arm after a hard blow of the fist, the taste of still-warm flesh forever fading from the mouth. Joe paced in front of the jungle gym, seeming restless as I felt.

"I'm here," I said, stroking the swing chain. "So let's hear it."

He draped his arms over the rusty metal bars, fingers picking idly at the peeling paint. "Feel funny lately," he said, staring down at the dirty yellow chips all curled up like skin flakes. "Feel funny right now."

I did too. Which wasn't the point. "Well? You wanted me here, I'm here. So tell me more about how you've gone behind everyone's back, lying, making up stories, disappearing for days at a time and never bothering to—"

"Jessie, you know, you just don't listen to me no matter what, you get your teeth into an idea of how things are and you won't stop biting, you won't—"

"You lied to me."

"You won't goddamned hear me when I tell you it's not that simple, even the flat truth's never that simple and if you keep biting that hard you're gonna break your jaw—"

"You told them I was diseased, Joe! You made them think I was a freak, something to run from, you threw me into the Rat nest without even—"

"Jessie?" He had my arm now and was grabbing hard, vicious, finger-bones sinking in and eyes urgent and almost feverish like it was him who was dying to hit me, again, like he was starving and the last lingering taste of meat from the bone was melting away, gone. "Jessie. *Listen.*"

The slow burn all through me was heating up, crackling hard and fast like the electrical current searing Stosh's bones as he fried and died his first death; I was twitching, struggling to evade not the hand clenching my arm but the overpowering ache in every cell, and then suddenly I was listening, listening just like Joe demanded, because I couldn't not hear it. The crash and chaos of two dissonant, discordant brain radios suddenly hearing secret harmonies, a mutual music low and mournful and so far beyond ordinary sound that I stretched out my hand as if I could try to seize it, felt Joe twine fingers in mine as gently as if all our young, old, inexorably crumbling bones might shatter. No triumph in his eyes, no smug glint of pleasure at distracting me from my own anger—he didn't do this. He couldn't do it.

You never know when a dance might happen, your head can't summon song at will. It just is. The melody is different every time, it vanishes from your memory even as it leaves a mark inside you that never fades, but as the notes played between us and grew faster and wild I knew just the tune I was hearing, knew exactly how it was and what it meant: *Last chance.*

I let Joe pull me up from the swing seat, and we started to waltz.

The moon was sickly and anemic, half dark (all dark, really, nothing but a dead thing's reflection of life and light), the air around us stank of disease. I can't hum or tap out the music that passed between us and I wouldn't ever try, it was something we never had before, ever, a dance that was all and only ours. Us, and nothing else, yet shifting and spinning in confluence with everything alive. Joe sidestepped us past the sandpit like it might swell over in a dry tide, pull us in to drown, and I slid my hand up and down his arm as if that could steady its continuous tremble: the signature, terribly gentle palsy of a bug-bare body, finally going to dust.

"You're not old," I repeated, as though saying it might make it true. "And I'm not changed."

His head was tilted back, lost in the notes of the calliope, but he still kept watching me. "I don't care what everyone keeps saying, Joe, I'm not changed—"

"You got Adriana." Here we go round the jungle gym, butterfly bush, abandoned swings. "So I heard. And Linc got Carny, which frankly does the whole universe a favor. Damned good work, Jessie."

"You want out," I said. "That's what this is. Isn't it?"

His denuded jaw grinned merrily away but his eyes were calm, the stony calm of someone who'd expected to be caught in a lie. "I don't know what you mean."

"This is why you got me out here, isn't it, Joe? Except you couldn't just say it, straight out, and I don't know why." Here we go round the stinking sands, so early in the evening. "Remember, after Lillian, we both agreed that if one of us got blinded like that, crippled, we'd send each other out? We wouldn't wait around again for Teresa to play hanging judge? But you didn't even have the decency to ask me first." Sticky dark wetness leaked from my eyes, smearing my cheeks as we spun. "I would have done anything for you, Joe, time was, and—"

"And I didn't need to 'just say it,' after all. Did I?" Joe's feet shuffled slower, easier, relaxing into the dance. "You knew. In the end. And that's something. Isn't it?"

"You lied to me right off, Joe." My stomach twisted, clenched. "You told Mags and Billy you suspected something about me was different. Didn't you? Something you couldn't quite see or smell, but it was there, just like with Teresa. Just like with the Rat. You thought." He was keeping us slow and easy when my feet itched to stomp the ground. "Because everyone's getting this sickness, this mutation, whatever the hell it is—and for some reason, you aren't. It's not happening. You're immune. Right? No new flesh, no new strength, and they all laugh at the old man who wanted to be a big noise and God forbid he say, Jessie, help me. Jessie, there's something freaky out there and it's stronger than us—"

"Listen to it, Jessie." His fingers kept clutching, hard and unyielding, their seething life gone so fast to dryness and bone. "Listen to it play. You heard it, right when I did. You've heard it all along. That's why I never had to say it—"

"—could never just say 'Jessie, Teresa's changed over,

the Rat's changed over, everyone's changing over, I'm afraid I'm the only one left, I'm afraid you're diseased now, I don't know if I can trust you, I'll get you to walk into the Rat nest and let all the sick-strong ones jump you, if you die then we're golden, you're unchanged like me but if you walk out again I know we're finished—'"

"Jessie—"

"It was a witch trial, Joe!" I was shouting now and I didn't want to, not over the music, not over the sound that was us and only us, but I couldn't stop. "So did I drown, or did I float?"

"Jessie?" Fingers around my arm, the softened sinkhole of my waist hard enough to hurt. "Adriana, Carny, you know what that means? Changed or not, it means you'll stay alive. You, Linc, Renee, you can defend yourselves. But me, Billy, Mags, Sam—Florian too, if he'd lived—we're weak and old and our time's done. It's not our world anymore, and we're walking targets—"

"I wouldn't let that happen! I'd—Jesus Christ, Joe, if I can fight, if I can fight them, I can fight for you!"

I was clutching back now, like I could drag him away from something nameless, all-pervasive, waiting there patient in the light and dark for its chance to grab him and feed. "I wouldn't let that happen to you! Don't you know that about me by now?"

The calliope notes skittered through our heads faster and faster, feeding on sorrow, anger, that strange heavy flesh smell rolling through the air. Then Joe laughed.

"Just tell me something, Jessie," he asked. "You never once, ever, cursed this reborn life? Trapped in the back of beyond, nothing to do but eat raw flesh and sleep too much and fight about nothing, all the best land gone to the best gangs long before you tunneled up and you can't even run away from it, you know? You can stumble, shuffle, fall on your ass without the fun of getting drunk, yeah, you can do that, but you can never *run*." He sidestepped and kicked at a half-buried stone, forcing it up from the dirt. "Decades stuck in this rotten shell of a body, covered in bugs—"

"You brought me meat that was supposed to go to Teresa." I was pleading with him now, and for what I didn't even know. "Remember, when I first tunneled up and the gang jumped me and I jumped you and I couldn't move for days after? I was this little suburban idiot and you taught me how to hunt, how to really fight, how to survive in the woods with no shelter. You taught me everything. We were . . ." The word sat in my head, limp and pathetic, and I said it anyway. ". . . special."

"Decades, Jessie, covered in bugs. Marinating in bugs. Do you know how much it itches when they really start hatching? You looking forward to that happening to you? Did you know you can go bugfuck insane, literally, because your skin won't stop twitching, crawling, jumping, all over you, all the time, waking, sleeping, no matter what you do? Decades like this, hiding, falling apart, doing nothing, being nothing. Centuries." He looked me up and down, shaking his head. "And at least I got a life beforehand, but what were you, fourteen? Fifteen? Christ. No growing up, no graduation, no college, no travel, no sex, kids, family, life—"

"—no job, no obligations, no responsibilities, no burdens, I'm living *now!* Right in front of you! I have a family now, and a life now—"

"And I was trying to look out for that, all right? For you! Just like we promised each other after Lillian, just like we said!" His voice was rasping and sharp, even as he swung me round so carefully like I might bend, snap, break. "You don't have any idea what it's really like out there now, Jessie, you never wanted to learn, I was trying to make sure you'd—"

"You can't leave me!"

An echo snaked sidelong through our song, the sound of something inside me bending, twisting, threatening to snap and break. I stumbled, almost tripping over Joe's feet, and he stopped where he stood as the echo grew louder, stronger, almost drowning us both out.

"You've got a life now, Jessie," he said. "That's what you said. And it's the truth. And one way or another, mine's running out. And we swore we'd never leave each other to die alone, we swore that—"

"I can take care of you. I can do that."

"That's not how it works for us, Jessie. You know that. So quit acting so damned sentimental, and just—"

"Stop telling me what to do. I am so fucking *sick* of you telling me what to do."

"This is what we promised each other, Jessie. You can't—"

"Stop it," I said, trying to bite back the echo, his words, all of it, just to hear the song of us and nothing else. I couldn't do it. "Stop."

"Listen to the music, Jessie," he said. "Just listen. For once. It's beautiful."

Stop telling me what to do, Joe, for once in your sorry afterlife just *stop*—but I couldn't help it, it was beautiful and it was ours and we'd never have it again, no matter if we both lived as long as Florian before we crumbled away, my feet stepped back and forth of their own volition and I was leading Joe now, we were leading each other. The rustle of the air through the spring-sprouting trees was our high countermelody and beneath it us, and nothing else, the sound of what we both were and had been since long before we both went underground.

"I could kill you," I said, quiet, soft. Mother to child. "I could kill you right now. Just like you wanted."

"And now I know I can't let you," he said. "Because you'd never forgive yourself. Just like with me and Lillian. Even knowing it's what I wanted."

We could have had this all along, could have had it right up to the end (whatever and whenever the end was, it wasn't this, I wasn't sick, he wasn't old—). But it was more important to test me. "Is this what you wanted?" I asked. "Everything the way it is now?"

Joe gazed up into the dark gray sky. "None of it's what I wanted," he said. Even quieter, and so sad. "But it's what we're all gonna get. It's what everybody gets in the end."

The most horrible part of all was, he wasn't lying. Not now, not anymore. *Died alone once, I'm not doing it again.*

A lifetime, an eternity ago he'd said it and I'd agreed with him, swearing reckless oblivious fealty like the infant idiot I was and now he'd gone and taken me at my word, taken me seriously like nobody ever had while I'd lived, believed *me* when I promised neither of us would go on without the other. But I could promise him anything, back then, because it'd never happen, we'd never die, I'd never leave. It'd never turn out he was so angry at being torn from his first death and so revolted by himself and so ceaselessly gut-twisting terrified of everything about this accursed reborn life that he needed me in ways I'd only ever imagined I needed him—Joe, I love you. Twisted-up as all this is you'd never have done it if you didn't love me. Why couldn't you just have told me, why couldn't I have *seen,* that all this time, since the very beginning, all you ever wanted was to go back to sleep, forever?

I wouldn't have called you a coward. I swear it. Because it's me, not you, who can't just face facts, see sense, lie down in the tall grass and accept that this is all we get, all anyone who ever lives ever gets no matter how good, how selfless, how beloved—

The music stopped. And we'd never have it again. Joe had an arm around me and he stopped us both short at the edge of the sandpit, the dry tide just past the swings that would never quite roll in—but it was rolling over both of us now thick and dense as felt, the smell of human flesh under a smeared-on cake frosting layer of undeath and beneath that, like a vein of ore in a rock, the oily chemical stench that first gave Teresa away. The sandpit reeked of it, the sandpit that was more than large enough to hide a body. Joe turned toward me and there wasn't triumph in his face, but remorse.

"I thought you'd have figured it out before this," he said. "Probably would've, if the dance hadn't—"

"Joe." The smell seemed to get stronger the more I stared. "What's in there?"

He shook his head. "I didn't want to see it. I didn't want to see any of it."

But he did see it, whatever it was. And he knew. All this time, he knew.

Behind me I heard the creak of footbridge planks and the rustle of branches, then slow cautious steps. Linc? I wanted Linc, Renee, anyone who was still truly *us* in the vicinity because something was even more wrong than I'd known and I was scared. From the corner of one eye I saw something with the gait of the cornfield folk, bobbing unsteadily on its toes like a cork in rough waters and throwing out hands to trees for balance as it approached. I didn't turn. Joe tossed a stone hard at the sand, and something quivered and shifted underneath in response.

"This world's not built for us, Jessie," he said. "It's not built for the risen-up, the mortal undead, not anymore. If it ever was. We're gonna get wiped out. We're being wiped out right now. So I wanted to live up to that promise we made each other, after Lillian. I wanted to make sure that one way or another, neither of us have to live like this anymore."

The steps stopped next to me, the strange smell now overpowering, and I felt a hand on my shoulder. I turned and nodded. I'd had a feeling it was him. The girl who'd vanished from the underpass, or him.

"Ben," I said.

He smiled from lips smeared with drying blood. His teeth were still like ours, longer and sharper than any hoo's, but they'd turned the gleaming white of high-polished bone.

"In the flesh," he said.

13

Ben just kept grinning and grinning. "So how's tricks, Jessie?"

Real words, articulated with full tongue and teeth. He was still there, still him—not like the cornfield people, those hollow rotten husks of their old selves—but there was a new hardness in his voice, an edge that could draw blood. His bitten arm was whole again, a thick solid sheet of flesh painted in a sleeve-sized bruise that flickered and wavered like pond water; fat veins cut through it like rivers in muddy ground. I couldn't help it, I reached out to touch and felt the smooth unbroken patina of living skin. Human skin.

"It was sticky before," he said, as I drew my fingers away. "Just like Teresa's. It hurt, like a big blister. But that passes. It grows over smooth and new and you feel just fine."

Almost hyper-human he looked, like a comic book character with pumped-up, bulging muscles and the sickly bluish pallor of cheap ink. "So fast," I said. Faster than Teresa, than the Rat, than I'd ever seen.

Ben laughed. "Day or so." He flexed a muscle and watched it twitch up, back, elastic as rising bread dough. His fingernails were pink again, solid in their beds. "Things are speeding up. Changing again. I've been hanging around the woods until I got used to it. Watching you kids stumble every which way trying to find me."

The flaky charring on his face was gone too—he might never have been burned at all. He might never have died at all. I didn't realize I was backing away until Joe's arm tightened around my shoulders.

"I was going to kill you, and then myself," Joe said, quiet like we were still alone. "So we wouldn't be the only ones stuck and unchanged—and then you kept talking about being tired and there was something in your eyes, something all glassy and strange like you had a fever, and I thought, it's happening to her too. The Rat were getting hungry, Jessie. This thing, whatever it is, it makes you strong and it makes you hungry—they're hunting down the unchanged, killing and eating them, like deer, like hoos, and I thought, if she fights them, if she fights Teresa, and she dies, she's out of this misery. If she lives, she's becoming one of them—and there's a place for her in this hellhole." He gripped even harder. "You guessed right, Jessie. That's what we do when we love each other, Jessie, we make sure we're not left to the wolves. We agreed on that. Just like you said. That's why I wanted you to kill me out here, but then I couldn't do it, I couldn't ask, because you'd never forgive yourself if you said yes—"

Ben let out a phlegmy, choking cough of a laugh. "Holy Christ, Joe," he said, wiping clear, human tears from his eyes, "but you really are one passive-aggressive son of a bitch."

"Well, I'm just sorry you never did get her to fight me," said a new voice, emerging from the trees. "I can always use a good laugh."

It was only by the long black hair that I recognized her. Teresa's face was smooth and whole as any real human's, her skin satiny with renewed life and her voice, her hoo-talking voice, pouring syrupy good cheer over a bed of ice. Trailing behind her, crouched down and cringing like a beggar tugging on a millionaire's sleeve, was something with ashen, blue-tinged skin and trembling muscles and swollen hands and a stench pouring off him strong enough to choke, a slurry of sulfur and acetate and motor oil and pure putrescence overlaying human, barely human, formerly human flesh. It looked up at me, its gray hair greasy and lank, its eyes filled with the desperation of the starving.

"I'm so hungry," it said, in Jim's voice. Grabbing at Teresa's arm in earnest now, barely seeming to notice as she shook him off. "Please."

Teresa laughed, then patted him like a little misbehaving pet. "You hoos don't do all that well when you get this, do you?" she mused, lips twitching and curving in a smile like a paring knife's path through a peach. "Guess you should've thought of that before you went and bug-sprayed it everywhere you could—"

I pulled at Joe's arm, insistent as a panicked toddler. "What is this? Joe?"

"I told you, Jessie," he said, staring down at Jim like a reproachful zoo animal at its keeper. "The world's not ours anymore. There's something loose out there, and it's changing everyone. I don't know how it started, or who started it—"

"Please just give me something to eat." Jim was stumbling toward me now, the cornfield rot in his eyes, his skin, his quavering desperate voice. "You owe me, Jessie, I'm your brother, you owe—"

"Don't you talk to me!" I bared my teeth at him, pulling free of Joe's grasp to shove him from my path. "You did this? You made this disease, in your damned lab, just like the Rat said you did? You turned them and Ben and Teresa into *humans*?"

I spat the word, making it the epithet it had always been among our kind. Teresa laughed, the same hoarse mucousy laugh as Ben, and Jim cradled himself in his own shaking arms.

"I don't understand you," he said, rocking back and forth where he stood. "You don't talk right. You've got this too, I can tell. I can see it in your eyes. But you still don't talk right yet. I need a branch." He started laughing, hollow and frantic. "I need a branch—"

"Tell her what happened," Teresa ordered him, singsong, glee dancing in her eyes. Her human talk. Her human tongue and teeth. "She wants to know. Tell her, and you can have something to eat."

"Lisa saw you." Jim looked from me to Joe to Ben, eyes full of sorrow, seeking someone, anyone, to offer him meat and pity. "That day, visiting your grave. She came back crying, she threw up, she said it was horrible, that it was *you* staring at her out of this rotted shell and how much you must be suffering, how much pain—"

"I was never in pain." I had to keep control of myself, had to keep him talking, to have any chance at all of learning why we were all standing here right now, but even knowing he couldn't hear a word of it I couldn't stop. "I had somewhere to go, somewhere to be. I had people like me. I had myself. I had a life, my own life, I had friends, I had someone who loved—"

I couldn't finish that sentence. *Had, had, had.* All going. All gone.

"I don't understand you." Jim shook his head. "You're still trapped inside a corpse. But you recognized Lisa, me—I always knew you all kept your minds, your memories, I *knew* it, and they wanted me to kill you. My own sister. My father. My mother. All over again." He doubled over suddenly, clutching his stomach, and when he raised his head again he had the glassy-eyed glitter of barely suppressed agony. "I wouldn't do it. I was going to bring you back. All of you. Make you human again. Alive. Bring you back from the dead." He doubled over again, his head whipping back even as his body pitched forward. "And it worked," he gasped. "It worked."

He started laughing all over again, laughing like Ben, like Teresa, hoarse and thick like he was choking up a lung. The glassy, glittery sheen of his eyes was the same as theirs now too, exactly the same. Not just pain, but madness.

"You owe me," he repeated with a feverish conviction, even as he made those shallow, gulping sounds of someone trying desperately not to be sick. "You owe me. I did this for you, Jessie, I did—"

"You did shit," Ben sneered, folding his arms. "Another nasty little hoo with his rotten little stories—"

Jim shook his head fervently. "Teresa's right. I told you the truth, we collected bodies, your bodies—oh, God, please, I need to eat, I'm so hungry—"

"Talk," Teresa said, her voice hard and smooth as gunmetal. "Let her hear it. Why shouldn't she? We all love a good story, helps pass the time of night. And hoos pissing in their own soup is the best story ever."

"Zoonotic infection." Jim grabbed at a low-hanging tree branch, clutching and swaying to keep himself upright. "Contracted from another species. Somehow. This strange, mutated *H. pylori.*" He licked his lips, steadying himself, that old science-lecturer look sparking for the briefest of moments on his face. "The lab got ideas, started tinkering. If they could mutate it more, make it an active contagion, wreak havoc with your digestive tracts, maybe they could somehow starve you out. Just seed your habitats with it, watch you wither and drop—nothing else had worked, nothing. Tried everything. They even had smallpox samples, Jessie, what the hell, it worked on the Indians, right? You have no idea what we've been doing out there, another reason no unauthorized humans are—"

He let go of the branch, crouched down and was violently sick all over the ground. Teresa watched him, impassive, mildly amused.

"So they invented something to eat us up from the inside," she said, grabbing Jim's shoulder and hauling him, moaning, upright. "Make our guts one big ulcer. But this one here had his own experiments, his own ideas—"

"I saved you," Jim whispered, a hand with skin like a deflated balloon sawing back and forth, back and forth over his dirtied mouth, and his voice rose higher and louder in a croon of thwarted fury. "I was part of that lab team, I worked on this and I monkey-wrenched it! I sabotaged it! I altered the bacterium again, I switched it out, our lab infected the woods, the beaches, every habitat, every place we knew you were with *my* bacterium, and it worked! All those undead bodies with holes all inside, but it didn't matter, they were stronger! They could eat anything, they stopped decaying, they grew new flesh—I did it!"

He rocked back and forth, back and forth, crouching with a palm pressed to his stomach like it might split open. "*I made you what you are!* I saved you! I brought you back to life! I saved you, Jessie. I loved you so much it's killing me, it's killing all of us, I've made you human again and we're all dying because of it and, Jessie, oh my God do you owe me. You *owe* me."

His face was flickering, wavering, changing like the great bruise of Ben's arm, tenderness and revulsion and gentleness and hatred coming and going too fast to pin down. Too quick to distinguish each from each. Ben, supremely unimpressed, leaned against a cottonwood with the old fedora pulled over his eyes and the blood visibly pounding through his veins. Joe just nodded, like none of this surprised him at all.

"I told you, Jessie," he said. "I told you. Everything's changing. Everyone."

"Except for you," said Teresa, grinning.

Joe's eyes looked dull. "Except for me."

"Contagious," Teresa noted, grinning wider as she gazed at me. "Contagious as the common cold. And it's still mutating, getting faster, getting more wicked, and turns out humans aren't the least immune. You have no idea what it's like out there, Jessie, out where the hoos—"

She stopped for a moment, her face contorting like Jim's, then with visible effort thrust her shaking hands into her pockets. She looked like she had that day in the park, with the matches, when she'd been trembling all over with hunger. Like Rommel had, when he screamed at Carny for more food. "No idea," she said, still twitchy. "Jonas Salk over here, he got it. Up to his tongue in it, no surprise. Whole damned lab brought it home to all their families—your family. Those idiot hoo-kiddies, sneaking around the beaches, they brought it back too. You've seen 'em, the sick hoos. Rotten inside and out, falling apart, starving for food but can't keep a damned thing down—"

"How much of this did you know?" I asked Joe, like Teresa wasn't even there. Maybe if I concentrated hard enough, she and what was left of Jim and this whole horrible dazed-up nightmare would just melt like flesh in the fire, disappear. Only Joe and Ben would be left, the real Ben, the old Joe, shitting themselves laughing at their giant-ass prank. I'd beat them until they were oozing from every pore. It'd all be okay. *Shit, Jessie, you shoulda* seen *your face.*

"Not everything," Joe said. "Not enough. All the little bits and pieces, they just . . . didn't make sense." He stared hard at Ben. "I didn't want to see it."

Jim was crawling near our feet, shoving dirt in his famished mouth, spitting it out again with sounds like crying. "I told them. I told them just like you said, I told them, now you have to give me—"

"It's a hoo-epidemic now," Teresa said, watching him in barely veiled delight. "Can't just toss them outside the town gates anymore, say good riddance, it's everywhere. Rotting, starving, crazy, all of them. There's meat riots. Hoos eating their pets, their children, forming hunting gangs, devouring anything they can find. Eating garbage. Eating filth. Eating everything. But none of it stays down. They just keep getting sick. They just keep dying."

"I'm hungry," Jim wailed. "I'm starving, I can't stand it—"

"That germ of theirs just keeps mutating." Teresa kicked him in the side, watching him convulse and retch. "And the hoos just keep dying. And me, I just keep laughing."

She sucked air between her front teeth, an idle whistling sound, like cannibalism and extinction were just a dull end to a rainy afternoon. Air between her teeth. Breathing like a human breathes. All to bring me back. To make me live again. All this, all this deception, all this sickness, all this horror, those cornfield hoos, Ben, everything, it was my fault, it was about me, it was all to try to make *me* human. Because I couldn't have just watched Lisa from as far away as I made Renee watch her family—not me, because I'm so fucking special and the rules just don't apply to me, I had to try to talk to her, I had to tell her I was there, she had to tell Jim. I was the original contagion. Me. My grief for Florian, my constant companion like a sharp lake stone pressing into my side, drained instantly away: I was so glad he was gone, that he never lived to see this. Never lived to see what I'd done.

Jim was by the sand pile now, digging around its edges, letting out choking, sobbing breaths. The pile moved again, shifted. It shouldn't have been moving. There wasn't even a breeze.

"What's in there?" I said. But I knew, I already knew.

Teresa snorted in derision and Ben smiled, rather gently. "Poor, loyal old Sam," he said. "I knew he'd come looking for me, all along I knew he would. So I waited. I thought he didn't make it, when I bit him, so I buried him. Shoulda been more patient, let the magic do its work—like now. See? Go on. Watch."

As we watched, the lumpy, stinking sand shifted and roiled. A hand came out, and another, and a pair of flailing arms in a sand-caked, moldy suit jacket and then a pair of old dusty eyes, still squeezed tightly shut.

Ben crouched by Sam's side, shoving Jim away. "I was hoping he'd wake up in time," he whispered. "See? Nothing scary, it's just ol' Ben and ol' Sam out on the town—"

"You killed him," I said, and the nest of knots that was my gut tightened into hard little buds of fear. "His best friend that he loved, and you—"

Ben laughed, a gentle indulgent sound. "I didn't kill him, Jessie—anything but. Look at this. Watch. Wait."

Sam's eyes clicked open, wide and startled and lit up with hunger.

"Now watch *this*," Ben said. And he reached down to poor dazed, trembling Sam, and ripped a hand through his guts like a saw tearing through a down pillow. Blood gushed over the sand—pure red human blood spraying our feet and legs. I jumped, shouting. Teresa laughed. Jim grabbed at the fouled bits of sand, frantic, sucking them dry. Sam shuddered, moaned, collapsed back into the sand pile—

And then his eyes clicked open again, staring impassively down at his own flesh as the organs knitted themselves together, as arteries and veins resealed themselves and muscle, fat, skin crept over all of it like a smooth blanket pulled over ulcerous legs. Drying blood soaked his clothes, made a huge scab of the sand. His eyes, looking at me, weren't old Sam's old eyes, and they weren't any sort of creature's I recognized at all.

"I'm hungry," he said, his voice sharp and cold as Ben's, and glared at me like a stranger, like a hateful thing blocking his path as he wrenched himself to his feet. "What're you gaping at, you little shit? Go get me something to eat."

"Sam." I wanted to cry. Where was my poor, funny old Sam, who loved flowers and hated hunting, who only needed a warm spring day and Ben to be happy, who was too old to move this quickly? "I'm so sorry—"

"I'm *hungry*," he snarled, his eyes feverish like Rommel's, like Jim's, and lunged toward me and Joe. Joe turned and kissed me, a brush of nonexistent lips and bone-stripped jaw, and grabbed me in a hard, hurtful embrace.

"I'm glad you were here with me after all, Jessie," he said. "Later days."

He shoved me away from him so hard I stumbled, lost my one-armed balance, fell heavily on my side. Sam knocked him flat to the dirt and he didn't struggle, just lay there with his face open and expectant and before I could shout or plead, before I could get back on my feet and fight, Sam snapped his neck between two fully fleshed, powerful hands. He kicked in Joe's skull the way I had Adriana's, staining the grass with a burst of brains and bugs, and Joe's body convulsed one last time like his limbs were hooked to wires and then lay still. Dead meat.

Teresa giggled, watching. I would have hit her, I would have broken her open but some sort of hazy web had wrapped itself around me, keeping me from moving at all. Sam crouched over Joe's body and tore with smacking, furious noises at his bug-hatched flesh, crunched through bone with sighs of satisfaction. Eating rot. Relishing dust. Then Ben couldn't take it anymore and hunched beside him, twitching to feed, and Jim was crawling toward his body too and Teresa, and I couldn't look anymore, I couldn't. Scavengers. Human buzzards. Cannibals. That's what Jim tried to make of me. I hunched down like Jim with my hand against a tree's knobbly bark, sick, so sick, I couldn't stop.

Sam was crawling through the sand now, alongside Ben, both of them digging feverishly for more meat. Jim was groaning, holding his stomach, starting to cry in earnest as the pains inside wouldn't go away. Teresa, her arms folded, watched me with malicious glee. There was a streak of tarry black at the corner of her mouth.

"He asked me to bite him," she said, her lips dancing merrily at the thought. "He begged me, after I did in Ben. Because he just couldn't make the change. Everyone else catching this new germ, but not him. I laughed in his face." She shook her hair from her eyes, her long wild hoo-thick hair. "He just wasn't worth the bother. Worthless, from start to finish."

Jim had crawled to the clearing's edge and was heaving and spitting again, just like the cornfield hoos, everything in him coming up. Sam and Ben pulled at Joe's remains, Sam crunching a mouthful of purloined bone and not letting go even as Ben kicked and punched him in an increasing fury: whap, cry, swallow. Whap, cry, swallow. Sam got the last bite, and Ben let out a sound like a rabbit's death scream and they *ran* after each other into the woods, ran like the feral, damaged human beings they'd become, so fast, such a perfect interlocking flow of muscle and bone that watching it I felt like I never had before: crippled. Left behind.

There was a mess of bone and dust and crushed skull and drying coffin liquor near the slide, something reaching from it still with the bare semblance of an arm, and that was all that was left of Joe, and we had just been talking, dancing and I'd told him that I could kill him, kill him right then and there, and the thought of it made me shake all over as I let out a shuddering cry.

"Jesus," Teresa sneered, tossing that thick black hair over her shoulder. "You'd think she actually lost someone *living*."

"I'll kill you," I said, and I'd thought and fantasized it dozens of times, hundreds, but this time I felt so cold and tense with purpose that I knew I really would. "I killed Adriana, I can kill you—"

"Adriana was still transitioning," Teresa said, hitching her shoulders back like she was shrugging off a coat. "Not me. You wanna try it, bitch? Come on. This has been a long time coming."

I made a fist of one rotten, stiff, creaking hand—this really was it and we both knew it, but I had to try, didn't I, for Joe, for Ben, for poor old Sam? "You're the worthless one," I said, as we circled one another, as Jim lay there watching us, stretching out a hand, weeping. "And you're bragging about it. You're sick. I wouldn't be like you, I'd rather kill myself than be like you, insane, crazy, sick, a cannibal—"

"Don't worry," said Teresa, slowly advancing on me. "None of that will happen. You'll just be dead. That's all you'll ever be."

Jim made an urgent moaning sound and then something came flying from the trees, hitting Teresa smack, smack on the shoulder, the cheekbone. Red blood streamed from her face as she whipped around, snarling, and then she was ducking handfuls of lake stones, hurled with undead force. Linc and Renee staggered out, unchanged still, vibrating with tension and fear as they clutched their weapons in their hands. Sticks and stones. Linc looked from Teresa, to Jim, to the remains lying at the foot of the slide, and I didn't have to explain. "Oh, Christ," he said, and started laughing like he'd never stop. "I knew it. I always knew it."

Teresa raised up a warning hand, her wounds from the stones already healed. "Private business, kiddies. Very private. Turn around and leave right now, or you won't walk away alive."

Linc snarled, a blessed display of teeth and black rot. "What makes you think you will?"

Teresa was all smiles, all happiness as she advanced on them both, running zigzag and forward and back in a bizarre, mocking little dance just to show how fast she could move. "Jessie," said Renee, full of urgency but none of her old teary panic, "what do we do?"

"She needs to breathe!" I shouted, as Teresa turned and leapt for my throat. "She needs to—"

She hurled me into the blood-soaked sand pile, yanked me out and slammed me over and over against the swing set poles, until coffin liquor streamed into my eyes and a cheekbone snapped and collapsed. Air, my brain chanted frantically over and over, *she* needs air again. I don't. Teresa threw me on my back and I reached out and squeezed, trying to get her nostrils and mouth in one grip and of course I couldn't, of course she bent my arm backward and then backward again until there was a long loud splintering crack and I screamed, and screamed even harder when she jumped on my legs, breaking a femur, wrenching and pulling. Something tugged and tore and snapped, and then one of my legs was gone below the knee and I'd barely felt it, in fact I felt nothing below the chest at all.

Linc howled, a long screech of fury like a song for me, as he grabbed Teresa and held her face down in the sand pile. Renee kicked hard and Teresa's skull split open, bone and hair flaring in a fan and brains leaking into the adulterated sand. Then it knit itself together again, closing as neat and fast as Florian's had opened in death, and she rose up in a spray of dust and grabbed Linc around the neck, wrenching forward, backward, breaking him open along the spine like a gutted fish still flopping for the water. Renee was on her, screaming, trying to pull her off, and then Teresa got a hand wrapped around Renee's throat and they were both staggering through the sand in their murderesses' dance while I rolled, so gently, down a long red tunnel. Renee wasn't moving anymore, she wasn't moving, the dance was all Teresa's. Wake up, little Renee, wake up. Linc, don't die—

Renee lay on her back, motionless, eyes staring vacant and hollow into the night sky. Linc was on the ground beside her and Teresa straddled him with guttural sounds of delight, teeth ripping into his face, fingers tearing the flesh from his arms. Something thick streamed from Linc's stomach, soaking Teresa's shirt, and I just lay there too, watching, the tunnel walls contracting around me. My cheek was oozing dark syrup from where a lake stone clipped it as I fell; my arm, what was left of my legs wouldn't move at all. I was back in the coffin, staring up immobile as the lid slammed down for good. Teresa bent over me, her mouth melting before my failing eyes into a chasm the color of bleached bones.

"Close your eyes," she murmured. "It'll go so much quicker—"

Wordless, ceaseless screaming erupted in a flood behind us, sirens crying out after the bombs had dropped. A thunderclap of running feet, bare, booted, belly-white, blister-red, forest-filthy, and through the pillars of legs I saw Ben, Sam, a Rat here, a Rat there, fleeting glimpses of the streaming hair and long grasping fingers and blackened eyes of strangers rushing in to help us die. Ben ran straight for Teresa, wrenched her off me and hurled her on her back with a bellow of triumph. Jim was cowering on the ground now, moaning in fear, sobbing in pain, grabbing for the underbrush like he could tunnel inside it and bury himself forever away from what he'd done, and then he was lost in the swarm and I couldn't see him, I couldn't hear anything but teeth crunching through bone and Teresa shouting, then howling loud enough to shake the earth. Then nothing.

Sam bent over me, his mouth still thickened with blood and black bile. I closed my eyes, waiting and remembering the deer, the hoos, the stray dogs and squirrels and raccoons and possum and countless other helpless stupid little animals we had cornered and killed. Not so stupid as us, reduced to this. What did a deer think of in death? No fear, if you were a deer you wouldn't have any of this sort of knowing fear, you'd just remember how the sun streaked the river when you bent down to drink, how the branches curved and arched like a curtsey to let you pass through. The taste of ripe berries on the twig. The axe-edge of winter. The spring. The night.

The moon.

BOOK THREE

Resurgam

14

I smelled rain approaching and the air felt strange, heavy
with quiet and emptiness, as Florian and I walked together
along the dunes. I wasn't sure what I was walking on, one
leg gone and the other broken beyond repair, but somehow
I was upright. The rain smell burned off as quickly as it
arrived and the sun suffused a thick wall of clouds, turning
everything pearly luminous gray.

"Is this heaven?" I asked. Someone was screaming, horrible breathless screams like muscle tearing off the bone,
but even that couldn't shatter the peace.

Florian smiled. "You just leave that be till you're all
used up."

"Weren't you watching that fight?" I picked up a lake
stone, tossed it in a wide arc at the water. "I am used up, old
man. Far out and floating. See?" I pointed at the bloated,
torn-up body bobbing on the Lake Michigan waves. "There
I am."

The screams from somewhere else didn't stop.

"That?" Florian looked scornful. "That ain't nothing but
the water. If you're smart, you'll stick to the sands." He dug
a toe bone into the damp sand near the shoreline, gone dark

from the rolling waters. "This is where we all came from. This is where we were born."

"So that's true then?" I picked up another stone. "Something happened here, ages ago, something that infected all the sands? Got into the air? Was it a meteor?"

"Infected all the sands," Florian said, an echo instead of an answer. "Got into the air. Strangeness everywhere. Sickness everywhere. Death everywhere."

His toes pushed deeper into the sands. Near the shoreline, if they're dry enough, you can get them to make a little sound underfoot, like the sound when you crunch through hard snow except fuller, heavier, almost melodic like a flat, subdued musical note. Singing sands, they call them. But here it was all waterlogged, sullen and quiet. The screams that much louder. Like sounds of childbirth. Born times three.

"The screaming sands," I said.

"The sands started this," he said. "And the sands'll finish it."

"I'm already finished." I flipped the stone, the silvery pink of a salmon's skin, over and back in my palm, raised my arm to throw it. "I'm done, I'm through—"

He grabbed my wrist with the strength he must have had when he was young, new-hatched, when my hoo-self was still centuries from birth. "Stop that," he hissed, wrenching the stone away and brandishing it before my face like he might strike me with it. "You stop wasting all them bits and pieces, tossing them away. They made us what we are today. They're what woke us up from death. What made us. What'll keep you walking. These are *us*."

"Igneous," I said, taking the stone back from him. I cradled it in my hand like it might break. "Sedimentary."

"Metamorphic," he said. His eyes were suddenly sad. "Meteoric."

"I'm dead. Done. Finished."

"This'll keep you walking." He closed my fingers around the stone. "Keep you walking till you get to the sands."

I shook my head, laughing. "I'm *at* the sands, old man!" I shouted. "I'm here! I'm in front of you! Can't you see me?"

I tried to let the stone go, drop it back where I'd found it, but somehow my fingers kept clutching it tighter and tighter the more I tried to let it go; its edges dug into my flesh and I was laughing harder, laughing hard and breathless like screaming and I couldn't stop. Florian didn't seem to hear. He shambled away, tottering slowly and then running on his tinder-stick legs, and then he became a huge fattened tick of a deer. The stone became my hand and I slashed his throat with nails grown to long bone-white spikes, heard the poor deer sigh and collapse like Florian had at the moment of death. Blood soaked the sand, rising higher and higher with the incoming tide. I spat out mouthfuls as Teresa's drowned, howling corpse bobbed and floated toward me, rose up and grabbed my throat, pulling me under—

I jolted awake, flailing. I lay on something hard and cold and my right shoulder felt funny, like a weight was pulling it down. My legs ached—legs. My legs. Not numb, or severed, or dead. I tried to sit up, just to check, and it was like pulling a concrete block by twine. Then some heavenly smell drifted past me and there were hands propping me up, holding the bit of heaven just under my nose. It was very dead, whatever it was. My stomach was a hollow husk, dry and thin and feeling like it might tear in two.

"Eat," said the voice. A woman's voice I almost knew, from somewhere.

I ate and ate and ate and didn't look at what I swallowed, just grunted like a kiddie for more. I tried to sit up again because I still had that strange feeling in my shoulder, I had to check, and then I was staring down at my arm, at my hand. My hands. My *two* hands, firm and pink with the skin gathered just right at the knuckles, little pintucks of flesh with no swelling or decay. The nails embedded so tight, so solid at the tips. My *hands*.

I dropped the piece of maggoty carrion I'd been devouring and felt at my face, at my mouth where a soft cushiony lip line now masked my teeth and jaw. Lips were such nasty rubbery things, what did I need with them? Why bother growing them back? My cheeks had gone almost plump and it hurt to touch them, like a big blister. I spat into my hand, and got something streaked with black but turning unmistakably clear. I sniffed my skin. Pure, unadulterated hoo.

My stomach buckled, twisted, but I didn't get sick, just sat on the feeling like an egg until it subsided. Happy now, Jim, wherever you are? I'm not giving you a goddamned thing to eat, I'm keeping it for myself. Eating filth. Eating anything. My hands shook and I grabbed the piece of dead flesh back, swallowed it down in huge tearing mouthfuls; it was delicious to me now, that was the worst part. Happy now?

Someone sat close to me, too close, watching me eat as she made soft munching noises of her own; long straw-dry hair, half bleached blond and half grown-out brown, brushed my face. I turned, and immediately I recognized her. It was the woman from the woods, the one Florian and I saw die, the one whose car came sailing into our parking lot a lifetime ago. Her skin was pink again, not the bluish-black of her transitioning time, and the thick anxious arch of her brows, the curve of her jaw as she bit into her meat and the querulous quirk of her chin, all made up a face I'd known long before, should have known right away when we met again. Standing over my gravestone wiping teary eyes, big bewildered brown eyes I'd looked straight into, back at the park, but never saw for themselves. Opening her mouth square in a scream as she turned and ran. Falling over sick, dying, right at my feet; the shape of her so familiar but with a new liquid, a livid death-liquor, poured inside it so everything about her looked distorted, wobbly, a gelatin torn in two as it separated from the mold. I should still have known. I hadn't wanted to. Just like with so much else.

"Do you know who I am?" she asked.

I nodded. My sister Lisa shook her head, the feel of her hair against my skin like an itch.

"Then you're one up on me," she said. "I don't know if I'm me anymore. But I'm not like the others—like some of the others. Some of us did keep our heads. Or find them again, after a while, for whatever good it does us. Then there's everyone else."

She put a finger to my cheek, so cautious, like the cheek-bone might shatter beneath her touch. "It's good to see you again, Jessie. Even like this."

Good to see me like *this*, again. But not the other way. I had nothing to say to that, absolutely nothing, so I kept eating.

Lisa twitched as she watched me, then grabbed another piece of flesh from the corpse lying next to us and devoured it in two large bites. She was painfully thin, cheeks bending inward like scooped-out gourds and eyes dark-circled and hollow.

"You didn't recognize me at all," she said, licking her lips for the last traces of the taste. "Back in the woods, I mean."

"Your hair," I said. I held out my hand, my right hand, my new right hand, for more meat. "You still had brown hair, when I saw you last. And your face, when you were sick. It was all . . . distorted." The swollen bluish-blackness of her as she staggered up to me and Florian desperate for recognition, starving for squirrel flesh she couldn't keep down. I shuddered. "For a minute, I think, I wasn't sure, but—even your voice sounded different."

"I don't like remembering it. Actually, I don't remember a lot of it." Lisa shook her head. "I wish I could have explained, but my brain wasn't working right. I think the change is a lot rougher on humans than on . . . what you were." She pulled at the cloth of her jeans, twitching, twitching. The shy, soft timidity she'd always had, the pliancy like she was made of a putty you could stick your thumb in deep and yank into any form you chose, had hardened with age or sickness or both, turned her nervy and brittle. "Your face was a hell of a lot different too, when I saw you, but I recognized you. I knew you right off. Your eyes. I can't believe you couldn't see it was me, my eyes, something that—"

I put down my bit of rotten meat and stared into her face, hovering whiny-needy inches from mine. "Someone I love is dead," I said, slow on each syllable. "Dead and eaten. My friends are dead. They tried to help me, and because of it they're dead. They're all dead and thanks to *your* brother the ones who aren't dead are monsters like they never were before and everything I loved is gone and I've apparently turned back into the thing I most hate in the world, so can you give me a fucking break for five minutes or do I have to shut you up the hard way?"

She didn't have anything to say to that so I finished my meal, almost bringing it all back up again in a giant Billy-style belch. So many words all at once, so fast, so effortless, completely distinct, so much tongue and teeth! That couldn't have been me talking, it was a fluke. I grabbed another piece of rottenness and chewed as I looked around. We were in the old abandoned church out on the highway, the floor still covered in brown bloodstains and the powdery remnants of dry-sucked bones. And new corpses, our meal, dragged here who knows when by the Rat or maybe some of them *were* the Rat, I couldn't tell, not anymore. Like it mattered. Anymore. I glanced up at the balcony; we were alone, at least for now. I couldn't stop staring at my new hand.

"It's because you lost it in death," Lisa explained. "When the truck hit you. That and your legs. Anything you lost dying you get back. If you were born without it, though— tough luck. That was disappointing for a few people." She shrugged, actually looked like she might laugh. "Life's just never fair."

"Where are the rest of them?" I asked, more to hear myself talk than anything. Still my voice but it had gone cold, sharp-edged and rat-a-tat staccato, like Ben's or Sam's, like one of the women in those old noir movies: *Johnny, don't ya see I had ta turn ya in! Yer a rotten bum, Johnny!* "The others. Where'd they go?"

Lisa shrugged. "I've been at the wood's edge for a while, I just followed them back in. There's gangs like that every-where now, running around. Just looking for more food." She laughed, a flat, toneless sound. "All anyone anywhere can think about, more food. More food. But it's all running out."

I thought of Linc, kicking and flailing on the ground with Jim, his own gang tearing into his flesh, and decided to think of something else. There were new, dangerously thin walls up in my mind that wouldn't let me think of Joe at all, wouldn't let me remember just what that had been like; the walls hemmed me in like a box, a flimsy magician's cabinet that could collapse on me in an instant, so it took all my concentration to keep the walls standing upright, myself safe inside. Sam's face, alien, twisted with starvation-fueled hate. Renee, staring with dead, hollow eyes up at the moon.

"Jim said you lived with him," I said. "In Mom and Dad's old house. He said he locked you inside when you got sick."

"I got out," she said softly.

"He never mentioned that."

"They'd have found me anyway. Probably killed me. Him too. They were asking him questions. He worked in the labs. It'd got out that they did something, maybe, that helped cause this. Everyone was getting sick. I'd disappeared all of a sudden. They knew what was going on." She pulled herself to her feet, paced back and forth before the altar. "Jim was—I saw him, in the woods, after he got sick, I can't believe that was just days ago, I, you're right. I barely knew him. It's not like someone just being dead." She shuddered. "We were all we had left, Jessie, that's the thing, and I . . . wasn't doing well. He was so good to me, it killed him inside too when you and Mom and Dad—but he held it all together for me. Because I just couldn't. He took care of me, when I needed it. And then at the end, when I needed it again. At least he tried to. I don't know what he was doing at the labs, he wasn't supposed to tell me but I don't care what anyone says, Jessie, I don't believe for one goddamned second he had anything to do with—"

"I asked you one simple question," I said. "I don't want to talk about him again. Ever. You talk too damned much."

And it's because of you. Because *you* came home and said you'd seen me, because that made whatever Jim was holding together inside go flying in all directions and look what he's done now, Lisa, look what he's done trying to save the day like he did when we were all alive. Alive before. Salvage Thanksgiving. Jump between me and Dad. Shout at you, try to get you mad enough to stand up for yourself at long last. Kill the whole world to try to get me back. It's all down to me, Lisa. And him. And you. You were right, Billy. Hell of a family affair.

Lisa stared silently out the remnants of a stained glass window. I got up too, my whole skin tender and almost raw, and began searching for more food. It was hard, in fact almost impossible, to think about anything else; my box's flimsy walls were holding up easier than they should have, because even as words like *alive* and *human* and *Joe* and *Linc* and *Renee* and *sister* kept flitting through my head my mind kept pirouetting away, lighting right back on *food, hunger, food.* It wasn't like before, the bursts of flesh-lust that subsided the second the meat slipped down your throat—this was constant, insistent, tugging at every corner of my body like a whining toddler who wouldn't let go. We'd stripped the corpses to nothing, a pair of piranhas on a picnic. I wrenched off bits of bone, ate them barely tasting them, and suddenly Lisa was right beside me feverishly munching her share.

"You've been out for days," she said. "Eating in your sleep."

I cast around my memory, dredged up nothing but the horrible screaming from my dream. "So what'd I miss?"

Lisa didn't answer, just popped bits of vertebrae whole in her mouth. I searched the pews for more bodies, allowing myself shock at how easily and quickly one foot slipped in front of another, muscles flowing like liquid with every long loose step—no more jerking stiffness, no more stagger. So much easier to keep my balance too, with two arms. It was like dancing and I might have enjoyed it, except for the growing, unshakable sense of panic that there was no more food in the church, that there might not be any more food anywhere and where had all that meat and bone gone, the heavy weight of flesh distending my gut just minutes ago and now I might never have eaten at all? I scratched at one of the dried bloodstains on the floor, trying to bring up some of the brownish powder, then crouched and put my tongue to it to coax it back into liquid. I tasted the sandy edge of concrete, and kept licking anyway.

"What are you doing?" Lisa demanded, right behind me.

I jumped backward, the heat rising to my new face, and snarled at her. She just shrugged again, like nothing surprised her, and handed me pieces of skull, a sucked-out bit of femur. As I gulped them down and licked my fingers clean she glanced out another of the window holes, the spring breeze wrapping half-bleached hair strands around her face, and sighed. I touched my own hair, touched it with my new right hand; it was one huge snarl, but thick and covering my whole scalp once more.

"Is this how it happened to you?" I said. "Like this, but worse?"

"First, you're so sick you can't eat anything. Hot, dizzy, aching, weak. Your skin turns blue. Then blackish. Then . . . rotten. Oh, hell, you saw it." She shook her head, remembering. "And it feels raw, like a huge blister. It's hard to breathe. A lot of folks died in that stage of it. Just asphyxiated. Then you get hungry. Ravenous. All day. All night. But you're sick along with it, can't stop throwing up. Then . . ." She shrugged. "You either die for real, like you must've thought I did, or you're out cold for a while and then you wake up like this." Her voice was dull and indifferent, like a comedian weary to get to the punch line and crawl offstage. "For better or worse. Sometimes you're a little crazy, right after you do wake up again. Happy crazy. Furious crazy. Crazy like you can't stop laughing at everything, right before you kill it—"

I remembered the gleeful, deranged glitter in Ben's eyes, the all-consuming chill coming off Sam like winter breath. Poor Sam. "I've seen," I said.

"Well, that's what it's like for humans anyway, living humans. Your kind too, I guess. It used to take weeks. Now it's hours. I guess the virus mutated again—"

"Bacterium," I said. "But this goes away, right? Feeling like this?"

Lisa hesitated. I thought of Teresa's trembling, Rommel's bellows of famine. Food. More food. I'm hungry, goddammit. Ben, bitten, his arm gone rotten, dead. He and Sam.

Except not. *You're out cold for a while and then you wake up like this.* Hot, dizzy, aching, weak. Like I'd been feeling, before Teresa ever attacked me. Just like Joe said. He was right. All along, he was right.

"Are any humans left?" I asked. "Is anyone immune to this?"

"A few. I think. If they can outrun all the sick ones like me, who'll eat anything they can—a few. Very few. I don't envy them at all."

Immune, just like Joe. Who got tired of running. "It goes away," I said. "Feeling like this."

"It did for a while." Lisa turned to me, arms wrapped around herself, around her stomach aching like mine. She crunched another mouthful of bone fragments. "Then it comes back. The hunger comes back. And it's even worse than before. And then, at the very end . . . well. You can't eat at all. You just waste away."

I slipped a hand into my pocket, gripping the lake stone that sat there like a long-ago promise, like a reproach. *Stop wasting them bits and pieces.* Why should I, Florian? Just because they're all I have left now of *you*? Of anyone. The blistery feeling making my skin twitch and shiver subsided, receded as I stroked its surface, like something was gently touching me in turn. Florian's pouch of stones still rested on my hip but someone had undone the ties holding it in place while I was out, retied them in an inept bird's nest of a knot. Lisa must've been looking for more food. Stones were one of the few things my teeth, my good old undead teeth now stolen from me forever, hadn't been able to crunch through. More food. We needed to look for more food. Run away from this horrible place where my afterlife ended, was stolen away. Where Joe, Linc, Renee, the Sam and Ben I'd known had all died, because I couldn't hide and keep still around a grave-haunting hoo. Hunger and shame. And grief. Nothing else to offer Lisa, or anyone. I clutched the stone tight as I could.

"I have to get out of here," I said.

"Might be smart. There's all sorts of gangs and mobs

wandering around out here now, looking for more meat. They'll strip your forest clean in days. Every animal they can hunt. Until they start dying too." Lisa looked thoughtful. "Though if we just lie low for a while longer, until they do—"

"I have to get out of here."

Lisa stared at me for a minute. Then she nodded. "North," she said. "Toward the cities. The dying part of the plague's in full swing up there. Bodies everywhere. There'll be a lot more to eat."

Her voice was detached and casually distant but the flicker of horror in her own eyes, at herself, made her suddenly seem more like my Lisa, the sister I'd known living, than anything in her face, her voice, her hair reverting back to its old nondescript brown. Those things, those physical things, were mere familiar signposts along the road to her but that moment of shame, disgust, grief, all-consuming famine, that was the destination. I knew that place so well already, in such a short time. The look died in her eyes just as soon as it sparked.

"Can you walk okay?" she asked, as she twisted her hair into a chaotic ponytail.

"Never better," I said, and almost laughed to realize it was true. "Lisa?"

"Yeah, Jessie?"

"I'm so hungry."

It just came out and I was so embarrassed saying it, teary embarrassed, like a little kid needing the bathroom for the fourth time in a row and it really felt as urgent as that, worse. Lisa didn't laugh, though. I saw anew just how thin her face was, how her beautifully taut unbroken unrotted skin outlined every bone in her wrists and arms.

"So am I," she said. "So is everyone. Like I told you. Don't worry, though—if it comes to that, you're probably strong enough to fight me off."

Ten, fifteen, twenty miles up the empty highway heading past Morewood, through the long-abandoned remains of Taltree Acres, veering toward Lake Station and Gary. I didn't speak, just kept feeling my chest expand full of air by slow degrees, let it out, take it in again, over and over like it'd never lost the knack; *I breathe now*, I kept thinking, breathing with my lungs, it was so awful and so dependent of me, the thought the earth that gave birth to me could now suffocate me filled me with horror, but still I drew in long, short, fast, slow breaths until I hiccupped and grew dizzy, amazed at the sheer novelty. And my hand, my new hand, my new arm! And how quickly, easily my legs swung forward and forward again, like they'd been born to the task! Neither of us seemed to need rest, never mind sleep.

What stopped us was hunger, the need to pause every half hour, every quarter hour, every tick on the stopwatch to gorge on possum or rabbit until bloated and sick and then feel it all melt away in a mile. We didn't find much possum or rabbit either, as we retraced Lisa's path: She was right, the forests were being stripped. By the time we hit the old u-pick blueberry farm on the Lepingville outskirts we were chewing fistfuls of weeds, cursing the sweet wonderful berries denied us because summer hadn't hit. At least it made it easy not to think about Joe or Renee or Sam or Linc. Too much. The flimsy box walls in my mind wavered, but they held. Who did Lisa think about? Jim? That guy Jim had mentioned, who didn't stick around? She'd gone so quiet, chin dipped to her chest in a posture of mobile defeat, I was scared to ask.

When we got to Lepingville proper, the trees suddenly gave way to empty car washes, deserted office parks, abandoned strip mall after strip mall after strip mall; lots of abandoned cars now too, no more clean deserted roads, but nary a body in sight. Lisa abruptly came to life, yanking me right off the roadside.

"More gangs up here," she muttered, as if we were house-safe crouching in a six-inch ditch. "We're a moving target."

"We'd be one anyway. Let's hit the fast-food places, they might have supplies in storage, meat patties—"

"I told you, they've already beat us to it—you've been a little isolated, haven't you? You were lucky." She laughed, squatting there in the dirt. "Lucky, lucky. Nothing to eat here. Nothing to eat anywhere."

She'd used herself up, I realized, in the retrieving of me and now was falling back into some sort of habitual starved torpor. So why even bother rescuing another mouth to feed? The surge of irritation I felt was another welcome distraction.

"I'm looking anyway," I said, and ran across the road before she could stop me. She was right, of course: Burger Mart, Steak Shack, Mambo Italiano, the Mexican Grill, the Texas Grill, the Hawaiian Grill, Al's Country Grill, all looted and stripped to the Formica and that too was scored deep with toothmarks. The stench of leaking gas was everywhere. At least there were still those lovely little packets of ketchup, relish, honey mustard, steak sauce, mayonnaise, jam, dozens of them that we popped into our mouths whole and let burst on our tongues.

As we walked on, spitting out plastic scraps, all else we found to eat were chewed-up bits of bone lying near the shells of cars, thrown into careless heaps like the remains of a jumbo-bucket chicken dinner. Through it all the seagulls still swooped and strutted around the empty parking lots, pecking at the garbage and rising upward with slow, mocking ease whenever we tried to catch them. The smell of burned flesh, a mere hint in the air just outside town, grew stronger and more acrid the farther we walked.

"I told you," Lisa said, stuffing her pockets with bone leavings and shaking hard with hunger. "Nothing to eat anywhere, until we get to the cities. Maybe not even then. Nothing to eat except us. Tell you what, I really miss when all that ate humans were walking corpses you could outrun without trying. We were so spoiled. We didn't know how good we had it."

"I didn't eat humans," I said.

She made a harsh sound barely disguised as a laugh. "Then you were definitely a cut above us."

A few more miles, and we started seeing signs of life: actual dead bodies mixed in with the skeletons (bird-pillaged, barely any flesh left for us), a few random figures wandering slowly, haphazardly around the parking lots with too little purpose to be an actual gang. As we watched they hunched in a circle, tearing a corpse to bite-sized pieces—a silent, weirdly harmonious scene—except for one who seemed confused and just kept squatting down, standing up, squatting again yards from the actual meal. Suddenly he collapsed where he stood, sinking to the asphalt and going instantly still. His friends, busy eating, didn't seem to notice.

"Oh, good," Lisa whispered, her eyes glittering, and we almost ran across the highway: Only one of them looked up when he heard, but he just bent right back over his food. We tore off handfuls of corpse flesh and barely bothered chewing before we swallowed, too tearfully grateful for actual real meat to savor our meal, and I was in such a thick haze of hungry oblivion that when I felt something tap my shoulder I shouted in surprise.

Lisa growled like an undead, jumping to her feet ready to fight. It was another fellow from the group, this one older and even more gaunt, more of a starveling than Lisa. He raised his hands in surrender, then motioned toward his friends: One of them had grabbed a matchbook from somewhere and was building a fire with scraps of wood, roasting the last bits of corpse to a turn. He nodded at the fire, then the piece of flesh I gripped in my hands. It could've been a trap, I supposed, but what's life without risk? I walked over and watched him fuss silently over the fire, blowing at it until it leapt to life, then move back so we could all cook our meals.

"Thanks," I said.

No reply. It felt weird holding our food directly over the flames with our hands, seeing my own flesh go boiling red and then blacken and instantly heal again, but it's not like we had any sticks and I didn't feel a thing but a vague, faraway warmth. Cooked meat, it turned out, was so incredibly good I almost moaned biting into it. The others ate too but more slowly, indifferently, and one of them dropped his last bit of meat to the blacktop; they all shuffled away, abandoning the fire as they headed past the intersection and toward the county line. The second they were gone Lisa ran for the fire, trying to roast half an arm whole over the little flickers of flame.

"God," she whispered between bites, shaking, "the fat just gets all hot and sizzling, it's—God—"

Maybe the one we were eating would have offered us a place by the fire too. That bothered me, and the thought that it was supposed to bother me didn't help (talk about your useless, bygone sentiments), but what scared me was that the others didn't want his flesh anymore—that's what the fire was really for, I could see it, a bit of novelty to try to coax themselves to eat. Was that what awaited us, after this horrible hunger finally ebbed? Lisa said so, by the end you couldn't eat at all. And apparently, from the way my own charred flesh healed in seconds, the way Sam and Teresa got right back up again after being smashed in two, you couldn't even kill yourself. You had to let yourself be scorched by famine, seared as if someone took a slow blowtorch to every cell, and then feel it consume you from the inside out, Prometheus and the vulture in the same body—

The liver. Lisa hadn't found the liver yet, the guts, she was too human to know they were the best part. I tore at the corpse, determined to get them before her, and when I raised my head again I saw an old gray-headed fellow on a rusty bike watching me from the roadside. I just stared at him, and he must've been a true hoo because he moaned aloud, the *waaahh* of prey that knew it was only a matter of time, and pumped the pedals so hard down the road shoulder I could hear him wheezing and gasping even as I laughed. Off he went, right into the arms of our new friends.

I could have caught up with him, and eaten him, yes. Easily. That second. But looking at his crumb-encrusted beard, the parka deflated from all the holes where the cotton batting escaped, his shoes splitting off from the sole, I thought it was damned unfair to kill someone just because he couldn't buy the fleeting protection of a car.

Lisa saw us both from across the parking lot, saw his bike becoming a vanishing spot in the distance and ran to me in disbelief, too late to get him. "You're crazy," she shouted at me, licking traces of blood and melted fat from her fingers, hands, forearms like a manic cat. "Absolutely out of your mind, you're completely stupid and crazy, it must run in this family. Why the hell did you let him get away? You think that much fresh meat just waltzes by every day?"

"I didn't want to kill him," I said, and left it at that. "It wasn't fair."

"Fair?" I saw her fingers twitch to slap me, but she was too smart for that. The words surged from her hard and fast like Mom when she really lost it, like Mom when she was angry she couldn't just let herself haul off and smack you. "So you let him go and now what, Jesus gives you a cookie? Like he's not gonna die anyway, probably a lot slower than we would've done it." She grabbed at the viscera, cramming a fistful into her mouth before I could snatch it back. "I can't believe you don't get it yet, how many ways do I have to spell it out, the world is ending, starvation or being eaten alive is all we've got to look forward to, and you—"

"Sorry," I snarled, grabbing another fistful from right under her grasping hand, "but the world isn't ending. We're ending. Every other species alive'll throw a big party, now that humans have finally gotten what they deserve right at the hands of one of their—"

"God, I don't believe it—the same animal rights bullshit you were spouting when you were alive, at least then you were too young to know better. It's pathetic." Lisa gave me a shove. "You're actually glad this is happening, aren't you? The zombies' big revenge on the humans? You're glad!"

I threw her to the tarmac, punching and kicking until she shrieked. It felt incredibly good to have two working fists, the only thing about this horrible meat-body I could learn to love. "I was minding my own damned business when your species decided to screw with ours and destroy us both," I snarled. "We were all minding our own business and I wasn't hurting anyone, you did it, *he* did it, but you know what? I am glad. You think I want to be stuck in this filthy human body any longer than I have to be? With you for company? Hovering over me breathing into my face, pissing, moaning, whiiiining poor you—"

"Just you wait," she sneered, exactly like Mom now. Spitting image. "Just wait until you really start starving to death—"

"Anything for some peace and quiet!"

I marched over to the fire and stomped it out, feeling a detached sort of interest in how my bare feet didn't melt or char, and then headed for one of the empty strip mall shops to rest, alone. The fabric store was relatively intact and with bedding to boot; I picked around until I found an unrolled bolt of something that felt flannel-like, wrapped myself in it and curled up with my back to a sales counter, imagining it was Renee or Linc I felt pressing against me. I started to shiver. Then an actual draft blew right over me, making the fabric ends flap like flags; someone had opened the store door.

"Jessie?" Lisa murmured.

I didn't open my eyes. She lay down next to me and I wrapped the flannel tighter around myself. She pushed in closer, and slowly a bit of our warmth seeped into each other's skins. Even through the layers of cloth her shoulder blades, her elbows were jutting and sharp.

"I'm sorry," she said.

Whatever. I'm sorry, you're sorry, we're all goddamned sorry. Mom was always sorry too. I didn't answer, just felt for Florian's little bag of stones and cradled it close in my hands. That and Lisa were all I had left now. Just like that wretched old hoo and his bike.

"I miss my daughter," Lisa whispered, her voice shaky and full.

Daughter. Daughter? I had a niece? Had. I didn't dare ask what had happened to her. For a second I thought Lisa might start weeping and keening like in the movies but instead she just lay there, dead quiet, her sharp-chinned head tucked against my arm. Gradually her breath became slow and even, and I pulled free carefully as I could.

Peace and quiet. Too dark now and too quiet, and they were all slipping back to me through the cracks in the walls: Linc, Renee, Joe, Ben, Sam, Florian, my parents, tugging at bits and pieces of my mind until I felt sucked dry and exhausted. My grandmother. Mags and Billy. That poor bastard on the bike. The niece I'd never had. Lillian. Annie. When I was still dead we beat this kind of rank sentimentality out of each other, but now here I was revived and stuck with nothing ahead of me but the two things I'd hated most about living: tedium and loss. What the hell was life anyway, but one long meaningless slow-motion act of loss? Like a big brimming jar inside you that kept tipping over and spilling, tipping and spilling, until you were down to your last swallow and had no choice but to go forward and forward and forward slowly sinking from thirst.

And so what do you do when it's gone, when even the dark wet stain on the inside of the jar has dried up and faded away? You don't die, you just realize you'll never be free again as long as the memory of the full jar is with you, as long as the echo of what you once had calls out to you. Like how long after Joe found me and I had my new family I could still hear bursts of my parents' brain radios, very late at night as they wandered east through Indiana and Ohio, and then there came that moment when I couldn't pick them up at all: a light shining from a farmhouse window on some dark, empty highway, streaking brightly across your windshield as you drive past, and then fading. And then gone.

I reached toward Lisa again and groped for her hand. She stirred awake, fingers grabbing mine and pressing hard.

15

All up and down the road leading north, just the dead, the dying and us. Corpses piled everywhere, soon-to-be corpses wandering aimlessly, indifferently along the roadside, no fighting for our food other than with rats and birds. Lisa was actually scared of the rats, jumping and shuddering at those hostile squalling chirrups, but I just took my share of bites: Only one thing could kill us now, and rabies wasn't it. Besides, she was more than happy to eat them, once I'd snapped their necks. I was the Little Red Hen at the End of the World.

The hunger kept growing worse. We ate and ate and ate, freshly killed, weeks dead, long-rotting things without discrimination, without tasting, and it melted away in the time it took to bite and chew. Restaurant ketchup, honey, shredded potatoes gone rancid. Blackened supermarket produce, rock-stale cereal, smashed-open cans of creamed corn and tomato paste and cold salty soup. The trees confused me at first, it was spring budding season and they were still bare as winter, then I realized the branches had been tooth-stripped, from berries to bark. Underfoot large, uneven grass patches were missing, torn out in hungry fistfuls; we grabbed some ourselves, trying to fill the empty spaces inside.

"I can't stand this anymore," Lisa wept, as we licked at fistfuls of salt poured into our palms, gnawed twigs and chicken bones, targeted the ever-multiplying rats. "I can't. I just want to die. Why can't we die?"

"Don't tempt me," I snapped. "You sleep a lot more than I do."

"Do it!" she screamed, holding her arms out like I might shoot her in the chest. "I don't care anymore! I don't! This is hell!"

Oh good, unhinged melodramatics! That would help! Typical human and no, I *refused* to start thinking of myself as one too. "Speaking," I said, as coldly and calmly as I could muster, "as someone with a little actual afterlife experience? This isn't hell. There is no hell. It's just what your kind always do to the world in one form or another, so pull yourself together and keep walking."

"Why!" she shouted, shaking me hard. "For what? We're out of the damn woods! Isn't that what you wanted? There's nothing else out there, we can fucking stop now! What the hell are you looking for? *Why are we doing this?*"

I squeezed the lake stone sitting quiet and patient in my pocket, willing it to keep me calm, keep me seeming rational even though I knew I'd gone crazy: All I wanted now was the beach, I wanted to see it, feel the sands underfoot before I died. The sands I'd never walked on as a hoo, that I'd ignored entirely while I was undead, now that I was born times three suddenly I wanted them, needed them, so badly that the yearning had swallowed me whole even as hunger hollowed me out. I missed my beach. And it wasn't even *my* beach— except maybe it was, maybe it really was, thousands of years ago, just like all the stories said, maybe it was the whole reason I'd become what I was. So I wanted to see it, just the one time. To see just where I'd come from. To say good-bye.

I turned my back on my sister and continued down the road. The stone deep in my pocket, the little bag of them weighty at my side: Florian was right. Hunger or no hunger, they kept me walking.

Lisa followed behind me, stumbling over her own feet,

sobbing under her snot-clogged breath. The rats swarmed around us, single-mindedly mean in a way I'd grown to admire; bare dead branches and bones snapped almost apologetically underfoot. Move. Ten more miles, fifteen, fifty, a hundred and fifty, twenty thousand. Look. All the town gates swinging wide open, security fences torn up, guard booths long deserted. Eaten-up corpses (not enough, nothing was ever enough), houses trashed inside and out for any trace of food (we tore them apart all over again anyway), whole neighborhoods reduced to smoldering cinders from a leaking gas main or arson or flamethrower panic or someone's fucked-up try at roasting remains, the poor dead torn-apart dogs and cats and rabbits and coyotes (but we finished off whatever was left). The stench coating our mouths. Vermin everywhere. A kiddie of two or three lying facedown by the roadside in a brackish rain puddle, naked, gnawed-on. Our stomachs growled at the sight. We didn't touch it. A woman, also naked, stumbling dazed down the road's shoulder, cradling something in a blanket in her arms, something stinking and buzzing with flies—

I don't want to talk about it.

Another torn-up security gate, the electronic sensors smashed, the metal warped and buckled like a neck wrung in a giant fist. A long stretch of railroad track surrounded by overgrown, leaf-stripped trees, dilapidated food-trashed wooden houses peeking out from the foliage, the soil underfoot pale and full of sandy grit: the outskirts of Prairie Beach, a little shore town that Gary swallowed up and annexed a hundred years ago or more. Up north, at long last. How far were we from the beaches? I didn't know this place, had been here maybe once while I was alive, just knew that if you kept going north far enough then boom, smack, water. I should've let Joe take me here, when I'd had the chance. A hundred years ago or more.

"I need to rest," Lisa said, quiet enough that I knew she wasn't kidding. She shook like a scrap of paper twisting in the wind, her face a hollow-eyed smear of chalk. "Okay? More walking later?"

"No more walking," I promised. Plague-converted hoos weren't as strong as my kind, that much was becoming clear, or maybe it was just she'd been sick that much longer. I was an asshole for pushing her so far either way, but I had to. I had to get here. I couldn't explain. "Over by the trees. We'll rest there."

Across the road was something that looked like a little nature preserve, sand-duneish prairie cheek by jowl with the coiled gray guts of a power station and another abandoned supermarket. Lisa and I looked over at the supermarket, mouths watering though we knew it'd be an empty looted box, and then we saw someone alive near the opposite end of the preserve, his back to us, a black coat far too big for him flapping in the breeze as he stood over a neat line of corpses.

We ducked behind a knot of debarked trees to watch. He hovered over the bodies, closing eyelids, preparing his little makeshift morgue for funerals that would never occur. Unaltered hoo, then, either that or like us but past wanting to feed. Either way, we'd be doing him a favor. And it felt like decades since I'd eaten anything blood-warm and freshly killed.

We crept forward quietly as we could, Lisa letting me set the pace. He was careless, not minding the perimeter as he worked, and while he stood there rolling and unrolling his coat cuffs like someone fussing with a venetian blind we came within ambush distance unnoticed. A glint of metal caught my eye and I saw the shovel leaning against a nearby tree. If I'd only had this body while undead, this speed, this ease—in one amazingly easy movement I rose to my feet, grabbed the shovel, crept behind him and put all my strength into a blow to the back of the skull.

He staggered, stunned, but his brains stayed inside his broken head: One of us, then, we'd have to fight. I so badly wanted to fight. He whipped around, snarling in anger and pain, and I struck again and again with Lisa kicking and punching from behind, bludgeon blows that healed within seconds but still got him down to his knees, curled up in a quaking ball on the ground. I raised the shovel in both hands, aiming for the neck, and he pulled himself upright and lunged for my legs.

"Jessie!" he shouted, clutching at me in entreaty. *"Jessie!"*

I stood there, the shovel still held high. He crouched in that ridiculous black coat, a tangled mess of dark hair falling over his thin, sallow, homely face, and as I looked into Linc's eyes I dropped the shovel and started to laugh and laugh and couldn't stop. Then I started shaking, still laughing myself watery-eyed and sick. Lisa lunged for him one last time, and he turned and, as pure afterthought, punched her breathless. The hilarity of that almost doubled me over.

"I saw you being eaten," I pointed out, and got quite giggly at the thought of it. "I saw—"

"Jessie," said Lisa, her meal snatched right off the plate, "you're doing it again. Stop it—"

I couldn't stop. Linc had my arm and was saying something about being left there half-dead, there was this huge fight, wasn't it just his destiny to get lost in the shuffle, if I greeted my friends this way what would I do if the Rat revived, and I just mopped my eyes and gasped for breath. He kept stopping to kiss me, again and again. The touch barely registered. Lisa followed sullen and drained behind us as Linc led me down a hill slope and into a thick, denuded copse of maples, full of thin, sick near-corpses just like him, just like me. They huddled together in their own little groups, watching us with such mild, distant curiosity that I knew they were dying.

"Look what I found!" Linc shouted, raising my arm up like a winning prizefighter.

They looked at me and went right back to huddling and shuffling in silence, but then suddenly one of them came running. A blond girl with a beautiful face, head-turning even wasted to bones and nothingness, came up to me, took my arm and sat me right down in the dirt.

"We thought you were dead," Renee said calmly, and

then almost broke my ribs in a huge sharp-boned hug. "We were out, and then . . . we just woke up, I can't explain—"

"Same here," I said.

"Linc was hurt and we couldn't have fought and any minute we expected—we were so damned lucky." She jerked her head toward Lisa, her expression hostile. "We thought she took you away to eat you—"

"That's my sister," I explained. "Lisa. She got me out. She's all right."

"Oh, the gratitude," Lisa called out bitterly. "Warms the cockles."

"I don't know why they left us there," Renee said, ignoring Lisa. "They must've been looking for food, any kind of food, but they wanted to fight even more than that. So they just left us there to rot. Thank God." She rubbed at my face like a mom with a toddler, scrubbing away tear streaks and blood and dirt with her sleeve. "When we woke up some of them were still wandering around the woods, getting weaker, and we all sort of drifted up here together." Her eyes flitted around the preserve, resigned and sad. "That was a few days ago, I guess. The Rat was there fighting, Jessie, you should see them now, they're all so sick, the gang's fallen apart—"

"Hey, we did okay," said a new voice, the scraped-clean shell of its former self. "For a while."

A blanket-wrapped wraith stood over me: Ron, Rommel's second in command from the Rat. I laughed again, knowing I sounded crueler than I felt, but he just shrugged and grinned. "Man, Jessie," he said, "you got some crazy shitheads in your family, you know that? Sicking up the whole world? Just to prove he can? And Rommel and I thought we were nuts—"

"Where's Rommel?" I asked. "Where's Jim?"

"Rommel's dead." Something that looked like actual sorrow flitted over his face, almost too quick to catch. "The lucky son of a bitch. As for your crazy shithead brother, who goddamned knows, he sure didn't look too good when we—"

"Is anyone gonna feed us?" Lisa demanded, embarrassingly whiny. Renee tossed a rock at her, barely bothering to look up.

"Be nice to her," I muttered under my breath. "She's my sister; she got sick. She lost her kid. For all I know, she may have eaten her."

"My whole family's dead." Renee shrugged, and blinked hard for a moment. "We found their bodies. At least it was quick. I'm going to pretend it was, anyway—"

"Never mind what we saw getting up here," Linc said. He shuddered. "Or what we did. We're here now." He nodded toward the others. "I'm starting to wonder if we're the last ones left. Anywhere."

For all of that, he couldn't seem to stop smiling. He kissed me again, taking my face between his hands and planting a wet smack right on my forehead. Ron snorted at the sight and Renee, so beautiful even starving that it shocked me, grinned at us both; I looked down, embarrassed again, and I saw my sunken wrist, every tiny bone risen up to the surface. I'd been inhaling meat, sucking down marrow, chewing wood, feasting on filth but it was starting, the big reversal. Just like Lisa had promised. I was a little kid staring down from the high high peak of a metal playground slide, impatient and hostile screams coming from the ladder behind me, my stomach falling as I realized the length of the shiny-hot drop.

Linc put fingers to my cheekbone, slid them to the jaw. His fingertips were amazingly cool and light. "You're hollowed out too," he said. "Worse than us."

"We were so strong," said Renee, with no regret, just a sort of wonderment for glories long past. "For a few days. And so hungry. And now . . ." She laughed. "We can't eat anymore. Can't eat anything. Can't make ourselves eat, can't keep anything down. Hair's starting to fall out too. And I'd been so glad to get it back."

Wasting away. I didn't even get the glory part, I was too busy being delirious. I put an arm around her and squeezed for a moment. Then I picked up her hand, studying it, the hand that had scrubbed the mess of fighting and crying from my own face: It glinted faintly in the sunlight, rings piled indiscriminately atop each other on the nearly fleshless fingers like horseshoes on a stake. Teresa's rings. Silver filigree, a sterling turtle with little opal eyes, a whole stack of what looked like dirtied white gold wedding bands. A garnet in a nest of tiny tarnished leaves.

"I wanted them," Renee said. She had a look in her eyes like the night we'd fought the Rat except quieter, harder. "So now I've got them."

"They won't do you much good now," I said.

"They're worthless," she said. "But they're a good reminder."

I thought about that, and nodded, and let her hand drop.

"Well, I'm still hungry," Lisa said, her voice loud and defiant. "And it doesn't look like there's too much competition for the eats, so what do you say, Jessie?"

Renee shrugged, not taking the bait, and glanced around the silent encampment full of emaciated faces. "No, you're right," she told Lisa, "none of us can eat, and you already saw there's some food over by the trees—"

"I still think we should bury them," Linc said.

"And I already told you, don't waste what energy you've got left," Renee replied, with a sharpness that told me this wasn't a new argument. "Jessie still needs food too. Eat what you want," she called out, "but do it over by the hillside, not here. We want to keep this place halfway civilized, while we can."

Lisa ran feverishly for the corpses. I looked into Renee's and Linc's solemn faces, saw how even Ron had turned quiet and weirdly pacific in his dying, thought of the hoos who'd let us share their fire, and felt ashamed of myself. Linc must've seen it because he patted my arm, understanding in his eyes. "It's easy for us to act civilized, now," he said. "I mean, there's nothing else left we can do."

I avoided his gaze. My stomach was still growling for more but even though that had been all of us here, every one, I still felt too embarrassed to go scuttling for food. I fumbled with the knot on Florian's stone pouch and slipped it off my hip, sat holding it in my lap. It was starting to feel heavy. Much too heavy. Renee actually smiled at the sight, slipping a ringed-up hand into her pocket and producing a stone with striations like mother of pearl.

"We took them with us," she said. "All the ones we could pick up." She curled her fingers over it, holding on tight. "I feel a little less sick when I have one in my hand. Makes me think of things before. Another good reminder. Funny, huh, how even when you know it's all in your head—"

"Why did you come all this way?" I asked. The pouch's bulging, blunted edges were, in fact, reassuring to the touch. "It's not any better here. Worse."

"Damned if we know." Linc laughed. He slipped a hand into the pouch, pulled out a green stone, stroked its surface. "Not any better? You're being nice, it's hell up here. We just . . . felt like we had to be here." He dropped it back inside, fished around again, pulled out a gray one. "Like we had to die here. I don't know why."

"I miss the beaches," Ron said, watching Linc's hands with a vague, but unflagging, interest. "Used to like it here. Even with the fucking scientists maggot-crawling every-where trying to tag your every move—"

My beach. Miss my beach. Get me my beach. The scientists. Octave Chanute. That would be right near here, the nearest beach, just a little farther north. Jim's lab. Where it all began and not just in happy sand-strewn myth-time, where whatever the hell I am now was born—you wanted to go back to what made you so bad? See where you came from? Here's the belly of the goddamned beast, have a grand old time sloshing around inside. I felt like laughing myself.

"How far away is it?" I asked Ron. "The beach."

"Ten more miles? Little less? Fuck, I don't know." He clutched the blanket tighter around him. "Doesn't matter now. Too damned far away."

Ten miles? That was nothing, Lisa and I had gone so much farther to get here, Ron, Renee, Linc so much farther still—and now that I'd made the mistake of giving in to Lisa's exhaustion, sitting down, the thought of even one more mile made me shake where I sat and cling to the stone pouch like the edge of a life raft. Linc let the gray stone slip back inside and I retrieved it, held it in my fingers, slowly squeezed with all the strength I had left to make its edges crumble into a fine, pebbly powder; we'd eaten that too, Lisa and I, licking at the chalky remnants of rocks and concrete and chunks of asphalt as we crawled up north. I squeezed harder. The lake stones wouldn't crumble, chip, crack, not for anything. Linc smiled at the sight.

"We tried that too," he said. "When we were still hungry. Almost split our teeth trying to bite them." He gently took the stone from my hands, slipped it back into the pouch. "Just as well. They're all we have left of . . ."

He trailed off. Everything. That's all they are. All we have now. And each other, for a few more days, a few more hours. Linc wasn't lost. Renee. Maybe that meant that somehow, somewhere out there, by some crazy fucked-up miracle, Joe—

Enough. Tarry black blood and a few random bits of broken bone, one still stretched out like an entreating arm. Nothing. Nothing for anyone. Just like he wanted.

Linc pulled himself off the ground and motioned for me to get up, led me toward the others. "There's someone else here," he said. "I don't know if you'll want to see them, after—but they're here."

Ron trailed behind us, like he had nothing better to do (and still, even now, I had to remind myself he wouldn't jump me, that Rommel wasn't in the trees coiled and ready to spring). Past the huddled masses, all shivering though the day was spring hot, and then Linc took me down a hill slope and toward the preserve's tiny visitors' station, a concrete box sitting on a broken bit of parking lot. A body lay outside the restrooms, curled up in a familiar posture of approaching death. Standing over it, stomping his feet and laughing at nothing, was a bag of bones with Ben's broad, angular face. He caught my eye and without thinking, I backed away.

"Jessie," he said, with an oblivious, crazy grin. "It's so good to see you again, Jessie, we gotta get the old gang back, we were over there and now we're here, I don't know how we got here but we gotta all get back together, we gotta show the Rat that's not their land—"

"Jesus," Ron muttered, shaking his head. "If you were gonna try to cave someone's skull in, Jessie, why couldn't it have been him?"

"Calm down now, Ben," murmured the body at his feet, every shaking muscle evidence of the effort it took him to speak. "Calm down. It's all right."

Sam. I knelt down by his side. His face was weary, resigned, almost serene in its utter lack of hope. Just like he'd always looked, since first I'd met him.

"It's good to see you again," I whispered.

"You can't mean that," he said, and I actually got a smile. "Not after—"

"Yeah, I do," I said, patting him gently on the shoulder. He was himself again, the plague-madness had passed. I always had a weakness for the old ones. "I do. How long has he been like this?"

Sam smiled again, slow and delicate like a hairline crack spreading through porcelain. "When we stopped being hungry, and he realized what we'd both done."

"We gotta get the old gang back together, Jessie." Ben crouched by us and rubbed his hands together like he could abracadabra himself an appetite, teeth chattering, shivering head to toe. His skin was tinged blue, like Lisa in her transition. "We can get the old gang back together, get back into the forests where there's some really good hunting—"

"There's no more hunting, Ben," I said. "Not now. There's nothing left to hunt."

"It's true," Ron said, and grinned proudly even as he shivered and stamped his emaciated feet. "We stripped those woods clean. Everything we could eat. Didn't do us any damned good, though."

Sam lay there on his side, moaning like Florian when he was dying. A thin little thread of his blood went drip, drip from a wound on his hand, then the vein sealed itself shut once more. My mouth watered and I put a hand to it quickly, stanching the flow. He raised his chin, his eyes glassy-bright marbles shining with pain; the thin little tufts of gray hair on his head were falling out again, his skin the color of ash.

"Joe," he whispered. "I'm so sorry—"

"It's okay," I said, and it was. Even though it never would be, it was. "You couldn't help it. And he wanted to die."

Sam shook his head and moaned again, in pain or shame or both. Ben stomped his feet harder, faster, like he could crush whatever was killing all of us underfoot, then suddenly lay down next to Sam and closed his eyes. "Calm down, Ben," he muttered to himself. "It's all right."

Ron shook his head and started walking back up the hill; none of the Rat ever could abide it, babying the unfit. Sam watched until Ron had vanished over the hill crest, then dropped his head with relief and grabbed at my hand, at Linc's.

"I want to go," he said. "I—"

A fit of coughing rattled him and Ben squeezed his own eyes tighter shut, twitching and crying like a scared dog. "Calm down, Ben," Sam said, gasping for breath, and squeezed my fingers. "Second time now, that I cut my throat and it didn't do anything. First time, undead. Second time, this." His expression turned hard, urgent, cold. "No third."

I turned to Linc; this was his gang and Renee's, or at least that's how I saw it. He nodded. "Go get Renee," I said. "So she can say good-bye."

Linc nodded and walked off. To find Renee, so she could say good-bye. So after that, she and Linc would have first crack at some fresher meat they might actually be able to keep down. I told you we were never sentimental. A little breeze drifted over the lot carrying the fragrance of the lilac bushes near the restroom doors, tiny scrubby lilacs giving us a last burst of sweet scent before they died. I remembered that deer hunt in Great River and Lisa, already sick unto death, nearly crashing her car in that other parking lot. Just a few months ago. Decades of days.

Footsteps were coming back down the hillside. Linc. Renee. Lisa. Some other, strange faces. News traveled fast.

Sam lay there back to back with Ben, like sleeping in the old days, and kissed my hand with a sweep of cold, dry lips.

"Make it quick," he whispered. "For us both. Make it quick."

We did. We feasted, that night, on Sam's body, on Ben's. Even Linc and Renee ate. And we were all starving again in under an hour.

16

Lisa held my head as I got sick, sick everywhere, puking up everything I'd ever eaten. The thought of meat, of any meat, still made my mouth drip drool and my stomach tighten in anticipation, but then it kept tightening and tightening like an iron band until the meat rocketed back up again and my throat burned with acid. Lisa's own puking marathon had ended hours earlier and now she was even sicker, shivering furiously no matter how warm the sun and the old, telltale blue tinge creeping over her skin like mold blooming on bread. Full circle, I thought, huddled on my knees and clutching my middle, trying to will the iron band to loosen. Full circle.

"Help me out here, Rob," Lisa said softly. "I need—"

"Ron."

"Whatever. Give her some water, we can both keep that down. I think."

Since her own hunger dissipated Lisa had grown still and calm, her famished combativeness draining away like dirty water down a storm drain. Ron hovered around her in a way that made me laugh; subtle as a train wreck, he was, even now. He held out a half-empty water bottle and I gulped until the acid taste in my mouth started to fade.

"This part's the worst," he assured me, "where you're still hungry but can't eat. It'll pass."

I crouched down to be sick again. I still couldn't get used to this, a Rat as our new best buddy, there had to be some scheme behind it and could I please stop being nauseous for just five minutes, that's all, so I could put together what it was? Lisa shivered holding me and Ron patted her arm, shaking himself.

"Why don't you go bother Renee, and leave my sister alone?" I said. "You never cared before, as long as they were blond—"

Ron just laughed, glancing at Lisa with the old slyness. "I don't see big sis here complaining—"

"You're sweet, Jessie," Lisa said, voice barely above a whisper, "but he's all right."

"He was happy about this," I told her, wiping my mouth. "He was attacking anyone who wasn't sick, a lot of folks who were, before it all went south, if that's your idea of sweet—"

Ron just laughed, tossing a drained water bottle over his shoulder. "Hey, well, shit happens. I dragged a crate of these from the grocery store, back when I could still carry stuff, I'll go get another. You're gonna be sick for a while here."

He walked off into the trees. I could see the effort it took for him to keep moving, the constant ripple of shivers and tremors gripping every muscle and how he had to stop every few yards just to rest. Then I was sick again, everywhere, my eyes watering and throat raw; there was no more relief in between bouts of vomiting, just the dread of when it would happen again. Lisa cradled my head against her arm, mopping the cold sweat from my face. I was starting to get cold too. Soon I'd be Saint-Vitusing through the daisies just like everyone else.

"Could I ask you something?" I said. "And don't go all nuts on me. Your daughter." I hesitated, when I felt her shake a little bit harder, but I had to know. "Did you . . . kill her or something? Did you?"

Lisa actually laughed, an abrupt, constricted sound like

someone spitting something solid from between their teeth. Then she stroked my head, sighing. "Karen had leukemia," she told me. "She died before any of this. Her father couldn't handle it and took off. I don't know where he is. Was." She cradled me a little closer. "Only three years old, my Karen. This family's had more than its share of fun, let me tell you—but I'm glad. I'm so, so glad she's dead."

"Sorry. Stupid question, I guess—"

"No, it isn't. Traveling the road out to you, I saw . . ." She shuddered, her body stiffening against mine. "Never mind what I saw. Even what we both saw, it was nothing like what I saw. But it's a perfectly logical question."

I brushed my hair out of my eyes and when I took my hand away, saw it covered in sweat-dampened strands: That was starting then too. Sick all the time, hair falling out—maybe someone had set off a bomb or something and we didn't know it. No dust clouds blotting out the sun, though, no silhouettes blossoming on the walls—just bodies everywhere, bodies in rows and piles and heaps and torn-up pieces for the birds and rats and dwindling ranks of the hungry. My own dying flesh. Six more corpses beside me, right now, losing their rigidity and swelling up with gas; Linc had stopped trying to move them, it was too much for him now. He, Ron, Lisa, Renee and I huddled in our own little group just like the others, half-dazed and moaning every now and then when the shivering or the bone-ache or the waves of nausea got to be too much. After Ron got back with our water, his last big burst of energy, he just curled up and trembled against Lisa's shoulder for hours.

"I hope there isn't really a hell," he said around incessantly chattering teeth, "or I'm so fucked."

"What do you call this?" I demanded, rocking back and forth against the aching in my legs, my back, my head. "If this isn't hell?"

He let out a little bark of laughter. "Real life. That's what I call it."

He burrowed under his filthy blankets and quit talking altogether. I lay down on my side, shivering and rocking and sometimes crawling a few feet away to vomit up bile; the chewed-up grass and soft powdery dirt felt like ground glass against my palms and knees, my skin still intact but tender as a great spreading blister. Linc kept handing me water bottles from Ron's half-empty carton, but I wasn't the least thirsty anymore, didn't care about the taste in my mouth anymore. My hair was coming out now in clumps.

"Over soon," Linc whispered, his arms around me from the back and Renee's from the front. "It'll be all over. For all of us."

It hurt horribly where their bones pressed against my skin, I winced and tried instinctively to ease away, but I was too scared to be alone. Other groups kept their own vigils, crouched on their own desert islands of misery, and I heard coughing, vomiting, crying, snatches of prayers, attempted jokes, dazed monologues of shock and loss. I lay there clutching one of Florian's lake stones in my hand, pale pink with a silvery sheen like salmon skin, and that hurt too but I couldn't let go of it, the thought of losing my grip on it filled me with a vague, nebulous panic that made me hold on even tighter even as the touch made my palm throb with pain. I was too exhausted to stand upright. I couldn't sleep.

Mom, Dad, if you're out there—no, I know you're dead. I'm sure of it. I just know. Sam. Ben. Joe. My Joe. Billy, Mags? Maybe they made it to the next county, maybe it hasn't spread there yet. Maybe chickens are penguins. Karen, my niece. Rommel. Maybe Jim, Teresa, how many more. All the Rats. All the Flies. No National Guardsmen coming to help us, no Red Cross, no Marines, no search-and-rescue teams, no paramedics, no government researchers, no special army divisions, no nothing. Just all of us, dying together, the county or the state or the whole country or the world. Well, why not? Why shouldn't the world end now? Stranger things have happened. Like me, the should-be skeleton, being here to see the end at all.

I really thought there'd be some soldiers, at least. Secret government lab cooking up an antidote. Red-faced vigilante guys raiding the gun stores, whooping righteously as they pumped us full of rounds: "Humanity" 187, Mutants 0. That's how it always happens in the movies. I used to like the movies. Maybe all of this is just a big movie, and I just have to wait for the credits to roll. Soon, very soon, we'll all be safe and well, the screen will go black and all the lights will come up.

Linc curled up with his head in the crook of my elbow. I loved them, I thought as I held them and felt them tremble, I loved them both, and I loved Lisa, and I loved Joe no matter what he'd done to me, to us, it didn't matter, he'd been as sad and lost as Sam ever was and I loved him, and I loved Sam too and I loved Billy and Mags enough to hope, against all common sense, that they really were safe. Even Ron, I could love just a little bit now. Teresa and Jim could go fuck themselves, I did have some limits, but it was amazing just what a love-number dying did on your brain. Useless, worthless sentiment, love—it didn't do anything but make you feel weirdly gentle and benevolent in a way that meant your brain, your sharp, suspicious, protective brain that got you through two deaths and two rebirths in one piece, was shutting down and couldn't do a thing for you anymore. Goodbye, brain, and thanks for thinking me out of a hell of a lot of trouble. This one, though, it's way beyond us both.

My head dropped down and I floated quietly away.

I struggled to my feet and stood there weaving, dizzy. I was alone in our great chewed-up dying prairie patch, and at the same time I was on the shore of Lake Michigan watching the choppy gray waters roll and subside, looking like bumps and waves in a big blanket of plaster. Drying paste. Sand coated my feet and they stung terribly; I tried to brush it off, wincing as the grains adhered to my blistering skin, and when I looked up again Florian was standing there watching me stork-hop around the shoreline. Still skeletal, still with the old death's-head smile.

"I told you it was beautiful," he said, gazing out happily at the granite-colored waves. "Missed my beach."

The beach became the prairie became the woods, and the trees had regained all their eaten-away bark. I was hallucinating, then, just like I'd thought. I didn't care. This might be my last chance to talk to him. "I'm dying," I said, and started to laugh. "For once, I'm really, truly dying."

"Could be," he said, looking thoughtful. "Could be."

"I don't want to die." Now I was nearly giggling. "I want to *be* dead, like I was. But I don't want to die."

Florian mulled that one over, the trees flickering and fading before my eyes and the underbrush again becoming sand. "That case," he said, "you won't."

"How senile are you, old man?" I brandished another clump of fallen-out hair. "I mean, look at me—"

"World's turning," he said, as we walked along the empty shoreline. "Earth's turning. The soil's turning over and the earthworms are all wriggling out to play. Omega's gone back to alpha and you and your friends, the ones still left? Soon you'll all be coming back. Once you make it over here. Once you're back to the start."

I thought that over, shaking the strands from my fingers. "And what the hell is that supposed to mean?"

He just stared at the water, toe bones digging idly at a clay-colored lake stone stuck fast in the wet sand. Enough. "What does that mean?" I repeated, and grabbed his shoulders and shook until I heard the rattle of dry sockets, felt dust caking my fingers. "What's that mean?"

"Ain't no need to get so riled," he muttered, pulling himself free.

"Why do you keep coming back?" I shouted. "Why do you do this to me? Nothing's been the same since you died, everything's gone to hell and everyone's so sick and I'm stuck in this horrible living body and everything we had is gone and I'm dying and I don't have time for—"

"Time?" Florian laughed, a lighthearted consumptive wheeze. "You complaining about time now? You're still dead to me, Jessie, whatever body you're in, and us dead folk have all the time in the universe, all the time ever made. And you know it. So quit moaning."

The old Florian, that was, kind even in scorn. My anger faded and I shrugged in reluctant agreement; he smiled even wider, that seamed skeletal dusty smile, and I felt a flash of nostalgia at the sight of his teeth, those long cylindrical undead-teeth that looked even longer in the absence of gums. Seeing them, you knew where hoos of old first got the idea of vampires. I wrapped my arms tightly around myself, though all my shivering had mysteriously stopped.

"I keep coming back," Florian continued, "'cause I know you'll listen." He patted me on the arm. "No matter how mad you are. Ain't no use in talking to anyone else, I was dead to them long before I ever crumbled into dust. But this ain't a pleasure trip. I'm here to tell you what to expect, so you'll know how to behave when it happens."

"I love you," I said, and blinked back actual saltwater tears, not coffin rot. That still startled me. "If you hadn't died—"

"They'd have killed me." He picked up the loosened stone, tossed it at the water. "Even without all them new diseases changing everything. I was useless to them, and we ain't sentimental."

"If my brother hadn't—"

"The sickness would've come anyway," he said, shaking his head impatiently. "Your brother ain't so important to all this as he thinks. Quit wasting your energy on him, you seen he lived long enough to get his punishment. Things happen like that, ain't no point in celebrating or getting sad about it. I'm here to tell you that I seen it all. Everything. And I know what's coming next."

The wind picked up, rustling the rags of my clothes and making the trees shake and bend; we were back in the forest, though still on the beach. "Where are you now?" I asked. "I mean, where are you, really?"

Florian looked confused. "Inside your mind," he said, scratching his back against a tree. "Where else would I go?"

"Is it just here, this sickness? Or is it everywhere?"

He laughed, wriggling his shoulder bones more vigorously against the bark. "Everywhere. Some places worse than others, right around here it's especially bad, but everywhere. Government's broken down, military's all dead or dying, not enough survivors to rebuild a damned thing—you seen it where you are, you should see what the bigger cities look like. Bodies all over, filth, typhus, hepatitis, rabies from all the rats. Gas explosions, fires, everything looted to the foundations. Folks walking around brain-snapped 'cause they turned cannibal. Well, you seen some of that yourself. Can't even feel sorry for some of 'em, they keep trying to shoot stuff like in the movies even though they know guns don't do a damned thing—" He sighed. "Well, hoos have simple brains that don't take in new facts too easy, we knew that already. But they're gonna have to get used to a whole lotta change now, real quick. A whole lotta forever change."

I picked up another lake stone, a greenish one, pressing the smooth dampness hard against my palm. "Then it really is the end of the world."

"It's the end of this world." Florian shrugged. "It's the end of their world. But it ain't the end of the *world*. There's no real end to anything, you should know that by now."

He reached a hand up to the fruit-laden branch of a pear tree, mysteriously materialized on the shoreline. "We've come close before, to having things like this, having a world without *them*. Other times, other epidemics. The Black Death, so-called."

So-called, yes. I couldn't help smiling because I realized I knew them all, knew them from the whispers when I was first alive, knew them from my very first days aboveground: all the wars, famines, natural disasters the hoos kept insisting were nothing to do with us, nothing at all, and they knew far better than us just what a lie that was. "The Great London Fire," I replied. "So-called."

"Chicago Fire too. I remember that one. Always trying to keep us down by burning us out." Florian chuckled, tossing a pear from hand to hand like a baseball. "Didn't work. The Thirty Years' War. The '68 Pittsburgh massacre. The 1918 'flu' epidemic. All them supposed serial killers. We've made our mark, pet. But the hoos never expected to lose for real, to have to turn the whole earth over to us and our kind, and it's actually happening." He handed me the pear, solemn, like a gift. "Don't really know what we're meant to do with it, tell you the truth, but we're stuck with it now."

"But *I'm* human again, I'm one of the ones—"

"You ain't human," Florian said emphatically. "You got the outer shell, you got the flesh and the breath and a couple of the appetites, but you ain't any more human than you were the day I met you. Thank Christ." He grinned. "You're just a hell of a lot more *living* dead than you were before. The hoo-folks that caught this, like your sister, same thing. The true living dead. Some of you, you'll survive this—not many, not easy, but you will. It'll burn off like any other disease. You and a bare handful of true humans, the living living, but they ain't my concern and they ain't gonna be in a position to tell you anything. You'll rule the roost. Back to the start, back to the way it was thousands of years ago, when that meteorite that made us what we are first landed. For the first time in forever."

I gripped the pear, nails sinking into the unripened flesh. "Then it's true. About a meteor landing and changing everything, the dust or radiation, or something, all those stories—"

"Humans think they've always been in charge of the planet, up till now." He shrugged. "They're wrong. We used to have hold of it, way back when. Lost our grip. Don't know how, don't know why, but we did. Now we're back. You're back. The hoos that are left don't like it, well, that ain't your problem. The weak don't get squatter's rights."

"But it'll just be us. I mean, the people who died, hoos, undead, whatever, they're not rising again, I haven't seen a single one resurrect. They're just plain dead." I clutched the pear harder. "So they're never coming back. Sam's not. Joe's not. And you're not."

Florian reached out and stroked my head, not seeming to notice when another clump of hair came off in his fingers. "Can't say as I want to come back, Jessie. I got a nice life here, in your memories, you made the beach just like I wanted it. And that's all I ever wanted. You got folks who love you too, so you'll always have someplace inside them to go." He appropriated the pear with a reproving glance, like I'd swiped it from him. "So go back now, quit your moaning and wailing and just get ready to die. Or to live."

"How can any of us live through this? We've got no strength left." I grabbed for his hand like it could hold me upright. "No appetite. No place to go. Nothing."

Something blazed fiercely from Florian's eyes, not anger but some breed of almost lethal determination, subsiding quickly as it sparked. "No place to go, Jessie? No place at all? You know better—there's always one last place for you to go. Underground."

The beach faded, the woods, Florian himself. I was standing in grass now, overgrown neglected grass thick with weeds; before me were uneven rows of gravestones, behind me a large arching metal sign and the torn-up remains of a barbed wire fence. Calumet County Memorial Park, my "resting" place. I wandered among the broken markers and gaping dug-up graves never filled in; up the aisles, down the aisles and there we were, in a little family plot under a big yew tree stripped of its leaves and lower bark: my mother, my father, my newly added niece and me. A small crooked marker stuck in the middle like an apology: JESSICA ANNE PORTER, MARCH 23, 1986–AUGUST 14, 2001.

I leaned forward and read the inscription over and over again. Such a tiny little hiccup of life. Ridiculously sentimental, giving over a whole precious piece of earth to house the remains of a nobody among billions because you maybe vaguely thought you loved them. I shut my eyes against the hard glare of a strangely harsh sun, and when I opened them again I saw markers for all the Flies in a row next to mine, markers in all the colors of Florian's lake stones, laid out like the teeth of a great sad smile. WILLIAM NOWAK, 1901–1939. Billy. Stabbed in a bar fight. MARGARET MAY O'SULLIVAN, 1889–1922. Maggie. Diphtheria. SAMUEL JAMES MORRISON, 1925–1970. Razor to the throat. BENJAMIN FRANKLIN JONES, 1942–1968. Bullet to the head. TERESA KENDAL, 1945–1980. Cancer. JOSEPH ANTHONY

MORELLI, 1939–1958. Car crash. Copycat. RENEE NICOLE ANDERSON, 1990–2006. Brain aneurysm. AARON DAVID LINCOLN, 1974–1990. Blunt force trauma. FLORIAN BROWN, 1712–1801. Old age, in his sleep. So rare.

I stumbled, walked, ran up and down that whole sad-sack, bad-luck row, feeling the life flowing from the pores of the stone—all that life flaring, pushing furiously against the confines of flesh, bursting outward and upward in a great gorgeous liberating explosion called death. Billy drowning as the blood slowly filled his lungs, Maggie's throat swelling permanently shut, Joe meeting a metal guardrail at sixty miles per hour, Ben's skull flying into jigsaw pieces, tumors devouring Teresa's lungs and liver and bones like us devouring a fresh-killed deer. Sam's one moment of true happiness, the industrious glee of the suicide as he picked up the razor. The sudden *snap* inside Renee's head as the swollen artery burst. Linc's terrible, practiced resignation as the punches and kicks came down harder and harder and then, too late, finally stopped.

The graves yawned open like jaws and I leapt into the space marked for me. I breathed in the dirt, let it fill my nostrils and mouth like solidified air and then the dirt turned gritty and grainy and damp with lake water and it was deep beige sands, singing sands, it was strength and nourishment and happiness, it took the blue tinge from my skin and the last traces of nausea from my gut; I tunneled like a sand crab into the next open grave, the next, the next, the collective release of life flowing straight into my bones. I had the strength of dozens, hundreds inside me, all that death, all that life, which was the same thing, exactly the same thing. I surfaced from the dunes and ran faster and faster across the cemetery, which was the forest which was the lakeshore again, relishing the pounding glare of the setting sun, there was so much life-death-life fighting to fit itself back in my bones that this poor body couldn't contain it, I was coming apart, shattering shaking like Florian disintegrating and I laughed out loud, shouted for joy as I flew into a billion particles of life, death, dust—

"Jessie? Jessie!"

I was back on the prairie preserve, nothing but dry grass and dead bodies. Renee leaned over me, looking apologetic. "You were crying," she said.

I put my hands to my face, feeling the traces of damp. Lisa was wide awake, sitting expressionless next to a body covered in dirt-stiffened gray blankets. Linc sat up next to me, almost groaning with the effort. "Ron's dead," he murmured. "So quick, while you were sleeping. Took this sudden deep breath, and never let it out again."

Someone else breathing in the dirt, then, no fool he. Dirt nap. I almost laughed, around a rush of true sadness. Thanks for the water, Ron, and I sincerely doubt there's a hell, though you won't get Valhalla either. I patted Lisa's hand, drawing a reluctant smile, then grabbed Linc's arm and drew him closer.

"We have to start walking," I said, urgency and agitation making my voice rise high. "North. To the beaches. We have to get there. We've got to go now. Our graves are there. We have to get back to our graves, to where we're all buried."

I knew from Linc's expression what I sounded like but I didn't care, I had to tell everyone before the dream faded and blurred. "That's how we're going to get better. That's how we'll get well—"

"Jessie," Renee pleaded, "stop."

"I'm not gonna stop, dammit! I'm telling you, I saw Florian and he said it, hell, he said it to us back when he was dying, you heard him, we all have to go back, we have to get to the beaches, get underground—"

"Shut up," someone groaned, and threw a branch at me. It landed about four feet short of the mark. "Crazy bitch."

"She's going delirious," someone else said. "Just like that Ben. Don't listen."

"We have to go back—"

"Jessie." Linc took my face between his hands. His fingers, his arms trembled uncontrollably. "We're not going anywhere. Ever. For anything. This is it."

I was shaking with illness and the need to yell at him,

explain, drag him there by force, but holding myself upright took too much effort and my outburst had worn me out. I curled up obediently on the ground, Linc stroking what was left of my hair: I needed to rest and gather what strength I had, I needed it because I was going, I was going with or without them and then I could show them, explain, I could bring it all back to them and they'd *know*. Linc rested his cheek against the top of my head. Keep being sweet, Linc, you do that now dying's made all the caution and doubt in you burn away, but I'm still going no matter what and I'm making you and Renee and Lisa better again if I have to smash all your heads in to do it. You can't stop me.

"We felt this way too, before," Renee said, consoling, comforting, as she settled back against my side. "Like we had to be somewhere, had to get somewhere important, like this here was just a way station, and it was right near us but we couldn't . . . well. We just couldn't." She pulled my head onto her shoulder. "I guess this is as good as any place, now."

"I guess so," I said.

A way station. That's exactly what this is, Renee. But you don't want to understand, maybe you're just too worn out now to understand, so I'll have to leave off explaining it. I need to rest. I need strength, if I can ever muster it up again. Useless goddamned body, useless undecayed invincibly strong body eating itself up from the inside out.

"Good as any place," Linc repeated. He sounded so tired it made me want to cry. An old cat weary of life, trying to hide in a closet or under a table away from pain and death, no fear anymore of the vet or his needle. "Good as any."

There was something about that sand, Florian said, back in the woods, back when we were both undead, an eternity ago. *Something about it.*

"My stomach hurts," Renee mumbled, quiet and resigned. "It's burning."

You lay down in those sands to sleep, woke up every night feeling good. Barely rotted at all. Want to see a loved one rise from the dead? Bury them in a good sandy soil.

Near the lake coast. The sands started this. And the sands will finish it.

"Drink some water," I said, reaching a hand out and resting it on Renee's hollow, tensed-up gut. Rubbing. "Is there any left?"

"We gave the last to Ron," Lisa said. Expressionless still. "Sorry."

"I can't keep it down anyway," Renee whispered. "Never mind."

It's our own Mother Earth, the beaches. The sands, they keep you young. You'll all be coming back, once you make it over here.

I reached out for the pouch of stones I'd untied from my waist, pulled it to me, rested my cheek on it like a sharp, unforgiving pillow. *No matter where I been, if I had these with me I always felt like I was safe. Them bits and pieces made us what we are.* My face hurt pressed against it but that old feeling was back too, the prickly pins-and-needles skin-itch traveling from the stones through the leather to me like a quiet, reassuring electricity, like the stones were alive, aware, sympathetic, offering up a bit of their own immutable life to the dying. *Get my beach. My lake stones. I'll live.*

Crazy. This was completely crazy. But it had to be true. Somehow. Florian wouldn't lie.

Renee pulled my head onto her shoulder again. Lisa lay down, an arm around that pile of dirty blankets. Valhalla. *I'm inside your mind, where else would I go?* I tried to imagine Ron's beach, what he'd want to have around him for eternity, clearing a little space inside my skull for him like I had for Florian, like I hoped Linc or Renee or even Lisa would do for me. Motorcycles and electric guitars roaring day and night, air hazy with hashish smoke and barbecue, naked blondes, oceans of beer. Lots of enemies, he was never happy without a fight. Ron's beach was easy. When that was through, though, I had to make a world for Sam and for Ben, poor wretched Ben, and for Joe, my fucked-up unhappy Joe, and for Billy and Mags dying somewhere far away, and for Lisa and Linc and Renee in case they died before I did, I couldn't leave my own loved ones with no place of retreat. Miles to go before I slept. Ten miles, Ron said, maybe less, maybe more. I'd soon find out.

Gardens. Sam's beach was an easy one too, flowers upon flowers. He loved flowers, more than people. More than himself. I lay there thinking of half-stripped lilac bushes, funeral wreaths, great fistlike clusters of small, wild roses. Beach roses.

The stones in my pockets tingled and sparked and burned so my legs twitched, almost jumped with the sensation. Good. Give me some more of that life inside you, you little bastards, just a sliver, just enough to go ten miles and back, maybe less, maybe more. I'm onto you now. The bits and pieces that woke us up from death, that keep us safe. Alive. Florian wouldn't lie.

Lisa wept in her sleep. We pretended not to hear her.

Linc and Renee lay there moaning in exhaustion, pain, sadness, and finally after minutes stretched to hours they dropped off. I waited until their strange humanlike breathing was deep and steady, then I eased myself away and reached quietly into the stone pouch, taking a few more to fill my pockets. I left the half-emptied bag resting between them both, then forced myself to my feet by slow degrees: up on my knees, let the spinning dizziness subside, now on one knee like I was proposing to Ron's corpse, straighten my shaking buckling legs and *make* them pull me up, slow, up—

The one who'd called me a crazy bitch was watching me now, curious. He leaned on one elbow, salt-and-pepper hair falling into his eyes, the jacket thrown over his shivering shoulders caked in dirt and blood. His mouth twisted up and puckered as I held out my arms like a toddler, took a few vertiginous steps.

"So where're you going?" he mumbled, his voice thick with hostility and disease.

A transformed hoo, not a former undead like me: I could tell, I didn't know how but it was like a smell he and Lisa and the others like them gave off; if they weren't family I didn't have any more time for them now than I ever did back in the woods. Where am I going? Where're *you* going, hoos? Straight into the evolutionary crapper, looks like, don't call, don't write. What a crying shame.

"Any place you won't be," I said, a little steadier on my feet. "Nobody'd blame me."

"Fucking zombies," he snarled, hand groping around for something else to throw and not finding it. "Still sticking together whispering your little plans with your own kind, even now, fuck the rest of us we can all just go to hell—"

"You're already there," I told him, swaying like a sapling in a hailstorm and grabbing for the stones in my pockets. Keep me upright, keep me moving, just a little bit. Please. Just a little bit. Linc, Renee, Lisa hadn't stirred. "So congratulations. Send a postcard when you get a chance—"

"Bitch," he spat out, as I turned my back on him. "Crazy rotten chewed-up dead bitch."

Probably, yeah. More than likely. But the beach, the sands, the rocks. Get there, and we'd live. Florian said so. Jim. Rommel. Ron. They couldn't all be lying.

Everyone lies, about everything, that much I should've learned by now. After all this. Everyone alive including me just lies and lies and lies. Lies like a rug. Stop all this craziness and just get ready to die. It's not hard. You've done it enough before.

I pushed through the torn-up trees and started walking.

17

The moonlight was dim and watery and the roadside dark; the store signs' neon, the sulfurous road flares, all extinguished by the breath from some great invisible mouth. The grass was scratchy-dry and the dirt a soft mealy itch against my bare feet and it was so quiet out here on the roadside, so still, I hadn't realized until now how much noise we'd all made there on the prairie preserve: the crying, mumbling, praying, groaning, puking, cursing, the continuous sound of the breaths of the dying growing louder and faster and then, with long low gasps, stopping forever. All switched off now, like a bulb shorting out in a lamp.

I grabbed at the edges of the safety fencing swinging open and useless around abandoned homes, dragging myself along, the deep slicing cuts from the fences' razor-edged metal healing within seconds, such a worthless new bit of superhumanity, we're all dying anyway so what's a severed artery or two even matter? Keep walking. Keep walking. My balance veered and everything crashed and tilted inside my head and my lung-breaths were tight painful gasps, I was going to be sick, I got sick all over someone's lilacs and crouched moaning on the ground for far too many minutes but I had to keep going, moving, force myself north. The beach is where this started. The beach is where it ends. Where is everyone? Was Linc right, and it really is just us remaining now, all of us dying on that patch of prairie? I hope this is still north, no compass, no company. Other than a raccoon darting back into the ruined foliage quick as it emerged, no sign of life.

My head hurt so much. Dazed heavy-lidded exhaustion pinching the bridge of my nose. Throbbing in the temple. Tightness at the back of my skull like I was tensing myself for a high hard blow from out of nowhere, like when I'd hit Linc with that shovel. I wanted Linc back, Renee, I just found them again and they wanted me there with them and now I'd die alone, lost. My own damned fault. The air was wet and cool and the tree branches swung, a susurration against the dark gray night and I was so thirsty, I lay down with my cheek to the damp sandy dirt and licked at a little divot in the ground full of rainwater. All around me remnants of dead bodies, chewed-up tossed-away bones I'd have scrambled for just days ago, half a corpse right there with one arm still stretched out, pleading—

Joe. My poor, unhappy, angry, fucked-up, sweet, hard-hearted, treacherous—if I just hadn't let my sister see I still lived, you might be alive today yourself. Or maybe not. You always wanted to die just as much as Sam but I wouldn't see it, I didn't want to know. But you wouldn't ever really look at me either, now would you? Guess we're even. Come back, baby, I miss you. It makes me feel horrible how much I liked Linc handing out kisses and putting his arm around me because that's not right when I just lost you, Joe, come back and set my head straight, you knew how to do that, you found me first, way back when—

COMMUNITY GARDEN. That's what the sign says, here on another wrecked-up fence. Snarled knots of ripped chicken wire, everything eaten down to the roots. Sorry, rabbits, none left for you. So damned sorry.

Crawl. Stumble. Crawl. Push through grass, gravel, leaves, underbrush. Stop to lean against another tree, don't dare lie down again, you'll never get up, hold on to those stones you brought with you like they're your last chance. Burning, tingling, almost twitching like big lumbering jumping beans as they press against your fingers. They made you what you are. Them and Jim. You don't look like a monster, not anymore, but you are one. All because you couldn't stay hidden in the trees where you belonged, where all monsters belong, hidden in the dark and the tangled thickets. No sense of shame. Thinking you actually have a right to the sunlight, to the roadside, to look at your own grave, to hold out your rotten diseased hand to someone living and intact like they shouldn't scream at you, run away, tell all their friends they just found another one for the fire—

Chicken and shrimp shack. One of those signs in front where you slide the letters onto little wire brackets, the brackets all rusty now, the peacock blue shack paint peeling right off. Sitting here in the middle of nowhere. Where the hell was the beach? Ten miles, maybe more, I had to have gone at least two or three, my whole body was shaking like Florian's in death when he finally gave up and flew apart, no fucking stones could help him then. Joe, Linc, Renee, Sam, Lisa, somebody, get your asses over here for Christ's sake, I don't want to die alone. Florian. This is your fault I'm stuck here. I started crying as I hung on to that rusty sign, clear human tears rolling down my face. Let's all just stop being sick and dead and dying and go eat chicken and shrimp, how about it? I'll have a hush puppy, some pie, all you can get here if you don't eat meat—no, not the pie, bet anything the crust's made with lard. It doesn't matter. That's not the point. Let's just *go*.

Keep going.

Sit down for a minute. Lie down. Just for a minute. No more.

The buzzing like flies, all in my ears. I remembered that sound, from dying.

I was lying in someone's deserted yard, under a sky awash in moonlight; no bodies here, just piles of rusted, broken farm equipment. An abandoned farm out by the county park, one I remembered well for its pear trees clustered near a weed-choked former vegetable garden, its ruined henhouse with the collapsed roof a faded, but still incongruously vivid peacock blue. How the hell did I get here, from the shrimp shack so many miles north?

I pulled myself to my feet and stumbled toward the henhouse, confused and a little afraid, and night suddenly became day and the farm stood beside a highway, near a rolling green expanse of beautifully tended gravesites. The graves yawned open and blurred figures jumped in and out, laughing, voices rising to children's playground shrieks. Clusters of trees, thick with ripe berries and farmhouse pears and the frothy pink-and-white blossoms of early spring. A soft rushing sound behind me alerted me to the water, choppy Lake Michigan waves swirling against a distant, wavering shoreline. The farm was part of the graveyard was part of the sandy-soiled forests sitting on a dune crest above the lake; I could walk to any of them, easily as crossing a deserted small-town street. Other than a deer wandering placidly through the dune trees and the laughter of flitting ghosts, I was alone.

God, I thought, stomping rotten pears underfoot as I walked closer to the shoreline, this must be it. Dead. All alone now, just like Florian on his beautiful beach. I didn't want to be alone. Where were my parents, my friends, the other dead/living dead/undeads wanting to fight for my turf, was I stuck here now myself, by myself, forever—

Behind me came a soft, quiet *click*, a disapproving tongue against the roof of a hoo-mouth, the cocked trigger of a gun. One foot in farmhouse dirt and the other in beach sand, I turned, very slowly, and when I saw him I threw my head back and started to laugh. He just shrugged, like he understood.

"Mind if I smoke?" he asked, holding up the ignited lighter.

I shook my head. Jim or the thing that looked like him lit up, inhaled with a deep sigh of pleasure and slipped the lighter into his pocket.

"Is this real," I asked him, "or am I just dreaming it? Lately I'm never sure."

"You're dreaming me," he said, with another deep breath of smoke. "In a way. But I'm still real."

"Am I dead?" I asked.

Jim took another, unnaturally long draw on his cigarette, looking me up and down with the easy, wary, arm's-length nonchalance I remembered well from when we were all alive. It drained out of him like blood from an embalmed body after I died, Mom and Dad died, Karen my niece died, Lisa got sick, he dragged himself and all of us with him over the edge. So am I dead? How many kinds of living and dead and living dead and dead living had I been in just these few months, these few days, after the stasis of plain old human living and dying? I deserved some kind of existential medal.

"Let's put it this way," he said. "You're definitely not talking to me for your health."

"So what'd it feel like, when you first got sick too?" I reached up to one of the pear trees, plucking a ripe fruit. "I would've given a lot to see your face, when you finally realized you'd screwed yourself just like you did the rest of us."

Jim, or this thing, creature, entity that looked like him, thought that one over. "You're not fooling me, you know," he, or it, said, still puffing away. "Losing me and Lisa hurt. A lot. And finding us again hurt even more. I know you missed me. Just as much as I missed you, however much you shoved it deep down inside because undeads aren't meant to see humans as anything but meat. Just like humans must only see the undead as monsters. Doesn't always work that way, though, does it?"

"You killed me," I said. "You took what I was, the way I knew myself, and you destroyed it."

"I was a good man," said Jim, the cigarette poised in his fingers as though it hovered, untouched, in the air between them. "That's the thing, Jessie. I started out as a very good man. I missed you. I loved you. I wanted to help you. I wanted to give you back the life you'd lost." A hollow, abrupt little laugh. "And just look how that turned out, eh?"

My fault then, I guess. Always my fault. After I never asked for this, any of this, would have thrown it back at him and snapped his neck if he'd ever dared propose it to my face. And of course, that's why he hadn't. Coward. Coward. Every fucking hoo alive nothing but a miserable self-centered coward.

"I don't have time for this," I said, turning back toward the dune crest. "I have to get to the lakeshore."

"Good luck on that." Jim rolled the cigarette between his fingers, this way, that way, and smiled. "I'd say you've got about half a mile left in you before you fall over for good and the rats get another meal, so you might as well just stay here, get to know the place, talk to me like a civilized human being—"

"I'm not human," I said, hard and cold. "No matter what you've tried to do to me, I'll never be human again. And I'm so goddamned glad of that, you have no idea, so don't you stand there after all this and whine about how you wanted to 'help' me. One lie after another."

"Well, of course I lie." He shrugged. "All the time, it's my main source of fun. Only about the trivialities, though. The bigger things . . ." Another draw on the cigarette. "The thing is, there really are some big, stonking, undeniable, universal truths that human consciousness, any sort of consciousness, just can't wriggle out of facing. And guess what?" He leaned forward, confiding and quiet. "I'm one of them."

Jim's smile grew wider and wider. The flesh on his face split bloodlessly open so I stared into grinning skull-like jaws and eyes grown dark and hollow and wide like corridors to another universe, hallways you could walk down forever without reaching your destination. The face of Death, which was really the face of Life, which were both sides of Eternity and I should have known all along, I should have known—but that there really was *a* Death like in all those movies and books, that was new. I tried to rustle up some legitimate awe and fright, for politeness' sake, but sheer dearth of energy made me fall back on confusion. He, it, just smiled, utterly unruffled, still sitting there in the split-open shell of Jim's dead body.

"Were you ever really Jim?" I asked, resisting the urge to touch him. Touch it. "I mean, was it him I was talking to, back when we first met, or—"

"Oh, that really was your brother. All full up with plans and schemes and crazy delusions, thinking he could turn what I was already putting into motion to his own advantage. And to yours. He really did want to help you, you know. No lie." It, he, crushed the cigarette underfoot and lit another. "Ridiculous little nutter, playing at the eternals, imagining he mattered—I'm not crying hubris here, you understand, I don't judge or condemn. It was just embarrassing to witness."

The cigarette smoke trailed from his mouth, nose, ears, the dark open pits of his eyes. "But that's all right, you know. He made a mistake, trying to do something good for everyone, and that gave me the foot in the door I'd been needing. He'll be dead soon, if he's not already. But you—you seem to be hovering, one foot off the cliff edge, and I can't for the life of all figure out if you'll jump." He blinked, bits of ash drifting from behind his eyelids as they opened again. "So I thought we should have a little talk, just to clarify your goals. So to speak."

"You don't just take us whenever you want?" I stared out past the trees, at the merry figures leaping in and out of their own gravesites; flashes of color were all I saw, quick and fleeting as lightning bugs.

"Oh, I could," he agreed. "But the ones who fight and fight and fight, they intrigue me. So stubborn, for no good reason." He inhaled again, smoke now seeming to leak out through the pores of his skin. "Ain't no need to kick up such a fuss. You already figured out it's all the same thing in the end, death, life, the big merry-go-round, but you keep doin' it anyway. Befuddles me, Jessie, I don't mind saying."

Florian's voice now. Utterly natural, somehow, to hear it from the split-wide death-mouth that wasn't Jim's—Florian, Jim, had I really been talking to someone else all along? My only real friend. Friends, though, they have agendas just like everyone else. Death's was obvious. And yet, if Death really was Life, in the end . . .

"So what do you want from me?" I asked.

He pointed the half-smoked cigarette at a pear tree. It flared into flowery life, grew glossy leaves and great fistfuls of ripe beautiful pears, dropped them as one to the ground and withered in the course of seconds.

"Wanna play a game?" Joe's voice now, the teasing affectionate timbre that used to make my stomach tighten in the most pleasant way. "Life and I have been playing forever—but letting it win all the time, just because it seemed like I was supposed to, that got boring." He settled back against an apple blossom tree, and the pink petals littering the grass instantly turned sickly brown. "So let's try mass death out for a while, see how the planet copes with it. Can always change my mind, wipe all of you out later and restore the living—so how about it? If you win the game, you get to live." He gestured around us, at the trees and grass, the berry-covered clusters of bushes in between the graves, the long line of the lakeshore below us. "And if you lose, this isn't exactly the fires of hell. So what do you say, Jess. A game?"

"I don't know how to play chess." I cradled the pear in my palms. "And I'm really bad at riddles. And I have to get to the lakeshore."

He laughed, patting the grass next to him affectionately. I didn't sit down.

"Aw, give me a little credit, Jessie," Billy's voice argued. "Not that kinda chickenshit game. I was thinking more . . . a wager, y'know? I ask questions, make a little instant bet with *mi compadre Vida* what your answer's gonna be and may the best entity win. You. Forever." He smoked down the cigarette, ash floating from his skin as he stubbed it out in the grass. "So whaddaya say?"

"I say that's a riddle. Or a trial, which is even—"

"It's a wager, based on honest inquiry." Jim's voice, again; I must've hit a nerve. "I have no particular answers in mind, and I'm accusing you of no crime. Your lot always tries to play these little semantics games to stall for time, it's quite boring. Let's start."

"Let's not," I repeated. My body was shaking again, the heat of fever sending it paradoxically cold, but I felt completely calm, focused, stubborn as hell. "I've got things to do."

He motioned to the graveyard, the trees and grass around us, the dune forests and the lake. "You can only pick one of these places to live in forever—graveyard, orchard, beach. Which do you choose?"

"The shores of Lake Michigan," I said. "Which that beach isn't. I have to go there now. Good-bye."

He lit another cigarette, casual as if I were playing along. "You can spend eternity with only one person, the others you'll never see again. Just one. Who do you pick?"

I pointed the pear at him, small end forward, like some fat mutated gun. "Everybody dies alone," I said. "So I guess that'd be myself. But that's as may be. I'm going to the beach, not eternity, and I intend to have company."

The two halves of Jim's shell were withering, like the peeled skin of a fruit left out in the sun; trails of gray smoke now streamed from Death's/Life's every pore and orifice. I think I was starting to make him angry. Good.

"Eternity eating only live flesh or dead meat. Which one?"

I watched the deer stroll through the dune forest and bend down at their ease to feed, the squirrels amble up and down the tree trunks. "I'll feed off you," I said. "That way I get both at once, and won't have to hurt any animals. But there's plenty more at the lakeshore, I won't have to choose. I'm going there now."

He shucked the last remains of Jim's skin like an uncomfortable sweater. The face-splitting grin, the dark bottomless hollows where eyes should have been, the skeletal nakedness were like Florian's body at the very end and I felt a strange, nostalgic sadness, remembering his eyes melting from their sockets like ice cream in the sun, the knocking banging bone-to-bone tremors that scraped him into dust.

"Ice cream in the sun," he, it, murmured as it stared at me. "That's as good a question as any. Vanilla or chocolate?"

"Butter pecan." I held tighter to the pear, as if it could

protect me. "I think. I don't remember what ice cream tastes like anymore."

"Apples or oranges?"

"Raspberries. Blueberries. Turkish delight, what the hell do you care?"

"A train leaves San Francisco at five P.M. going east at ninety-five miles per hour, and another train—"

"I'm leaving now," I said. "I'm going."

"You're not going anywhere." He had human eyes again, very suddenly, and they gave me the pitying glance you offer a drunk, a bum on the street. A stupid child. "Nowhere ever again."

When he rose to his skeletal feet he towered over my head, casting a shadow that blotted out the trees, the shore-line, the sun. I was in the dark again, lying in a wooden box in a concrete shell in an oblong of dirt; I was walking under a new moon watching the human world wind down and die, every light burned out, shot out, useless and extinguished. Lying in the woods, torn limb from limb, waiting to be eaten up just like Joe. He, it, them, loomed over me with eternal light in one eye, eternal night in the other. Judge. Jury. Executioner.

"You lose," it said.

I'd always known. We always do. Lose, that is. We never know or learn a damned thing.

"Are we being punished for something?" I asked.

An almost dainty snort of derision. "Don't be stupid."

"So you're just bored. Want to shake things up a little. All of this really means nothing."

It shrugged and laughed, a dry hollow chortle. "I keep trying to explain to you, I don't test, I don't judge, I don't calibrate, I don't *care*. This is just how it is. Has always been. May always be." He, it, put a hand on my shoulder, bare finger bones thick with dirt and the desiccated remains of skin. "And now it's time to go. It's time for all of you, every one of you, to go."

Time to go. Time to give up the ghost, hand over my poor body like some sort of worn, creased-up pool pass. Because you say so, even though you've got billions, trillions, just like me but I need *this* body to get to the beaches, to save everyone, it may not be much but it's all I've got, this poor little body shaking and trembling with starving sickness, its scalp nearly bald. (I had a damned potato skull, not like Renee's, thank God I'd never tried shaving it while I was alive.) It belonged to *me*, however many times it got ripped to its roots and changed all over again, and it wasn't such a bad thing to have: the arm that hugged Joe (before he turned on me), the fist that fought Teresa (and lost), the hair (all fallen out) Linc liked to stroke when he thought I was asleep. A weird sensation, feeling a protective, maternal sort of love for your own remains. Motherly narcissism. Sick, really, when you thought about it. But that's too bad. It's mine. Not yours.

"I'm not going," I said. My fingers broke through the pear's thin skin, sinking into the soft, overripe sugar grit of the flesh beneath. "Sorry. I've got things to do. Not now."

"You don't get to make that decision," it said. Its bony hand tightened. "It's time."

"You have billions just like me," I said. "Trillions. You'll never miss just one—"

"Each one unique." It stared right through me, sweeping over me with a blinding sulfurous searchlight and suffocating shadow: eternal light, eternal night. "Each one itself. Each death really *does* diminish, Jessie—human, inhuman, man, woman, child, infant, animal, insect. There are no trivial losses. Which, of course, means I make no trivial gains. I can't do without you, Jessie. Without you in particular."

"You'll get me eventually anyway," I said. I felt no fear. Fear and panic wouldn't penetrate here, wherever this place was, perhaps because they meant nothing to this entity that ruled it. "You can wait."

"You're so sure about that?" The death grip on my shoulder was tightening, crushing, hard enough to snap bones, but I felt no pain, no pain just like no fear. A little attempted inducement, that, a silent hard sell. "Maybe if I don't get you now, I won't ever get you at all. I mean, a smashed-in skull won't kill you anymore, or being torn limb from limb, or heat, or cold, or rot, or overwork, or a knife blade, or bullets, or flamethrowers—"

"You said it yourself, didn't you? You can always change your mind and wipe us all out. So you don't need me just now."

Silence. Then those skeletal, preternaturally strong fingers had me fast, crushing me in their hold like grain between millstones; my feet flew straight off the soft grassy ground as I dangled before the light and night of bottomless eye sockets, above the yawning chasm of a dark, sticky mouth.

"You belong to me," it whispered. "Since before you even existed, all of you have always belonged to me."

That great hole of its mouth was wet and black, oozing with murk, like coffin liquor from a gutted undead. Like a primordial mud, bubbling up from the earth back when it was new: death, which was life, which was exactly the same thing. That's the thing, isn't it, I thought, as I dangled over the defanged precipice, waiting to be swallowed whole: You're right. You've always had me. Which means you'll always have me. Which means you don't need to take me now, you don't need to take me ever, you're inside me and a part of me just like Florian and Ben and Sam and Joe and Ron and my mother and father and all those other losses that've gone into the making of me—why the hell do you need my poor pathetic *corpse* to make that real, a flesh-and-blood tool you'll just let sit unused and rusting in the box? How can you be so fixated on the least important thing?

"Your pleas don't move me," said its voice, not coming from that gaping canyon mouth now but from somewhere far beyond. "Not at all."

Pleas? Fuck pleading. This is just how it *is*. I need this body, not you. You've never needed to take our bodies to have us and maybe you'll understand that now that Death rules the earth, these are my legs and not yours kicking at the air, at the bubbling tar swallowing them, my hands trying to pry your fingers free, my teeth scrabbling for a sink-hold on your nonexistent flesh, I'll take your eyes, I've done it before, I'm not going—going to die—I'm not going—the sky blotted out, sticky wet nothingness, choking and drowning and I can't go now, I need to get to the beaches, I'm not letting you, I'm snarling and growling like the old days and my hands are throttling your great bony throat the beach is gone the trees the graves are gone the deer the night the moon the great black tarry mouth I'm not going with you I'm suffocating I'm dying I'm not—

The night sky, not wet overwhelming blackness but a distant, peaceful deep gray. No graveyard. No farm. I lay curled knees to chin near a rusted-out marquee sign next to a peeling, peacock blue abandoned shrimp shack on a roadside in Gary, my road, my shack, my world. I was sick again, bile coating my throat and mouth, but when I was gasping and finished, my gut actually subsided, my stomach unknotting and breath slowing to normal. Breath. Normal. I'd never get used to having working lungs. I was drenched in sweat, soaked head to foot and shivering, but I could move without every muscle clenching, stretch my legs without spasms, when I raised my head the earth didn't dip and spin but stayed courteously still.

I rose to my knees, then my feet. Shaky, still shivering, weak and hollow-limbed but steady enough. Shockingly steady. My clothes, skin, what was left of my hair were grimy, stiff, maddeningly itchy with the layers of dirt, sweat, blood, dried puke, hardened grease, streaks of feeding fat and I had a sudden, powerful urge I hadn't felt since before that long-ago car accident, years and years past: the need to bathe. It actually made me laugh. Laughing hurt, wore me out.

I was clutching something sticky and sugar-grit soft tight in one hand. I opened my fingers and saw not rotten pear but the hard remains of a lake stone, snapped into pieces. The stones none of us could break open, grind, crush, bite down on for trying. Like blood from a sliced vein, juice from a ripe fruit, something oozed from the pieces and ran onto my skin: tarry and black like coffin liquor but as it hit the air it dried out, hardened, became grainy and lighter colored and seeped grittily from my opened fingers onto the ground. Sand. A low-humming, barely audible singing sand. Where it touched my skin I felt soothed, stronger, like something inside it was buzzing and burrowing deep into my cells and nerves to protect me, restore me. Keep me walking, when I should long since have been dead.

Meteoric. Metamorphic.

As I thrust the stone pieces and sand traces into my filthy pocket I heard a soft quiet *click* behind me, like a flicked cigarette lighter. I turned, a rabbit scuttling swiftly into the underbrush at my movements, and saw facing me something small and recognizably human but covered in a greenish tinge, the verdigris of rot, bits and pieces of her swollen tight with decomp gas. One side of her face was smashed beyond repair, the intact eye staring out from a fistful of crushed bone; the right arm dangled useless by her side, held fast by the thinnest possible strands of tendon and luck. Limp auburn hair with faded pink streaks, greasy and stiff with layers of dirt. Bare, swollen, blackened feet. An old T-shirt and jeans gone to soiled rags.

I gazed at myself, my old lost self with her gas-bulging eyes and wary, moldy, unreadable face, and then she bubbled, warped like a fading mirage and the thing that looked like Jim took her place, calm, smiling, flicking cigarette ash at a moth wheeling overhead. The moth seemed to freeze in midair, dropping dead on the dry, brown grass; he picked it up, breathed on it and it twitched, walked across his palm, flew swiftly away.

"Guess you weren't as sick as you thought," he said. Cheerful, serene as the clear night sky. "My mistake. But we'll just wait and see how that all works out."

He picked up a heavy, battered rucksack lying on the ground between us and slung it over his shoulder like he had all the places in the universe to go, endless countless cornfields of dead and dying to try to comfort and feed.

"Later days, Jessie," he said. "Much, much later."

He turned and strolled off, whistling tunelessly as he lit

up another cigarette, and disappeared. Didn't vanish, didn't dissolve like a ghost, just kept walking in the opposite direction like any other living creature until he'd become a fly-speck in my vision, until I lost him.

I slid my hand into my other pocket, finding the intact lake stones I'd brought with me; I pulled one out, curled my fingers around it and squeezed, hard as I could. It didn't break. Or crack. Or crumble. It just sat there, smooth and impenetrable, tingling faintly against the skin of my palm. A magnet, shivering at the touch of iron filings. I held it to my ear. Heard nothing, nothing at all, for many moments, then finally picked up the smallest note, fainter and more elusive than any sea sound from a shell: that same low, quiet humming of the sands. The echo of a meteorite hurling through space, about to hit a glacier-scooped lake bed and split open and change the earth's history forever. The background sound of eternity.

I put it back in my pocket and headed for the waters.

Overgrown trees and brush. Waist-high unmowed grass, just like our county park. Billboards, some looking decades old and worn to flapping paper scraps, for gas stations, restaurants long since closed, a car wash, a radio station, fast-food places, all the detritus of hoo-life. More broken security fences, torn-up barbed wire, an abandoned guard post with a spent flamethrower cartridge, all the evidence of what had once been us. My hands were steadier now, the tremors fading; the bluish tinge starting in my skin was gone, beneath all the dirt it was pink again and moist with sweat. My scalp itched, I reached up to scratch, and pulled at some of the remaining strands of hair: thin and brittle, but they didn't fall out. I still had to stop every quarter mile or so to rest, retch, yield to aching muscles and queasy stomach, but getting up again was mere torment instead of agony. Keep going. Keep walking. The sky was slowly lightening, from charcoal to iron. How much longer? How many hours more?

A set of railroad tracks, the ties split and broken. Someone had tried gnawing at the wood beneath the metal, it had all splintered. The death stench everywhere around me seeped into my pores like a noxious steam; I was no longer inured to it, it was no longer the alluring aroma of food or the comfortable stink of my own flesh. Which truly, desperately needed a bath, shower, decontaminating scrub. Joe and Ben used to walk this far every goddamned time the spirit moved, they never fell on their asses like whiny little kiddies. Keep going.

A warped, broken metal gate higher than my head, trying to block the road forward. Guard posts with the doors swinging wide open. NO UNAUTHORIZED PERSONNEL BEYOND THIS POINT. Florian could bend an iron streetlamp post in half when he was young, did they really think we couldn't tear through something like this without trying? But of course it was to keep other hoos out, not us. We came and went as we pleased, and they wrote each other little "scientific" papers about what they saw of us. Guess it helped pass the time. A lone body in one of the guard booths, swollen with gas and buzzing with flies. Not diseased; from the look of her, she'd been shot.

Not chewed on either, not at all. One of the first ones I'd seen in a long time who'd been left alone. Whether that meant anything, other than there were too few of us left alive and hungry to scavenge her, I didn't know.

The sky overhead had faded to pewter, suffused with a dim, dull but gaining light. The dawn's early light. As I pushed through the gate my legs hurt horribly, the muscles like rubber bands snapping hard and brutal against my skin with every new step. The road past the gate grew narrow, winding, the tree limbs and underbrush crowding in from all sides. Apartment buildings, a restaurant or two, a pharmacy, a tiny supermarket trashed to its foundations and a pile of broken glass, then nothing but the greenery, the bodies and me.

I could smell it now, beneath the stink of all-encompassing death. The lakeshore. The dampness all in the air like expectation, a pregnant pause before the cries and whispers of the tides. The stones and broken bits of stones in my pockets vibrated, buzzing against the cloth, then started letting out a steady, audible hum. The road turned again and the over-growth opened up, and with no warning I stood before a long, clear, endlessly wide expanse of sand and sky. Tall, waving beach grasses on either side of the road, a pale gray and softly glowing sky that seemed to run toward the water and then fly up higher and higher taking with it all the stink of decay and disease and sickness and horror; even the bodies strewn on the roadside looked calmer, quieter, like they'd all just fallen asleep.

The Octave Chanute Lakeshore Park. Says so right there on the sign. My beach. Finally. Snuck right up and ambushed me, there in plain sight. All I had to do was—

Sit here and cry again. Just for a second. It felt almost like the stones were crying alongside me but that was just knowing I was going to die alone after all: There was no way I could ever get back to the nature preserve, much less try to drag Linc and Lisa and all of them here, I had no more strength, I'd used up my whole fever-break on this wild life-chase and now—

I stumbled past the shell of a small Greek-columned, open-air building, built from blocks of worn sand-colored concrete. The old bathhouse, a Prairie School architectural landmark from back at the turn of the century before they started restricting the beaches to the researchers and us. I'd seen pictures of it. Stand up on the second floor, all open columns and roofed-in balcony space, and you got a sweep-ing view of the water. Past that, maybe a hundred yards away up on a high ridge, another, far bigger building. The same rosy-sandy concrete brick, Greek columns, lines boxy and graceful all at once, except this building was as closed and forbidding as the bathhouse was open: narrow half-hidden doors, tiny windows too high to reach, towers on either side of the sprawling main building with dark, slanting, over-hanging roofs like arms stretched out to protect something fragile, signal the world to stay away. For all that it sat defiantly approachable there in a large patch of tree-covered parkland, no fencing around it, no guard posts. No signs.

I didn't need a sign, I was certain what I was looking at. The lab. The thanatological lab where Jim had worked, where he had dragged our dead back and cut them open. Where they spent all their time trying to figure out how to kill us, where they first sprayed the grounds, the trees, the dirt, the air with a mutated pesticide that did them all in. Where I was born times three even though I didn't know it—no. That was the doing of the rocks, the sands, the remnants of our long-ago meteoric mother. *Our* Mother Earth, just like Rommel said, when all this time I'd thought it was the dirt where I'd been buried. Right here. My real parentage, my family. The sound of the water shushing against the sands came up soft, insistent, faint in the distance.

Was anybody alive in there? Anybody at all? Quiet, everything still closed off and shuttered when every other house and building I'd seen was—no. One of the lab's front doors was open and looked bent on its hinges. A couple of those little second- and third-story windows were nothing but dark holes. A body or two, lying there on the walkway, rotted, forgotten. Another fortress turned mausoleum. My questions might all be there, but none of my answers.

I turned my back on it and stood facing the water. Expanses of tall waving beach grasses, a tree or two outlined stark against the sky, and in the middle a narrow path of foot-beaten sand leading straight down the long, sloping duneface to the shore. If I was wrong, if it wasn't here I was meant to be, then I belonged nowhere.

Why hadn't I made Linc and Renee and Lisa come with me? Insisted, while I still had the chance? Too late to go back, to retrieve them. They might already have died. I didn't want to belong here alone—

The sand underfoot was thick-layered and heavy and the grass stems, as I grabbed at them for balance, cut and sliced at my skin. The pearl gray sky and dark blue water met at a horizon line so straight and sharp it looked drawn with a ruler; the waves rushed in, the tide rushed out, with the endless repetition of a heartbeat, the gulls circling in constant call and response. I half-walked, half-slid down the dune-face, resisting the strange urge born of exhaustion or sadness or some newer, unnameable impulse entirely to start crawling through the sands, let them get against my skin and in my nose and mouth and bury me, take me back underground. The stones in my pocket had gone suddenly, abruptly quiet.

As I reached the bottom of the ridge and the trail gave way to the wider beach, the sand strewn with old cigarette butts, dead twigs, bits of driftwood, I saw them. They were curled up and burrowed down in the sands, like Florian and I had both done in my dreams, lying with their backs, limbs, faces all covered; their fingertips clutched and bore down, holding on to handfuls of grains and sinking in past the wrists. Third-borns just like me, dazed, half-bald, blue-tinged and exhausted and wasted-thin despite all our obscene feasts of dead flesh, trying to bury themselves alive, get back underground. Dozens of them, all over the shore sands like burial mounds, like a cemetery full of undeads all tunneling up and breaking through.

I stared at them and the sands beneath my feet seemed to rise and fall with the strange lung-breaths they, we, all took like the humans we weren't, with the sounds of our newfound heartbeats regular as the tides. My heart had started again too when this plague changed me, just like my breath, I hadn't even thought of that until now. I put a palm to my chest, to feel it, and the others squeezed their eyes shut and moaned in pain or just stared up at me, incurious, so calm. One of them held up a hand, gaunt and withered, like Florian's before he went fully skeletal.

"You're still sick," he said. His voice was trembly and soft but had an undercurrent of steel; pale sands matted the lenses of his glasses, his dark brown skin like a half-frosted cake. "I can smell it on you. Come lie down."

I wanted to lie in those sands and sleep and sleep so badly my whole body ached, but I had to know first. "Will it make me better?"

"I don't know." He turned onto his side, trying to push himself in farther, feet pedaling at the sands to make his sleeping hole, or his grave, that much deeper. "I just had to be here. Had to get here, somehow, before I died."

A few yards away another one was digging a hole for herself, stopping every few moments to be sick, arms trembling and spasming with the effort but bringing up only pathetic handfuls of sand every time. I wanted to go help her. I had to lie down.

Bodies were everywhere, actual corpses, gull-shredded and swelling up with gas. Other figures wandered aimlessly over the sands, human, third-born, I couldn't tell, some the ghastly blue-black of the actively dying. Nothing I could do for them now. Or Linc. Or Renee, or Lisa, or Sam, or Joe, or anyone at all, but there was that woman trying and failing to tunnel underground and I had to help her, after I'd caused all this without ever intending to I had to help someone other than my own damned self—

She fell to the sands before I could reach her, no more digging, hands still trembling as she lay there. One of the bruise-colored dying, his breath an uneven, rasping moan like the singing sands in pain, came up to her and kicked her, hard in the head again and again, like undeads skull-stomping after a fight; she made a horrible sound, an almost indignant gurgle twisted into a wet, choking scream, and crumpled up unmoving and silent.

The buried ones just lay there, unmoved, as if they'd seen it all before. They probably had. The one at my feet turned his head away.

I took a step forward. Her attacker pulled a small knife from his pocket, hands shaking worse than hers had. Still human, then, a sick human: no undead's or third-born's good sharp teeth. He sawed pieces off her, his pound of flesh, but as soon as he'd crammed them in his mouth he spat them out again, moaning, the same shame and revulsion and uncontrollable hunger I'd seen in Lisa, killing that squirrel in the forest, in the cornfield people retching up everything they ate. His breath grown louder and keening, he pulled himself upright, licked at the knife's edge, coughed wetly, threw it down next to her body like it'd bitten him.

He turned and stared at me, his mouth a rictus of false cheer, his eyes full of despair and madness and silent begging to be kicked dead himself, thrown clear of his own misery. He was almost bald now, thick thatch of prematurely gray hair reduced to bitten-away threads, his cheeks concave with the plague's starvation and his lips gone black beneath the smear of bright red blood. He stretched out a hand, his whole arm convulsing, and the loosening nails curved backward, sank deep into his sand-caked palm.

"I always knew I'd see you again," said Jim.

18

I thrust my hands into my pockets. The stones sat there against my fingers, just ordinary rocks now, no tingling or humming or singing, but the touch of them reassured me just the same.

"Are there others with you?" I asked. I hadn't seen anyone I knew, down in these sands, but that signified nothing. "How did you get here?"

"Two hands," he said, like he hadn't heard me. "Two hands, there in your pockets. I did that for you." He weaved side to side, sliding on the miniature sand piles his feet had made, making wet hacking sounds every time he drew breath. "Lips, a tongue, a larynx. You can talk to me again like a civilized creature instead of grunting and drooling like your tongue got cut out, *I* did that for you, I—"

"I could talk to you before," I pointed out. I was easy, quiet, a trainer facing a mad dog. "We talked a good long time, actually, it's just you only bothered giving me half the truth—"

"You owe me," he whispered, with the same feverish, glassy-eyed hatred I remembered from the woods. He yanked at his remaining hair and another handful came out, easy as a tuft of cotton candy off the stick. "Look what I've done for you! Look what I've done for all of them! Every one of you! And this is what I get for it!"

His shaking, jolting arms motioned furiously at the buried ones, at the sky growing lighter by the second, then he seemed to lose control of them and they dropped helpless, still trembling, to his sides. I stared out at Lake Michigan, that horizon line drawn so solid like it was underscoring the whole world: *And that, as they say, is that.* The ghost of the Chicago skyline floated out there, an unbroken distant blue-gray shadow so shockingly clear I could make out each individual skyscraper, the antenna on top of the Sears Tower. Some of the buildings looked shorter than they were supposed to, their top ends jagged and uneven. A dark haze, drifting from some of them, that might be ash or smoke.

"Lisa's with me," I told him. "She passed through the other side of this, like I did. She's one of us now. But she's sick again, like we all are—"

"Fuck Lisa." He spat on the sand, scrubbing the drying blood from his mouth like he'd just realized it was there. "You're sick? *You're* all sick? Look at me! Look what you've done to me, look what all your kind did to—"

"You never told me she left." I picked up a bit of driftwood, crumbly and fragile from all its time bobbing on the waves. I wanted to go back to speaking with a tree branch, back to when my own enforced silence, Linc's and my ability to talk right over his head, still gave me the protection of distance. When I could pretend this dying man, my brother, was just a stranger in a foreign tongue. "You said she got sick. You said you locked her up. You never bothered telling me she got out."

"Fuck all of you." Jim spat again, aiming for my feet and missing. "Her too. All of you. All you that changed. You're all monsters."

The tide rushed in, soft, undisturbed, and back out again. Something bloated and missing an arm, a leg, came in with it, deposited like a cat's gift of a dead mouse on the sands. I wanted to lie down so badly, never get up again.

"You said there was something strange about the sands

here." I took another step toward Jim, dropping the drift-wood in case he thought it was a weapon, and he bared teeth that were long and grayish and visibly loose in the gum. "That we live longer here. That the sands make the dead revive. Your lab up there, you said it had geologists that—"

"She said I was scaring her." Jim kept lurching foot to foot, stomping at the sands now, wasting his last energies trying to keep upright. "Before all this happened. I told her I could bring you back. You don't know how she cried after she saw you, she said it was horrible, you trapped in that rotting body, that it was like watching you being tortured— I promised you to her. Her daughter, I promised her little girl back. Mom and Dad, I *promised* her, I made a promise, I—"

He started to cry. Snot-choked sobs out of honest grief for me, for Karen, Lisa, himself, crying like I'd only ever seen when the black Lab he'd had since he was six had to be put down and stop it, Jim, stop it, you're evil, you're crazy, don't make me remember the person I really knew, stand here and watch yet another person I love wash away with the tides. Loved. Even worse. I reached out a hand, and he backed away from me like I was diseased. As, in fact, I was.

"Then she said I was scaring her." He scrubbed at his mouth again, furious, sawing his hand back and forth like he could cleanse away his own words. "That it was wrong, think-ing you could bring back zombies, monsters, make them human again, it was 'wishful thinking,' it was 'against God,' I should stop, I was so 'obsessed' I was scaring her—"

"The stories about a meteorite." I reached into my pocket, showed him the cracked bits of stone, the dried-up sand from inside them. "I've heard them. Is it true? That something landed here, thousands of years back, and this stuff got into the sands? In the dirt? Is that what your geologist pals were—"

"She threatened to report me." Jim was panting now, loose teeth grinding together, rage building big and swift beneath the teariness like Dad when he was feeling put-upon by the world, really angry. Exactly like Dad. "Can you believe it? I bust my hump for her, for *you*, for this whole fucking family, for half my goddamned life, and all I get in return is the bitch threatening to whistle-blow to my own boss, turn me in, after everything I'd done for—so I didn't have any choice, Jessie, I had to lock her up. Okay? I had to lock her up, I didn't want—and then she got sick." He laughed. He actually laughed. "She got sick."

I put the fragments of stone away.

"Did you make her sick?" My voice didn't waver, I felt what was surely the same strange, unshakable calm I'd seen in Lisa's face as she lay dying; that, and the cold certainty I already knew my answer. And I'd felt sorry for him. I'd *pitied* him. "Did you use her, after you locked her up, experiment on her like some sort of guinea—"

"She got sick!" Jim roared at me, all rage, Dad's rage, eating up that weak rotting body from the inside worse than any disease. "She got sick, we all got sick, this wasn't supposed to happen! It wasn't supposed to be that there was a war, and your kind won it! You! The walking corpses, who already lived out your goddamned lives! You won! All without firing a fucking shot!"

The gulls cried out overhead, circling, sailing over the waters in the serene knowledge that none of this was at all bad for them. Something else was washing ashore, less recognizably human than the last one.

"We didn't win anything," I said. "We're extinct now, the undead. Just like humans—worse than humans, I've seen living humans, I haven't seen any more of us. You've wiped us out. Your bosses should be thrilled to—"

"I should have killed you." He wrapped his arms around himself, clenching up with shivers. His discolored skin looked baggy and loose. "I should've gone back out there with a flamethrower and roasted all of you to ashes. Monsters. Monsters everywhere. Tell Lisa not to worry anymore, you had a good quick death."

"We're all sick," I said. "Dying. But something about those stones I showed you? These sands? I think they're why Florian, my friend, he was so old, they're why he lived so long. Those stones I showed you, they were his. And I think they're why I'm not dead now. That maybe, somehow, they're making me better. Am I right?"

"You won. Congratulations. You all fucking won."

"Am I just crazy, Jim? Or am I right?"

"You owe me. I gave you this, all this, you owe—"

"You experimented on Lisa, didn't you?" I advanced on him, slow, easy. "To punish her, or because you were so panicked by then, because of all this, that you convinced yourself you were doing her some kind of favor. But she got away from you. Sick as you made her, she got away." I started laughing too, I just couldn't help it, as I looked around the beach, at the half-living burial mounds surrounding us. "We all did. The whole world got away from you—"

"We knew there was something here." Jim sat down heavily on the sand, his last reserves draining away and gone. "Something that created your kind. Maybe something that cheats death itself, that—there was a meteorite that hit here, five, ten thousand years ago, when the lake was still forming. Some sort of protean matter in it. Got mixed up in everything, saturated with it, it changed the whole composition of— what're you asking me all this for? Why? That was the geologists' lookout! I was in biology! It was our mandate, I wouldn't go along with it, they wanted us to wipe you all out—"

"And you have," I reminded him.

He glared up at me, breathing hard, his fury draining away like filthy water down a sewer and leaving behind Jim again, Jim in those jaundiced eyes, that horrible sloughing cyanotic skin, full of the terrified bewilderment of any creature human or otherwise sick unto death. Like Lillian, belligerent but still sobbing, broken, begging me and Joe not to stomp her. And I'd had to—

Not this time. Whatever he's done, to Lisa, to me, any of us, leave it. I loved him, once, and he made a mistake, and he's dying because of it and I'm just too damned tired to want to punish anyone. Never mind everyone else who died because of him, I can't help them. Can't help anyone. And there's nobody here to force me to hurt him now.

"I'm sorry," I said. And I was. "Later days."

I turned to walk away and sloughing rotten arms reached up, grabbed me hard around the knees and slammed me face-first into the sands.

I inhaled without thinking and I was choking, gasping, sucking in mouthfuls of grit; my throat was coated and caked with it and I flailed, panicking, then something in me remembered the deep-down gravesite dirt and that impenetrable concrete grave liner crumbling into powder and I stopped fighting it, I just lay there and tried to breathe it all in. Just like when I first tunneled up. *You're still dead to me, Jessie, whatever body you're in.* My head spun and chest seized, goddamned accursed dead-living body screaming for oxygen, but I made myself lie there still and just as Jim loosened his hold, thinking I'd stopped fighting, I broke free and found the open sky. Retched up sand, sucked in air, as I grabbed Jim's arms and twisted them behind him. He kicked, legs shaking, and cursed as his feet flew wide.

"No," he whispered, thick and congested with hate. "You don't get to survive. It's not fair. You're coming with me—"

I was panting, dizzy, spots dancing before my eyes, and the sands we wrestled in were so soothing, so welcoming. *You're still sick. Come lie down.* My eyes kept closing, my whole body screaming for rest, surcease, sleep, and weak as he was that let him twist free and grab me again, try to use his weight against my own wasted gaunt bones. He rolled me on my back and his mouth gripped my shoulder but his teeth couldn't get purchase, too loose, too blunt; my hands reached around his neck and throttled, no pity left, nothing in his eyes now like Joe or Lillian or anyone else I could ever have loved. He flung an arm wide, convulsing, I could have laughed just then at the spasmodic helplessness of it, and then that hand reached into the sands and retrieved his knife and something thrust into my side like a fist blow to shatter bone, like my flesh was a greenstick branch being torn slowly in half with every nerve twisting, agonized twisting, refusing to snap. I arched up and I screamed, and screamed.

Jim shouted with laughter, triumphant, and as the hole in my side began tightening and knitting together quick as he'd torn it he stabbed me again, again, the chest, the stomach, what flesh was left on my arms. It wasn't killing me and I barely had a chance to bleed into the sands before my body healed itself but it hurt so much, hurt like my hands in that meat-fire on the road never had; vomit pooled in my mouth, I howled in anger as much as pain and scrabbled for the blade, let it slice deep into my fingers as I finally got hold, and then Jim wrenched it away and thrust it straight through my throat.

I gurgled, a wet thickness bubbling from my lips and nostrils; my hands flew up frantic to pull the horrible suffocating thing out, I was gagging on blood, smothering, then I remembered Linc during the fight with Carny, so long ago, five or ten thousand years ago. Breathe it all in. I let my arms go limp, let the deep red spume ooze from my teeth, closed my eyes to Jim and the rising sun.

The sands were a great, gentle palm cradling me as I lay there, staining them deep red, and my instinctive panic receded like the tides; I wouldn't actually drown in my own blood, just like I'd known back in my coffin I wouldn't die needing breath. I waited. Let Jim keep me pinned until he was sure I'd stopped struggling, then felt him roll off my body. He put fingertips to my temple, brushed back a stray, broken strand of what remained of my hair.

"I'll bury you," he whispered. He was breathing hard, from satisfaction or fear or just the disease slowly shutting down his lungs. "Nobody'll touch my sister. Not for food." A wet strangled cough. "Good, quick death."

He tugged hard at the knife, yanking it from my throat. As the blade slid free my eyes flew open and I grabbed him around the neck, shoved him into the sands and punched hard, again, again. Congratulations, Jim, you pulled it out, do you get to be king now? How about now? He thrashed and gasped like a fish on a boat deck and his flesh slid off in thin, frayed ribbons beneath my fists as I struck him, more, again. You lied to me, you hurt Lisa, you used her like one of your poor fucking guinea pigs lab rats cats dogs monkeys you can't leave anything alone, you couldn't leave me alone, everyone's gone thanks to you and I'm stuck here myself, all by myself, forever—my torn throat had closed itself up tight and all that came out was muffled sounds like screams and I couldn't stop, he was screaming now too, crying—

Break his back, a little voice inside me whispered. *His spine. Take his eyes. Do it. You know you wanna. What good is he to anyone?*

I pulled back, panting. Jim lay there, torn up, used up, trying to breathe and wasting it all on sobs. That little voice, still whispering incessantly, was thin and anemic and so tired, the ghost of someone I wasn't anymore; that bloodlust, that unceasing need to feed on flesh, on fear, on fury, it was nothing but the light of someone I'd once been streaking blindingly bright across a ghostly windshield, fading, now gone. The crashing synaptic drums, pounding piano, hard screeching electric guitar that had thrummed inside my head, kept me running for nine constant years, all gone silent while I wasn't even listening. My ears rang with the lack of noise. The burial mounds around me were all quiet too, only the gulls and the water and the faraway-seeming sounds of the few other humans wandering the beach, dying.

I'd loved him, once. That, now, was enough to make me stop. He was gone anyway. Out of my hands. And I was just so tired.

I let him go, gripping the knife he'd dropped. Lay there on the sands, exhausted, unmoored, as he tried to pull himself upright, only got to his knees. My fists had stripped his face, the wet tissue paper of his flesh nearly down to the skull; he snuffled away tears and glared at me with eyes that were Jim's, then a mad terrified stranger's, then his once more. Flickering and changing too many times to track. Jim comes in. Jim goes out. He shoves a knife through your snout, your spout.

"This all started because of you." The words were squeezed from his throat, congealing into low groans like dried-out glue from a half-spent tube. "Long as you live, maybe you'll live forever, thanks to me, just never forget that, Jessie. All this happened, all of it, because I tried to help you—"

"I never wanted your help." My voice was the spent, hollow shell of a snarl. "Never. I knew what I was. I was making my own way. It's because *you* couldn't stand the thought of how I looked, and sounded, and smelled—"

He fell forward, curled onto his side, laughing at nothing as he lay there with his limbs clenched tight and trembling. Like Florian, in his final minutes.

"You couldn't leave it alone. You couldn't just let me live it out, go to dust and die again like I was meant to—" I was close to crying again, choking it back into harsh, shallow breaths.

"I wanted to help you," Jim repeated. "And I did. But they'll get you now." He'd buried his head in his arms, rocking back and forth where he lay. "The lab. Couldn't all have died. Some of them lived through this, passed through it. All their research—figure it out—they'll kill you. They'll find a way—kill all of—"

His words twisted into a long, low moan and his body contorted, convulsed. Get up. Stab him, kill him, like you did for Sam and Ben. A mercy. Don't leave him like this. Do it.

I couldn't move. The sands had me now and I was drained of energy, anger, cradling the knife in my hands like it could actually protect me and too spent to dig myself into the dunes. Somebody help me. Help me go to sleep. Jim cried out, wordless, again. I stared past him, at the corpse of the woman who'd been his last attempted meal.

"You were right," said a soft, steady voice close to my ear. The man who'd told me to lie down, there in his own proper burial mound a few feet away. Unmoved by my plight, or Jim's. "The whole world got away from humankind. There's nothing you can do for him now. Not for any of them."

"Help me!" Jim was up in a crouch now, trying to crawl,

skin peeling from his arms and legs as he infant-crept, shaking, retching, over the sands. Every syllable was pain twisted into speech. "Please! Somebody—"

"Ain't nothing you can do for him, Jessie. Not a blessed thing."

Florian's voice. I knew Florian wasn't here, that I'd just conjured him up in my head because I was so worn down and afraid and lost and watching my last family die, surrounded by strangers beyond caring, and that made me curl an arm over my face and let tears drip onto my dirt-stiff sleeve. I wanted Florian back. I wanted everyone back. I wanted to wake up back in the woods with Joe and Sam and Billy and everyone all laughing at me, getting on my ass about my shit-crazy dreams, and if that couldn't happen I didn't want to wake up again at all.

"Somebody help me! God—"

Who did Florian want back? His children, of course. Who else? What about the man buried next to me? Was he here all alone too, a burial mound with no family, no visitors? Nothing you can do. Maybe he was talking to himself, as much as me. Trying to let himself off the hook for still being alive. But then none of this was his fault, was it. Not like with me.

I felt better, lying there. Still sick, still tired unto death, but better. Like I really would get up, fullness of time, brush off the sands, start walking again to God knows where. I didn't want to. So damned much walking. Where would I go? What would I do? I already went through this once, back at the cemetery, and I didn't like it—

"Jessie!" My name, shaped into a scream. *"Help me!"*

Another knife jab to my gut, my heart. Stuck in my throat so I can't even cry. Go away, Jim. Please. I can't help you.

"Jessie!"

Stop, Jim. Stop. Just stop.

"Jessie! Are you out there?"

Something wrong with his voice, suddenly. Didn't sound right. Didn't sound like his at all.

"Jessie!"

Dying did a number on you, I should know. But I was pretty sure it wouldn't make a man sound like a woman.

I forced myself up, swaying on my own hands and knees there in the duneface. I saw people a few yards away down the beach, a man and a woman, some sort of motionless burden slung between them with arms and legs dangling and strands of half-fair, half-dark hair covering its face. Another illusion. I'm quite the conjure woman, these past few weeks. I watched it in silence.

"Jessie!"

My tongue felt thick suddenly, unwieldy. Dried up with sand and tiredness and the fear it really was all just a mirage. The words came out in a croak:

"Renee?" I waved an arm, the knife blade glinting in the early sun. "Linc!"

Linc. Renee. Renee made a sound like a sob and they were staggering toward me now, overwhelmed by the weight of Lisa's body, not losing but gaining substance and fleshy solidity as they came closer. I tried to get up, walk toward them, but all I could do was keep reaching out my arms as they stumbled over the duneface, skirting corpses and burial mounds with their feet sliding back and forth like they were negotiating winter ice. What would these beaches be like, in the winter? Freezing weather had been our friend once, preserving decaying flesh, making the chittering crazy-itching bugs all slow and stop their feeds to hibernate, but if fire couldn't kill us now maybe ice would do the trick. Linc was shaking violently, every muscle clenched and twitching, and with each step Renee's entire face closed up with pain. Lisa was unconscious, each breath a scared skittering cry, her skin gone fully blue. They collapsed on their knees before me, Lisa dropping facedown like a bundle into the sands.

"I had—this dream," Linc managed, out of breath, gulping like he was fighting off being sick. "Florian. The beach, it, the sands are—"

"I know," I said, to try to spare him the effort of talking. Renee was doubled over coughing, a wet nauseous sound. "Florian said—"

"Renee had it too." He coughed like she was coughing, quickly turned his head away, but nothing came up. "Same dream. We woke up, you were gone. You were right. Should've listened to you, but—had to follow." He took another long breath, his face gray. "Lisa wouldn't stay behind. Brought her with us. She's dying, Jessie." He touched her hair, not flinching when a hank of it came off all over his fingers. "Humans can't take this disease like we can—"

We can't take it either, Linc, not if that woman Jim tried to feed off is any sign. This is our last chance right here. I tugged at Lisa's shoulders, Renee helping me roll her over, saw peeking from the knuckles of Lisa's fist clenched tight as rigor mortis the smooth, green-gray surface of a lake stone.

"She wanted one," Renee explained, looking guilty like she'd filched it from me. Still coughing. "She said—it felt good in her hand—Jessie, you'll think I'm nuts but I swear there's something about those things, it's like they made us stronger or less sick or—"

"You're nuts," I assured her. No time to waste on what Florian, Jim, Rommel all told me, what was sitting there in my own pockets. "Help me dig her in. Hurry."

"What are you—" Linc and I were already raking aside armfuls of sand, scrabbling with what energy we had, while Renee watched in consternation. "Don't cover her face like that, she'll suffocate!"

"No, she won't!" I reached over and gave Renee a shove, just like the old days, I had no time for this, she and Linc didn't have time for this. "You said I was right about the beaches, are you gonna just sit there now? The sands are what—Jesus Christ, Renee, will you get off your ass and help us!"

"Help me!" Jim screamed, crawling in a circle, limbs spasming and blackened with encroaching death. "Jessie!"

Linc got Lisa's shoulders under a layer of sand, worked on a deeper pit for her legs. He gave me a wary glance. "That sounds like—"

"Jim," I said, and didn't elaborate. The sands I was digging in warped and wavered suddenly, like someone had tossed a grainy handful at my eyes, then it passed. Linc stopped for a moment and hugged me hard.

"Please, God!" Jim was slowing down now, the circle contracting. "God! Help me!"

A little cluster of hoos, blue-tinged, rotten inside and out, stood a few feet removed, shaking, shuffling. Watching him in anticipatory silence. I dug and dug like a mother rabbit, a dog in a garden, getting Lisa farther down. Safe, from all of this.

"The sand," Renee said, pushing more of it over Lisa's arms and, still with some hesitation, her face. "And the stones. Is that why Florian wanted—" She looked up at me, stricken. "We could have saved him."

I shook my head. "That wasn't sickness, just being old. He was ready to go." Lisa still had a faint, wavering pulse but her wrist, her palm were growing cold. "No matter how long they'd kept him alive before."

But he still wanted them. Because they were something he loved. Something that kept him safe, all those years. I brushed some of the sand away from Lisa's lips and, crazy wild hair of a notion, dug into my pocket for the broken fragments of stone. Slipped a few of them into her mouth. Covered her up again, to let her keep breathing it all in.

Would we all be able to die, still, even after all this? If one day we just decided, like Florian, we were ready to go?

I lay there next to Lisa, half-buried myself, an arm flung over her pile of sand. *Go on along, pets. I'm tired.* Linc and Renee lay next to me, all of us cradling Lisa against ourselves, holding on to each other.

"I'm sorry," Renee said, watching as Jim hauled himself upright one final time. Each limb stretched, agonized, on an imaginary rack. His body trying to blot out the rising sun.

"Nothing we can do," I said. Another shadow passed overhead, a gliding gull. "Nothing."

Jim let out a sound, a low yowling noise like a cat about to be sick, and then the yowling became a long, high, enraged scream and he collapsed where he stood, crumpling slowly to the sand, screams cut dead as suddenly as a radio snapped off in mid-broadcast. His feet, his hands twitched, jerking away from the heat of some phantom fire, and then he was still and silent.

More shadows. Those hoos, as once were, days or hours or minutes from death themselves, slowly staggering toward his remains. One of them gazed down at me, staring straight into my eyes, desperation and remorse and the feverish, overpowering urgency of famine turning her eyes to dark dank holes. What the hell did she want, forgiveness? Permission? Don't look at me, bitch. I've got problems of my own.

"Get out of my face," I whispered, and held up the knife. "Just get out."

Drool snaked from her blackened lips, gleamed on her chin, then she and the others had Jim by the limbs, trying to work up the strength to drag him away. Linc reached out a hand, actually trying physically to turn my head from the sight. I shook free, and watched.

"Was anyone still alive back there?" I asked. "When you left?"

"Some," said Renee. She'd closed her eyes, her face now pressed into the sands like they were the mound of a use-worn pillow. "Not many. Not very."

"We have to get back." I tried to sit up again, only managed to balance on an elbow. "Bring them here. They might get better. Like these others."

So many burial mounds, all around us—so many? Not so many. A few dozen, at the most. Two dozen, more like. That was all. All that was left. Assuming they all lived.

"We'll get back," Linc assured me, fingers curling around mine. "As soon as we get some rest."

"It's actually not that far to walk," Renee added. Her face was chalky pale, her hands shaking with fatigue; the sand covering them roiled and sifted like little beetles were crawling underneath. "We can get back there, bring them with us. In a few minutes."

A few minutes. Hours. Days. My arm hurt and my head was heavy so I lay down again.

The hoos had Jim's body now but their strength was ebbing too, they'd only managed to drag him a few feet away. They squatted over him, moaning, then bent their heads down and tore at his flesh, trying to bite deep. One of them had a knife too, a big sharp thing like hunters carried. The blade covered in rust, or dried blood.

"It's not fair just to leave them there," I told Renee and Linc, almost belligerent like they'd been fighting me about it. "We have to go back. We have to get them."

"We will," Linc promised. His eyes were closing too, his hand slipping from my grasp. "We will."

They'd got the knife deep into Jim now. Sawing at him. Blood oozed thick onto the duneface and a couple of other hoos crawled up, groaning, grabbing handfuls of drenched sand. Like Sam, after he woke up again. At least he was out of this now. Him and all the others.

I knew her, I suddenly realized. The one who'd been staring at me. I knew her. She was one of our neighbors, three or four houses down the street in Lepingville: Mrs. Finnegan? Ferguson? I'd forgotten. Had a dippy border collie that got into everyone's garden. Brought us platefuls of Christmas cookies. She snatched a handful of torn-up flesh from another sick hoo, punching him hard, weeping as she bit down, and I turned my head away.

"Look at the sun instead," Renee said. Her eyes were open again, staring straight up; tears rolled along her cheekbone, disappeared near her ear. "It's beautiful. It really is."

Gold and tangerine and rosy pink, flooding my eyes. I squeezed them shut, it was too much, and sunspots pulsed and floated in an orange film behind my lids.

I wonder what she brought to the house, to Jim and Lisa, after our funerals. She was the sort who would have. Lasagna? That was about right. They always bring things you can spoon out and cut up. Out of nowhere random thoughts of food flitted through my brain, wandering bright and sudden as those sunspots, sense memories I thought I'd lost forever making my mouth water: pancakes thick with syrup. Potato chips. Fresh strawberries, the tiny bruised ones straight off the vine that burst open the second your tongue touches them. The vegetarian chili Mom sometimes made just for me, everyone else would whine if they didn't get their damned ground beef. Butter pecan ice cream. The warm, twitching, blood-soaked flesh of a rabbit, deer, squirrel, duck, possum—human? No. Not that. Not ever again. I couldn't actually be getting hungry, normal hunger, conventional, mundane, everyday hunger free of bloodlust or starvation, right here, right *now*. Was this all part of getting better? I couldn't be lying here, like this, knowing what was happening just a few yards away, thinking about goddamned strawberries and—

My eyes flew open and I dug at Lisa's sand pile in a sudden, frantic fear that we really had suffocated her, that she'd somehow tunneled downward and downward into the dune-face and we'd never find her again, while I lay here, like an asshole, daydreaming about pancakes. My fingers found her collarbone, slid up her throat, pressed against the slow, weak but still persistent pulse like we'd both stop breathing forever if I let go. Renee reached up, took my other hand.

"We won't get back," I said. The hoos were stumbling away from Jim now, wobbling as they walked, smears of flesh and slicks of blood covering their chins, chests, arms like they were babies missing their bibs. "For the others. Not in time."

"No," Renee said softly. "I guess we won't. But we would have. If we could."

We would have. If things had only been different. I hoped that was actually true.

I looked away from the hoos and into the eyes of the man from the neighboring burial mound, the one who'd lain there through all this like all the rest of them, silent and indifferent. He was sitting up now too, still half-submerged in the sands. I didn't hate him, for just lying there. Why should I? Why should he have taken special notice, really, of that woman dying? Jim and me fighting? Any of this? Some live. Some die. Other than saving yourself, maybe a few others if you're truly lucky, there's just nothing you can do.

You hungry too, Mister? I bet you are.

The morning sky was an intense, almost hurtful blue, barely a single thread of cloud to stop the light from pouring in and I kept squinting, pained, as the sun made its ascent. One of the hoos covered in Jim's blood fell over, twitching, convulsing like Jim had. Lay still. The others just kept on walking. Flesh without agency, even as they fed and pitched forward, their brains slowly, inexorably starting to shut down.

"They're dead," I told the stranger. As if he couldn't see it for himself. "Aren't they?"

"Yeah, they're dead," he said. His voice was weary, full of the useless knowledge of how it all might have been, if things had only been different. "They're all messed up."

19

We could have stayed. There was plenty of room and only a few dozen of us left. We did, for a while, up in the big lab: It was ransacked, of course, equipment broken, papers indecipherable, some chewed up like papier-mâché. Filing cabinets emptied. So much for playing detective after the fact.

I couldn't stand it. Couldn't look at the beach without seeing Jim, silhouetted against the sun screaming in death. At the trees without waiting for Joe, Florian, someone to emerge, tell me to get my ass back to the deer hunt. At my own hands without hoping for the sprout of new rot. I hoarded food I didn't need. Started fights. Then Renee got her head split open, fighting over a dented double can of goddamned creamed corn, and so the four of us picked up and headed back east.

We stuck to the coastline, following the shore. Empty steel mills, rusting rail track, darkened casino signs, vacant lots unfurling in green ribbons from behind hulks of machinery, and then we were back in tall sharp grasses and sandy dune soil. The gravel road widened, the woods' end marked by a faded sign reading WELCOME TO COWLES SHORES. We'd crossed over into the next county while we weren't watching. Lake Michigan looked gray and choppy out here instead of deep blue, stretching out to the horizon like a blanket of living frost.

"This is it," I said, standing on the dune crest. "This is where we're meant to stay."

"How can you be sure?" Lisa said. "How do you know?"

"Pick a house," I told her, and ran toward a row of abandoned cabins, remnants of long-ago summers before the beach became contraband. Our homes now, side by side: Lisa's, Renee's, the one Linc and I share. Behind them, where the sand reverts to woods, we've put a circle of lake stones around the trunk of an old tree. This may not be where he was asking for when he died, but it'll still always be Florian's beach.

The humans know we're out here. They stay away. Stories go around about how those who wander into the sands never return. They will not fight us on the beaches. It's not true. It'd be too much like cannibalism now, even though we're not really them and they're definitely not us. Too few of them, anyway. It'd be like basing every meal around black truffles.

I don't think any humans who got the plague reverted back: They either became one of us, like Lisa, or they died. Almost no humans left, from what I see, and no true undeads at all. My former kind, extinct. Our progenitors, rapidly getting there—

Well, hello there, Joe! Kitty-Joe, that is. Just got back from Kokomo. So many ferals out here, reverted pets, long-time strays. Joe's a king ratter, him and Kitty-Mags. Sam's fat and lazy, Billy's purely vicious, Teresa's so little and shy I never see more of her than a gray glimpse of fur. Good to have all the Fly-by-Nights together again, though, one way or another.

I get upset when they disappear, when they die. Renee does too. Lisa thinks we're crazy. She never liked cats.

Lisa won't talk about Jim. About what he did to her, to us, what things were like before she got out and ran away. She claims she doesn't remember. I know she's lying. She won't let me say a word against him, gets angry and stalks off if I try. Linc doesn't act like that when I talk about Joe, ever. You might even say he's been pretty patient.

Linc says I should write all this down, everything that's happened to us. Everything I tell him. He thinks someone, someday, is gonna want to read it. Renee says so too. We'll be history someday, she says, in the far future. Our kind will want to know just where they came from. And I can tell them.

Sometimes Renee and Linc, and I can't say I blame them, are both completely out of their minds.

Winter's in the air now, I can feel it, and Lisa's nagging about insulating the cabins. Why bother? We get cold when it snows, it's already snowed once or twice, but no frostbite; long sleeves are all we need. Colds, stomachaches, deep cuts, sprained ankles, they never last. No need to waste our time bundling up and hiding away.

"We have to keep busy," Lisa keeps saying. "We'll go crazy otherwise. Every day just like every other."

She wishes she were human again, I think. Sometimes. Then we find another human body by the roadside, naked, battered, half-eaten by animals, and she changes her mind. If she still had her daughter, it'd be different. I know it would. But there's nothing I can do about that.

Our kind are regrouping. We hear talk from our foraging expeditions, strangers on the road, of more and more folks drifting into Prairie Beach, coming together, or at least side by side. Happy-slappy little post-necropolis. Lisa would go back. She'd go back tomorrow. Renee? I don't know. Linc, thank God, thinks like I do: People fucked with me all my life, he says, and kept right on fucking with me after I died. Why the hell would I give them a third chance?

I'm afraid of what will happen if I'm around people again. Just look what's come of us all, because I decided to try to say hello.

Sometimes I think what Lisa really wants is another baby. Is that even possible now? We don't menstruate, she or me or Renee. I haven't heard tell of any of our kind getting pregnant. So much for Linc and Renee deeming me the wise old ancestor with the funny folktales. I'll tell them the stork really *did* deliver us, and took a giant, wet plopping shit all over humankind in the process. What can you do, eh, kids?

I hope Renee stays. Somehow, when I wasn't looking, she and Linc became the friends I never had when I was alive, most of the time I was undead. Lisa, though, I don't know. But she doesn't know about me either, so I guess we're even.

If we could talk about Jim maybe things would be different.

I was walking in the woods the other day, wandering around like old times. Just enjoying the tall oaks, the last ragged remnants of scarlet and yellow leaves, imagining what the lilies and columbines and feathery clusters of ferns would look like again in the spring, and then I saw something that looked like Jim but wasn't, rucksack slung over one shoulder, strolling along no more than a yard removed. He turned in my direction and my body went cold and then hot in that hoo-way I'd never get used to, an icy flush of anger and fear as I stood there, rabbit-still, waiting to be swept into flood-lit shadows of endless light, endless night—

Then I blinked, and he, it, vanished.

The next morning, Linc pulled me aside. "I saw a man in the woods," he said, "the other day—"

"I know," I said.

"He just disappeared. Right in front of my eyes."

"He does that," I said. We went to work on the vegetable garden, laying down dead yellow and scarlet leaves for mulch, and didn't mention it again. He does that.

And what happens, if he ever decides to stay?

There's a metaphor in all this somewhere, Linc says. Looking and sounding like Ben, the old Ben, thin arms folded and a battered cloth beach hat pulled over his eyes. Linc died young as I did but he still looks so old sometimes, weather-beaten, freeze-dried, tanned hide stretched over wire. Just like me. I love him and I don't want Death to stop and stay for him, or Renee, or Lisa, but I can't do a thing about it. Just like when I was first alive. Just like after I died.

So really, what's new? And if this isn't anything new, and it never was in my hands, ever, then what's there to fear? Or maybe it's that the fear is all part of the love, inextricable, and you just can't have the one without the other. It would figure. Just another way other people are a pain in the ass.

Which makes as good a conclusion as any. If I ever did go and tell this whole story to anybody else.

Tonight's sunset was like streaks from a jam jar, marmalade and blood orange and raspberry spilled across the sky, and we sat up to watch, Linc with an arm around me and Lisa half asleep with her head in Renee's lap. It'd been a good day. The deer were jumping, like they got a prize for volunteering themselves, and we'd built a fire, roasted our meat, feasted like kings and queens at the end of the world.

"I miss dessert," Lisa said, her voice low and easy with tiredness. "Not stale grocery store candy either. I wouldn't mind a cake."

"In what oven?" I demanded. "Plugged in to what outlet?"

"*Solar,*" she said triumphantly, raising her head with a little smirk. "Weren't you Miss Environmental while we were alive? You should've thought of it. All you need is tinfoil and a box. I know there are books about it."

While we were alive. Lisa'd never talked that way before, not so easily. Maybe she'd finally accepted she was one of us. Time would tell. And we had that much.

The sunset lost its tangerine streaks, turning dull orange and then dim orange-yellow; then the sun seemed to fall, very slowly, the old optical illusion as the sky went dark. We waited, squinting with sun and sleep, until the last bits of orange and purple and magenta were faded out and gone.

"It's beautiful," Renee said, watching the cold silvery waves crest and spread against the sand. "It really is."

Linc nodded. Lisa, who'd dropped off, started awake with a face-splitting yawn. Stomachs full. Time to sleep.

As we headed back up to the cabins, the oak tree branches flapped hard in the wind, like kids' hands fervently waving, and then subsided; a possum froze, let out cautious sniffs as he passed us, then just ambled away. Linc and I stood in the doorway, watching the night come drifting in all around us. The trees rustled again in the breeze, then turned still and quiet.

This story's for you, Florian. And everyone else I ever lost, even the ones who tried to lose me first. Enjoy eternity. Come visit if you like. I've been in and out and on the threshold enough times to know, the door's always open. Even when it looks like it's been slammed in your face.

Enough talk. It's getting dark.

TURN THE PAGE FOR A SPECIAL PREVIEW
OF JOAN FRANCES TURNER'S

FRAIL

When I was fourteen there was a security breach near the intersection of Seventy-Third and Klein and my mother killed her first intruder, and her last. She was on the six-to-three shift and I had guitar lessons a four-toll drive away in Leyton and she was supposed to pick me up straight from school, so we could hit U.S. 30 before the evening checkpoints started. But she didn't show, wasn't answering her cell, so I just sat there in the cafeteria, waiting, inhaling traces of stale crinkle-fry grease and watching the sky fade from drab blue to deep gray. Dave, one of the janitors, was mopping the floor like he wanted to slap its imaginary face and Ms. Acosta slipped and skidded in the wet and almost fell. I was glad to see it after all her clucking to my mother about slacking off and bad attitudes and "*twoooo*-antsy" (that's how she pronounced it, all bird-whistle fluttery like a comedienne in some old movie). She saw my lips twitching and glared at me, got what my mother called a cough-syrup smile right back, and I was reaching for my phone again when the warning siren kicked to life.

Louder and louder, that singular cadence distinguishing it from tornado and fire alarms: *aieeeow-oooo, woooo-owwwww*, low and moaning like an animal in pain. A very particular animal, creature, inhuman thing, that one-note wail all it had left for a voice. Onomatopoeia, we'd just learned that in English: natural sound encapsulated into speech, like a captured insect buzzing in a new-made bottle. *Onomatopoeia, onomatopoeia*, the word kept winding and tongue-twisting through my head. Remain in your seats. This is only a test.

"Damn," Ms. Acosta said, going pale under her orangey streaks of foundation.

"They're just testing it!" Dave shouted over the noise, supremely bored, nails raking at an angry pink splotch on the side of his neck. "The sun hasn't even set, those things are barely awake—"

The intercom snapped on. *"Code Orange alert,"* said a woman's voice, prerecorded, urgent but serene. *"Code Orange, located at—Klein—and—Seventy-Third—"*

"Halfway across town." Dave shrugged, and kept squeezing out his mop.

"Please lock all doors and windows and seek basement shelter until the all-clear sounds. If you are outside please seek the nearest safe house or other accessible building. It is a federal crime to deny shelter to any person seeking refuge from an environmental disturbance. Code Orange. Code Orange . . ."

"Just what I need. Haul it, Amy." Ms. Acosta swept my backpack off the table, grabbed it like it'd burden me too much to run from the crippled hordes. "Dave? Move it! Let's go!"

"They're halfway across town," I said, and folded my arms. No wonder I couldn't reach my mom, there hadn't been a Code Orange in years and never with her on shift. If I could somehow get over there I could watch her toast their asses, maybe flick one with my own lighter if it tried to run away—

"Amy, I swear to God I'm not in the mood—Dave? Dave! Put that mop down and let's go!"

Dave just snorted. "Jesus Christ, Alicia, calm down. They

move about two miles an hour and they ain't gonna roller-skate over here—"

"Fine!" She flapped her bony bangled arms at an imaginary audience, the only one that'd applaud her dramatics. "Fine! I'm not your mother, you get a leg torn off like Cris Antczyk did don't bother hopping over to me for sympathy— *Amy!*" The siren kept sounding, Dave nonchalantly fussing with his dirty yellow plastic bucket and CUIDADO: PISO MOJADO sign. "Get up. Follow me. *Now.*"

I got up. Shoved my hands in my pockets, feeling with fingertips for my school ID, town ID, curfew card, access gate e-pass. Followed her a few steps, sizing up her scuffed beige pumps with the one loose wobbly heel, my black flats. Then I ran, sailing over the damp linoleum, Ms. Acosta stumbling and screaming, "Amy, *goddammit!*" and Dave shaking his head laughing but I was already down the hall, out the steel double doors, the approaching sunset tinting Sycamore Street in a lurid orange wash and the sirens making the air tremble and throb.

My chest was a hot hollow husk but I was laughing as I ran, nobody can catch me, everyone else was basement-bound but I was going to see an honest-to-God living dead body get exactly what it deserved. I'd never seen one in the flesh, not even by the roadside, and even on the news all you ever saw was "dramatic re-creations" and shitty movie CGI—I was gunning for the real thing and to see my mother do the deed. She'd get a raise, a promotion, if she faced it down. She could do it without puking or fainting, not like so many of the men. All their big talk. I was proud of her, still one of the only women on the security squads, and this wasn't just to gawk and rubberneck. It wasn't just for me. After everything that happened you have to understand, I'm not lying, this wasn't all just about—

I'm getting ahead of myself. Sorry. You start to ramble, blither, when there's nothing left to talk to but the air. Ms. Acosta, she'd tell you all about that, if she were still alive.

The little white stucco house on the corner of Sycamore

and Cypress had gone creamy pink, quivering like a slab as the sunlight went rich and deep; I tunneled through their lilacs and kept on going. Seventy-Third's halfway across town, Dave was right, but Lepingville wasn't that big a town. As I veered off Maplewood I could already see the police cars and fire engines and Lepingville Civic Security vans blocking the streets, great grapelike clusters of red, blue, bottle-green flashing lights. I picked through backyards and easements looking for the best vantage point and completely by accident I saw her, framed perfectly by the gnarled, curving tree branches around me: my mother, an ambulatory burnt marshmallow in thick padded charcoal-gray fatigues, coppery hair twisted up at the back of her head, waddling down Seventy-Third calm as you please as she fitted another cartridge to her flamethrower.

Everybody in town joked about intruders but they were still scared shitless. My mother, though, she'd grown up over in Gary with no alarms, no fencing unless you put it up yourself, nothing but a half-defunct PA system, your basement and you. Anything could happen, any time, and you had to keep cool or you'd go crazy. I wanted to be cool, *sanguine*, just like her. I wanted her to get that piece of walking ant bait, the raise, the promotion, she got so much shit from the men she worked with and she deserved this chance, it *wasn't* just all about me—

There it was. All alone, standing there in front of the torn shrubbery and rusted, broken fence point it'd ripped down, arms dangling and limp, perfectly quiet but with its long pearl-gray teeth bared and grimacing. A bloated, brackish, muddy mess, a first-grader's art project shaped with careless palm-slaps into a too-angular skull, a smeared nubbin of a nose and horribly thin fingers; something about those fingers, the way each one was a perfect sticky twig of tacky clay not yet softened to full rot, made a horrible shiver rush up my back, my chest going hot and tight in disgust.

It was a man, had been a man, its penis swung limp and useless from its gaping trouser holes but more indecent than the sight of that ever could be was the smell. You can't imagine the smell, so strong and sharp and porridge-thick that I gagged, gasped as it rolled over me, my lungs squeezing shut under the assault: an overpowering gaseous stink that wasn't even a proper smell of death but of *life*. Nasty, fetid, wriggly life, bursting in horrible exuberance from that thing once a man, fields of mold blooming on fabric and skin, grubs and bluebottles breeding, hatching, crawling from the crevices around eyes, nose, crotch, armpit, elbow crooks, eating and being eaten from the inside out—the police and firemen heaved and retched but not my mother, she didn't even flinch, just pulled on her breath-mask and stood her ground. Kill it, Mom, for God's sake kill that *smell*. All the rest of them just watching. Like me.

They stood aside, the other security guys, they left her to it all alone: The bitch thinks she can handle it? Yeah, we'll just see about that. Cowards. She walked right up to it, there in the middle of the street. The cops raised their guns. Bullets wouldn't kill an intruder, but wounding it might buy some time. My mother took her time. Why shouldn't she? It couldn't run, it could barely walk. Its kind relied on ambush and paralyzing panic.

I stuck a jacket fold to my nose and crept nearer, keeping to the trees. I never even considered how trees, bushes, dark shadowy overgrowths where they could lie in wait were their friends, how I'd never smell others coming over this one's reek. *Sanguine*. That word sounds a lot better than *reckless*.

It made a sound, looking at my mother, and the noise it made sent a strange, prickly disquiet through me because it wasn't like in the movies, it wasn't the right sound. It was a low, full moan that bore an edge of surprise, a living human's dismay and uncertainty turned to stretched-out toffee in that undead mouth. It kept staring at my mother, wide gaping eyes from the collapsed ruin of a face and make it stop, Mom, tell it to knock that off; it's not hungry, I can tell it's not. It's like it thinks it knows you, somehow, from somewhere.

The stench was so awful my throat closed up; I was making little *huhh, huhhh* heaving sounds I couldn't stifle, warm acidy puddles pooling in my mouth. Kill it, Mom. Make it stop.

She took off her mask. The cops, the security squadron muttered in confusion but nobody tried to stop her, they weren't taking a single step closer than they had to. The thing moaned again, an oh-shit, what-now, what-do-I-do noise and some of the squadron snickered. My mother wasn't laughing. Her eyes looked like that thing's voice sounded.

"Get out," she said, her voice shaking. If the smell was getting to her, you'd never guess it. "Go back through that fence and get out."

Why was she talking to it? They didn't understand us. They were beyond speech. She took a step forward, tugging her boot from the soft thick dirt. The thing didn't move.

"You're trespassing on human territory!" she shouted, a strange, strident agitation buoying her voice up over the squadron vans, into the trees, as she rattled off the black-book gobbledygook it couldn't possibly understand. "As a civic security official I am authorized to use all necessary levels of force to address Class A environmental disturbances by Indiana Code Section 17, paragraph 8(d)—"

It made another sound. *Oooooo*, it went. Still looking my mother up and down, like it knew something about her and had no idea what to do with what it knew, and then *ooooooosssss*. Airy, hollow whistling, trying to make sounds a rotten tongue, lips, palate wouldn't allow anymore. *Ooooosssssss*. And it took a step forward.

My mother didn't move. The squadron snapped to attention; you could see it on their faces, fear, and some smirking, because they thought she'd frozen up. It wasn't that, I knew it wasn't, but something was very wrong and even over the horrible stink of living death you could smell, feel, hear the wrongness all concentrated in her voice as she raised the flamethrower and screamed, "Get out! *Get out!*"

It opened its mouth again, making softer, cow-lowing cries like it wanted to wheedle her into something. Coax her. It stumbled forward, slow as they all do, holding out its arms.

I don't know what I was expecting to happen when it

caught the flame. Maybe that it'd drop to the pavement and lie there like a proper corpse, a genteelly singed peaceful stinking dead body, or give a little *pop* like marshmallow char in a bonfire and collapse, instantly, into a sighing pile of shitty muddy ash. But instead it stood there with its puppet arms waving, each filthy rag of clothing a tattered fiery flag, and then its mouth opened and jaw came unhinged around a long, hard, sustained scream of agony. Not like the alarm siren, not like in the movies: It sounded human, the sound of those screams was a human being just like me or my mother or Ms. Acosta or anyone else in such awful, unimaginable pain they'd do, give, promise anything to make it stop but there was nowhere to go, no way out. It couldn't run, not like a panicked human on fire. Instead it rotated in a slow tottering circle. It sank to its knees, groaning and sobbing. And it rolled on the ground. And it bubbled, and cooked, and slowly died.

The firefighters moved in to keep the grass from igniting; didn't matter if they doused the flame, the heat would still keep working its way in, sloughing off rotten skin and bone. It was covered in sprayed-on extinguisher frost now, a grotesque Christmas window mannequin with arms curled into useless, foreshortened boxer's fists, and the screaming wouldn't stop.

The smell, as it burned. Kept burning, even without any fire. Mom. I need you to make it stop, now.

She sat down hard on the grass, watching it writhe and sob and burn, and someone grabbed her and dragged her to the vans. It was crying now, full-throated sobs of pain as its bones disintegrated, skin falling off in thick charred pieces like slivers of briquettes from a barbecue. The same sort of dirty gray ash. They'd surrounded my mother now, going Good job, Lucy, you *did* it, you fucking toasted it, just listen to it wail, and I ran from my hiding place because I couldn't stand it anymore. It *had* to stop crying, she had to make all this stop happening and go away, tell me it wasn't really a person and everything would be—and that's when she saw me, and shoved them all aside to get to me.

"What are you doing here!" she shouted, pulling me out of the path, away from the sobbing howling skeleton lying in its own ash. "You're at school, you're in the *shelter*! Why aren't you—goddammit, can't you stay out of trouble longer than five minutes at a time, why are you here! What the hell are you doing here!"

I didn't have any answer and my mother grabbed my arms in a pincer grip and shook me, yelling things I couldn't hear, and Ms. Acosta was suddenly right there puffing and panting in white sneakers like nurse's shoes, and my mother screamed at her to mind her own goddamned business for once in her life, and I wrenched free and ran fast as I could from the smell, the shouting, the cries of pain that just kept growing louder. It all got lower and fainter, faded out entirely around Hollister, and I sat there on the sidewalk like my mother had on the grass, letting my nose and ears fill up with the clean airy quiet. A good hour, maybe more. The color faded and retreated from the sky, everything bathed in the soft formless dark.

I went home and threw up and then sat in the basement, on the cots we had set up in case of tornadoes or what had just happened, and that's where my mother found me. Staggering tired, she looked drained dry, a dried streak of something like blood except sticky and ashen smearing her cheek. She didn't yell at me, we had the leftover baked beans for dinner and went straight to sleep. The next morning and all afternoon she just lay there, quiet, staring at the wall next to her bed. And the day after that. And the day after that.

My aunt Kate said later my mother hadn't been right in the head since my father died, that even before that she'd been strange. Off. A lot of people said that, about my mother. But I knew her, and they didn't, and all I'll say is that after that evening something inside her seemed to bend and twist like that thing's rotten twiggy fingers, tearing in two without making a sound. She never cried. She wasn't the type. She never talked to anyone. She could take care of herself. She went to work. She came home. She asked me about school, how anyone smart as I was (ha) could be barely passing history, asked me about my music, cooked the pancake dinner we ate every Friday she was off-shift. No more lying around in bed. There was no time, and she liked to keep busy.

And then one winter morning a year later, when I was fifteen, I woke up and she was gone. No note.

She used to go out sometimes at night, long after dark, when she thought I was asleep; all she'd ever say was she was taking a walk. Walking for hours, sometimes not coming home until dawn. That was so reckless I got scared, even knowing I couldn't stop her, that her job meant she knew "stranger"-danger better than I ever would, that like everyone else she never went anywhere without her lighter. I'd lie there half-awake, drifting, as the sky lit from iron to pearl, and sometimes I'd fall back into thick heavy sleep and when I woke she'd be lying beside me on the bed, fully dressed, snoring. We never talked about it. Always, no matter what, she came back.

They found her LCS jacket, folded neatly at the edge of a forest preserve a half-mile outside the town gates, her badge and ID in one pocket. The jacket's too big, but it's warm. I like to imagine it's what got me through this past winter.

If you're going to get anywhere in life—this is how I see it—it's important to always show the truth of things, even when it doesn't make you look good. Even when it makes you angry. You have to be honest, no matter what, or it all just goes to shit. So the truth is that she's not forgiven, my mother, for what she did. I have the power of forgiveness in me and it's the only power I have left; I wave it inside my head like a July sparkler, letting the little line of fiery floating light it traces in the dark mark out the saved, the damned, those forever left behind. She's not forgiven. My father isn't forgiven, for disappearing while coming home from the mill when I was five. Ms. Acosta isn't forgiven, for . . . I'd thought we finally understood each other, when there was nothing else left. But we didn't. That dead thing isn't forgiven, ever, for spreading its filthy contagion of crying, pain, despair—

No, I change my mind. I forgive it because it hurt so much. Only for that. Just like I have to forgive my uncle and aunt, for getting so sick. The way everyone got so sick, the way everyone died—human, zombie, everyone. Everywhere. Except me. I'm one of the only ones left.

Last spring, a year after my mother disappeared, it started. A plague. A famine. Everyone around me got sick, a disease nobody had heard of, no doctor could diagnose. It made people hungry—no. It made them ravenous, insane with hunger and the more they ate, the more the disease ate at them, turning them to great gobbling mouths crammed with meat, drink, garbage, soap, grass, paper, tree bark, dirt, insects, vermin, antifreeze, glue, face cream, Styrofoam, gammon, spinach, anything, anything they could chew or swallow. They attacked and killed their pets, children, each other. For food. Everything they'd ever feared the intruders, the real flesh-eaters, might do to us—

But the undead too. Even them. They got sick too.

But not me. I don't know why. I hid and kept hiding until the sickness burned itself out, hit a peak and a slope and finally the living, the undead, every eating thing couldn't eat anymore, didn't want to. After all that, they starved to death. The disease binged on them, gorged itself sick, and then it purged. And they all died.

No. Not *everyone*.

Some who got this sickness—living, undead, didn't seem to matter—they survived the ceaseless hunger, the self-starvation afterward, and became something else. They look human, some of them used to be, but they're not. Not anymore. As strong as zombies ever were, even stronger, but they don't rot, they don't decay and no matter if you stab, shoot, starve, freeze them, drown them, smother them, torch them with fire, they can't die. They heal right before your eyes, and it's the last thing you see before they kill you. Fast-moving, fast-talking, fast-thinking as humans. Strong as zombies. And no matter what, they can never, ever die. The intruders are dead, but they've left a new generation behind. So many of them. So few of us.

There were only four of us in Lepingville who stayed human, who never got sick, and I'm the only one who got through last winter. And it was a mild winter, this year.

I don't know what I'm going to do. I've got no idea what I'm supposed to do now, and there's nobody to tell me. One foot in front of the other, my mother always said. Step forward, keep going even as your feet sink into the soft lawn mire all around you, the *shuuuck* of your shoe yanked from a pocket of mud making you flinch like a starter pistol just went off by your ear. Keep going. Somewhere. You'll figure it out. You've got no choice.

I think somehow, from all her years working cheek by jowl with death, my mother sensed this was coming, the way animals sniff out impending earthquakes and flee. She was going to take me with her, but it was too dangerous and she knew someone would take me in, they have to because it's a felony otherwise, and once the sickness ceased she'd find me and we'd figure out, together, what to do next. I couldn't die, we had to find each other. I didn't kill myself. I didn't starve. I didn't freeze or get sick or butchered for my flesh, I didn't ever mean to do what I—*I stayed here*. I have a right to be proud of that. I stayed.

That's what they tell you, when you're little. Right? If you're lost, stay right where you are. Somebody will find you. It's inevitable. Someone. Somewhere.

I'm still waiting.

Even vampires have monsters that they're afraid of—
and Anita is one of them . . .

New from #1 *New York Times* bestselling author

LAURELL K. HAMILTON

KISS THE DEAD

An Anita Blake, Vampire Hunter Novel

When a fifteen-year-old girl is abducted by vampires, it's up to U.S. Marshal Anita Blake to find her. When she does, she's faced with something she's never seen before: a terrifyingly ordinary group of people—kids, grandparents, soccer moms—all recently turned and willing to die to avoid serving a master. And where there's one martyr, there will be more . . .

"Long before Stephenie Meyer's Twilight series and Charlaine Harris's Sookie Stackhouse novels, [there was] sexy, strong-willed vampire hunter Anita Blake."
—*USA Today*

"Hamilton remains one of the most inventive and exciting writers in the paranormal field." —Charlaine Harris

laurellkhamilton.org
facebook.com/laurell.k.hamilton
facebook.com/ProjectParanormalBooks
penguin.com

M1035T1211

Explore the outer reaches
of imagination—don't miss these authors
of dark fantasy and urban noir who take you
to the edge and beyond . . .

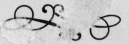

Patricia Briggs	Anne Bishop
Simon R. Green	Marjorie M. Liu
Jim Butcher	Jeanne C. Stein
Kat Richardson	Christopher Golden
Karen Chance	Ilona Andrews
Rachel Caine	Anton Strout

penguin.com/scififantasy